Khammaan Khonkhai's life experience accounts for much of the vivid detail that distinguishes this novel. He grew up and taught in a rural village in northeastern Thailand, and later continued his education at Prasanmitr College of Education in Bangkok and at the University of Northern Colorado. He has published many novels, short stories, and articles in Thailand. Three of his publications have won awards from the National Books Committee and another has been given by the Bangkok Bank Ltd.

Gehan Wijeyewarnede is a member of the staff of the Department of Anthropology, Research Scholl of Pacific Studies in the Australian National University. He was born in Sri Lanka, and was educated at the Royal Collage in Colombo, the University of Ceylon in Peradeniya and King's College, Cambridge. He has taught at the University of Ceylon, Singapore and Washington (Seattle), and has published papers on agriculture, kinship, and ritual in North Thailand.

AF869226

The Teachers of Mad Dog Swamp

Khammaan Khonkhai

Translated by Gehan Wijeyewarnede

SILKWORM BOOKS
1992

ISBN 974-7047-05-5
THE TEACHERS OF MAD DOG SWAMP
Khammaan Khonkhai
Translated by Gehan Wijeyewarnede

English translation © Gehan Wijeyewarnede, 1992 All rights reserved.

Original published in Thai by Karavek Publishers, 1978
First Japanese translation translated by T. Tomita,
published by The Imura Culture Centre, Tokyo, 1980
First English translation published by University of Queensland Press,
St. Lucia, Queensland, 1982
First published in Thailand by Silkworm Books, 1992

Silkworm Books
54/1-5 Sridonchai Road, Chiang Mai 50000 Facsimile 66 (53) 27-1902
Mailing address: P.O. Box 76, Chiang Mai 50000, Thailand

Cover design by T. Jittidejarak
Cover photograph from the film's poster "Khru Ban-nork"
Typeset by Margaret Tyrie
Printed and bound by O.S. Printing House, Bangkok

Distributed to the book trade by
Books and Magazine Distributor (Thailand) Co., Ltd.
Tel. (02) 393-5532, Facsimile 66 (2) 396-0973

CONTENTS

TRANSLATOR'S INTRODUCTION TO 2nd EDITION

It is ten years since the publication of the first edition of *The Teachers of Mad Dog Swamp*, and fifteen since the genesis of the original Thai when the film director, Surasi Phatham, approached the author, Khammaan Khonkhai, with a proposal for a film about rural schoolteachers. Given the author's strong didactic intentions, it is not inappropriate to ask: 'How has the novel stood up to the passage of time?' The author's own assessment in 1988 was that 'not much has changed', though he goes on to make clear that the lack of change he refers to is in moral rather than material conditions.

Attempts to bring modern development to the northeast region have accelerated throughout the last decade and the regularization of relations with Laos has undoubtedly brought greater material prosperity. It was also a period of continuing migration to Bangkok, so much so that concern is now being expressed as to the actual population of the capital city. An increasingly significant proportion of the population registered in the northeast may actually be resident in Bangkok. This creates problems for Bangkok, but must add to the material resources flowing back to the northeast. Khammaan Khonkhai's view, however, was that the greater availability of material goods has not changed the basic exploitation of the poor and their inability to defend themselves. This is perhaps an issue that requires closer analysis.

There are two topics that I would like to raise, very briefly, in this 1992 introduction. 1992 is without doubt a date that will be remembered in Thai history whatever the immediate consequences of the events of May that year. Our view of these events, while they have hardly been resolved, is that the Thai military have been forced to reconsider their understanding of their role in Thai politics, and they, and the world, have been alerted to a strong middle-class claim for an alternative agenda. That this claim is student led, I think, links it with some of the preoccupations of this novel. One could say that the demands of the rural schoolteachers of Mad Dog Swamp, particularly of its hero, Piya, are those of the demonstrators of May 1992: a rational, more humane, equitable society, a Thai society, but part of the modern world. The 1992 message of *Khru Barn Nork* is that the forces which so impressed the world in May 1992 have long been part of Thai culture, of Thai society.

The other issue is more specific. The tragedy of the novel arises out of the selfish exploitation of the country's forests. Within the last few years, disastrous floods in Thailand forced the government to put an end to legal logging within Thailand's borders. This event coincided with the policy of the Burmese government to conduct a firesale of that country's own resources to enable it to finance its civil war against the people of Burma. The Thai military in particular have grabbed the opportunity and there is now probably more timber moving through Thailand than ever before. It was very disturbing, early in 1992, to hear young men talking about taking photographs of these timber collection sites and timber transport vehicles and the feelings of fear and menace which, their attitudes conveyed, surround these activities. Khammaan's 1988 comment must be taken seriously. The moral climate has changed little since the 1970s.

Changes to the translation have been minimal, though some mistakes have been eliminated. I apologise to my friends and colleagues for one such correction in particular which they have used, with some glee, in teaching.

My thanks are due to Ria Van de Zandt, Karen Hall and, in particular, Margaret Tyrie for the preparation of this manuscript, and to Margret Wijeyewardene for the proof reading.

This translation, as was the previous edition, is for Richard B. Davis.

June 1992

A NOTE ON THE ORTHOGRAPHY OF THAI WORDS

Thai words have been used in the text of the translation for three general reasons: to retain some of the flavour of the original; because an English rendering seemed awkward; or because no satisfactory equivalent was available. The transcription used in the text aims to enable the reader unfamiliar with anthropological or linguistic conventions to reproduce something of the Thai pronunciation. A glossary is provided at the end of the book which gives the word as spelled in the text, a phonetic transcription using the Mary Haas system for the representation of Thai (but excluding tonal indications), and the English gloss. Not all Thai words for fauna and flora used in the text have been included in the glossary. Botanical identifications are given in footnotes. For readers unfamiliar with Thai, I should explain that *ch, th,* and *ph* represent aspirates which contrast with the nonaspirates c, *t,* and p. Therefore, *ph is* pronounced as in the English *pot,* never as f, and c is never pronounced as k, but as an unaspirated voiceless affricate. The contrast between *t* and *th is* similar to the difference between the initial consonants of the French *tout* and the English *two.* The author's pseudonym Khammaan Khonkhai is spelled, at the author's request, to conform with the romanization used in the Japanese version.

G.W.

FROM THE AUTHOR ON THE PUBLICATION OF THE SEVENTH PRINTING

Khammaan Khonkhai

The novel *Khru Barn Nork* helped both Thai and foreigners better understand the conditions and way of life, particularly, of rural teachers in the northeast of Thailand. Those who already had some knowledge were given greater understanding and those who knew little have made clear to me the sympathy aroused in them when their attention was drawn to these conditions.

The occasion of my writing the novel was the invitation by Duang Kamol Entertainments to take stories from my book *Banthük khorng Khru Prachaban* (Records of Rural Teachers) and make of them a feature film with the title *Khru Barn Nork* (Rural Teachers). I volunteered to write a new book in the form of a novel of that name mainly because I had many more details I wanted to include.

I began writing the book at the beginning of 2520 (1977) and finished the final draft towards the end of that year, though it was not released till the beginning of 2521. While the book was being prepared, the film team was already working in the village where I was born, and in the first five printings published by Karawek Printers of Advance Media Ltd the cover photograph as well as other photographs in the book were stills from the film included on the decision of the publishers. The sixth printing by Bannakit Press changed the picture on the cover, but used some of the old photographs inside.

In the Japanese edition translated by Professor Takejiro Tomita of Osaka University there were drawings of Thai fishing implements mentioned in the novel, as well as a photograph of the translator with the author. Otherwise the book is in Japanese script which I cannot read. The only Thai is on the cover, the title *Khru Barn Nork*. In the English edition translated by Dr Gehan Wijeyewardene of The Australian National University in Canberra, there is a section explaining Northeastern Thai words in English and the title was changed to *Teachers of Mad Dog Swamp* which in Thai translates as *Khru haeng Norng Ma Vor*.

In 2528 (1985) Dr Gehan informed me that there was someone interested in translating the book into Dutch, but there has been no further news and I can only guess as to whether it was translated without permission or not at all.

The fact that *Khru Barn Nork* was widely distributed in many foreign countries has meant a greater understanding of the Thai countryside and its teachers, abroad. I have had many letters from American students, asking about me and my life and for explanations of aspects of the novel to help them in their studies. The novel has helped to create a greater understanding of rural Thailand than I had anticipated.

When we compare the essence of way of life of the people and teachers of the rural northeast before 2519 (1976) with this year of 2531 (1988), there is not much that has changed. Some superficial changes have occurred such as the increase in the availability of material goods. Thus roads have improved and communications are more covenient, electricity and electrical goods such as television sets and refrigerators, vehicles such as saloon cars are more available. But people are still poor, lack many necessities, are oppressed and exploited, and have no power to defend themselves whether in economic, social or political life. The condition of the poor and exploited in the northeast has not changed between 2519 and 2531 - it may even have become worse.

Khru Barn Nork is a novel, but it is a novel reflecting the truth. I have only tried to set out those conditions which create problems in our society so that the members of society may recognize and understand them. I have no answers to these problems. It is the duty of all of us to find ways of alleviating these problems through mutual effort, contributing whatever we can to their solution. We do not have to await the birth of a second, or a third, Khru Piya to do this.

Bangkok
December 2531 (1988)

TRANSLATOR'S INTRODUCTION

Khammaan Khonkhai (the pen name of Sompong Palasoon) now works in a specialized agency of the Thai Ministry of Education.[1] He has a deep and varied experience within the teaching service, his first post being in a village school in the province in which this novel is set. He has been a newspaper commentator on educational affairs since 1967, and since 1975 has had a dozen novels published in Thailand, four of which have won national awards. The precursor to this novel was a collection of stories on rural teaching (*Banthyg khong Khru Prachaban*). In the Introduction to the Thai original of this translation he tells us that he was asked by a young filmmaker from Northeast Thailand, Surasi Phatham, for a script based on the earlier new script describing in detail the life of both rural teachers and the country people of Isarn (the northeast region of Thailand). The movie of *The Teachers of Mad Dog Swamp*, *Khru Barnnork* (literally, 'Rural schoolteachers') was the outcome and was released in 1978.

A recent account of the development of the modern Thai novel describes how, during the 1920s, a close relationship grew up between the cinema industry and a new generation of Thai writers. In those early days it was the translation and retelling of foreign film scripts for a growing reading public. Wibha Senanan says that many writers now well known got a large part of their experience

[1] He is now (1992) the Deputy Secretary-General of the Teachers' Council of Thailand.

of Western fiction through this type of writing.[2] The tradition has continued as the Thai cinema emerged, and it is therefore not unexpected that this novel had its first appearance as a successful film. When the book was published shortly afterwards, it became a best seller, going into its third printing within a few months. Since then there have been two more.

Rural schoolteachers and teaching are often in the news in Thailand and the theme was clearly suitable for a successful novel - perhaps more so than may seem to be the case elsewhere. The government recognizes the potential of rural schoolteachers for shaping attitudes and changing values, and, therefore, their importance in the long political struggle that continues in the countries of Southeast Asia. There is also the traditional reverence accorded all teachers (the Thai *khru* comes from the Sanskrit *guru*, and Khammaan Khonkhai ends his Introduction by invoking a blessing in thanks to all his teachers). It is hoped the reader of the translation will gain some insight into the nature of Thai society, the interplay of tradition and modernism in contemporary Southeast Asia, as well as into the reasons for the novel's success. The purpose of this Introduction is to fill in some of the background which a Thai readership would take for granted, and to make some suggestions as to the importance of the novel in a wider context.

There is much in the novel which is reminiscent of the popular Thai cinema. The forces of good and evil are sharply drawn, villain and hero conform to recognizable types. The former is a money-hungry businessman

2 Wibha Senanan, *The Genesis of the Novel in Thailand* (Bangkok: Thai Watana Panich, 1975), pp. 67-68.

battening on a populace corruptly administered. The hero is young, idealistic and devoted to the public service to which he belongs. The plot is fairly simple and has elements of what might be considered to be melodrama. Yet, it would be very wrong to dismiss the novel as merely a popular film script. The intention is serious, almost didactic, and its history seems to suggest it speaks to an important section of modern Thai society.

Despite its popular elements, the story is handled with a delicacy and gentleness, particularly when it deals with love and sex. In the body of the novel there is occasional violence, but two of the most important of these incidents are genuinely funny rather than anything else. The novel does not exploit the obvious. Rather it spends much time in descriptions of everyday activities, the preparation of food, and village celebrations. In my opinion, its main concern is the communication of identity, as I hope to show later in this Introduction.

For the benefit of those readers who are unfamiliar with the history and culture of Thailand I give a brief account of the socio-cultural background. Thai-speaking Buddhists comprise the overwhelming majority of the population of modern Thailand. The language, Thai, belongs to a family of languages which continues to puzzle historical linguists. For the sake of convenience it is usual to use the term *Tai* to denote the languages which go to make up this family, and their speakers, and *Thai* the languages and peoples of the modern Kingdom of Thailand. In the late 1950s it was estimated that there were 30 million speakers of Tai languages - this figure is of course now exceeded by Tai speakers within the boundaries of Thailand. The area of dispersion is considerable - from 7° to 26° North and 94° to 110° East, yet the languages are remarkably homogeneous suggesting a relatively recent common ancestry. Some languages, like Ahom (in Assam), are now extinct. Others, especially Thai and Lao, have acquired an extensive foreign word stock which has changed their character in many important ways.

Tai-speaking kingdoms in Southeast Asia may have appeared about the 10th century AD. It was till very recently believed that the spread of Tai peoples occurred as a consequence of the fall of the Nanchao kingdom of Yunnan to the Mongols in the 13th century. Historians no longer accept this hypothesis and many historical linguists now believe that the centre of linguistic dispersal was from somewhere in what is now Vietnam.

Modern Thai history claims its origin in the Kingdom of Sukhothai - established in the early part of the 13th century. Sukhothai however was one among a number of kingdoms, some Tai, some not, vying for supremacy in the area. It was Ayutthia, founded in 1350, which presaged the modern Thai kingdom with its capital in Bangkok. Thai consciousness of Sukhothai is inextricably bound up with the discovery and deciphering of the stele of King Ramkamhaeng (c. 1275-1317) by the great King Mongkut (1851-1868) who with his son King Chulalongkorn laid the foundations of modern Thailand. This inscription has become a pre-eminent symbol of the origins of Thai nationhood - one former Prime Minister wrote of a portion of this inscription that no other Thai writing has moved him more with its beauty. It is natural that Sukhothai should have the place it does in popular thought. Modern historians, however, have questioned this interpretation.

Until the latter part of the 19th century, though many of the outlying principalities enjoyed a considerable degree of administrative autonomy, the ideology of Southeast Asian monarchy was always one of centralized power, and the technological advances of the 19th and 20th centuries have been well used to serve this end. Thailand is now among the most centralized societies in the world - despite recent attempts to redress the balance. Administratively, politically and culturally Bangkok is the absolute centre. For many public servants posting to the provinces is virtual exile. It is only barely twenty years since there were any universities outside Bangkok. In 1964 only 400 of over 78,000 students enrolled in universities and colleges were in provincial universities - about 300 in Chiangmai University and 100 in the only university in the Northeast. The position now, though still overwhelmingly in Bangkok's favour, is much better. This is connected with increasing concern and respect for regional culture.

Despite its importance, there are few detailed descriptions if life in Bangkok available to the foreign reader. One of the best of these is the thesis on a Bangkok slum by Akin Rabibhadana.[3] Much more is known about the details of life in a rural community, the setting for much of this novel.

Administratively, Thailand is divided into some seventy provinces (*changwat*). The chief adminstrator of each province is known in English as Governor, in Thai

---

3 Akin Rabibadhana, 'Bangkok Slum: Aspects of Social Organization' (PhD thesis, Cornell University. Michigan: University microfilms 1975).

phu wa ratchakarn changwat. He is a senior official of the Ministry of the Interior (*Mahart Thai*) and is in theory held responsible for everything that goes on in the province. Other departments will also have provincial heads stationed in the provincial capital and there appears to be a measure of uncertainty as to their responsibility to the Governor at the other end of the building - or down the road. There is an appointed provincial council made up of senior government officials and private citezens and its function appears largely advisory.

Provinces are divided into districts (*amphur*), presided over be a *nai amphur*, usually translated as 'District Officer'. Each relevant department has a district-level head and staff as appropriate. Below the district level, adminstration is effected through village officials. Villages are officially designated and defined. These may often be recognized as distinct residential units by the casual observer, but sometimes boundaries may appear to be quite arbitrary. Villagers choose one of their number as headman - *phu jai barn*. He is recognized as such by the district administration and is paid a small stipend. Villages are grouped together into *tambon*, a unit sometimes translated into English as 'commune'. One of the headmen, or some other suitable man is elected as *tambon* head (*kamnan*). This official does not appear in the novel. Headmen and *kamnan* may often be quite wealthy and powerful men; in other cases they are little different from their fellow villagers. They are, however, typically men in the middle. They are called on to deal with a host of intra-village problems, settle dispuites and give advice.They are also called on to enforce administrative decisions and to convey government policy to villagers, and they are held responsible by administrative officials for the well-being and good behaviour of their communities.

The Thai government service reflects Thai history. Its origins lie in the amalgam of practices and ideas which accompanied the growth of early principalities and city in the Interior *(Mahart Thai)* and is in theory held responsible for everything that goes on in the province. Other departments will also have provincial heads stationed in the provincial capital and there appears to be a measure of uncertainty as to their responsibility to the Governor at the other end of the building - or down the road. There is an appointed provincial council made up of senior government officials and private citizens and its function appears largely advisory. Provinces are divided into districts *(amphur),* presided over by a *nai amphur,* usually translated as 'District Officer'. Each relevant department has a district-level head and staff as appropriate. Below the district level, administration is effected through village officials. Villages are officially designated and defined. These may often be recognized as distinct residential units by the casual outside observer, but sometimes boundaries may appear to be quite arbitrary. Villagers choose one of their number as headman *-phu jai barn.* He is recognized as such by the district administration and is paid a small stipend. Villagers are grouped together into *tambon,* a unit sometimes translated in English as 'commune'. One of the headmen, or some other suitable man is elected as *tambon* head *(kamnan).* This official does not appear in the novel. Headmen and *kamnan* may often be quite wealthy and powerful men; in other cases they are little different from their fellow villagers. They are, however, typically men in the middle. They are called on to deal with a host of intravillage problems, settle disputes and give advice. They are also called on to enforce administrative decisions and to convey government policy to villagers, and they are held responsible by administrative officials for the well-being and good behaviour of their communities.

The Thai government service reflects Thai history. Its origins lie in the amalgam of practices and ideas which accompanied the growth of early principalities and city states into the Ayutthian empire and the later Bangkok-based kingdom. Some of these ideas were derived from Hindu-Buddhist traditions and reflected ancient views of the nature of kingship, the nature of the state, and its relationship to the cosmos. Nineteenth century reforms initiated by the monarchs Mongkut and Chulalongkorn and twentieth century revolutions together with pervasive Western influence have made Thai bureaucracy at least superficially like that of most other contemporary states. Nevertheless, one commentator, William J. Siffin, writing in the mid-1960s, claims that the dominant value orientation of the Thai bureaucratic system is not 'productivity, rationality and efficiency', nor is the authority that brings 'order and impetus to bureaucratic action ... primarily the legal authority of the Weberian model so often applied in the study of Western systems'. Siffin goes on to argue that the fundamental values of the Thai bureaucracy are 'hierarchical status', 'personalism' and 'security'.[4]

The issue is a complex one, but essentially seems to involve the notion that, whereas the individuals who make up any bureaucracy are concerned with the continuing existence of the system, in the Thai bureaucracy this aim takes precedence over its instrumental functions. The issue is not whether corruption and inefficiency are characteristic of one system and not of another. I mention Siffin's views here, because the novel seems to suggest that some Thai have similar views of their bureaucracy.

Two aspects of the civil service (i.e. government servants excluding members of military) are relevant to an understanding of the background of the novel. First, personal rank and administrative function are generally co-ordinated, so that reference to a man's job identifies his position in the hierarchy and by implication his position in society. The service is divided into five classes, each in turn divided into three grades. The hierarchical principle manifests itself at the lowest level in the 'salary step'. Each year an official is expected to rise one step, there being four in each grade.

The largest units within the administration are the ministries. These are divided into departments, each with specified functions, and these are further divided into divisions and sections. The lowest class is made up of nonspecialized clerks, and, in the Education Ministry, most local teachers belong in this class. In the next class are officials in sections, and chiefs of sections ('Section Head'

---

4 Siffin, William J., *The Thai Bureaucracy: Institutional Change and Development* (Honolulu: East-West Center Press, 1966).

in the novel) in the class above that. Chiefs of Divisions are in Class One and the highest, known as the Special Class, has most senior officials of a department.

The other topic of relevance is recruitment, which is by examination at either fourth or third class level (the two lowest). Entry to the third class is usually restricted to college graduates - so that all the teachers addressed as *acarn* are at least of this rank. There is no system of central examination. Examinations are held by the employing agency, usually the department. Notice of examination is publicly made, but with such little fanfare or notice that applicants are mostly informed by word of mouth. In the novel the provincial authorities hold the exams for recruitment to the teaching service. The implication is that the exam is held annually to coincide with the qualification of graduates from the Teachers' Colleges.

The topography of the village of Norng Ma Vor as it emerges through the story recalls much that is typical of Thai villages in general. But obviously villages vary enormously, and the particular layout chosen by the author is not fortuitous. There is a distinct residential area in the centre of which is the village hall, which later becomes the newspaper reading room. The school and the monastery are outside this area and separate from it. This is made quite clear by detailed descriptions of journeys from the residential village to these two places.

It is not uncommon that monasteries are surrounded by residential areas, but one also finds them on hill tops or other locations quite separate from the lay communities they serve. The location of villages and monasteries are interconnected, but only partially. The position of a village is largely determined by economic, ecological and, sometimes, administrative necessity. For monasteries certain locations are traditionally more likely to be sacred sites than others - natural formations, such as hills, cliffs and caves. Other sites with no obvious features may be linked by legend and tradition with ancient monasteries and therefore be chosen to build new ones. The major link between village and monastery is the mutual dependence of layman and monk. The monk needs the laymen to supply his sustenance, for food, labour and materials for building and all other demands the world may make. In turn, the layman needs monks so that they may perform those meritorious actions which will bring him well-being in the future - in this life or in some other. It is one of the paradoxes of the monk-layman relationship that the more a monk is removed from the world, the more meritorious it is to offer him alms. A practical balance is often struck by the monastery being situated in a place that is accessible, but not too near the village.

In former times the monastery was the only school there was. Today, village schools are also often at a little distance from the village, perhaps for the more mundane reason that a sufficiently large piece of land is difficult to find within the settled area. Nevertheless, monastery and school are part of, but separate from, the village. It is clearly the author's intention to stress this separation and to associate Piya and 'Carn Khen with this. They both choose to live away from the village, they are more serious and thoughtful than the inhabitants of the village, and the villagers ultimately fail to understand this desire for solitude.

To return to the role of the monk - it would be wrong to stress only the monk's separation from the laity. His is ideally, and ideologically, the Middle Way. Sometimes monks may fundamentally influence the way in which a village conducts its affairs. In many areas prized possessions, communal or individual, are kept in monasteries - as are the competition drums in the novel. In the towns and cities wakes are now held more and more in the monastery compound; in Barn Norng Ma Vor they are still held in the house of the deceased.

The business affairs of monasteries are conducted by the abbot and a lay committee. Effective control seems to vary greatly, sometimes the abbot exercising iron control over finances, building policy, etc.; elsewhere, powerful laymen may make the final decisions. One might speculate that Piya's uncle, the abbot of a monastery in Bangkok, would exercise a great deal of authority himself. Ecclesiastical matters are more formally controlled through a hierarchy with the Supreme Patriarch *(Sangharaja,* lit. the king of the order of monks) at the head of a governing council and ecclesiastical administrators at each level paralleling the secular system. Fully ordained monks must be males over the age of twenty-one. Those below that age may be ordained as novices. Although novices may be ordained anywhere by a single qualified monk, for 'higher ordination', the full ordination of a monk, there must be at least four qualified monks. The ritual can only take place in the sanctified *uposathagara,* commonly known by the short form *bot*. Not all monasteries possess such a sanctified area. The ritual of sanctification requires royal permission and a royal grant of land.

Villages may also have various shrines and officiants connected with religious practices of a different kind. These should not be seen as being in competition with Buddhism, though some monks and orthodox laymen might disapprove of some or all of them. In Isarn, the northeast region, the village is likely to have a shrine to a protective deity. Rituals at this shrine, performed at least once a year, are likely to be conducted by the *thaw cam,* sometimes called a 'brahmin', who conducts the *su khwan* ritual at the marriage of 'Carn Kern's son, and gives magical-herbal treatment to Mae Kham. Protective domestic spirits are also found throughout the Northeast, but not a great deal is known about their operation. Much more is known about North Thailand, and a brief comment here will also allow me to say something about domestic and household organization.

The family and the domestic unit as well as the village are associated with folk religious practices, and the clearest evidence we have on the operation of kinship-based religious practice comes from North Thailand. In this region matrilineal groups, that is groups of persons related to each other only through women (mother, grandmother, etc.), perform rituals together and each group is under the protection of a particular spirit. Most often it is women who are active in these rituals, though men are entitled to take part and sometimes do. In the Northeast we have at least one report (significantly from the province in which this novel is set) which identifies matrilineal groups with a recognized leader who acts as 'adviser and arbiter in matters concerning blood relations ... (and) also acts as mediator in communication with the kin group ancestral spirit'.[5] Other writers have described Northeastern Thai kin groups as being bilateral - the members of the group being related to each other through both male and female links, though, as throughout Thailand, residential groups are likely to form around a core of mother-daughter-granddaughter. One of the reasons for this familiar pattern is the Thai practice of keeping one's youngest daughter at home. She is often expected to bring her husband to live in her parents' house, which she inherits when they die.

The case of Mae Kham and her family illustrates other situations which may be frequently encountered in real life. The old woman lives with her young grown-up daughter, Phayorm, and school-going son. Though even property-owning widows or deserted wives may head such households, it is true that isolation and poverty create a vicious circle. Mae Kham has been deserted by her husband who has run off with a younger woman, and the older woman has had to sell her land to survive. In real life, deserted wives often find another husband, but one can imagine the circumstances that might have worked against re-marriage in this case. These circumstances also make it likely that the daughter's husband will either live with his wife's family or take her whole family with him. So that both expected patterns of domestic relations and the exigencies of life may lead to the mother-daughter-granddaughter configuration in the formation of households and even the associated kinship-based ritual groups.

---

5 Klausner, William J., *Reflections in a Log* Pond(Bangkok: Suksit Siam [distributorsl,1972),pp.57-58.

Households or individual families tend to organize their own economic affairs. There are exceptions to this, such as when a man, or sometimes a woman, may preside over a compound made up of the families of his or her married children. The headman's wife refers to such arrangements when she says that if they had grown children in the village they could help them cultivate for a share of the rice. Typical arrangements are also implied by Mae Kham who says that Phayorm helps farmers with their rice cultivation in exchange for rice. When the headman is transplanting his fields, Phayorm is one of those engaged. In North Thailand, traditionally, such work would earn about twenty or thirty litres of unhusked rice per day. There is much variation in the formation of these labour teams. Some cultivators may call on a regular group of kinsmen and neighbours, others take whoever turns up, and a few try to do all their cultivation using the labour available within their own household or calling on only very close kin. Cultivators work for each other, keeping strict account of obligations to each other. Landless families are paid in rice, though in recent years payment in cash has become common. In the novel the headmaster's wife says she and her husband would depend on hired labour were they to cultivate rice. She further indicates that casual labourers need the protection of a patron, who must be persuaded before he will release his client labour. In that village, this patron is likely to be Lung 'Carn Kern.

For Thai rural folk, particularly those without land or with inadequate land, the year's supply of rice for consumption is the most pressing need. The arrangements by which they acquire rice on credit, as described by the author, appear widespread throughout the country. Clearly these are arrangements which are exploited by the greedy and the ruthless, but they can also occur among villagers whose only motive is to help a relative, friend or neighbour. The high rates of interest, although conducive to exploitation, appear to arise from the system itself, and one should remember that the contracts are nearly impossible to enforce if the borrower defaults.

Northeast Thailand is part of that very restricted part of Southeast Asia in which glutinous rice is the staple. Certain references in the novel may not make a great deal of sense unless the reader has some idea about the use and the requirements of this food. The starch molecules of glutinous varieties differ from those of the commoner non-glutinous varieties, so that they are not edible, at least not palatable, when boiled. Glutinous rice, therefore, when used as a staple must be steamed. It is used in many parts of Asia in the making of sweets, sometimes mixed with a non-glutinous variety, but as a staple, its use is largely restricted to valley-dwelling, Tai-speaking peoples of North Burma, North and Northeast Thailand, Laos and Yunnan Province in China. There is some evidence that its use may have been more widely distributed in proto-historic times.

The rice is steamed and then packed in woven rice containers. When required during the day it is taken out and eaten cold. A lump of rice is taken in the fingers of the right hand and compressed either in the fingers or the palm of the hand so that it forms a ball in which the individual grains are tightly packed. This may then be dipped in a relish and eaten, or eaten with a piece of meat, fish, pickled vegetable or a spoonful of curry. The aim is to flavour the rice. It is non-absorbent, and no attempt is made to mix it with the curry or relish as is often done with non-glutinous rice. This would result in the grains falling apart, making it almost impossible to eat. Non-glutinous rice has prestige value in Thailand - it is known as 'the rice of the lords'. It is part of that cultural complex which is defined as proper, refined, desirable. The reader may notice that where the eating of rice is actually described in the novel, it is of the glutinous variety. The occasions are in the home, a small party of intimate friends, and at work in the fields or in the forest. On formal occasions such as the teachers' dinner or the opening of the new school house, food is mentioned, but not the rice. The reason for this is that it would be obvious to any Thai that 'the rice of the lords' was eaten. Glutinous rice, however, is strange to most Thai, and its mention creates the rural and regional atmosphere.

Decisions made within the village, affecting the village as a whole, are perhaps always the result of achieving consensus. Where practical matters are concerned, self-interest is an effective inducement. In the North, where locally maintained irrigation systems are still very common, the farmers organize themselves, appoint leaders who make decisions and enforce sanctions on those who default. Such systems work very well - but anyone who is not directly involved will only work if he is paid an appropriate wage. Where the central government requires work done, the force of state power is applied to compel such work to be done - though this has become much rarer. Where villagers can be persuaded that a piece of work is in their interests, the authority of village officials and public opinion may often suffice. In the novel there is a suggestion that the road into the village was built in that way - as was the original school house and the newspaper reading room. There is also the suggestion that a man with Lung 'Carn Kern's power could make or break such projects at will.

The occasion on which the village acts to settle a dispute is one of the vignettes of the novel. The young teacher Phisit is forced to pay compensation to a young girl he has seduced. Such incidents are not uncommon and it is often a young teacher or other government servant who is involved, as nothing is to be got out of a young man without property or status. A government servant is a sitting duck because of the very strict rules which, on paper, control the private behaviour of Thai government servants. The newspapers from time to time report the punishment, sometimes the dismissal of officials for such things as illicit liaisons between two officials. I know of no published account about the actual application of these rules, but we may guess that such disciplinary measures are often selectively applied for reasons of internal, or even national, politics. A man like Phisit, without proper connections, would be very vulnerable to a demand for official action.

Before I leave these discursive ethnographic comments, there is one theme of the novel which deserves some attention. Crucial to the plot is Piya's attitude towards nature and the protection of the environment - particularly the forests. The denuding of Thailand's forests has for many years been a matter of widespread publicity and concern. There are grounds to believe that the great natural wealth of the teak forests of the North has been irreparably destroyed. Successive governments have been concerned and have attempted to reverse these trends, but have been overwhelmed by corruption, greed and sheer lack of interest at all levels of the society. Foreign greed and thoughtlessness has not helped either. Even on this issue the novel reveals a complexity which needs a certain amount of exposition for the foreign reader. The despoliation of forests is perhaps primarily the consequence of large-scale illegal felling for commercial purposes, ultimately organized by robber barons such as the one depicted in the novel. But one should emphasize the 'perhaps'. A great deal of clearing is done by villagers of a variety of statuses - landless peasants and small entrepreneurs included. Increasing population pressure has pushed the landless into forest reserves. There is very little the government can, in all conscience, do about it. But its effects are likely to be more serious than even the felling by unscrupulous timber merchants. Villagers are also allowed to fell timber to build their houses. On occasion some even resort to the stratagem of throwing up something that looks like a house, using the most expensive timber they can find, and then selling it, as a house, to a timber merchant. The cumulative effect of all this is disastrous.

The novel suggests that the attitudes towards these matters are complex. Piya's and the author's views of conservation are clearly widespread among thinking Thai - and there is no particular reason to suppose that there is anything particularly 'modern' or 'Western' about these views. The author uses 'Carn Khen, the defender of the traditional way of life, as also the proponent of a sensible attitude towards the use of natural resources. It is nevertheless true that, quite apart from the vulgar exploitative attitudes which are not the prerogative of any particular society or culture, there are certain views of man and nature which may surface at many levels of Thai culture. Again, I should make clear that this type of view is probably common to all people with an agricultural past - but we are here concerned with a Thai version of this and its significance for the novel.

Piya's view that the presence of forests is necessary for the rainfall which feeds the farmers' crops is dismissed as 'madness' by those associated with the illegal fellers of timber. 'Madness' is also the accusation regularly made against the behaviour and the ideas of 'Carn Khen. What then, in the view of the villagers, should be the attitudes of sensible folk? Richard Davis has encapsulated a number of related attitudes in the dichotomy between 'settlement' and "forest' (specifically in Northern Thai peasant society, but perhaps more widely applicable). He writes,

> The forest is the domain of wild animals, spirits, and uncivilized aboriginal hill peoples. There is no 'natural' beauty. All beauty lies in human settlements ...[6]

This is a pervasive view, not only among rural people but with manifestations among the urban and the middle classes. (The word usually translated as 'nature',*thammachart*, is a learned borrowing from the Pali and doesnot usually mean 'forest'.) In 1979 I was in the beautiful Inthakhin valley some fifty kilometres north of the city of Chiangmai. A large irrigation dam, the Mae Ngat, was in the process of construction and was then a large

6 Davis, Richard, *Tolerance* and *Intolerance* of Ambiguity in Northern Thai Myth and Ritual', *Ethnology* XIII, No. 1 (1974) pp. 1-24.

unsightly gash across the stream and the vegetation. Standing at one end of what would be the dam, one looked across rice fields and signs of human habitation to rings of mountains, one behind the other, receding into the distance. It was a Sunday, but there was a young engineer on the site, and he could not contain his enthusiasm. In words, he painted his picture of what it would look like, and there seemed no doubt in his mind that, quite apart from utility, it was going to be more beautiful than it ever looked before. Repeatedly the word was used, *thammachart*. Having seen other irrigation works in Thailand, it was not difficult to see what he was talking about. Not only would there be the concrete presence of technological achievement; there would be carefully tended green grass, dazzling arrays of flowers, summer houses, pathways, statuary. It would be a place to which visitors would come from every part of the country, lovers, children, old folk - a place that would give inestimable pleasure. And if such visions were good enough for the creators of Versailles and Hampton Court, why should they not be good enough for that young Thai engineer? Ethnographic particularism should not blind us to the fact that this is merely a Thai interpretation of a widespread phenomenon. The novelist uses his knowledge of the variety of attitudes that go to make up this phenomenon - the dependence of poor village folk on the edges of the forest for their very survival, its more rational exploitation by those with greater courage, and the opportunism of those who whole-heartedly exploit the superstition and fear of the rest of the population. We are tempted to impute a particular view to the author, but we should not forget that the views of Piya, for instance, serve a function within the novel and it is as a presentation of a variety of views that the treatment of this theme should be considered.

A brief word on the province and region in which the novel is set. The province of Ubon Rajathani (Ubon for short) lies in the northeast region of Thailand, known in Thai as Isarn. It is a plateau region bounded by the mighty Mae Khong river to north and east, and by ranges of mountains in the south and west. It is drained by tributaries of the Mae Khong, one of which is the Mun on which the city of Ubon stands. The region is held to be the most backward of Thailand - in economic development and standards of living. This stems partly from its geography, but also from history, when it formed a buffer region between Thai power in Ayutthia and the Khmer.

Many take the view that the northeasterners are Lao rather than Thai. It is true that many of the major dialects and material culture, and to some extent custom, are closer to Lao than to Thai. Nevertheless, in this novel there is no mention of such an alignment. Though Northeast Thailand has been the scene of continuing insurrection in modern times, there has been little suggestion that this activity is directed to unification with Laos - either the kingdom or its successor, the people's republic. The truth of the matter probably is, that though general northeastern culture is more Lao than Thai, the mosaic of dialect and ethnic groups that go to make up the people of Isarn have come to identify with the Thai state rather than with any other.

In modern Thailand, as I suggested above, regionalism, dialect and folk cultures have come increasingly under pressure - perhaps not so much because of the centralizing policies of successive governments, but as a consequence of the spread of education, transport, newspapers, radio and television. All these maintain and enhance the preeminence of Bangkok. The capital draws the young, the ambitious, the talented. Its way of life, its language, its modern entertainments and urban values act, and have acted, to erode the strength and variety even among the Thai-speaking Buddhists who make up the overwhelming majority of the country's population. The novel may be looked at as the author's confrontation of different ways of life. The life of remote northeastern villagers, that of a specific group, the village schoolteachers, and of the provincial bureaucracy seem to confront each other as well as the author's own consciousness. Together they present a composite picture held up to the view of the young of the capital, a social category symbolized in the opening scene of the novel, a category of people the author clearly sees as in danger of growing apart from its own origins, its own sources of strength. This audience is part of the novel itself, for Duangdaw, Phisit and Ekachai belong to it.

It is from this elaboration of the multiplex nature of a modern Asian society that the theme of 'identity' emerges. My own reaction was probably very personal. In the first place, as an outsider trying to learn about Thai society, so much of the detail was vividly illuminating. The passing description of a gesture, an exclamation or the hint of an attitude would bring to mind a series of undigested memories, sometimes a sudden insight. In his Introduction, the author says he is concerned to depict 'the life of the rural folk of Isarn in the years 2519-20 (Buddhist Era)'. In fact there is more than just rural life - it is the conviction carried by the detail which conveys the feeling, 'This is Thai society'. In this sense the novel is an ethnography of Thai society and as such is concerned with the identity of its characters, of its audience and of the society itself.

The other part of my reaction to the book was perhaps even more personal. The author is concerned with a societal condition in which those with power, those economically, culturally and spatially at the centre of the society, are progressively alienated from nature and the folk society from which they all sprang. Because of Thailand's very special modern history, this alienation may seem less acute, much less a problem than it is in the many societies, and for millions of individuals, just emerging from a recent colonial past. But because the confrontation of colony and colonial power is absent, perhaps the consequences of the growing cultural divide may be better perceived. In the remainder of this Introduction these themes in the novel, and some of their implications, will be pursued.

Ostensibly, the author sets out to describe the way of life of a poor village folk of a remote area of the northeastern region (Isarn). He details their speech, their economy, their technology, their festivals and their food. He dwells on their poverty, their sickness, the meanness of some and the strength of character of others. He glories in the environment in which they live, the cycle of seasons, their knowledge and adaptation to it - yet recognizes both their ignorance and superstition. This folk quality is celebrated throughout the novel through the two characters, Piya and 'Carn Khen, as well as the author's own comments. The eponymous hero is the 'way of life' of the rural schoolteacher, the *khru bannork*. The relationship of village schoolteacher to village is already complex. As the novel makes clear, to the villager the schoolteacher is a government servant, and therefore a species apart. Nevertheless, he or she is part of the village community. This is expressed in the recognition that teachers are permissible, possible and highly desirable marriage partners. Outsiders are very likely to refer to schoolteachers as if they were members of the village. There is a positive valuation given to the fact of a schoolteacher being a local man, from the same province, and, as the novel indicates, a certain pressure is put on teachers to return to the village of their birth. This last point is significant. Piya has fetched water from the well, tended buffaloes and done all the things a young village boy does. His social mobility has been possible, not by being a monk, but through a monk, his uncle, the abbot of a monastery in Bangkok.

A good novel will often illustrate and encapsulate the sometimes long-winded results of social science investigation. Often, too, the novel may disclose, or draw attention to unconsidered aspects of the phenomenon. Social scientists have recognized for some time that the monkhood allows poor boys from a rural background to get an education and make their way in the world. There is less reference in the literature to cases such as that of Piya. They do occur, however, and may be of considerable importance in the society as a whole. One of the features of Thai social structure, known, but not adequately understood, is that despite the hierarchical nature of the society, its emphasis on relative status and class divisions, upward mobility is, and perhaps always has been, possible. In this respect Thailand shows more similarity to the post-war societies of the 'Western' world than to many other societies of Asia. One writer has suggested that, at least in the contemporary period, there is a parallelism in the rise of poor boys from the provinces to positions of political power through the army and the rise of village boys to ecclesiastical preeminence in the *Sangha*.[7] The movement, however, is not only through these two channels. Piya has been able to acquire an education despite the poor background from which he comes. Very early in the first chapter it is made clear that his contemporaries in the Teachers' College are determined to advance their careers and status in the world; some of them at least with backgrounds not dissimilar to his own. Piya himself renounces such ambitions - which is necessary for the internal logic of the novel. But there is no suggestion that his life up to that point is a unique phenomenon.

There are a number of these recognizable social categories sketched in the novel, some only fleetingly. One interesting case is Lung 'Carn Kern the village entrepreneur, who is on his way up quite another social ladder - commercial success through the petty exploitation of his fellow villagers. But it is with the teachers that the author is most concerned.

The world of the teacher connects in one direction with the village - the teachers have their origin there and that is where many of them work and live. In the other direction they connect with a world in which power is exercised, policy determined, and from which regulations emanate. The teachers may be sceptical and resentful at some of the

---

7 Tambiah, S.J., *World Conqueror and World Renouncer* (Cambridge: University of Cambridge Press, 1976).

decisions made, but there is no doubt that even the most sceptical share, as does the author, a sense of national will. Human frailty, ignorance and stupidity corrupt, but the protection and fostering of the total way of life must ultimately be acknowledged. This is best seen in the way the author handles the numerous social rituals of everyday life: dinner at a district restaurant, the opening of the new school, the headmaster entertaining his colleagues, the card games, and lunch at the noodle shop. Piya may be critical of the teachers' gluttony and drunkenness in public, and the author very often indicates his own attitude through his choice of epithets. Yet these scenes are lovingly described, they are part of the Thai scene, part of the way of life.

And so to the unseen reader! The vignettes of Thai life are for the benefit of the urban reader, perhaps prototypically the Bangkok student. The sophistication of metropolitan life, Western films and foreign philosophies divorce these people from the life of the village, even the life of the district centres. A life, which for good or ill, is ultimately the only one they can call their own. It is no accident that the novel begins in a ballroom. This is a symbol of the life Piya rejects, but to which the author addresses his novel. It is a long bus ride between that ballroom and the schoolhouse of Barn Norng Ma Vor, but, Khammaan Khonkhai seems to be saying, it is a ride the reader must take if Thai identity is to be understood, if it is to survive.

But what are readers of the English version to understand of this Thai examination of Thai identity? I would suggest two things that may be considered. First, it is a slice of Thai life seen through the eyes of a Thai observer, and therefore has the supreme virtue of telling us outsiders what Thai themselves consider important, particularly about their relations with other Thai. I hope the translation has retained most of the author's emphases. Because I see anthropologists and other students of Southeast Asian affairs as constituting a substantial proportion of readers of this translation, I would like to go into one matter in some detail. This is the use by the author of the resources of the language to indicate the complexity of relationship between the characters. In Thai, forms of address, reference and self-reference convey a great deal about the status of the persons concerned. The sets of terms concerned have no direct or systematic equivalents in English. This creates problems of translation, which I have tried to overcome through a number of fairly obvious devices, such as literal translation, and retention of the Thai term itself. In the process however much may be lost. I therefore give here a brief account of the author's usage.

Generally speaking, in the novel, men with status show the least variation in their pronominal use. Anyone, for example a schoolteacher, who has a position outside the village (being a government servant) will use *phom* as first person singular. Piya thus uses this term when talking to all his superiors, to Duangdaw and Phayorm, and to all adult villagers. In fact the only time he uses any other form in self-reference is when he talks to his pupils and uses the term *khru,* 'teacher'. Mor Sombat does not quite fit this pattern. For the most part his self-reference is like Piya's - except that he keeps less refined company and he uses the *ku/myng* form when for example talking to Ai Song, Sia Mangkorn's gunman *(ku* - I, *myng* - you). This covers most of the male self-reference. There are minor exceptions. We may note that the headmaster refers to himself as *lung* 'elder uncle', when talking to his niece Duangdaw, and as *phor,* 'father', when talking to Piya, whom he tells he is going to treat like a son; Phisit uses the familiar *chan* in self-reference to the young girl he seduces, and teachers refer to themselves as *khru,* their status label, when they talk to the young children. The only other usage that needs to be noted is Phisit's drunken encounter with Phayorm at the funeral house. He brushes up against her while playing cards, then claims this has given him luck and refers to himself as *phi,* 'elder brother'. This is normally a usage both friendly and respectful, but in this context Phisit suggests intimacy and is therefore offensive. I should hasten to add it is not only the use of *phi* which conveys the offensiveness. He addresses her as *khon suai,* 'pretty one', moving her suitor Mor Sombat to rage.

Women's self-reference appears straightforward, but is complicated by the fact that they often avoid the use of a first person pronoun. In the novel there are passages in which a female character makes very little use of pronouns at all. One example is conversation between Phayorm and Mor Sombat. The former finally uses *chan* in self-reference, which itself is fairly complex. The other young female characters use *nu*, the diminutive 'mouse', primarily used by and to children. Both Phayorm and Duangdaw use this form with Piya; Duangdaw even in the intimacy that danger brings towards the end of the story. The term is respectful and Duangdaw also uses it to the headmaster, her uncle, as well as to visiting senior government officials. But the term may have quite other connotations. This is not particularly obvious in the novel. Phayorm's use of *chan* to

Sombat does suggest she feels herself much more his equal (than she does with Piya) and, strangely, less intimate. Duangdaw, expressing her displeasure with Phisit, uses this same term. This should alert us to the fact that the words do have a wide range of meaning, and context can have a large part in determining their appropriateness. The older women tend to refer to themselves as *mae*, 'mother'. This tendency to use what are essentially terms of reference as pronouns, in the first person, is more apparent in second person usage. We have thus a number of terms, many of which I have retained in translation, titles of various kinds, used as terms of address. There are first, kinship terms: *phi*, 'elder brother or sister'; *aai* or *ai* (which I shall deal with in a moment); *mae*, 'mother'; *phor*, 'father'; *lung*, 'elder uncle'; *aa*, 'younger uncle' and variations of these. All of them, except *aai*, *ai*, may also be used as self-reference terms. Next we have a series denoting various statuses (excluding rank in government service). Examples are *thit, acarn*, *'carn*, *sia*. The last is a term derived from Chinese and means a business magnate. A Chinese businessman of lesser distinction may be referred to as *thaw kay*.

The terms thit and *'carn* need some explication. The latter is short for *acarn,* a Sanskrit derived word which generally means 'scholar'. It is widely used thoughout Thailand in numerous contexts. It may mean a monk or learned layman - learned in religious and traditional lore. In academic circles it means a university teacher, usually below the rank of a full professor (who is *sastracarn*). The novel uses the title for a teacher who is a university graduate. The abbreviated form *'carn* falls, partly, into a different series. Throughout Thailand there are terms used as titles for men who have served terms as monks or novices and then left the order; *thit* and *'carn* are two of these. In Isarn *thit is* applied to a man who has been ordained into the monkhood. The term *'carn* is a rank higher and refers to the fact that while a monk he has been honoured by the villagers with a ritual bathing (*hodphra*).[8]

The third set of titles are those associated with government service rank. The title *khru,* 'teacher', has been mentioned already. Another form of address used throughout the novel is *khru jai,* 'headmaster', literally, 'big teacher'. A similar term is *phu jai,* 'headman'. The government officials outside the village, who figure prominently at various points in the novel, are the Section Head, *hua na muad* (the officer in charge of education administration at the district level), *syksa* (short for *syksathikarn,* the head of the Education Department; at the district level, *syksathikarn amphur* and at the provincial level, *syksathikarn changwat*), *syksanithet* (the Education Supervisory Officer), and the *phu wa* (the Governor), more politely addressed as *than phu wa*. The relationship between the Section Head and the District Education Officer is confusing if one does not know that throughout most of the 1970s the Education Department in Thailand was under dual control. Finances were handled by officials responsible to the Ministry of the Interior, so that the Section Head is an official of this Ministry. The Education Officer belongs to the Ministry of Education and is in charge of educational policy. It is clear in the novel that at the district level this man has little work and less power.

---

8 See Keyes, Charles F., 'The Northeastern Thai Village: stable order and changing world ', *Journal of the Siam Society* 63, Part 1 (1975) pp. 177-207.

These titles become both forms of address and reference. As the ranks go up the scale of importance, the more likely it is that names are dispensed with altogether. This is partly a result of the fact that the higher the position the less likely it is to be duplicated. There is only one governor (*phu wa ratcha karn changwat,* 'he who administers the province') and his name may never be mentioned in ordinary speech. He is invariably addressed as *than* or *than phu wa.* All district and provincial level officials are likely to be addressed as *than.* In contrast, though headmasters are addressed as *khru jai,* they are referred to with the addition of the name - thus *Khru jai* Khammaw. In fact Headmaster Cantha refers to his colleague with the familiar *Khru jai* 'Maw.

Adult men are addressed by their titles. At lower status levels the name may be added. Thus Piya is *Khun Khru* to most people, *Khru* Piya to his colleagues and a few others, and *Khun* Piya to Duangdaw. She is *Khun* Duangdaw to Piya, until the end of the novel when she becomes *Khun* Aew, her nickname. Phisit, the younger harum-scarum teacher, is an exception. He is sometimes addressed merely by his name, and on occasions by Duangdaw as *khun.* The Section Head, displeased with Piya, addresses him as *khun.* The Governor, in a similar frame of mind, addresses Sia Mangkorn as *Khun* Mangkorn. A brief comment on *khun* is clearly required. Foreigners are often taught this word means 'you' in Thai. This is a mistake. It is true that in many situations it is a neutral form of address, to strangers, to colleagues or when the more respectful *than* may seem inappropriate. Nevertheless, as the novel shows, a switch to *khun* can indicate displeasure, because of its impersonality. The Section Head would refer to Piya as *khru* and the Governor refer to the business magnate as *sia* - indicating a recognition of the other's status and individuality. The use of *khun* switches to unrecognition and social distance. On the other hand, Piya and Duangdaw, by the mutual use of *khun,* indicate both their respect for each other and the recognition of each other's individuality - they are to each other not merely colleagues, not merely teachers. The use of *ai* or *aai* throughout the novel presents something of a problem. This word is always spelled the same in the Thai, *aai* with a falling tone. According to dictionaries of Central Thai, and in my experience, it is usually pronounced *ai* with a falling tone and its meaning is almost always derogatory. In Northern Thai there are two distinct words—*ai* with a low tone which is either derogatory or used familiarly to younger males, and *aai* with a falling tone which, in some provinces, means 'elder brother'. In rapid speech, though the appropriate word may be clear, it is not always possible for me to decide which word has been used. In the Isarn dialect, as it appears in this novel, the equivalent of *ai*, as used in the North, appears to be *bak.* When the author uses *aai* as a prefix to names, sometimes in narration, sometimes in direct speech, I interpret this to be a standard usage expressing, ambivalently, derogation and/or familiarity. There are a few occasions, however, when such an interpretation is not possible. The village girls address Piya as *Aai Khru,* as does Khamkong to Phisit when he takes her to the city. In these instances the term must be glossed as 'elder brother'. 'Elder brother' is in most, if not all, dialects a form of address used by women to boyfriends, lovers and husbands. I have retained the word *caw* as a prefix or title to the name of many young males. This is another word which carries some ambivalence. In one set of usages it means 'lord' and is an honorific, but that is not the sense here. When it is used before the names of young boys it is similar to *ai* or *bak* used in the same context, perhaps slightly less redolent of rural society and the countryside. When used with the names of young adults it is derogatory, suggesting officiousness, vulgarity or a touch of the hooligan; nothing clear cut, just a suggestion. The use of these prefixes or titles in Thai arises from a distaste for or awkwardness in addressing or referring to people only by a name. Although the author's sample does not cover the whole spectrum of address, reference'and pronominal use, the reader will appreciate their complexity in Thai.

The other set of concerns that arises from the novel also has to do with the complexity of language and society in the societies of modern Asia. In the Thai novel, one may identify at least three linguistic registers. There is first of all the peasant/dialect register - words which the author often translates into the standard language for the benefit of the common Thai reader. There is the formal language of the bureaucrat, a pre-eminent form of life in the kingdom. There is the language of everyday speech, the language of the newspapers, the slang and the newly acquired foreign words. The philology of the novel is as it were a history of Thai culture, of Thai society. Much of this must unfortunately be lost in translation. The implication of it for the readers of the translation should not be overlooked.

Whether the language at issue, the language of the village of Norng Ma Vor, is considered to be Lao or a dialect of Thai does not matter. The novel is in part a plea for the right of the language and the culture to a continuing existence, a plea for the preservation of cultural integrity. Equipping the rural young for a better life in their native Thailand does not, and must not, involve the suppression of their own folk culture. Much of Thailand's creativity must come from the rambunctious metropolis of Bangkok; but it seems as if the author is saying to the urban young - 'Do not forget the sources of strength that lie in your own origins'. What is involved may be set out by way of a brief comparison of the language history of Sri Lanka and Thailand. The British occupation of Sri Lanka fostered the growth of an élite educated in, and speaking, English as their major language. For many of this élite the local language became only a practical means of communicating with servants or in the market place. English was for them an instrument of political and economic aggrandizement, bringing great rewards in material terms, as well as giving them access to one of the great stores of literature both creative and technical. Many have now come to realize, however, that the price may have been excessive. The English-speaking élite of Sri Lanka not only divorced themselves from the creativity that lay in the community that surrounded them, the language they had come to think of as their own was grounded in an environment they would never see, in someone else's history, in someone else's society. Because the standards applied to their speech, their grammar and syntax, their idiom and intonation were decided in the metropolitan centre, that elite could never more have any significant effect on any language.

Superficially one may suppose that the position of the Thai élite was in stark contrast - the difference however is more subtle. The Thai elite, however divorced in political power and social position, always spoke, effectively, a similar language to those that made up the bulk of the population. Nevertheless, Thai history, like Southeast Asian history in general, and like the history of the metropolitan colonial powers themselves, has ample evidence of linguistic suppression. Southeast Asian wars were about people. Conquering princes, over and over again, uprooted whole communities to bring them under more direct control. In this process these communities could lose their language and ethnic identity and, within a generation or so, adopt new ones. The great difference between this situation and that under Western colonialism, was that, in the Southeast Asian situation, these communities became wholly part of the culture into which they were forcibly integrated. Under Western colonialism this rarely, if ever, happened. In Southeast Asia the history and linguistic experience of the conqueror became that of the conquered.

At the turn of the century when the Bangkok regime moved to consolidate its rule over the regions of Thailand, each region had a distinctive culture and distinctive language - related to each other, but different. Regions, sometimes provinces, boasted their own viable cultural and literary traditions. Over the last century this cultural independence has been eroded.

The standardization of language, and certain aspects of culture, has been part of the policy of modern Thai regimes. The system of primary schools with a bureaucratic teaching staff has up to now been its main instrument. In the past, governments have acted unwisely, though relatively mildly, in the suppression of regional cultures and dialects. It is not merely government policy, but the pursuit of social advancement, that leads to standardization. Central Thai language, a particular way of life, particular ways of eating, are prestigious, and government service, education and economic advancement recruit people to the uniformity of modern Thai life. High school children rebuke the foreigner for trying to speak the local dialect - 'it's not proper', 'it's not refined', one will be told. But there is a growing recognition of the value and the strength of variability. For instance, since its inception, the University of Chiangmai began teaching the fast-disappearing Northern Thai system of writing to undergraduates.[9] Today there is a small but dedicated band of scholars who are re-discovering and reworking a rich mine of their own history and culture. The people of Chiangmai have always valued and loved their language; the academic enterprise, one hopes, will now ensure its acceptance as part of the culture of Thailand. *The Teachers of Mad Dog Swamp* is another plea for the strength that cultural variety can give.

Writing this in Australia, as I am, there is a very specific purpose in making this translation available. This country's increasing involvement in Asia has among other things resulted in a continuing stream of novels set in the countries of Southeast Asia. As is to be expected, these are Australian novels set in Asia. They have primarily to do with Western European Man or Woman, usually speaking with an Australian accent, against the exotic background of Jakarta,

---

9 Most Northern Thai students would speak Northern Thai language in their homes.

Manila or some such city. There cannot be any objection to this - but the reader must beware that the exotic background is not mistaken for the reality of Asia. Let me, very briefly, indicate the kinds of things I mean. C.J. Koch's prizewinning novel *The Year of Living Dangerously* has many things in it which I enjoyed and by which I was impressed. But I have never been in Jakarta, and the book gave an impression of the city which I expect would be shattered if I ever went there. More recently, another novel set in Indonesia has appeared, *Monkeys in the Dark* by Blanche d'Alpuget. It is immensely disturbing to find that two of the bits of colour in Koch's novel also feature prominently enough in d'Alpuget's to be released as advance publicity in the *Canberra Times*. That the Ramayana Bar and the transvestites of Jakarta are integrated into their plots by both authors does not dispel the feeling that they have succumbed to the use of the obviously sensational. This kind of distortion to which the reader may be exposed, is something that anthropologists too may perpetrate. When I write on spirit mediums in Chiangmai, what inaccurate emphasis could I convey to the unwary reader. The foreigner's view is always selective, perhaps distorted. It seems to me therefore that there is a real need for translations of local Asian novels, novels written by Asians for Asian readers. Some of them at least can give a view of the society the foreigner can never get, and which is, dare I say, closer to the reality of the society as perceived by those who live in it.

There is yet another danger. The good popular novel may introduce inaccuracies and distortions without even appearing to do so. I cite two paragraphs from the same page of John Le Carré's *The Honourable Schoolboy:*

> Driving on, they passed a village and a cinema. Even the latest films up here are silent, Jerry recalled. He had once done a story about them. Local actors made the voices, and invented whatever plots came into their heads. He remembered John Wayne with a squeaky Thai voice, and the audience ecstatic, and the interpreter explaining to him that they were hearing an imitation of the local mayor who was a famous queen.

Why should one quibble with this? To me it throws in a reasonably accurate bit of local flavour, an interesting, and now much rarer, aspect of Thai popular culture. But a few lines above this passage, Le Carré has another little bit of local colour:

> They stopped, and a young monk scurried out of the trees carrying a *wat* bowl and Jerry dropped a few *baht* into it.

So much here is totally and offensively wrong. The unfortunate thing is that many readers who have heard such phrases as 'Buddhist monks' begging bowls' will not only accept the little vignette as authentic but perhaps absorb other notions about the behaviour of monks which can completely distort understanding of the society.[10] Perhaps Le Carré does not have to be right about Thai society; but

---

[10] In the Buddhist view monks do not beg. In practice they decorously make their rounds each morning with their bowls into which the laity are privileged to place food - not money. They certainly would not scurry. People see monks as providing them (the laity) with the opportunity to perform meritorious deeds.

Khammaan Khonkhai, and others like him, are Thai society and I close with the hope that what they have to say will become increasingly available to readers of English.

Gehan Wijeyewardene
The Australian National University
March 1981.

CHAPTER 1

The celebration that followed the award of diplomas was a big event in the lives of the young men and women who had just completed their courses at the Teachers' Training College. The large assembly hall was packed with people clothed in variegated colours under the neon lights and the multi-coloured spots. There were hundreds of them, the young teachers of the future, some with the first diploma, others with the higher; but now all enjoying the drink, the food, the songs, the sweet smells, and the movement of their bodies following the rhythm of the music which excited them and drove them on.

Piya, a young man who had just completed his upper level diploma, was among those at the celebrations. He had decided that this would be the last diploma for which he would ever sit. After much soul-searching he was determined that he was going to start earning his living, while many of his acquaintances had just as resolutely decided to pursue higher qualifications, and therefore more money, at other colleges and universities. This was the first time he had participated in such a celebration, as one being there by right, as it were. People called it a 'graduation celebration', but he did not see anyone bring their diplomas along. Most of them came to dance. Some quite shamelessly hugged each other, but most of them just swayed to the music, moved their bodies with the beat. Others seemed happy just making themselves tired. But there were also many who just sat and watched the others enjoy themselves - perhaps because they had no partners, or because they did not like to make an exhibition of themselves, or perhaps for some other reason. Piya was one of these. Bored with the dancing, he left the huge assembly hall, stopped a moment at the toilets, then walked outside into the cool air of the college grounds. He passed a few couples cuddling in the dark as he made his way to another building as brightly lit as the assembly hall - but here there were no people.

In this building an exhibition of the arts and crafts of the northeast region was being held. The exhibition had opened three days ago and would continue for another week. Piya had come every day, for he was a committee member of the Northeastern Cultural Society. 'Oh! It's Khun Piya! I wondered who it was.' The curator, who was keeping watch outside, greeted him as soon as he recognized him. 'It must be very pleasant over there. Why have you left so soon?' 'Oh yes, it's very pleasant. But somehow I prefer a little quiet.' He entered the building and walked down to a hall on the floor below. He asked the curator, 'It's not yet shut, is it?' then left him on his own to smoke his cigarette. The curator called after him, 'It closes at nine o'clock.'

The exhibition of northeastern arts made Piya very proud; partly because he had been responsible for its organization, together with many other students and teachers, but most of all because he was proud of the arts of the region itself: its basket work, such as the glutinous rice containers, creels, fish trays, wicker water pails, baskets, bushels and trays; its weaving and crochet work such as decorative pillows, women's cloths *(sinmi)*, silk sarongs, *pha khaw ma* (the narrow, open cloth worn by men); its musical instruments, such as *khaen* (a type of mouth organ), *phin* (a type of harp) which in the Northeast is called *sung*, wooden bells, strumming instruments and clappers. All these he had seen many times already, but he could not resist looking at them again.

The young man came to a large framed photograph, a sixty-centimetre enlargement, and stood silently in front of it. It hung in the middle of the wall directly opposite the main door. In the picture was a middle-aged woman wearing an old black striped local skirt and a single *pha khaw ma* wrapped around her breasts on the upper part of her body. She carried a little child on her hip, supported by her bent left arm. On her right shoulder she carried on a pole two large closely-woven baskets. In one basket could be seen a glutinous rice container and a mortar and pestle sticking out on top. On the other side was a closely meshed dip-net hanging by its round frame from the end of the carrying pole. The curve of the pole indicated the weight of the contents of the baskets. The expression on her face and her posture indicated clearly that she was hurrying on her way, the sweat lining her face, her body exhausted. Yet, her dark eyes shone with determination, just like those of the little child who followed behind her, carrying in one hand a creel and, tied on his shoulders, a fishing rod. Even though he was thin, with a distended belly, and dressed in only a tattered pair of shorts, he still wore an expression of complete enjoyment. In the background, rice fields stretched into the distance. Dead trees, known by a term meaning 'easy to strip', stood piercing the sky with their leafless trunks and branches.

Piya stared at the eyes of the two people in the picture, feeling their burden and their solemnity and, at the same time, letting his thoughts float to Isarn, his birthplace, from which he had come so many years ago. The sound of dance music which came noisy and insistent from the Assembly Hall slowly dropped out of his consciousness, being replaced by the soft, faint sounds of the *khaen* and the *phin*, whose plaintive melody, slow and sad, fluttered in his ear and gradually became louder as the rythm of the *ponglang* (a wooden gong) thrust itself into his imagination.

At that moment, the question he had been pondering for many days was answered. When he graduated, should he work in Bangkok or should he return home? He would return and become a teacher in Isarn.

About nine o'clock that night Piya returned to the *wat* where he was staying. The noises of the capital receded into the background as he entered the precincts of the monastery, which lay some way from the main road. He walked past the *bot*, the monks' residences, the *cedi* and the line of trees, all of which he had walked past many a time. Ten years he had come and gone this way, from the time he had left Primary 4 (which was as far as his village school went) till he had acquired his higher diploma. This place, like his home, had, as the Thai are wont to say, 'the image of coolshack', brought peace and happiness to body and mind. When he climbed up into the *kuti* in which he lived, he met Thit Phomma, a man from his own village who also lived there and whom Piya called 'uncle'. He had just returned from work.

'Why have you come back so soon?' Thit Phomma asked, with his face still buried in the newspaper in which he had been checking lottery numbers. 'I thought you were having a party tonight.'

'I saw no point in staying on,' Piya said, taking off his long-sleeved shirt. 'I don't know how to dance, and even if I did, with whom would I dance?'

'Oh! These things ... you should practise. If you are interested, you could learn any time.' Thit Phomma had still not raised his eyes from the numbers in the newspaper. 'Hell! What a pity! Missed by one number. Look at this! I missed the fifth prize by just one number. Mine was a "six" - they drew "seven". All the rest were right!'

'How did it go? How much did you lose this time?' Piya took up a *pha khaw ma* and changed his trousers. He knew Thit Phomma was besotted with gambling - particularly with the lottery. Nearly all the money he earned driving a motorized trishaw was thrown away in his pursuit of 'good luck'.

'Just a little. Two or three hundred baht, that's all. It leads me on like this! I just miss on this side, then just on that. Every time! If I get a good prize I'll go home and make an offering of *kathin* robes. I'll hire a band here in Bangkok and take it up with me.' Thit Phomma had come to Bangkok looking for work. He had first earned a living riding a pedal trishaw. That was ten years ago and he now drove a *samlor khryang*, a motorized trishaw. He had not changed much in that time, he still waited for his one great stroke of luck.

'I say, if you'd saved up the money you spent on lotteries, by now you would have been able to buy many tracts of rice fields,' the young man said. 'Does my uncle think he is going to live in Bangkok for ever?'

'I must stay on here. If I can get my hands on a large sum of money, I'll go back home and become a farmer.' Thit Phomma sat with one knee up, his jaw in one palm and elbow on knee. 'But you, Piya, will you be a teacher in Bangkok, or will you return home?'

'I am going home' Piya said without any hesitation.

From the place of his birth and early childhood in Ubon Rajathani, Piya had come to study in Bangkok. After completing Primary 4 he had gone to live with a monk in the district of Jotsay. This *Phra Khru* was only a distant relative - but he was the only relative on whom he could call for help. He went to him to continue his studies in Primary 5 in the municipal school in the monastery. Later he continued in the government high school and finally completed his teacher training at a well-known training college in Bangkok.

Living in Bangkok had not turned him into a city lad at all. Without exception, the residents at the monastery were from Isarn: the abbot, the other monks, the novices, the lay boys and those like Piya who boarded there, were all natives of the same region. Every day there were other relatives and devotees from the high plateau of Isarn who came to visit and to spend some time living in the monastery. They were never absent. Once a year Piya returned to see his relatives in the village, which was more than a hundred kilometres away from the provincial city of Ubon. His father and mother who had been, in the Thai idiom, 'like the protective shade of the bodhi and the banyan tree', had died before he had completed Primary 4. He had no fields, no house, no property of any kind about which to worry. Nevertheless he held fast in his innermost thoughts to the lifestyle of his childhood. Everything still remained in his memory and often occupied his thoughts -

the rice fields, the groves of forest, the hills and mountains, the streams and swamps; the drought and the dryness, the heat, the burning heat of the hot season; the green and plenty of the rains and the cold of winter. Whenever he heard the sounds of *mor lam*, the sound of the *khaen*, whenever it rained and the sound of thunder was heard, Piya, like all other children of Isarn, thought of his birthplace, his home.

At dawn, the day after the graduation party, Piya went to pay obeisances to the Venerable Uncle, the abbot of the monastery, who had taken responsibility for all his wants during the last ten years.

'What do you say *Bak* Khen, you've finished your studies now, haven't you?' the Venerable Uncle asked, using Piya's childhood name. 'Are you going to study some more, or are you going to work?'

'I want to teach in Ubon, Sir.' The young man bent his head and stared at the floor, polished to a gleaming finish.

'That's fine,' he said, spitting his betel out into a spittoon. 'Are you going to live in Ubon, or will you go home?' He meant to the village of his birth. By 'Ubon' he meant the town itself, rather than the province, which in Thailand always shares the name of its capital.

'That depends on where they want me to teach. The town or the countryside - it doesn't matter.' Piya gazed at the face of his benefactor who had bestowed on him the name he now used, who had raised him to adulthood 'with rice from the bottom of his alms bowl' and had enabled him to acquire his teaching qualifications. 'But I would prefer to teach in the countryside.'

'Go! Go back to our home! Go and be of benefit to your brothers and sisters' - a phrase which means 'to your fellow men'. 'As for us, we men who have an education, we should inform our fellows, enlighten them. Even if we don't have brothers and sisters of the same blood, all of us who live together on this piece of earth are brothers and sisters.' He continued to advise the young man on his work and how he should behave with others. It was somehow special, more special than the instruction he had received over the years. And when the day came for Piya to go to Ubon, the Venerable Uncle gave him a sum of money to tide him over till he was examined and selected to be a teacher. That day the young man of twenty-three years left from the bus depot at the Mor Chit Market in the long orange bus of the Transport Company for Ubon Rajathani, the province of his birth. He left with his diplomas and with his own sense of purpose.

CHAPTER 2

'They say the teachers' examination is tougher this year than last. Is that so?' the young man in a short-sleeved shirt and grey slacks asked his friend, seated in the liquor shop opposite the Rajathani Hotel. Work was over for the day.

'What does that mean?' Another man in a khaki uniform was putting away various things in his bag. 'Does it mean that the questions are hard, or that there are more people applying?'

'We know there are many applicants and few positions. What I want to know is ... they say there's a lot of money changing hands ... thousands of baht a time, sometimes tens of thousands. Is that true?' the first young man said, taking off his tie and putting it away in the pocket of his trousers. He ordered another bottle of soda.

'There is talk about money changing hands every year. The Governor and the Provincial Head have emphasized that anyone who knows for certain and has evidence that someone has paid money to someone else, should report it. Now there's only gossip - no one is willing to come forward and make a clear accusation,' the man in uniform said.

'I've been in many districts and have heard the teachers complain - this one's paid his money for his son to be selected, that one's paid money ...' The young man in short sleeves told of his own experiences. 'I just want to ask you, Khun Sutham, you are in charge of all this ... ask you straight what it's all about. I don't want to believe that there is all this bribery ... it has ruined the education system for long enough now.' Just then another man came out of the hotel restaurant.

'Come, join us, Sir!' Sutham stood up and invited the newcomer respectfully and then turned to his companion.

'Khun Vichai, meet Palat Koson, the Deputy District Officer, Amphur Muang[1]. We were just talking about the teacher selection examination,' he said, returning to the original topic of conversation.

'That's fine. I wanted to meet Khun Sutham, and here you are.' Palat Koson ordered a bottle of beer. 'I can't drink spirits. Has the committee for the teachers' examination been officially appointed yet, or not?'

'Not yet,' Khun Sutham, an official in the provincial administration of the Education Department, replied. 'But I guess, as the Governor has made his assistant head of a number of the committees, it is likely the Deputy Governor and the Head of Education will be on it.'

'My daughter qualified as a teacher this year.' Palat Koson went straight to the point, ignoring the fact that Vichai was seated with them. 'She can't go on to further studies, she must get a teaching job.'

'What level?'

'Elementary diploma. If she doesn't get it, she will have to study "twilight",' the father said, using the English word, with a worried expression on his face. 'But I'd rather she get a job. Is there anything going near the town?'

Khun Vichai did not look very happy. Acting as if he had just thought of something, he excused himself. 'I must beg your pardon, Khun Sutham and you Sir, Deputy District Officer, I think I've forgotten something at the

---

1 *Amphur Muang* - the district of the provincial capital.

office ... I don't know if they've closed up yet or not.' Making his farewell, he got on his motorcycle and made towards the office of the Provincial Education Department.

'Who was that?' asked Palat Koson. 'I didn't get a good look at his face.'

'Acarn Vichai, the new Provincial Supervisor,' Sutham explained, giving Vichai the title for a teacher with a university degree. 'He just graduated this year, but before that he was a teacher in Khemarat. He was in about the same batch as myself.'

'Are there vacant positions round about the city?' Palat Koson came back to the original question.

'There's a vacancy only in the school for the backward, Phi Palat; and that only because we gave the old teacher an opportunity to transfer and we left the vacancy open for one of the new teachers.' Sutham addressed the other respectfully as 'elder brother.'

'I am sure that won't matter. I only want my daughter to get in. I don't think there'll be any problem about the committee.' The *palat*, who had crawled up from being a clerk, carefully poured himself the second glass of beer.

'But I think you, Khun Sutham, are sure to have a colleague who is on the committee, or know an official who has a vote, and will cast his vote as every year. I'd like to leave my daughter's case to you ... concerning the other things, lets wait till later.' When he had finished speaking, he took out a name card and wrote his daughter's name and examination number on it and handed it to his companion.

When the final results of the examination were announced after the interviews, it appeared that 364 applicants with the higher diploma had registered, but in the first batch only 183 had been selected - equal to the number of vacancies. Piya was fortunate to be selected at number 23, well within the top half. Nevertheless, the school to which they were allocated were all with no exception, far from the provincial capital. Piya, when he read the names of the schools, had no idea where they were. He finally chose a school with a rather astonishing name.

'The school at Mad Dog Swamp! Barn Norng Ma Vor, in the *Tambon* of Phak I Hin. That is an interesting name!' He gave his decision to the official, after he had filled in all the different forms and finally made up his mind.

'Come back on the twenty-seventh for your papers of appointment to be taken to the District Office.' Khun Sutham, who was the official in charge, announced over the public address system in the assembly hall of the Provincial Council on the day the successful candidates went to choose their schools.

'We will prepare a document, one for each district. All of you chosen to go to the same district must go through the formalities together.'

Piya looked for someone he recognized, but there was no one. After he had chosen his school, Piya examined the list of successful candidates, but he still did not recognize a single name. He only learned that 1056 candidates with elementary diplomas had registered and only 347 had been selected.

On 28 May the new teachers who were to go to the same district as Piya - thirty in all - had arranged to meet at the District Office at 10.00 am. Among the group was one graduate with a bachelor's degree, Acarn Ekachai, who had been selected for the largest primary school in the district, that which stood just opposite the District Office. Twelve of them had the higher diploma and the rest the elementary.

Apart from Acarn Ekachai, the others, including Piya went their separate ways, each to his or her school away from the district centre. Among the sixteen youths who came there that day, some were neatly dressed and shorn, almost as if they had just left the monkhood, and then there were those wearing jeans and fashionably long hair. Among the fourteen women were some wearing black skirts and white blouses, like trainee teachers, and others dressed in fashionable, gaily coloured suits. But there was one whose face - mouth, nose, eyebrows, neck - was prettier by far than all the others. This one wore a matching skirt and blouse of expensive material, white with a sky-blue pattern - or was it blue with a white pattern? - and high-heeled shoes. She sat in the front row - Acarn Ekachai having carefully shepherded her all the way from the bus station in Ubon town.

'What's your name?' Acarn Ekachai whispered to the young man who sat silent opposite.

'Piya,' the young man answered softly, but clearly.

'You graduate from Ubon, did you?' Acarn Ekachai continued.

'I graduated from Phra Nakhorn Teachers' Training College in Bangkok.'

'Oh, Khun Piya! You are not a native of Ubon?' Ekachai suggested. 'Where do you come from?'

'Certainly I am a native of Ubon! I just went to Bangkok.' Piya was happy that someone at least was interested enough to ask him. 'I don't know anyone in this district - apart from you, Acarn, and our crowd here.'

In a little while the District Officer and the head of the local education office entered the meeting hall. Everybody stood up and respectfully greeted them. The District Officer looked around at the thirty new teachers and then sat down. The local education officer checked off the list of teachers, calling their names, qualifications and school. When the list was complete, Piya could remember the names of about five of his companions and he knew that the name of the girl in the blue outfit seated next to Acarn Ekachai was Duangdaw.

After that, the District Officer gave them a rundown of the district - its geography, its economy and social composition, politics and government, and then a highly condensed account of developmental policy for its population and plans for its defence. He then called on them to put their hearts into the performance of their duties. Finally, he told them that if they had any problems of any kind they could always send details of them to the District Office.

When he had finished and left the room, the head of the District Education Office went with him. Khun Sawad, the assistant to the Section Head, then explained to them the procedure for voluntary membership of the teachers' council. He invited the new teachers to join the provincial savings co-operative and the Funeral Benefit Society. The District Education Officer then came back and instructed them on governmental procedures and their duties in general, and specifically on what was expected of all teachers. He went on for about an hour and a half and finished round about noon.

A group of them, Acarn Ekachai, Duangdaw, Piya, Prasit and Bunchan, went for lunch to the restaurant opposite the District Office. Piya observed that Ekachai's intimate attentions to Duangdaw greatly increased when he invited her to have lunch. The young lady did not refuse and, following his example, invited others to come along with them. 'Khun Piya, you must have lived in Bangkok many years.' Acarn Ekachai continued his conversation, when they had all ordered their noodles.

'Yes, it was many years.' Piya did not feel like discussing his past history. 'I went to live with a monk as a monastery boy. My home is in Amphur Amnart. I am entirely a village boy. I am no townsman or city type.'

'What school did you choose, Khun Piya?' Duangdaw asked sweetly, as if they had known each other a long time.

'Barn Norng Ma Vor, in the commune of Phak I Hin. Where it is, I have no idea. I just saw the strange name and chose it,' the young man replied, smiling.

'Oh! I know it! My uncle is the headmaster there!' She referred to herself with the epithet 'mouse', a form used to and by children, but also commonly used by adult women, as a mark of respect, to both older men and women.

Duangdaw reached for the bottle of chillies pickled in vinegar. Acarn Ekachai quickly picked it up and made as if to serve her some, but the young woman insisted on serving herself.

'You've got to go south, about twenty kilometres. Mine is tougher than that, it's almost on the border. Perhaps Khun Piya will change with me?'

'I don't care where I go. All I ask is a school to teach in,' the young man said with sincerity.

CHAPTER 3

The winding, chalky road had been constructed entirely through the labour of local villagers. The medium-sized bus, of the type known in Thai as a 'two-rower',[1] crawled slowly along, overladen inside and out, the roof stacked with goods right up to the front wheels. It carried passengers and every imaginable kind of cargo. The sun was the colour of chewed betel, when it was not entirely obscured by the dust which rose behind the vehicle. As they approached the village, children playing by the side of the road stopped whatever they were doing and ran after the bus. Two of them, walking on stilts, made a good job of racing it as it strained in low gear behind a herd of cattle which marched ahead, filling the road as if quite oblivious of the horn which the driver kept sounding - long, short, alternatively, in concert with his feelings.

The bus stopped finally at an open space in the middle of the village. The passengers disembarked like ants from a disturbed nest. Piya gingerly lowered a gun handed to him from the roof, together with his cloth suitcase. He stood looking at the people and the various things in the bus in some bewilderment. Besides about thirty passengers there were a number of bags of cement, many boxes and crates of various kinds of goods, sacks of manure, and on the roof there were even sheets of corrugated iron for roofing - at least two loads of them.

---

1 *Sorng thaew* - two rows. The common Thai term for the small buses, privately owned, which are found throughout the country. They are usually fitted with two benches on either side of the passenger compartment.

'Does everybody who came with us live in this village?' Piya asked a middle-aged man, large of stature, with thick hair, large eyes and bushy eyebrows, who was standing staring at him with some interest.

'They are nearly all from here, but a few are from other villages. They take the bus and get down here, because there is no proper road beyond this village.' The man stared at Piya almost without blinking. 'You haven't been here before?'

'I am the new teacher appointed to teach here.' Piya tried to sound as polite as he possibly could. 'Khun Aa, could you please direct me to the house of the headmaster?' Piya respectfully addressed the older man as 'Uncle'.

'Follow me.' The man spoke curtly and strode off without looking at Piya, suddenly showing not the slighest interest in anyone.

Many who had been standing close by and who had heard the sound of their conversation, soon began to whisper together, and followed the pair with their eyes as they walked past a group of children, a flock of ducks, people carrying firewood and women shouldering buckets of water.

'Carn Khen, hey, who's that you're bringing along?' An old man stripping bamboo on his verandah had been talking to his wife who was busy feeding silkworms in a large bamboo tray.

'He looks like one of those students who came to our village last year,' his teenage granddaughter chipped in. "Carn Khen has a lot to do with that lot. Since he had that trouble and went and built his house out there, he doesn't have much to do with people in the village. Even when the old people beat the alarm, beat the *korlor*, he doesn't come to listen. These days the "venerable sir"', he continued sarcastically, 'only has to do with strangers. I should hurry to Headman Lua and tell him,' the old man said as 'Carn Khen led Piya past his home.

The two walked on, not saying a word to each other. Finally, the leader stopped, turned round and pointed at a wooden house built high off the ground, set back from the road about twenty metres from the village. 'That's the headmaster's house.' He spoke abruptly and walked off, as if uninterested in anything the young man might have to say.

Piya, bewildered, stared after him until the man took a bend in the road around a clump of bamboo and was lost in the enfolding dusk. He turned towards the teacher's house. The house stood among mango and carombola trees. There was a coconut tree by the stairs in front of the house. The yard was spacious, suitable for playing *takror* or for a badminton court. On the side of the house was a granary, which the villagers called a *law*. Under the house were a number of looms for weaving cloth. A motorcycle stood in a fenced enclosure. As he came closer, he saw a sign-board, green with white lettering, fastened on a post at the front of the house:

Khammaw Kaewsai
Headmaster Barn Norng Ma Vor

The young man climbed the stairs determinedly. An older woman emerged from the kitchen fiddling with a *pha khaw ma* which had come undone, rewinding it around her breasts.

'Whom do you want?' the woman, the headmaster's wife, asked him abruptly, in the manner and the accents of the local people. 'I've come to see the headmaster,' said Piya, raising his hands in a *wai*; 'I'm the new teacher come to teach at his school.'

'Oh! Is it the new teacher then?' the headmaster's wife exclaimed, looking as happy as if she had met her own son. 'I Si! Go, call the headmaster! Quickly! Oh, the girl went to draw water and hasn't come back yet. Just a moment, "this one" will go and call the headmaster. Sit and rest a while. You don't have to be bashful with us.' She rushed out of the house as if she had no interest in whatever it was that was cooking away in the kitchen.

Piya set his little bag beside him and sat down, leaning against a pillar, letting his feet hang down on to the outer verandah which was at a level lower than the floor of the house. The three walls of the area in which guests were received - used in fact for all kinds of purposes - were covered with a variety of pictures. Apart from pictures of Their Majesties the King and Queen and the three royal children, there were numerous pictures of groups, all framed and neatly hung. Most of them were old, so old that on some of them the lettering of the names of those in the pictures had faded and even disappeared. Looking at the pictures, one could infer that the owner of the house had attended many conferences and many refresher courses; at least six, for there were six group photographs. There was, besides, a portrait of a young man in khaki uniform. It must have been taken a very long time ago. The picture had faded and the hairstyle, which had the parting in the middle, gave an indication of its age. Piya guessed that this was Headmaster Khammaw as a youth. There was also a calendar from a bank, printed on expensive paper in clear tones, and another from a miscellaneous goods store in the district centre. The store had acquired a photograph of a film star and attached it to a piece of cardboard with the name of the store and a calendar block with daily tear sheets.

The house was reasonably clean. There were no cobwebs to be seen, but there was some dust on the floor. At the end of the outside verandah was a frame made of short pieces of bamboo for drying clothes. Below it was a tray-like container made of old cane water-buckets. In two of these were planted onions, two or three plants in each pail. Next to it were two large earthen jars for drinking water, placed on stands to raise them high enough from the floor so one could stand up straight and take water out of them. At the mouth of each was a scoop made of coconut shell. Over each platform on which the jars stood was a little shingle roof, each shingle a span in length. On the wall of the kitchen, by the door, were three calabashes hanging in a single chain. Between the kitchen and the house itself there stood equipment for spinning thread and winding it, known locally, respectively, as *kong* and *hak*.

From where Piya was he could see two closed doors leading into the house, presumably each leading into a room. The entire roof was made of corrugated iron, and the walls of shiny seasoned *takhian* [2] wood. There was no ceiling. From the central tie beam hung an iron hook on which a hurricane lantern could be suspended. Looking around, there did not appear to be any chairs or tables in the house at all. Nevertheless, Piya knew that this house would

---

2 *Takhian* - HOPEA ODORATA.

be by far the best in a village of this size. In any village it would be hard to find even two or three houses to equal this one, other than in the larger, more prosperous villages, of which there were all too few.

While he was occupied examining the house, he heard the voice of the headmaster's wife. 'There is no end to this gambling, is there? One of these days I'll get the police to come and catch the lot of you.' The woman herself appeared on the stairs a moment later, followed by a man whom Piya recognized as an older version of the photograph on the wall. He quickly raised his hands in a *wai*, sure that this was Headmaster Khammaw.

'*Sawatdi khrap*! Greetings, Headmaster,' he said.

The headmaster returned his greeting 'Sawatdi khrap! Have you been waiting long? You'll stay here won't you? When you've had a bath we can chat,' he said, using the balanced, repetitive '*ab nam ab tha*' meaning 'to bathe', characteristic of polite speech. 'Where's your bag then?'

'Here,' said Piya, pointing to his little bag. 'I've just got the one. I travel lightly.'

'Are you from Ubon? Where is your home?' asked the headmaster as he opened the door on the far right of the house. 'You can sleep here. There's no one here, it's just full of dust. What's your name?'

'Piya. My home is Ubon. I was born in Amnart. I've often lived in villages much more remote than this.' Piya followed the headmaster into the room, felt the close, stuffy atmosphere and smelled the stale, unventilated air.

'The windows are difficult to open and close. The wood's all warped and stuck,' the headmaster said, pushing one shutter open and letting some light into the room. 'I was wondering where you were from - and here you are, one of our own after all. There! Make yourself at home. Go have a bath! The bathroom's down below - go down the back stairs. I'll have the bed ready in a moment.'

'Thank you very much.' Piya was very touched. He felt he could not have been welcomed with greater warmth on this his introduction to being a country teacher.

When they had eaten the evening meal, the headmaster took Piya to the headman's house to introduce him and to inform the headman, as was customary in the country.

'Headman, Sir, are you asleep?' the headmaster called from the front yard of the house.

'Not yet,' came the reply from the house. 'Who is that? Is it the headmaster? Come on up. I wanted to see you, too!'

'About what?' said the headmaster, climbing up the stairs with Piya in his wake.

'People came and told me that 'Carn Khen brought some stranger into the village. I suspect he may be some kind of agitator. Oh! Who's that you've got with you?' The headman, wrapping his silk sarong around him, rose from the spacious floor and stared at Piya, whose face he could not see very clearly in the light of the flickering kerosene oil lamp.

'The new teacher who just arrived today,' the headmaster said, pointing to Piya.

Piya greeted the headman, going down on his knees to show his respect, and addressing him as 'father'. 'I just arrived in the bus this evening.'

'Oh! You're the one they said that 'Carn Khen brought, is that right?' the headman said, abandoning his suspicions with relief.

'I didn't know ... there was this older man when I got down from the bus. I don't know his name. He took me to the headmaster's house. He didn't speak to me at all, and as soon as he had pointed out the house he just went on his way.'

As Piya thought about the man a special interest in him began to develop, for at the very least the two of them shared the same name - Khen, Piya's childhood name.

'That's right! That's him, 'Carn Khen, the mad one.' Headman Lua laughed heartily. 'That fellow is no good. He likes shocking the villagers. He doesn't like living with others, he's gone and built himself a house outside the village - near the school. Don't trust him in anything!'

CHAPTER 4

Early next morning the headmaster went to school as usual, but today there was something unusual for the pupils and the villagers. The school stood on a little hillock outside the village, to the south. The village itself was situated on another little hill; between the two was a valley which, however, was not susceptible to floods as all the rainwater drained into a nearby swamp - the Swamp of the Mad Dog (*Norng Ma Vor*).

The sound of the headmaster's little motorcycle groaning, *phut phut*, up the hill to the school was not unusual. But today all the children, as one, stared at it as he came into view; for today he had a pillion rider.

'Last year there were three ... at the end of the term one was transferred and the other left the service. The District Education Officer said he would send us two replacements. Why we got only one I don't know.' The headmaster spoke against the wind, the sound of his voice competing with the four-stroke engine of his old-model 125cc machine - almost ready for the scrap heap.

'I have been teaching by myself since the end of last term. The new term's about a month old now.' The headmaster referred to himself with the word *phor*, 'father', expressing his affection for the young man, putting him in the position of his own son.

'How many pupils do we have?' Piya yelled over the sound of the motor and the wind.

'Ninety-eight - three more than last year.' I Thaw,[1] the motorcycle, slowly crawled to a halt with a sort of a lunge by the large tree in front of the schoolhouse. Piya dragged himself off the pillion. He stood up, breathing in deeply the fresh air of that late May morning, announcing to himself the beginning of his career as a rural teacher. The little boys who were playing under the eaves of the schoolhouse in the shade of the building stared at him, wanting to know who he was. There was a whispering among the older children; some said he was the new teacher, others the Development Officer; still others thought he was the Health Officer. Finally, the argument came to an end when Caw Khiaw, the son of the headman and the leader of the school children, decided for them.[2]

'That's the new teacher. Last night he came to my house,' the boy told his companions with pride.

Piya looked around with mixed feelings at the children surrounding him. He felt affection for them, and pity. The concern and the sadness came from the appearance of their bodies and their clothes. The expressions and complexions of many of them indicated a lack of proper nourishment. Their white cotton clothes looked brown, their shorts and shirts had lost most of their colour ... and they all had mottled black marks. Their behaviour and their speech towards guests and strangers were inclined to be hostile.

When the lad Khiaw said with certainty that the newcomer was the teacher, the kids' expressions turned to broad smiles. They tried to cluster closer around him,

---

[1] The headmaster's motorcycle and, later, Piya's bicycle are given pet names - *I Thaw* may be translated 'Little old lady'.

[2] *Caw* - a prefix used before the name of young males. Here, but not always, translatable as 'master'.

bringing to his nostrils the strong sour smell of unwashed bodies. Headmaster Khammaw finished putting away his motorcycle, turned around and yelled at them: 'Hey, you kids, get back! Don't crowd around like that, you smell. That's your new teacher!' The children went back to their play, but they continued looking at him with interest. The older children still stood a little way from him, whispering, but the younger ones went on playing. Most of them were playing a game whose name translated as 'the fruit of the moss, the shit of the elephant', and which involved gathering sticks at top speed. The boys were playing a game known a *Marg I*, and a game in which they divided into teams and chased and caught each other. Some children were still coming in. The white blouses and blue skirts in the early morning sunlight under a bright, blue sky was a sight that gladdened the new teacher's heart.

Piya followed the headmaster into the school building. The wooden building was a temporary one, put up many years ago but not yet complete. As it was, it satisfied the required standard - seven metres broad and twenty-seven metres long. The pillars of hardwood, each one tall and straight, held the shingle roof, each shingle an arm's length and a span broad. The pillars were proof of the quality of the timber in the region. Marks on the pillars, about waist high from the floor, indicated that the intention was to raise the floor of the building. At the moment, however, the floor was composed of round stones laid on the ground. The school had no windows, no doors - for it had no walls. There were, however, broad planks of unplaned wood forming a temporary wall on three sides, which protected the building from sun and rain. Inside the building the rooms were undivided, but the division into four classes could be discerned - the long desks at which pupils sat were arranged in four groups, and a blackboard was attached to a pillar in front of each group of desks. Each class had a desk and chair of rather poor workmanship for the teacher. There was one large cupboard situated behind Class 4. The cupboard, tables, chairs and the pupils' desks were all made of large planks of wood, the crude workmanship in the style of the villages of the forest on the plateau. Just from looking at these objects, Piya could see with no great effort that the forests of the area were highly productive.

'Our school used to be in the monastery. I persuaded the villagers to build this one about five years ago - without any financial assistance. They co-operated in sawing the wood, planing it and putting up this structure. As you can see, when it was just sufficient for teaching, they abandoned it.' The headmaster gave Piya a brief rundown on the history of the building.

'You see the timber for the joists, the floor boards and the walls are all there - but the villagers are not very interested in education. I've asked for money out of the budget, but the Section Head says we've got to wait, though we'll get it in time.'

Piya felt the headmaster was shifting the blame on to the villagers and asked, 'Whose work is this, that's already done?' He looked up at the roof, which had holes in it where the wind had blown out a number of the shingles.

'The villagers' and the teachers'. It was mostly the work of Khru Satharn. Before he was transferred Khru Satharn persuaded the villagers to come and help him, and they built what you see here. After his transfer, work on the building stopped.' The headmaster opened the cupboard as he spoke, picked up an old hoe with a jagged edge hung by a rope on the post inside the cupboard, and took out four exercise books with the names of the children written in them.

'Is it OK if you take Primary 3 and 4? They should be easy to teach,' he said, changing the subject and handing Piya two of the registers. 'I'll take Primary 1 and 2.'

'I can teach any of them,' said Piya. He opened the register and noted the numbers in each class. There were twenty-two in Primary 3 and eighteen in Primary 4. He wanted to ask the headmaster why he did not ask the villagers to help complete the school - but he did not dare. The headmaster soon spoke again.

'I don't like to ask new teachers with good qualifications to teach these low classes. You teach Classes 3 and 4. Classes 1 and 2 don't need to be taught all that much.' The headmaster's view was one widely held in educational circles.

8.45 a.m. As the sun rose in the sky, the May morning began to get uncomfortably hot. The headmaster took a large metal bolt from the cupboard, took the hoe by the rope and beat on it hard. *Kaeng! Kaeng! Kaeng!* The sound of the gong could not compare with that of a bronze bell, but the children stopped playing at once; the two groups playing games broke up and nearly all the children rushed off to piss in the grounds behind the school. The boys stood facing the bushes, the girls squatted on the ground. The sight of the kids all pissing at the sound of the bell would have surprised an urban spectator. But here in the countryside it was a familiar sight. The teachers instructed them, when they first came to school, that the children must perform their excretory functions before they entered the classrooms and thus save everybody a lot of trouble. In spite of that, every year in Primary 1 there were kids who, not daring to tell the teacher, made a mess all over the classroom.

In a little while the headmaster gave his hoe another two strokes. The children hurried to form a row in front of the wall, facing the flagpole. The pole was straight at its base, but bent visibly at its summit - leaning towards the schoolhouse. The tree trunk used for the flagpole had been like this in its natural state. Each class lined up in two rows, the girls in one, the boys in the other; the girls on the left, the boys on the right; Primary 1 in front, then 2, 3 and 4 behind them in order.

Piya came out and watched the children line up. He was intrigued by their orderliness, for since he first struck his hoe the headmaster had not come out to watch them, nor said a word to them. The kids lined up without any chatter or playing around. Only the young boy, Khiaw, walked up and down, seeing that the rows arranged themselves properly. One little boy rushed into the classroom and took the flag out of the cupboard the headmaster had opened. He brought out the flag and tied it to the rope on the flagpost. A little girl had been standing by the post holding the rope ready for him. The flag was new and unfaded, having just been issued by the District Office. When they were ready, the two of them hoisted the flag up the pole.

The headmaster struck the hoe again, one stroke. He firmly commanded: 'Respect the National flag! Lines straight!' Khiaw had returned and now stood at the head of the Primary 4 row. In a clear voice he led them in singing the first verse of the National Anthem, 'Thailand unites ...'

Their tone was good, but their pronunciation of the *ch* sound was not very clear: their timing and rhythm were both a little bit off - but you could recognize it as the Thai national anthem.

About eighty children had come to school that day. They sang the second verse and continued, finishing when the flag had been hoisted and was fluttering at the top of the flagpole. Though the words of the song, the melody and the rhythm may have deviated somewhat, Piya was satisfied that his new pupils had sung the national anthem very sweetly, and suppressed any doubts he had as to whether this procedure was as always, or put on specially because there was a new teacher that day.

After they had honoured the flag and recited verses in honour of the Buddha, still standing before the flag, Headmaster Khammaw stood before the flagpost between the clumps of yellow lantana and announced, 'I have good news for you all. Today we have a new teacher, Khru Piya. He comes from our own province, and speaks our own dialect. He studied in Bangkok for many years.' He said, using the respectful *than* referring to Piya, 'Khru Piya will teach Classes 3 and 4.' A rising murmur came from the children of these two classes, who showed on their smiling faces their satisfaction at this arrangement. The sound of their chatter rose and then slowly subsided.

'Piya, do you have anything you want to say to the pupils?' The headmaster turned to Piya, who stood by his side. The young man shifted his position so that he stood in front of the rows of children. He smiled at them, and spoke in polite tones.

'*Sawatdi*, pupils all, I am very happy to be able to teach you. The headmaster has given me Classes 3 and 4 to teach, but I believe a teacher is a teacher to all the pupils in every class in the school. I promise you I will instruct all of you, teach all of you, love all of you as if you were my brothers and sisters,' Piya said, referring to himself as Khru.

The headmaster put up on the blackboard a number of mixed problems in adding and subtracting amounts less than a thousand for the children of Primary 2. He then moved to Primary 1 for a lesson on reading, and put up on the board about ten words, all with the consonant *kor*, the first in the Thai alphabet, and the long vowel a. He used his pointer to indicate each letter and had the children repeat each sound after him. They then copied the words onto their slates.

As the children scratched away, the headmaster drew from his trouser pocket a packet of shredded tobacco and a roll of dried banana leaves, known in the region a *kor torng*. With great skill he rolled himself a cigarette on the palm of his hand, and lit it with a battered old brass cigarette lighter, the kind you light by turning a little wheel with your thumb. He lit the long cigarette with one flick of his thumb, the tabacco flared, and soon a cloud of white smoke hung over his head, like the cloud that hangs over an electrified rice mill. When the cigarette was about over, he stood up and walked towards Piya, who had taken the children of Classes 3 and 4 together. He had been trying to get to know them each individually. The headmaster beckoned to Piya who followed him out of the classroom, and whispered softly, 'You don't have to teach them anything much, a little reading, a few sums, that'll do. Put some sums up on the board and let Ai Khiaw see they do them. Let's go have a drink in the meantime.' Piya looked at his watch, which said it was just 10:00 a.m.

'It's Friday. Tomorrow Lung 'Carn Kern is giving a party - as teachers we must go, give the affair a little class, you know. They'll be filling up many jars of liquor - if we go now, we should be able to get a little off the top! I'd like to take you along and introduce you too.'

Piya looked for an excuse. 'That's OK, you go on ahead. I'll look after the children. Perhaps I may follow after twelve.'

'In that case I'll go on ahead. I'd really like you to meet them. Uncle 'Carn Kern is a very important man in the village. If you have any problem you can always depend on him,' said the headmaster, as he turned to walk towards his motorcycle parked in the shade.

When the headmaster had gone, Piya turned with some trepidation to the business of dealing with all four classes. However, everything went without trouble till the midday break. He walked up and down, observing the children who had brought their lunch with them. He noticed that the group of children who ate inside the classroom had curries or other dishes to eat with their rice. Those who sat outside, eating under the shade of the tree, were likely to have only glutinous rice with *caew* - a relish made with powdered chillies, onion and *pla ra* (fermented fish). Its full name was *caew pla daek*. He also observed that many childern ate nothing at all. He felt like asking them why they did not eat more nutritious food - but he knew the answer already. They were in a dry month. The only food in any abundance was various kinds of insects - such as *cinun, cipome, cudci* (various grasshopper-like insects) and the eggs of red ants.

He saw many kids eating their midday rice with fried *cinun*, fried grubs and fried grasshoppers, with signs of great enjoyment.

He walked up and down, observing the children, and after a while his mind turned to where he himself was going to eat. It was a question to which he found no answer. The headmaster had told him that he usually went home for lunch. The headmaster being absent, Piya had to decide whether he was going to brave the midday sun walking to the village and back, to eat at the headmaster's house, or whether he would perform an act of self-denial and forego his midday meal. He finally decided on the latter, thinking he would celebrate his first day as a teacher by doing without lunch.

When teaching was to begin again at one o'clock, the headmaster had not returned and the young teacher took all four classes himself. His method of dealing with this problem had not been set out in the teachers' training manuals. He set Classes 3 and 4 to read on their own, Class 2 to draw something out of their own imagination, and he himself taught the Primary 1 children the elements of reading. After about an hour he brought them all together again and spoke to them on a variety of subjects - whatever came to mind. He spoke about the political system, the duties of a citizen, cleanliness and sanitation, the conservation of nature. He ended by leading them in singing, and finally divided them into two teams to compete against each other in an extended relay race. He kept the children interested and entertained till three o'clock. The headmaster had still not returned. Piya announced that school was over for the day and let the children go home.

The children gladly grabbed their slates and books and excitedly rushed home across the school ground. 'The new teacher is a good sport.'

When he was putting the equipment away in the big cupboard against the wall, he happened to glance at the timetable affixed to the pillar, and berated himself. 'Oh hell! Today is Friday. We should have had prayers before school was over. Now I've let them go!'

About two o'clock that same afternoon, in the little wood outside the village, not very far from the school, the headmaster had parked his motorcycle beneath the shade of a large tree. Nearby a group of men sat, their heads close together, on a mat spread beside a termite mound.

'Oh! You're early today, Headmaster!' Thit Phun the banker raised his head, having collected his money and put the tamarind seeds in the bamboo container. 'Have you closed school?' Thit Phun's question was to the point, for whether the school closed or not used to depend entirely on the headmaster.

'Things are fine now. I've got a new teacher. I left him looking after the school.'

The headmaster sat down on the mat, close up against Thit Phun, the banker. 'I really decided not to come today. At noon I dropped in at Uncle 'Carn Kern's for a taste of his liquor. Thought it would be good to make up yesterday's losses.'

Thit Phun shook the bamboo container, which was the shape and size of a glass with a square bottom, its face polished smooth and shining. The four counters, tamarind seeds, rattled inside it like a cricket beating its wings. He then, quickly, but gently, inverted the bamboo on a small pandanus mat which was spread on top of the other mat.

'Even!' Siang Khampha wrapped his old *pha khaw ma* around his shoulders, and placed a twenty baht note, folded over twice, on the mat in front of him.

'Odd!' A young man flung two ten baht notes on top of it.

'Let me have ten,' said his friend, seated beside him, pulling out a ten baht note.

'No empty hands on the mat! Put your money on!' shouted the owner of the twenty baht note.

'All black!' The headmaster put down three ten baht notes. Thit Phun quickly gathered in the money in front of him, showing his intention of putting up the same amount as the headmaster if the contents turned up 'all black'. This meant that all four tamarind seeds would have to lie with their black faces upwards.[3] The headmaster would then win. Those who bet 'evens' would also win. If the counters fell two black, two white, all black or all white, it was 'evens'; any other combination was *khik* - in the central language *khi*, 'odd'. The headmaster's bet was an expression of his overconfidence, since the chances of all four showing either black or white was much less than the regular 'evens' where two black, two white, or all white, would win.

When all the gamblers had placed their bets, the 'croupier' lifted the *bang boke*, the bamboo container, with his thumb and two fingers, his ring and little finger sticking straight out, like the outspread wing of a bird. He slowly

[3] The tamarind seed is cut in half; the exposed inside is 'white' the hard outside 'black'.

raised the container, bit by bit, then suddenly whipped it away, bringing it sharply down, right way up, bang, in front of him. There in front of their eyes were the four counters all with the black face up.

'All black!' they shouted in unison, like the sound of a gunshot, followed by the swearing of those who had lost.

'Today you're hot, Headmaster, winning straight off!', Thit Phun said, counting out sixty baht. He then picked up the tamarind seeds and put them back into the bamboo container for the next throw.

When most of the children had left the school, Piya sat down, leaning against the back of a creaking chair. He was hungry and tired. There were still several boys hanging around.

'You still here, Khiaw?' He recognized Khiaw, the head boy, and beckoned to him. 'Come here! Come here all of you and talk to me a bit.'

Caw Khiaw led the group towards Piya with a friendly expression on his face. One of the boys, a thin little chap, so dark-skinned that his teeth and the whites of his eyes contrasted strongly with the colour of his face, Piya recognized as being in Class 3.

'I can't remember all your names,' the new teacher said, putting his hand on the leader's shoulder. 'Tell me your names once again, and I'll remember them for certain this time.'

Caw Khiaw gave him his name, then Iam, then Bunmi. The last, the little dark-skinned boy, gazed at the new teacher with trust and affection, but didn't seem to have the courage to speak.

'Go on Bak Siang!' Caw Khiaw coaxed. 'Go on, tell him your school name,' he said familiarly. He referred to the name by which the boy was registered at school, very likely a different one to that by which he was known around the village.

'Oh! Your pet name's Siang, is it?' Piya stretched out his hand and gently rubbed the tip of his shoulder. 'I'll call you Siang, that's OK.'

Piya then asked the four of them about the school. He found out that the previous year there had been three teachers: the headmaster; Khru Nipha, the wife of a border policeman who had come over on transfer and was here for two years - her health was not very good and she had retired; Khru Satharn had been appointed three years ago. The Class 4 pupils had been Khru Satharn's first batch when they entered school. It was Khru Satharn that the headmaster had credited with an important part in the construction of the school as it now was. It may have been his interest, his intelligence, his ability to get things done, or perhaps it was something else, which brought about his transfer to the big school in the district centre.

'Since you've been in school, which teacher do you like the best?' Piya asked the four children.

'Khru Satharn, Sir!' Khiaw jumped in, ahead of his companions.

'And what about you, Bunmi?'

'I like Khru Satharn, Sir!' he replied smiling.

'And you Iam?'

'Khru Satharn, Sir!' replied the curly-haired youngster.

'Siang?'

'Khru Satharn!' the dark-skinned lad said, avoiding his gaze.

'Why is it you all like Khru Satharn?' Piya knew he must try to find out about this man, for he had heard his name many times that day.

'He was good,' Caw Khiaw answered. 'He didn't beat us at all.'

'His teaching was fun. He taught us songs and took part in sport.' Bunmi said.

'Khru Satharn wasn't afraid of ghosts. He wasn't afraid of anyone at all,' Iam said of the old teacher, proudly.

'He was kindhearted. He really loved all the little kids,' said Siang.

Piya walked back with the four boys. The schoolhouse stood on a little hill, an attractive situation. Below, on the south side, was the wood, and about two or three kilometres beyond was the main forest. To the west was the swamp, which flooded and swelled to a large expanse of water during the rains. In the east were the fields, so interspersed with trees that in the distance they looked like a forest. These fields in fact lay in a forestry reserve on which the villagers had encroached, cutting down all the small trees and leaving only the big ones. The village itself lay to the north of the school. The walk from the school to the village was about a kilometre. As the path lay between fields, one could conveniently see the village from the school and vice versa.

They walked into the untended area beyond the playing field and Piya saw many wild flowers whose names he did not know, creepers and clumps of green bladed grass.

Numerous lizards scuttled into their holes as they saw the humans approach.

'What's that? Whose hut, whose abandoned house is that?' Piya pointed to a little hut which stood in the vicinity of the school to the west, between the school and the waters of the swamp.

'Khru Satharn's house.' Caw Khiaw said. 'Khru Satharn built it last year; he wasn't in it a year before he was transferred. The wind has nearly blown the whole roof away. During the day the little boys looking after buffaloes come and lounge about in it.

'And that one over there, whose is that?' Piya pointed to a house which lay at the edge of the fields between the school, the swamp and the village.

'Oh, that belongs to 'Carn Khen, the mad one,' Caw Khiaw, Bunmi and Iam all answered together.

The headmaster returned home about five o'clock that evening with a piece of freshly slaughtered beef tied with a strip of bamboo. He also had with him a pot of blood tied up in a basket to the back of his motorcycle, I Thaw. He was smiling broadly and called to his dear wife,

'Has Piya come back yet?'

'He's back. Have you been playing *boke* again today?' She glared at the man climbing up to the house and turned towards Piya, who had fallen asleep while writing. 'Is it true or not?'

'I don't think so.' The young man was not sure how to reply. He had no idea where the headmaster had disappeared to.

'Goodness, Old Woman! Stop complaining! Take this meat and mince it for us to eat, and be quick about it.' He handed his wife the meat. 'Is there rice cooked yet? I Si! Take these *makok* and *matum* leaves and *i lert*. Wash them to eat with the *larp*.'[4]

'Where did you get the beef?' asked his wife, speaking in dialect.

'I asked for a share from Uncle 'Carn Kern. Thirty baht was hardly enough for *larp*. I thought I'd show a little profit.' The headmaster had returned and begged the meat from his host, thinking his winnings were insufficient to make a meal of it. He walked to the water pot and washed his hands with the drinking water. 'I got the innards specially. Do you eat red *larp*, Piya?'

'I can manage', he replied, mumbling, as he came and sat down. In fact he did not like eating raw meat at all. 'Let me help with the food.'

The headmaster prepared the food himself. A large chopping block with a dirty thick incrustation on it was drawn out of a corner of the kitchen. The headmaster took the meat out of the bamboo strips which held it together. He picked out the meat still on the bone and pieces of stomach and put it in a pot with various vegetables which had already been chopped. The fillet and meat off the leg, of which there was not very much, he chopped very finely. He put some into a large dish and poured on it the *phia* - gastric fluids, in truth, digested food which the animal would have used to nourish its body. It was a green fluid from the small intestine. It was bitter to the taste. He mixed

---

4 *Makok* - SPONDIAS PINNATA, hog plum; *matum* - AEGLE MARMELOS, the bael fruit tree; *i lert* or *phak i lert* - various PIPER species.
Larp - a dish usually made of minced, seasoned meat.

up the fluid with the minced meat. He put it in the dish, not yet putting anything else in except the entrails, which had also been finely chopped, and which he sprinkled over the meat. After that, he sprinkled various condiments into the dish. He added, in proper proportion, fermented fish (*pla ra*), finely chopped green chillies, rings of onions, shredded kaffir lime and lemon juice; what could not be omitted from the *larp* was the parched rice - rice parched till it was yellow - and the finely pounded onions.

When all the ingredients had been put in, he used a spoon to mix it all up together. Mint may be added with the other condiments, or it may be added later. The fresh blood is also put in at the same time. This type of *larp*, in which the meat is cut into thin slices instead of being finely minced, is called *sokalek*. The headmaster had prepared the food with great speed. Most of the ingredients had been prepared beforehand - it was the chopping of the meat which took time.

The headmaster, having finished, went off to bathe and change his clothes. He put on a silk sarong without a shirt. I Si, the little servant girl, spread a cane mat on the verandah and brought out the bowl of *larp*. Piya helped by bringing out the glutinous rice container. The headmaster's wife drowsily tended the soup. When it was ready she ladled it out into a bowl and brought it out to place with the other dishes. The headmaster pulled out a jar of alcohol in which medicinal herbs were pickling. He poured himself a little cup and knocked it straight back. He refilled the cup and handed it to Piya. 'Drink this! It's a great appetizer. Liquor spiced with honeycomb, the stomach of porcupine and *talung*.' The talung here referred to a kind of brown langur. It was believed that all these additions to the liquor were a boost to one's health and strength - because the bees gathered honey from three thousand kinds of flowers, the porcupine ate three thousand kinds of root and the langur ate the shoots of three thousand varieties of tree.

Piya closed his eyes and determinedly forced down half the cup of liquor. It poured like fire down the throat, as if he had swallowed a whole bonfire. He hastily swallowed some soup, still unpleasantly hot, to wash down the liquor, then swallowed some more. It was his way of expressing his trust in the headmaster. According to custom, if a man poured you a drink you had to drink it all. To fail to do so would be a sign of disrespect.

'Oh, come on, try a little of the red *larp*. It's truly delicious.' The headmaster sucked in the meat, his mouth full, and followed it with a young *makok* leaf.

Piya helped himself to a spoonful. He steeled himself to put it in his mouth - just enough for his tongue and his teeth to be aware of it. The flavour was well blended, though slightly bitter. The meat, which he expected to be tough, was quite tender. He hurriedly bit off a piece of brittle *makhya* fruit to follow the meat down, then noisily sipped some more soup to wash it all down.[5]

'It's very nice, but it's a bit bitter,' the young man observed, not knowing that the more bitter the *larp* the better.

'Of course it's bitter. It's delicious. I especially asked for the *di*.' *Di* was the green liquid which comes from a little sac adjacent to the liver. It is bitter to the taste and used as a condiment to improve the flavour of the *larp*. 'Young people, that's the way they are now. Can't eat bitter things.

---

5 *Makhya* - Species of native SOLANACEAE.

Not long before we won't be having any of it any more.' Everyone fell silent for a while, their expressions showing satisfaction. 'You can board here,' the headmaster said. 'It's only those you see here. The two of us, Granny and I, and I Si, my niece. She can draw you water and pound your rice for you.'

'What about your children, Headmaster?' Piya was thinking of the photograph on the wall.

'I've got two sons. The elder one is still studying. The younger one is in Secondary 2. Both of them stay with their uncle in Ubon. They don't come home very often. During the holidays they come for about four or five days at a time. They say they miss all the comforts and conveniences of the town. The higher their education goes, the further they run away from the countryside.'

'Having two children, it's almost impossible to support them,' the headmaster's wife complained. 'We've got to send them many hundreds every month. If we had many children, like some others, we wouldn't be able to open our eyes, open our mouths like this at all.'

'Do you farm at all, Headmaster?' Piya's thoughts turned to the fact that many rural schoolteachers were forced to supplement their income through rice cultivation.

'Oh! Where will he get the strength for that?' the wife interrupted. 'If you get your children and grandchildren to cultivate, you could have them give you a share and save the cost of buying sacks of rice. When it's vacation, go and help them a bit. Formerly we used to hire labour to work some fields. We've given that up now. It's unpleasant. You've got to depend on them. When you have labourers - every one of them has a master whom you have to placate and depend on completely.'

They then got on to discussing the cost of Piya's board. Piya raised the subject, for he knew that living with a family was to impose a burden on them. The headmaster's wife decided on a sum of 150 baht a month. Piya would eat whatever they had, according to the custom of these people of the villages of the forest and the foothills.

'Things are very difficult, we always have trouble with food. When Khru Satharn was with us, he was very energetic. He was always off looking for crabs, fishing with the villagers. Whenever he had anything, he always helped with our food,' the headmaster's wife reminisced. Khru Satharn had formerly lived in this house.

'Talking about him, I really miss him,' the headmaster said, also reminiscing. 'He was a good man. Easy to get on with; would eat anything; keen; was really good with people. The villagers loved him; the children too.'

Piya felt they were all comparing him with Khru Satharn. He could not remember how often he had heard the name that day. He thought if it were possible he would do better.

CHAPTER 5

A wedding feast is known as 'eating *dorng*'. The term may refer to the carapace (*kradorng*) of a crab, of a tortoise or of some other animal. Some speculate that the word refers to *kiaw dorng* - 'relatives' - that it indicates the establishment of relations between the man and woman representing different families. Whatever its origins, the people of Barn Norng Ma Vor call it *kin 'dorng* - 'eating '*dorng*'.

Putting on a wedding feast, like other celebrations, is considered a social affair. All co-villagers should be invited and must be informed that so-and-so is putting on a feast with entertainment. The host at a wedding is expected to spend money on a celebration befitting his station - lest others think he is a man of small means. Uncle 'Carn Kern was the most prosperous man in Barn Norng Ma Vor. He may even have been the richest man in the commune of Phak I Hin. He had been ordained and had remained in the monkhood till he had achieved the status of Acarn. After he left the order he had prospered in trade - buying cheap and selling dear. He had begun by collecting forest products and selling them to traders in the district centre. Later, he had taken to acting as middleman, buying from the villagers and selling outside at a profit. It is a human failing that when we become involved in the business of buying and selling our original trustworthiness turns to guile and dishonesty. Charity and generosity, the characteristics of a true Thai, are lost, and we see in their place greed and selfishness.

Uncle 'Carn Kern was of a piece. As his business expanded and he gazed on the prospect of growing rich quick, he began to take advantage of his fellow villagers. He fixed his scales, he gave short measure, sold on credit, foreclosed and forced sales of possessions worth much more that the debt; and he pursued his favourite strategy - 'buying green rice'. 'Green rice' was rice still standing in the field. None of the villagers was well off. Though they grew rice, they did not have enough for their needs; either the rains had been insufficient, or they had not been as industrious as they should; they had gambled and had to borrow from Lung 'Carn Kern or buy on credit. They bought milled rice or paddy (unhusked rice), on the understanding that it would be repaid at the harvest together with interest at stupendous rates.

If one borrowed a hundred baht in May, one had to pay back 'a hundred thousand' of paddy at the harvest - that is, ten 'ten thousand', 120 kilograms, in December. Paddy was then selling at least at two hundred baht. If the farmer borrowed one baht of paddy, at the harvest he had to return two.

Uncle 'Carn Kern had, in this way, become the richest man in the village. He had a small rice mill, which was being converted into a middle-sized one. He had a 'two-rower', a bus which plied between the village and the district centre. He owned fields and gardens, herds of cattle and buffaloes. When he put on a feast at the marriage of his son, it had to be a grand one, so elaborate and sumptuous it would be remembered a long time. But, it should be economical; it should bring the greatest benefit, for the least possible expense.

That Saturday morning Piya and the headmaster arrived at Lung 'Carn Kern's house to find a confusion of people all dressed in the brightest of clothes. Two loudspeakers of the kind used on vans advertising or selling medicines were attached to a large tamarind tree in front of the house and the sounds of Thai country music were heard throughout the village.

Monks were chanting when the two men arrived. The headmaster led the young man to where guests were seated inside, and sat him next to the bride and bridegroom and the host. The room was full of people in devotional attitude who immediately began whispering, gesturing and pouting their lips, enquiring of each other who it was. Their interest in Piya soon dissipated.

The groom was a young man of about Piya's age. He looked a bit of a rascal. When offerings had been made to the monks, the groom looked at the young teacher in a way that suggested they were to be enemies from their first meeting. In truth, they did not know each other at all. The bride came from Barn Phak I Hin, the biggest village in the commune, situated about eight kilometres away. Not only was the bridegroom's family richer than that of the bride, but the ceremony was being held at the groom's house. Piya looked at the bride with some sympathy, but the groom still glared.

The monks were given their morning meal and returned to the monastery. Next on the agenda was the ceremony of 'calling the *khwan*', strengthening the life essence of the two protagonists. The vessel for the ritual was a large brass tray with a pedestal. This was beautifully arranged with all the necessary paraphernalia. There were the auspicious tinsel tree - gold tinsel made into a cone of many layers, one on top of the other - flowers, candles, incense, boiled rice, milled rice, packets of sticky rice, boiled eggs, bottles of liquor, and the sacerdotal thread for linking the wrists of the bridal pair. All these had been prepared and laid out in a special room. As soon as the monks had left the house an old woman brought out the *pharn*, the tray with pedestal, and placed it on a white cloth spread on a cane mat in the centre of the room.

The *thaw cam*, the officiant who would perform the *khwan* ceremony, usually called a Brahmin in the towns, was an old man wearing a white cloth round his waist and another wrapped around the upper part of his body. He came and sat by the tray with the ritual equipment. The bridegroom sat in front of him and the guests, friends and relatives sat in a circle around them, all with their palms together in front of them, in the attitude of devotion. The *thaw cam* chanted the sacred formulae. The headmaster came up and joined the circle, while Piya backed off and sat against the wall, with his hands together like everybody else.

The words the *thaw cam* chanted were in the local rural dialect. He began by announcing to all the gods and goddesses that this couple loved each other and were now married, their bodies devoted to building a family which would be prosperous, tranquil and happy. Then came the 'calling of the *khwan*', that is, the infusion of inner strength into both of them. They were then blessed, and prosperity and happiness invoked on their behalf. The chanting was done from a set of old palm leaf manuscripts handed down through many generations. The important and powerful quality of this ritual lies in the officiant having a voice that is cold and heavy and a manner dignified and deliberate.

Until the officiant reached the part of the chant in which the *khwan* is called, a couple outside kept calling 'Come! *der! khwan! err-ii*!' dragging out the two syllables *der err-ii*. When the correct point was reached, the entire company began to repeat this refrain: 'Come! *der! khwan! err-ii*!' all together, as loud as possible, till the sound became a concerted yell. The microphone picked up the sound and it boomed through the village and far out into the fields: 'Come! *der! khwan! err-ii!*'

Piya too was swept up in the excitement and helped swell the sound of calling the *khwan*. His mind went back to his childhood - when he was about seven or eight he had nearly drowned, and his mother had had the ritual performed for his benefit.

'Come! *der! khwan! err-ii*!' Piya joined in the second time round and thought to himself, 'They are calling for their own *khwan* rather than for that of anyone else.'

The *thaw cam* then took one of the eggs from the tray and cut it in two. He gave the egg to the groom who fed the bride with it, with all guests looking on. Then came the 'tying of wrists'. In former times the wrists of bride and groom were tied with the thread itself and with nothing else. Now, however, banknotes, ten, twenty, or one hundred-baht notes according to the station of the guest, are tied onto the arms of the couple. This money is a gift to the newlyweds. The parents cannot take any part of it as their share or as a contribution towards expenses. The headmaster turned towards Piya and said, 'Come here a moment. Come, tie the wrists of the bride and groom.'

Piya picked up a piece of thread, about a span in length which the headmaster passed to him. The crowd was pushing back and forth, making their way to the couple, tying their wrists and moving away. Some tied the wrists of one, some the other, some both. The method of tying was to loop the thread below the right wrist and then twist the ends together so that they would not come undone or the thread fall off the wrist. While doing this the guest or relative uttered any words of blessing or congratulations he or she thought appropriate. Those nearby would hold the hand or elbow of the person actually doing the tying, giving expression to their sense of community and sense of togetherness. Piya moved up to the bride. She was sweating profusely, moisture pouring down her forehead, and someone had to mop it up for her. He looped the thread around her left wrist and twisted the ends together, saying softly, 'May you have happiness and prosperity, may you have ever-increasing good fortune.'

'Thank you,' she said, avoiding his gaze, embarrassed. Both of them were quite unaware that the groom was glaring at them suspiciously.

A stream of dishes now emerged from the kitchen, dishes of *larp* and various curries. The guests sat in groups of four and five. The headmaster, Piya and the headman sat in one group, not far from that of the bride and groom and their hosts, Lung 'Carn Kern and his wife. The headmaster introduced Piya to the four of them.

'May I be as a son or nephew to you,' Piya said to the older man, respectfully.

'Fine! There's nothing to worry about here. Conduct yourself well and everyone will love you,' the senior citizen of Barn Norng Ma Vor said simply.

'I hope you stay long with us,' said Thit Kart, the groom, smiling. 'But those who were here before, teachers from other villages, none of them stayed very long.'

As the party progressed, Piya kept being pressed with drinks. Everybody seemed determined to drink themselves insensible. As they became more and more drunk they kept bringing him glasses of liquor. It was all a sign of friendship, but Piya saw it as more of an indirect route to murder. When his vision became blurred and he began to feel intoxicated, he excused himself and left, leaving the headmaster behind.

CHAPTER 6

During the first ten weeks of his appointment, Piya found that he was left alone to take care of the school almost every day. Headmaster Khammaw had business at the District Office, or he had to attend a meeting of local headmasters, or he sometimes just vanished for half the day. Piya was very tempted to ask the children whether it had been like this in the past.

'The headmaster doesn't teach much, Sir,' Caw Khiaw said one day, on behalf of his schoolmates. 'In the past only Khru Satharn and Khru Nipha did any teaching; the headmaster sometimes went to the District Office, sometimes went off to play cards or play *boke*.'

Piya was startled to hear these words from one of his pupils. 'Don't say things like that about the headmaster. Have you seen him?'

'Yes, I have,' said Caw Khiaw. 'The crowd that plays *boke* plays every afternoon, just here, by the school.'

Whatever conclusions Piya arrived at, whatever he guessed at after that day, he kept to himself.

Piya had his breakfast early and did not wait for the headmaster. In the morning he had boiled duck eggs mixed with fish sauce or fermented fish as a relish, with balls of glutinous rice. Two eggs kept hunger away till noon. After breakfast he hurried off to school again, not waiting for the headmaster.

At 7:00 a.m. when he reached the school, he found a number of pupils there already. He conscripted them to clean up the grounds around the school building, and to sweep out the waste paper from under the children's desks and chairs, with a broom made of the midribs of the coconut leaf. The rubbish he then had thrown away down the hill. Their work done, he called them together, sat them down on the ground under the eaves of the school and told them stories, each day two or three. He then let them run off and play as they liked.

Every morning he followed this routine and noticed that the crowd of children coming to hear his stories increased daily - many of them timing their arrival to escape the work, but catch the stories. Soon after he had started this, he got them to sing - first songs they already knew, then new songs he taught them. They learnt the songs and the tunes very quickly and soon sang as a group with great skill.

He later taught them various games and led them in playing them. He made them wash their hands after their play and wait quietly till it was time for the morning flag ceremony. Within a week the pupils were hurrying early to school for their morning's entertainment with the teacher. They all wanted to listen to his stories, sing along with him and play his games. But what gave Piya greatest satisfaction was the fashion in which the children sang the songs he taught them. Though the songs were not of his own composing, they were songs very suitable for this generation of children; songs that encouraged them to learn, songs expressing love of the nation and polity, and songs of city and country children popular at this time. In addition he took the opportunity of instructing the early morning attenders in good manners and deportment.

'I am very relieved to have a teacher like you,' said the headmaster one morning, looking Piya in the face and addressing him as father to son. 'Our village children are very tractable, they don't stay away from school without reason. Fine! Go ahead and good luck!'

'It seems to me that getting the children to enjoy themselves at school was a good way to make them learn. Besides, there is the consolation that getting them to school early would take a great burden off the minds of their parents and guardians,' Piya said, giving expression to some of his concerns.

'Their pleasure's all over when they get home. Do you know that they have been bothering their parents to have us teach Saturdays and Sundays as well?' The headmaster laughed. 'But it's no joke your coming to school early in the morning every day. It's quite a walk. Why don't you take that old bicycle that's under the house. If you have it repaired I am sure you could use it. The frame's fine, you will just have to get new tyres for it. It's mine - I've had it since I first started teaching. Since I bought my motorcycle I've forgotten the old thing.'

'Thanks, I'll have a look this evening and see what needs repairing.' Piya's face did not show his pleasure. 'I've been looking at that bicycle for a long time now, but I felt a little diffident about saying anything.'

The next Monday Piya had the old ramrod of a bicycle as his means of transport. He did not have to walk any more - or ride pillion on the headmaster's motorcycle. The old Ai

Krong[1] was an old model *farang* bicycle. The frame was sturdy and Piya had put on two new tyres. He had also replaced the brakes and fitted a pillion. He was quite a sight riding through the village - a tall man on a tall bicycle.

This morning he had arrived and joined the pupils at their tasks and then led the usual singing. Piya had often observed a man standing at the edge of the school grounds, watching them, but today the man seemed more intent, and seemed to stand there much longer than usual.

He stopped the singing for a moment and asked, 'Do you know who that is who keeps standing and staring over there?'

The children looked where he was pointing and burst out laughing. 'Carn Khen, the mad one, Sir!' one of them shouted, reminding Piya that he should have looked this man up a long time ago - he had procrastinated many days now.

The children continued their singing and 'Carn Khen disappeared behind a clump of trees when he realized he was being observed.

The headmaster arrived after eight o'clock; he parked his motorcycle and walked up smiling.

'We're going to get another teacher, Piya!'

'Who is it?' he asked, conscious of some slight excitement.

'My niece! I think she must have been appointed in the same batch as you,' he said, still smiling.

'She was sent to Barn Dorn Hen Om - almost on the border. Her father appealed to the *Nai Amphur* (District Officer) to have her transferred. They couldn't do much as

---

[1] Lit. *Ai*: familiar or derogatory form of address; *krong*: 'to rattle'.

she had just been appointed. Finally they agreed to send her home - to her uncle. Her father's satisfied.'

'A woman?' Piya had still no inkling that he knew the girl.

'That's right. She comes this evening. I just received a letter telling me about it. She'd sent a letter through the bus driver yesterday, but Ai Kart forgot to give it to me.'

During the day Piya kept worrying about the problem of where he was going to live. When the new teacher arrived, particularly as she was the headmaster's niece, she would have to stay with the headmaster. There was only one extra room in the house, the one Piya was now occupying. He could not possibly share the room with the new teacher. He would have to find new lodgings, or, if he continued to live in the headmaster's house he would have to sleep out on the verandah. This would not be impossible, but it would certainly be very inconvenient.

'Sir, what are the four requisites, Sir?' a pupil of Primary 3 broke in on his thoughts.

'The things which are necessary for life,' Piya explained, 'food, clothing, shelter and medicines for the prevention and treatment of illness.'

'Which one is the most important?' another one asked.

'I am not going to tell you, I want you to think it out for yourselves. Importance has to do with the use it has for our lives. Think of it like this - if you could choose only one, and none of the others, which one you would choose? That would be the most important.' Piya was keen on the children thinking things out for themselves.

'Medicines,' the young lad, Siang, answered.

'And why is that Siang?' the teacher asked.

'My mother is sick,' the dark-complexioned boy said in a low voice.

But for Piya it was shelter that was the most pressing problem.

During the lunch interval, while eating, Piya discussed his residence problems with the headmaster.

'It's been very convenient, in every way, but now that your niece is coming to live with you, I think I should make other arrangements. I thought I'd take this opportunity of telling you that I intend coming to live here, at the school.'

The headmaster looked puzzled. 'How are you going to live here at the school? There isn't even a room here! There's no problem about you living with me - we'll work something out about the rooms.'

'I'll come and live in that little house over there.' Piya pointed in the direction of Khru Satharn's deserted hut.

'The children told me Khru Satharn built it, but was transfered soon after. I thought I'd repair it - there's not a great deal to be done. It really only needs a new roof - and a small part of the wall. Living near the school I'll be able to do much more work.'

'I'd still like you to think about it first. I don't want you to go and live anywhere else,' the headmaster said. 'And I don't want you to take on all kinds of bother.'

'I've been wanting to move near the school for a long time,' Piya said, with truth, 'but I had no reason to raise the matter with you, Headmaster. As to comfort and convenience, there could be nothing better than staying with you. Even if I was in my own home it couldn't be more comfortable.'

'In that case I will have to help you to get Khru Satharn's house in order, before you can move in. But it's deserted here, at dusk and at night. It will be rather frightening all by yourself.' The headmaster still hoped to change his mind.

After school was over Piya mounted Ai Krong, his bicycle, and made his way to Lung 'Carn Kern's shop where he bought nails and wire. He borrowed a hammer from the headmaster and bought grass strung in bundles ready for thatching the roof. He made enough repairs to enable him to sleep there that night. Besides the headmaster, who lent a hand, a group of young boys, Khiaw, Bunmi, Iam and Siang, helped him with the work. By about 5:00 p.m. they had the essentials done.

'Let's go home, we can continue tomorrow,' the headmaster said.

'I am going to sleep here tonight,' Piya insisted.

'Hey! Sleep here tonight!' the headmaster exclaimed in surprise. 'What's the big hurry?'

'I don't need to consult a horoscope and look for an auspicious time. If I have a mat to lie on, a pillow for my head, that's fine,' Piya said, wiping the sweat off his brow.

'OK!' The headmaster gave in. 'But let's go home and eat first. You can then get a mat and a pillow and come back to sleep. There are lots of other things you'll need too.'

'Fine. May I continue to eat at your home, till I am settled in? I can then do my own cooking.' Piya gazed at his new home, satisfied.

CHAPTER 7

'There's a letter for you,' the postman yelled outside the monk's residence.

'Ai Suk, or whoever's down there, go and get that letter,' Luang Lung, the abbot, shouted back. In a little while, Caw Suk, a secondary school boy, crawled up to the abbot and respectfully proffered to him a letter in a long envelope. 'Open it and read it to me,' he said.

> Written at Barn Norng Ma Vor, Tambon Phak I Hin.
> Humble salutations to the beloved and deeply respected Venerable Uncle.
> I haven't written to the Venerable Uncle since I began teaching, as I have been overwhelmed with work and the business of finding a place to live. Everything is satisfactorily settled now. I am living at the school. I have repaired a little hut in the vicinity of the school. Once I moved in, it has proved a pleasant place to live. This week I have begun cooking for myself. There is no difficulty about it, I've bought rice, chillies, salt, *pla ra*, a mortar and pestle, and other kitchen utensils. I can buy various supplies from the villagers, duck's eggs and fish. I have a plan to keep chickens and grow vegetables. I want it to be a show piece for the children and villagers. I don't know yet what else I should do. My relations with the villagers are very good. For the most part the villagers are peace loving and encourage education. Some of them, however, are addicted to gambling and not

altogether trustworthy. But I haven't had any hint of trouble or disagreement.

We've had another teacher join us, which now makes three, the right number for our ninety-odd pupils. I am determined to perform my duties as a teacher to the best of my ability, both in teaching as well as in instructing the children in their duties as citizens; also in imparting to them a sense of virtue and propriety. I think all this needs to be done.

The money the Venerable Uncle gave me was not all spent. I have now got my first salary. I think I should be able to save some of it and I hope to come to Bangkok at the end of July. I trust that the Venerable Uncle and everyone at the monastery are in good health. I am keeping well.

With my humble salutations, love and respect.

Piya

At about the same time, at his little hut, the young schoolteacher was preparing the soil adjacent to the hut to plant a variety of vegetables. He intended planting lemon grass, sweet basil, chillies and local solanaceae - all frequently used and productive over long periods.

'Will they grow in the sandy soil? You'll be very clever if you get any return,' someone called from behind. Piya turned and looked and saw Thit Phun grinning at him. 'And where are you going to get water from? Plants are not made of plastic - they need water.'

'Greetings, Brother Thit,' Piya addressed him, smiling. 'I am just having a go, planting them for fun, that's all. I don't really know if I'll get a crop. It's better than doing nothing.'

'Go ahead, but I don't think it's possible. If you're successful, I'll really respect you.' Thit Phun, the croupier of the *boke* game, passed on.

The villagers were interested in the outcome of Piya's activities, for he was using the soil piled up from the excavations for the foundations of the schoolhouse. It really was sandy. But Piya treated it with the manure he laboriously collected from the fields and pastures, the droppings of cattle and buffalo. There was also the problem of water.

At this time there were two public wells the villagers used. One of them lay on the road to the swamp, near the house of 'Carn Khen, and the other, outside the village, on the other side. The school used the former well, which was about half a kilometre away from the school-house, about three hundred metres away from Piya's hut. Walking there and back, shouldering two *khru'* at a time to water his plants was going to be a laborious business. Piya decided he would dig a new well near his hut. But this was not a task he could perform alone. In the old days the whole village would get together for such jobs. Everyone who participated felt they were performing a meritorious action providing for the public good. It was often said, 'He who digs a well, or builds a resting place, he must surely acquire merit.'

In Isarn there are three kinds of wells. The ordinary well is just a hole dug to the required depth - usually from one metre to six metres deep; the mouth of the well perhaps two metres across. When water is reached, the digging stops. Water rises from the underground spring, but it was never known to overflow the top of the well. These wells are temporary; in the wet season the rains wash soil into the wells and close them up.

The second kind of well is called *sarng saeng*. *Sarng* means well and *saeng* refers to timber which is used to build a protective wall, preventing earth being washed into the well. This kind of well, like the ordinary one, has a mouth about two metres across and is the depth necessary to meet water - usually about five metres. Four hardwood posts, the size of houseposts, are then sunk into the well. Between these posts and the sides of the wall wooden planks are arranged on all four sides, from the bottom of the well up to the top. When one looks into such a well it looks like a rectangular box. These wells last a long time without collapsing, for the planks, the *saeng*, hold back the earth.

The third kind of well is called *sarng thor*. *Thor* here does not mean a 'punting pole' (as it does in the Central Thai language), but a large hollow cylinder which is placed inside to prevent the earth collapsing into the well. The inner cavity is about a metre in diameter. In former times it was easy to find trees with trunks large enough for this *thor* to be made of wood. Nowdays people prefer to use *thor* made of concrete instead. For some unknown reason, when a concrete cylinder is used these wells are not known as *sarng thor*.

The well near Piya's hut was of the *sarng saeng* type; that is, it was lined inside with planks and was about six metres deep. Usually, during the rains the water level rose to within a metre or two of the top, but in the dry there was water only in the very bottom of the well. Those who were skilled could pull up a *khru'* brimming with water, even in the dry season, as the water in the well was about knee-deep. Because the water table was so low, when many came to the well for water each had to wait his, usually her, turn. The spring could not fill the well as fast as the water was being drawn out. This queuing was known as *thar nam* - 'waiting for water'. The young lads and lassses loved the *thar nam*: it was an occasion for much chatting and flirting.

For drawing water, a bamboo pole was used - its diameter of a size to allow it to be held comfortably in the hand and its length the depth of the well. The end of the pole was cut into a hook for use with the *khru'* or a bucket. The pole was known as a *khan khor*. Each well must have its *khan khor*. Whoever came first, drew water first, according to his or her place in the queue. There was no crashing of the queue. To use the *khan khor* you hooked on the basket (*khru'*) or bucket and lowered it into the well. This was, however, not an easy task. If the person was unskilled the bucket could quite easily be lost in the water. If the water were deep and it could not be retrieved, it just had to be abandoned at the bottom of the well.

Piya found himself two empty *khru'* and walked to the well one evening. The young girls stared at him and giggled uncontrollably at the awkward and unusual manner in which he carried his baskets - even though he had drawn water and carried it home when he was a little lad.

'Aai Khru, youv'e come to draw water yourself, don't you want someone to come and help you?' a young woman standing slightly apart, teased familiarly. She meant, 'You live alone, don't you need someone to help you?' She called him *aai* giving him the status of elder brother. *Aai* means 'elder brother' in the local dialect.

Piya just smiled. He was not used to girls flirting with him. His smile provoked the whole bevy of young girls to laugh in concert. They quietened down as Piya spoke.

'I'd like to have someone help draw water and do the cooking, but living in a dilapidated hut as I am, who would be interested?' he continued, teasing them back. 'Pretty girls like you are better suited to living in wooden houses with corrugated iron roofs, not in huts thatched with *kha* grass such as mine.[1] But if anyone takes pity on him, it will be the good fortune of a poor teacher!'

'Leave your sweet talk! If you plant a carrying pole, it's not sugar cane. Even if you can eat it, it won't be sweet,' the first girl countered with a conventional retort in dialect. It was a sharp word designed to crush Piya and silence him.

'OK,' Piya said in a businesslike manner. 'We've all got to come far for water, isn't it rather tiring? Why don't we dig another well nearer to the village?'

'A well near the village is never very clean. Pigs, dogs, ducks, chickens, walk all over the top of the well - who will dare drink its water?' a young girl said firmly.

'Even if you don't drink the water, you could always use it to water your vegetables and your trees,' Piya argued.

'That's fine. But our elders didn't do it like that,' the first girl contradicted him.

Piya put his baskets down near the mouth of the well. There was a little slush around the mouth, as around any well. A young girl nimbly drew up a basket of water hooked on the end of the *khan khor*. It was difficult to

---

[1] *Kha* - IMPERATA CYLINDRICA.

believe this narrow-waisted, slight, fair complexioned girl had so much strength in her. When she put down her basket Piya reached to take the pole from her and draw his own water, but she said softly:

'Let me draw the water for you, teacher. Yesterday you let the basket sink - its always a nuisance trying to get it back, isn't it?' As she spoke she took Piya's basket, hooked it on the pole and quickly lowered it into the well. Her companions laughed delightedly.

'Oh! They go well together!' The girl who had squashed Piya with her *bon mot* made a suggestive sound. The girl drawing water went red. She drew up the first basket, lowered the second and filled it.

'Thank you, Phayorm,' Piya said to her, and turned smiling to the others who stood around. 'Thank you anyone else who would like to help me; all of you, Khamkhian, Bunkong and Sommai.' This amazed them all: in a few days he had learned all their names. Phayorm, who was somewhat uneasy, felt much relieved.

Piya placed the carrying pole across his shoulder, the two baskets with water at each end. He started off, towards his house, walking awkwardly, for he had not done this for many years. In his childhood, he had drawn water, pounded rice, and done all the work around the house like any other boy from the countryside.

When the young man had passed out of earshot and could not hear their conversation, the four girls began discussing him in the manner of females.

'I think Khru Piya has a girlfriend,' the one with the eloquent tongue offered. 'Whoever she is, she needn't worry about winning the lottery. He's an industrious lad, that.'

'I've never seen a teacher draw water. Khru Piya is the first I've seen draw water and carry it himself,' Bunkong, a round-faced, fair-skinned girl, observed quite accurately. The villagers of that area did not think it proper for a teacher to do any hard work. Teachers were government officers, persons of standing who did not need to engage in physical labour.

'Don't you feel sorry for him? If he can get one of the pupils to stay with him he wouldn't need to go to all this trouble. At least he could fetch water for drinking and bathing.' Phayorm, the red-cheeked girl, with long lovely black hair, wearing a black blouse with puffed sleeves, spoke to no one in particular.

'Well, why don't you go on and help him? You look good together.'

'Goodness, Elder Sister 'Mai! Don't talk rubbish. A poor girl like me wouldn't dare think of something like that.' She picked up her carrying pole and put it over her shoulder and said to Khamkhian, who lived in the house next door, 'Let's go, 'Khian, it's getting dark.'

After the arrival of Khru Duangdaw, the headmaster's niece and new teacher, teaching became a little easier for Piya. He no longer was left with the supervision of all four classes. The headmaster gave her the teaching of Primary 2 and, in his absence, the supervision of Primary 1. Piya continued to take Classes 3 and 4. He valued the extra time he had to teach them and to get to know them better, now that he was no longer bothered with Classes 1 and 2.

'Is Khun Duangdaw going to Ubon this week?' Piya addressed the young woman politely, one day, during the lunch break.

'I thought I'd ask my uncle for permission to attend to some business at the district centre on Friday,' she answered, using the diminutive 'mouse' to refer to herself. 'I don't really have any official business. Acarn Ekachai and I arranged to go to Ubon together on Friday afternoon. Is there anything you would like me to bring you?'

'No. I just thought you may not be going home this week.' The young man had not yet raised his head from the textbook on new methods in agriculture which he had had Duangdaw buy for him last week.

'Oh! Was there anything ...' She put down her *Women's Fortnigthly* on the table. 'I arranged to go to the cinema with a friend, there's an Alain Delon film at the Chalermwatana.'

'Oh no, there's nothing.' He looked up and gazed at the young woman, saying in a casual tone: 'Headman Lua has arranged for a village meeting on Saturday. The headmaster and I want to discuss the completion of the school building. If you could speak in support, I am sure another voice would carry a lot of weight with the village.'

'Oh, I don't think I would be of any help. Another thing is, mine was an ordinary appointment.' She meant she was not specially appointed as a rural schoolteacher. 'I want to get a transfer to the city. I certainly couldn't bear to live for years in the country like this.' There was a finality in the tone of her voice.

That Saturday evening, the beating of a *korlor* gave the signal for the headmaster and Piya to mount the steps of Headman Lua's house. The headmaster sat leaning on a post as close as possible to the betel nut container (locally known as a *khan mark*). It was a large rectangular container, decorated in the local fashion. The carved pattern however was now rather obscured through age and wear. The headmaster picked up a bit of tobacco in his fingers, and a piece of prepared dried leaf, and rolled himself a cigarette. He lit it from the kerosene lamp, made from an old milk can.

'Oh, Headman! This is a bit stingy,' the headmaster said, turning to his host who was seated nearby belching loudly. 'On days when you beat the *korlor* for a meeting, you should light the pressure lamp and give us a little more light.'

'It's a moonlit night. Why should I light fires, light lamps for nothing?' He turned to Piya. 'Well, how goes it, Khru Piya? Don't the ghosts bother you living at the school alone?'

'Not yet, Headman. Are there ghosts at the school then?' the young man asked, half in earnest - addressing the headman politely as 'father'.

'They say the ghosts used to be pretty fierce. But nowdays I don't think there are any. The ghosts and evil spirits have vanished - they are frightened of the noise of cars and trucks. They have all fled into the forest.' Headman Lua giggled, 'Hee, hee.'

As time passed the villagers dribbled in, climbing up to the house in ones and twos. Within fifteen minutes there were a dozen or more in the house. Others stood talking in groups in the courtyard. The headman called down to them:

'Who's there then? Ai Ma, Ai Phan, Thit Duang, Thit Phong - come on up. What are you standing there for? Is that what you came for? Ai Chom, beat the *korlor* once more, please.'

The young boy, whom the headman had addressed, jumped up and beat the korlor which hung from a post supporting the eaves, near the open verandah. The gong-like, resonant sound of the *korlor* drifted far throughout the village. The *korlor* was an instrument used to summon the villagers to meet. In this area all villages used a *korlor*. There were none using a drum, as in the song about Headman Li.[2] The *korlor* was made of hardwood, about 5-12 centimetres thick and more than a span in breadth and more than a metre and a half long. A hole is drilled through it for hanging in the headman's house. It's beaten with a hammer - again made of hardwood and known as *khorn ti korlor*.

Another half hour passed and the crowd had increased by no more than another five men. Altogether, with the early comers, about twenty people were present, mostly the heads of families and young ones.

'Hasn't Uncle 'Carn Kern come?' the headman asked of the meeting. 'If Lung 'Carn isn't here, we can't decide anything whatsoever.'

'It looks as if he won't come,' someone said. 'I saw him setting off by car for the *amphur*, with Sia Mangkorn. He may have gone straight on to the Provincial Office.'

'I don't know what we have here in this village that Sia Mangkorn comes so often,' the headman said loudly.

---

2 A comic song about a northeastern village headman which first gained popularity in the early 1960s.

'Who is it then, this Sia Mangkorn?' Piya whispered to the headmaster.

'Oh, he's a rich merchant from Ubon. He's got business of all kinds. Hotel, sawmills, ricemills, and I don't know how many other companies.' The headmaster stubbed out his cigarette and threw the butt into the space under the house.

'I've struck the *korlor* and called this meeting today.' The headman spoke in a businesslike manner. 'There are two or three matters of official business from the *amphur* - I'll take them up later. Let's take the important matter first, that is the building of the school. The headmaster and Khun Piya have asked me to call this meeting so that we may decide what should be done. It has really been going on for many years now, since the school moved from the monastery premises. The building has not yet been completed as we had originally planned.'

'I think we have sacrificed enough already - in money and labour,' Thit Duang muttered. 'It's now the responsibility of the government. Let the headmaster go ask the government for money to finish the building. Look at Barn Kud Pla Kang and Barn Norng Sa Nor, they got government money for their building. The villagers didn't have to pay anything. What's more, they were employed building the school and they each earned many hundreds of baht.'

Thit Phun, the leader of the *boke* gambling school and a well-known gambler in the district, supported Thit Duang. 'Building the school should be the responsibility of the teachers - after all, the school is like the teacher's rice field. It's how they make their living. The villagers found the money to build this much. The teachers should find the money to finish it. Don't trouble us any more about it.'

'What do you say, Headmaster?' The headman turned to the headmaster who did not seem very interested in the proceedings. 'Or will you rather have Khun Piya explain?'

'It depends on Khun Piya. It's all his idea.' The headmaster passed on the responsibility to the young man.

Piya altered his position to face the gathered crowd and spoke, slowly, clearly and melodiously.

'Friends, I recognize that everything you have said is perfectly correct. Nevertheless, I'd like everybody to understand clearly that the school is not the property of the teachers or of any particular person. The school is the property of the villagers, of every one of them. The children and grandchildren of each one of us can use the school, learn there and acquire knowledge of all kinds. The teachers treat the children quite impartially. If we have a good school, the children can study well and in comfort. They won't need to do their studies on the bare ground as they do now. I, and all the other teachers, are not going to be teaching here forever. But the school will be here. The school can't be transferred, or run away. Therefore those who are going to benfit from this school are all of us, the villagers of Barn Norng Ma Vor. It may be a long time before we get any satisfaction if we wait for the government to help us. The government has many other matters it has to concern itself with and, even if they do help, it will be many years before it happens. For all these reasons we should help ourselves.'

'That's enough! There's no need to make a recruiting speech. You sound as if you are trying to mobilize us. What do we have a government for if they can't build a school or build a new road for its citizens?' The loud voice was the voice of Caw Kart, the son of Lung 'Carn Kern, who drove a minibus between the village and the *amphur*.

'You're OK, teacher, but let's see; wherever you're from, you talk a lot, but I don't see you do anything.' After that there was some desultory voicing of opinions by a number of villagers, nothing of consequence and much of it incomprehensible. Finally the headman concluded that the villagers were not yet agreed on completing the schoolhouse themselves. Perhaps they should wait for the new budget. In the meantime the temporary schoolhouse would have to do. As for Headmaster Khammaw, he showed neither satisfaction nor dissatisfaction - no one knew what he had wanted.

The one who was sad, frustrated, whose hopes for co-operation had been damped and whose requests had been refused, was Piya. He promised himself, despite it all, that he would try to be as good a rural teacher as he could.

CHAPTER 8

At the end of July, the rains had not yet come. They were needed. The seedlings transplanted in the fields had begun to turn yellow without any moisture in the soil. People were saying the rains had failed again. Many who had not yet even transplanted had already gone to 'Carn Khen for rice for their daily needs. they had no idea whether they would be able to repay their debts come the harvest.

After the villagers frustrated his wish to complete the school building, Piya turned his energies to expanding his vegetable garden beside his little hut. From his textbook on the new agriculture, he contemplated a variety of new crops which he might try. He prepared new ground, planted much seed and watched as the shoots emerged. Though he watch them and watered them carefully as they grew, many lost their battle with the sun and the heat and died, while others succumbed to pests of all kinds. He was very disheartened.

The problem of water, he thought, he would settle by digging his own well. The first day he started work on it, at a spot near his hut, Thit Phun, coming from his gambling school, stopped and asked him, 'What are you doing, digging such a deep hole?'

'I am digging the well,' Piya answered, bent over, digging away with a hoe he had borrowed from the headmaster.

'What well?' said Thit Phun, not understanding.

'A well, for water,' the young teacher answered, still not looking up at his interrogator. 'That well's so far away, It's to much trouble carrying water up here. So I'm digging a well here.'

'What? All my born days I've never seen a man dig a well by himself. Is it possible?'

He looked doubtful; then, with a look of extreme scepticism he continued on his way toward the village. He was soon followed by another; but in fact this second man had been watching Piya from the start, since he had begun teaching the children to sing, since he begun to coming to the school to teach each morning. he had seen him move to the hut near the school and begin his vegetable growing enterprise. He had watched him lead his simple life, but always industrious, energetic. The man was 'Carn Khen. Piya had often chatted with him at his house by the edge of the fields.

'Oh! Uncle, Sir, you've come here today?' Piya greeted him with pleasure.

'Are you digging a well?' said 'Carn Khen, making clear he knew already.

'Yes, a well,' Piya said. 'The other well is too far away; I've got to make one closer to my home. I've no idea how deep I'll have to dig before I hit the water. Perhaps it'll take two or three days.'

It's shouldn't be too deep. You should find water at about two metres. But digging a well in the rains is against all the rules. the old folks didn't go for it much.' 'Carn Khen gave his opinion.

'Why was that, was there some reason?' Piya put the hoe down on the ground and wiped the sweat out of his eyes.

'I don't know. Perhaps there was no shortage of water during the rains and nobody dug well then. They may have thought anyone digging a well in the rain was a queer sort of person.' 'Carn Khen abstractedly examined the dying plants. 'Go ahead. Don't pay too much attention to what people say.'

The day after school closed, early in the morning, Piya suddenly found himself with lots of helpers. He had Caw Khiaw, Caw Iam, Caw Bunmi and Caw Siang, the darkskinned lad who didn't talk much. Nevertheless, he liked to hang around the teacher, always offering to perform small tasks for him. The whole group came to see what he was doing and immediately volunteered their services. Caw Khiaw jumped down to the bottom of the hole which Piya had dug the day before - about the metre depth. He used a short-handled hoe to dig the earth and put it into a basket (*pungki*) which the three others hauled up on the rope. the headmaster, Duangdaw and Piya, wearing shorts and no shirt, stood nearby watching.

'If any of you are tired and want to stop or want to go home, please stop. I'll have your fathers and mothers complaining that the teachers are making you work,' Piya told the children.

'How clever you are, Khun Piya,' Duangdaw said. 'Whatever it is, you do yourself. You grow vegetables for yourself. You dig your own well. More than that, the kids love you - the whole school does. You really make me envious.'

'Don't be envious of me, Khun Duangdaw, you have many things I don't have, and which I am sure I'll never have in this life.' He turned to the headmaster. 'Isn't that true, Headmaster?'

'Oh, I don't know. I have no idea what you want, Piya,' the headmaster smiled.

'Happiness. I want happiness for myself and for others,' he answered with conviction.

'How about this?' the headmaster said, changing the subject. 'Come and eat at my place this evening. There are three teachers coming from Barn Phak I Hin. We are in neighbouring schools and visit each other often. We're pretty friendly. Some other day I'll take you when we meet at Barn Phak I Hin. It's a big village. Pretty girls! You haven't been yet, have you?'

'Come along, Khun Piya. I'll be the hostess and show off my skills,' the young woman coaxed.

'OK, I'll follow you in a little while,' Piya said, walking to the mouth of the well.

'It's enough if we go down fifty centimeters today. Another day or two and we should strike water.'

The sun was near setting and, looking from the hut on the elevated school ground, it glittered on the surface of the water of the swamp. The green rice stalks around the swamp looked like the forest surrounding an oasis in the desert. On the fields at slightly greater elevation there was not yet a single stalk of rice. The ground was dry and without colour.

Piya turned his gaze away from the west towards his own vegetables, which were in the same condition as the rice fields on elevated ground. He looked then at the soil from the well, which lay beside it and hoped again that they would strike water tomorrow or the next day. He closed the door of his hut and locked it with a small brass padlock which would not have resisted any determined effort to break in. Its only use was to deter the casual passerby. He got on his bike, Ai Krong, and rode down the hill towards the village and the evening meal at the head master's house.

'Oh! You got here just as we were talking about you,'

said Headmaster Khammaw as he introduced him around. 'Piya, meet Khru Cantha, the headmaster of Barn Phak I Hin, the chief school of our area. This is Khru Thongsaen and Khru Visarn, both of them from Barn Phak I Hin.'

Piya raised his hands in greeting and sat down, joining the circle on the floor. In the centre there stood a 'flat', a halfbottle of rice whisky, and two bottles of soda. Khru Duangdaw came out of the kitchen and greeted him in a bright, friendly manner.

'Oh, you've come, the energetic schoolmaster! I guarantee the food's going to be all eaten today.'

'What are we going to get?' Piya asked, smiling broadly.

'Wait till it's served. I am not going to tell you yet.' The young woman turned back into the kitchen.

'We're going to have pork today. I wanted to roast it on a spit for us to eat - but the animal was a little too big for that so we've barbecued some and minced the rest.' The headmaster poured some whisky for Piya. 'Not roast pig on a spit today, nor will we have "pig *harn*", the headmaster said, playing on the similarity of the words *han* and *harn*.[1]

'What is "pig *harn*"? I've not heard that before.' The new teacher was puzzled.

'What we call "pig *harn*" is an animal that many have contributed to buy,' Khru Thongsaen explained. when we have an opportunity to get together, we have it slaughtered. We add in the cost of the drink and everything else, and divide it up amongst us.[2] Usually the convenor pays for it all and he collects the money from the others at the end

---

1 *Han*; here meaning 'to turn round on a spit'.

2 The word *harn* means 'to divide'.

of the month. This we call "pig *harn*". Sometimes its "beef *harn*" or "chicken *harn*"; depends on what you want to eat.'

'No "pig *harn*" today, that's guaranteed,' the headmaster affirmed loudly.

The little servant girl, I Si, brought out the barbecued pork. In fact it was more like scorched pork, for the ears, the liver, the skin from the back of the neck and pieces of meat about the size of the palm are placed directly on the red hot coals and turned back and forth till cooked. The meat is then cut into pieces of a size suitable for eating. Dipped in fish sauce it was an excellent accompaniment of the whisky - particularly the skin on the back of the neck which was called *nang khi hart*. It was nice and crispy to chew.

Khru Duangdaw followed soon after with plate of fried spare ribs, hot, and smelling delicious.

'This is all my own work,' she said, and sat down not talking a great deal of care, as she was wearing jeans. She settled down, seated in women's fashion with both feet tucked under her on one side, neat, tidy everything in order. 'The only things I can cook which are edible, are scrambled eggs, boiled eggs and fried dishes like this.'

'You'll soon be a grand lady and won't have to go into the kitchen. All you'll have to do is point your finger and eat.' Headmaster Cantha gave the girl the benefit of his observations. 'These days the young men are not interested in the cooking ability of their wives. They only want them to be pretty. Don't you agree, Piya?'

'I have no idea,' said Piya, as he picked up a piece of spare rib and put it in his mouth. 'I haven't yet thought about marriage, and I don't know how one should choose a wife. It's very tasty, Khun Duangdaw. Is this your lack of cooking ability?' He turned and smiled at her.

Khru Visarn, who was about five years older than Piya, look at the youngest of the group. He poured himself some whisky and stretch his glass towards duangdaw. 'Have some, a light drink with some soda.'

'I don't think I can take it. If it was beer I could manage. At home in Ubon my father always keeps some in the fridge.' Duangdaw at first refused, but then accepted the glass, which she placed in front of her. The roar of a powerful motorcycle came out of the darkness and stopped in the middle of the yard in front of the house. They stared out and saw a young man wearing brown jacket. His dismounted and climbed up to the house as if completely familiar with the place.

'Greetings, Headmaster.' He was in his thirties, wore his hair fashionably long, falling down to his neck.

'Oh! Headmaster Cantha, Khru Thongsaen, Khru Visarn, you're all here. What are you all celebrating here?' He grinned at them, as he knew them well, at the same time greeting each with his hands together. He sat down, joining the drinkers, though no one had yet invited him.

'Where have you been, and what you are doing her, Mor Sombat?' the headmaster asked, showing his pleasure at seeing him.[3] He introduced Duangdaw and Piya. They greeted each other in customary fashion, all three holding this position, waiting for one of the others to speak first. There was no great hiatus however, for Khru Thongsaen asked Mor Sombat, 'Where were you last Monday? I brought my wife to see you, but you weren't there so I took her to the provincial hospital.'

---

3 *Mor* is a title used for medical practitioners of all kinds, and certain other specialists.

'Oh, I went to see a patient over there in Sabaeng - and spent the night there,' Mor Sombat answered quickly. Sombat was an unlicensed practitioner whom the villagers considered very skilful and gave the status of "doctor".

'What's wrong with your wife?'

'I don't know. She's pinning for "the white fish of the fields". She'll be OK for three days and then will run a temperature for four. One moment it's her stomach, the next her head. I took her to the main hospital, but it was no use whatsoever. The medicines alone cost about a hundred baht.' Khru Thongsaen expounded on his wife's problems. The phrase "to pine for the white fish of the fields" was a local idiom referring to a poor state of health, continuous aches and pains, the inability to eat anything at all without suffering some reaction. The only thing that could be eaten was a species of fish, "white fish of the fields", a species of carp.

'Mor Sombat, you must be a rich man,' Khru Visarn chipped in. 'Everybody in the *tambon* knows you. You have so many patients calling on your services, you seem to have no time for a wife and family. You must be earning ten, even hundreds of thousands.'

'Nonsense! Everyone's got the wrong idea.' The unlicensed doctor, who had served with the Army Medical Corps, poured himself some whisky and noisily drew into his mouth some larp which the headmaster's wife had just placed in front of them. 'This constant running around with my motorcycle breaking down is no way to make a lot of money. I don't deny I'd like to make money, but I don't know how to get the money out of patients. They suffer from every imaginable kind of disease, and sometimes I can't even recover the cost of the injections I give them.

We rural folk are like flowers in a single field - you see these sick people and you've got to feel sorry for them. I treat them and hope they'll pay me later. If I were rich I'd buy myself a car, not ride this dilapidated motorcycle.'

Piya's interest in the doctor was aroused. From what he heard from time to time, Mor Sombat was much trusted by the poorer villagers. He saw now even those of the station of village schoolmaster were his clients and took their families for treatment to him.

He asked, 'Where do you live, in case I need to come and consult you?'

'I live at Barn Khok Klarng, the village just beyond Barn Phak I Hin. From Barn Norng Ma Vor, if you take the "development" road, it's about nine kilometres. I find my living mostly in this *tambon*.'

Piya concluded at once that Doctor Sombat was not really a doctor, or an official of the Health Department. He had used the phrase 'find my living in this *tambon*'. If he were a real doctor he would have lived at either district centre or in the city. If he were a health official he would not have used the phrase 'find a living'. But Piya did not dare pursue the subject. He felt it would be unsuitable on this his first meeting.

'You seem to come to this village very often. Do you have a lot of patients here, or is there some other reason?' Headmaster Khammaw asked, smiling. He had heard the village gossip that Mor Sombat was courting a local girl, but he did not know who she was.

'Both. I first came to visit a patient, but later I found I'd lose sleep if I didn't come,' the young doctor hinted at his involvements.

'That's the way it is. When a young man is far from

his young lady, he has to go looking for her.' Khru Visarn turned to Piya, 'And Khun Piya! Do you have a betrothed somewhere - or not yet? Or does your heart just flutter around Barn Norng Ma Vor?' He looked towards Duangdaw, who looked quite composed.

The headmaster lit the pressure lamp and hung it on the metal hook which was suspended from the rafters. They finished eating and chatted a while. The headmaster picked up a used pack of cards and passed them to Khru Visarn. The four teachers arranged themselves for a game of cards.

'OK, let's try out our skill a bit. We get to meet only once in a while. Mor Sombat, what about you?' The headmaster looked at Piya. 'Do you want to watch, or are you going home? You look as if you can hardly keep your eyes open.'

'Yes, please excuse me. I think I'll go home.' He raised his hands in farewell to each of the four guests, and then turned towards the kitchen. 'Khun Duangdaw, I'm leaving. thank you very much for the fried pork. It was delicious.'

She came out and stood on the verandah watching him mouth his bicycle, Ai Krong. 'Good luck. Tomorrow I'll fry some more for lunch.' She gaze after him as he vanished into the darkness, feeling a stab of anxiety for her colleague. She changed clothes for her bath, and when she had finished went off to bed, leaving the five men to their card game.

Piya got back to his hut about eight o'clock. He parked his bicycle and walked to the well. Two days' digging had resulted the depth perhaps just enough to cover a child's head. He thought to himself that there should certainly be water within three metres of the surface. With water so near the house, there were many thing he could do. Beside having water for drinking and cooking, it would be convenient for the children, who would no longer have to cart water from afar to fill the stone jars for the school. The most important thing, however, was that he would have water for his little kitchen garden. He picked up a pebble and dropped it in to the well. He thought he heard a splash, but did not trust his ears. He tried another pebble, and there was a splash again. Some water had already flowed in to the bottom of the well. He grew excited and want to tell somebody about it, but there was no one around and he had to keep it to himself till the morning.

His happiness turned to something else when he got to the hut and saw his lock had been force open. The little brass padlock hung down with the hasp which had been pulled off its attachment to the door. Piya hurriedly lit the lamp and examined his belongings. He found signs that they had been disturbed but nothing was missing. He possessed no valuables anyway. He decided the thief had probably been looking for money rather than anything else.

The young teacher had been much tried and his emotions were confused. He sat on the verandah outside the hut on the long bench which he had made specially for sitting out on and enjoying the breeze which blew from the direction of the great swamp. Lights flickered in the neighbourhood of the water, revealing the villagers fishing. Lights also still showed from 'Carn Khen' s house. He could just hear the wavering sound of the *khaen*. Usually young men came blowing the *khaen* when they were courting their sweethearts in the village. He was curious as to which young man was unusual enough to play the instrument outside the village. At first he thought his nerves were playing tricks on him and he did not believe his ears. He paid more attention and was certain it was a *khaen* he heard. What was more, the player was highly skilled. The rendition of every tune was far superior to that to be expected from courting youths. he wind that blew from the rice fields made the sound of the instrument louder and more distinct. Piya belonged to the generation too young to know the names of the tunes. He knew from his uncle the abbot, who loved to listen to traditional plays on the radio, that the *khaen* had many tunes, each of them named. As he listened he realized the music came from 'Carn Khen's house. he had known 'Carn Khen for two months now, but this was the first time he realized the older man was skilled player of the instrument.

Piya forgot his door and the broken lock. Later he decided he would not say anything about it to anyone. He thought now about his guitar for which he had saved and on which he had practised since he started work for his diploma. He now could play a number of songs. He had wanted to bring it with him, but Ai Suk, another nephew of the abbot, who was a student in Secondary 3, had become devoted to it and had not allow Piya to take it with him. He recalled how Ai Suk had said to him, when he had come to Ubon for his departmental examination, 'Goodness, you're going to be earning now, in a few day - let me have the guitar. you can buy a new one.' Later when he caught the bus for Ubon he had only taken a single bag.

The sound of the *khaen* now made him miss the guitar. He felt he should have some kind of musical instrument to keep him company and to dispel his loneliness during the long evening hours.

CHAPTER 9

Three days later the well was ready and Piya could draw water for his use. At about two metres he had hit a spring and the water flowed so strongly that they could not dig any deeper. He found a plank which he placed by the side of the well. He got a bamboo from 'Carn Khen, suitable for use as a *khan khor,* for the schoolchildren to use in their daily task of filling the school jars to the brim. In addition, they began to help Piya water his vegetables which had begun to wither. With this new attention, they slowly recovered. Around the flagpole they had planted flowering plants, a variety which could stand extremes of heat and rain. These now began to flower as they too got their share of water from the new well. Without trace of withering, they bloomed - alternate clumps of purple and white. The surroundings of the flagpole changed from a wilderness of dry bushes to attractive rows of green, purple and white.

'You seem to like these "everlasting flowers" very much,'[1] Duangdaw had said the day he planted them. 'Is there some history to it?'

'If there is, I suppose it must be my old teachers. Every Teachers' Day, wherever I was, in addition to the *phraek* grass[2] and the *makhya* flowers, there always was a tray of these everlasting flowers.' The young teacher had perhaps found an answer, but then he really got to the root of the matter. 'Really, I like all kinds of flowers, I think they are all very beautiful. But when you have to grow

---

[1] 'Everlasting flowers' - GROMPHRENA GLOBOSA, globe amaranth.

[2] *Phraek* grass - CYNODEN DACTYLON, Bermuda grass.

them in these kinds of surroundings, like the school here, you've got to plant some species that will keep growing without being watered every week and which will still flower abundantly.'

That morning, it was the first Monday in August, according to usual practice there would have been no school. It was customary that the school took vacations from the first of the month. But this year, school had not closed. The rains were much later than usual, and there was no water in the rice fields for the transplanting. The school really followed the dictates of the weather. Most villagers were rice cultivators and when it was necessary they asked that the school be closed to allow their children to help in the fields. Piya woke early, dressed, had his breakfast and went out to look at his vegetable plot. Everything was in order. The children were drifting in, in little groups. He felt he had been responsible for an increase in the children's love of the school; they came early now, in increasing numbers. Even the headmaster and Duangdaw had been forced into coming early.

The sun beat down fiercely from a cloudless sky, even though it was still early morning. Piya gathered the kids together in the space behind the school - a sandy spot, protected by the shadow of the school while the sun was still low in the sky. This early morning gathering had now almost become part of the curriculum. He began by telling them stories, some of them true, some of them from texts, and others local folk tales. The children were both entertained and informed. Piya knew how to choose stories that would keep their interest and were at the same time suitable for children their age. He was a good story teller and he gave the occasions variety by breaking for games and singing with them. When they had sung a song extolling the joys and freedom of living far from human habitation in the middle of the forest - a prospect few would encounter, except in songs - Piya asked:

'Who knows why rain falls?'

The kids looked silently at each other. Finally Khiaw, the leader of the school and first in most things, put up his hand. 'Because the heavens weep,' he said clearly.[3] The other children giggled at his play on words.

'The gods bathe, Sir!' another lad said, and his companions greeted him with more laughter. As he sat down he turned to the boy next to him and said angrily, 'Well, that's what my father told me.'

'OK! Who else can answer? Go ahead, you don't need to be afraid of being wrong.' Piya pointed at Bunmi. 'What do you say, Bunmi? Why does it rain?'

The young boy stood up and said: 'I don't know, Sir.'

'Siang! What makes rain fall?' He pointed to Siang, who sat nearby.

'Because there are clouds,' Siang answered - but mixing local dialect and standard Thai. The children laughed delightedly. The inhabitants of Isarn had one notable characteristic: if one of their number mixed dialects through a slip of the tongue, they thought him old fashioned and a bit of a rustic.

'I don't see why you should laugh,' Piya said, smiling. 'Siang was quite correct. "Sky litter" means "clouds". If there are clouds it's likely to rain. Let me explain.'

---

3 The phrase 'the sky roars' or 'weeps' is the common Thai idiom meaning 'it thunders'.

Just then the headmaster and Duangdaw arrived and the children turned round at the sound of the motorcycle. Then they turned back immediately to listen to Piya.

'Rain is but water that falls from the sky,' Piya began. 'Rainwater originates in the water on the surface of the earth, and that water, the water of streams and swamps, originates as rainwater. I am sure you've all observed the swamp by the school, Norng Ma Vor; in the rain it's full, in the dry season the water's very low. Do you know where it disappears to?'

They were all silent, not one daring to speak. As Piya was about to continue, there was a noise from Caw Siang.

'It dries up,' Siang said and again evoked laughter from his companions as he used a dialect word which could be used of water, but had unpleasant connotations. Siang was upset. Whenever he opened his mouth, everybody laughed.

'Siang is right. Don't you laugh at him.' Piya tried to ease matters, then continued.

'The water that evaporates,' he said, using the same word Siang had used, then following it with the more acceptable central Thai expression, 'a part of the water vanishes into the atmosphere. Or, in a manner of speaking, it disappears into the sky. In fact it doesn't disappear at all. It changes into water vapour, which is invisible. Water from streams, swamps, ponds, wells, even pots and jars, it all evaporates. The hotter it is, the more evaporation there is. All this water vapour gathers together and appears to us as clouds, or as they say, lumps of *khi fa*,' he said, repeating the dialectal expression Siang had used. 'Some clouds we see are very light and float high up in the sky. Others look heavy and come much lower. When the clouds reach a lower temperature they release their water as rain. One of the things which makes the atmosphere cooler is the presence of forests. The thicker and more luxuriant our forests, the cooler our weather. That is why the government forbids the cutting of timber and the destruction of forests and why it encourages people to plant trees and protect the forests. It improves our climate and increases our rainfall.'

When school assembled for regular classes, Piya continued to talk to Classes 3 and 4 about rainfall and forestry. That afternoon he had the fourth class children dig ditches to bury the rubbish left over from the rubbish they'd buried the previous week - together with that newly accumulated. Each ditch was roughly a cube with a metre edge. The ditches were scattered around the area which was considered the boundary of the school grounds. Some were full of rubbish and dried leaves, others of animal manure, mixed droppings of cows and buffaloes.

'When the holes are full of rubbish and compost, we'll cover them up with soil and plant various kinds of trees - one in each ditch. They should grow well, grow tall, quickly, as the rubbish acts as manure, food for the trees; we must keep the soil at the base of the tree always moist,' Piya explained to the children.

He had said to the headmaster that he thought this was just as important a part of teaching as the lessons in the classroom. He had told the children that when the rubbish was well composted they would plant mango and tamarind trees in the ditches, in time encircling the entire school compound.

Later that afternoon, when school was over, Piya walked down to the house of 'Carn Khen, 'the solitary one', who could be said to be his closest neighbour. 'Carn

Khen's wooden house stood high off the ground - a small house, perhaps just right for a single family, but too big for the single man that lived there. The roof was thatched with *kha* grass. The use of this grass stretched so far back into the past that it had given the word *langkha* (roof or house) to the Thai language - that is, the house that is thatched with *kha* grass. The floor was made of planks of good timber, but the walls were screens plaited from long strips of bamboo. These screens, known as *lai khup,* were beautiful to look at, very skilfully woven. The doors and windows were also woven bamboo screens. Piya had not seen bamboo screens used for doors and windows before, nor had he seen protective walls of bamboo which combined strength and delicacy in this manner. The frames of the screens were made of hardwood beautifully planed and finished. The houses with bamboo walls that he had seen usually had unstripped bamboo poles used for frames and were tied together with bamboo strips or jungle vines - not carefully nailed as this one was.

Seated on a litter under the house, 'Carn Khen was weaving a basket for glutinous rice. By his side stood a number of completed glutinous rice containers, piled on top of each other. In one space between the pillars of the house was a pile of neatly arranged split firewood, each stick cut to exactly the same length, testimony to the meticulousness of the householder. Next to the firewood was a pile of bamboo, sawn into sections and stacked away in similar fashion. Above Piya's head, tied to the floor beam of the house was a bundle of fishing rods and *ngaep sai kop,* an instrument for catching frogs. These were woven of yet another kind of bamboo. There was, in addition, a *tarng barn,* a bird trap made of netting. Everything was delicately made and beautifully finished, testifying to the skill of the craftsman.

The host invited Piya to climb up to the house for a chat. It was very hot, and in truth it may have been more comfortable below the house, where the slight breeze made it cooler. Piya, however, said nothing and followed his host.

The steps leading up to the house were the type which leaned against the platform. There was a rise of about one half metre from the top of the steps to the house floor. On either side, at the top of the steps, was a carved tiger head. By the side of the steps was a platform for a water jar, as was customary in Isarn. This was specially made from the trunk of a species of pandanus as tall as the floor of the house.[4] The important thing was that there should be three branches on which to place the water pot. Usually the branches still had green leaves and flowers with green unfurled centres which perpetually gave off their scent. Piya also observed the water scoop which lay covering the mouth of the jar. The handle was made of rosewood,[5] beautifully carved as a Naga head - the end being the Naga's open mouth.

The host spread a mat and invited Piya to sit. Piya looked covertly around and observed that though this man in his late forties lived by himself, the house was spotlessly clean, with everything in order. Everything in the house, the utensils, the furniture, the tools, all bore witness to the fact that the owner was a skilled craftsman.

---

4 PANDANUS TECTORIUS.

5 Rosewood - DALBERGIA LATIFOLIA.

'How's the well? Do you have enough water for your wants?' were the questions asked by the man everyone said was mad. His speech gave no sign of madness.

'It's fine. I keep drawing water the whole day and it's never empty. The kids draw water for drinking and for watering the plants. I also get them to bathe every day after school's over, before they go home. Oh! Not everyone. Just the little rascals who look particularly dirty.' Piya enumerated the uses of his well.

'And how are the vegetables doing? I haven't been that way for some days. It's been so hot these days, you must be having some trouble. The young rice plants are so yellow, they look quite scorched. I don't know what ill-omened thing has happened that there has been no rain.'

'Carn Khen chattered away, as if he was quite uninterested in what had brought Piya to visit him.

'The other night I heard you play the *khaen*. It was very pleasant,' Piya began. 'I worked out it must have been you playing. I'd like you to teach me.' Piya remembered the first day he had met him, when he got off the bus at Barn Norng Ma Vor; he had addressed the older man as *aa* (younger uncle) and he used the same term of address now. This was suitable. If one compared ages, 'Carn Khen was four or five years younger than Piya's father.

'I was very interested in the music you were playing,' he continued. 'I am terribly sorry I have never had the time to learn to play our local music.'

'What have you played before?' 'Carn Khen asked, staring at Piya as if he expected to find something in his face. 'If you're going to study music, you've got to begin young. But if you are really interested, you can still learn.'

'I've played the guitar - a *farang* stringed instrument, the kind you pluck. I've never played a wind instrument,' Piya explained.

'Blowing the *khaen* is difficult. It has seven notes like the stringed instrument, but the arrangement of the notes doesn't follow the arrangement of the scale. Also the left is not the same as the right. It's perhaps better you learn to "hit the log" rather than blow the *khaen.'* 'Hitting the log' was playing the *phin*. The *phin* or *syng* was a three-stringed instrument, like the Western mandolin.

'That depends on you, whatever you think is suitable.' Piya was willing to take his advice. 'But where am I going to find a *phin* for sale?'

'They don't make them for sale. Each one is different, each musician makes his own. If you are really interested, I have one which you can use - you won't need to go looking for one.' The host stood up and went into the room with a friendly smile on his face. He returned in a moment with a three-stringed *phin,* finely carved and beautifully finished. Piya could not understand why the villagers called such a talented man 'mad'.

Before he handed Piya the instrument, 'Carn Khen tried it out, accompanying himself as he sang softly in a clear, resonant voice, the tune and rhythm animated.

'That's a nice song, what is it?' Piya said, happily.

'I don't know what it's called; the musicians with the players like to sing it when the hero and heroine stroll through the forest. You may call it the song of lovers engrossed in each other.' He passed the *phin* to the young man. 'Try playing it. It's not difficult. The kids, your pupils, Bak Khiaw, Bak Siang, they've all come and learned from me. They can all play it. Take it, play it, it'll prevent you being lonely. I am very happy to give it to you.'

When he got back to his hut, Piya almost forgot to eat, he was so engrossed in his new instrument. He tried strumming it and found it was not very different from other stringed instruments. He tried out songs he'd learned on the guitar and felt he didn't do too badly.

It was very hot, but towards midday the oppressiveness increased. Shortly afterwards a gentle wind began to blow, slowly increasing in strength. Rain began to fall, lightning flashed and there were repeated claps of thunder. The rain fell so heavily - as they said - 'that eyes had never seen nor ears heard.' The young teacher examined his roof with a flashlight. It seemed it had not yet been blown away by the wind. But the rain water dripped through in many places - he was lucky his bed was still dry. When he had shifted all his belongings so that he was sure they would remain dry, he covered himself with a blanket and snuggled into bed with a heart happy on behalf of the farmers who would now have enough water for their rice fields.

Piya woke early the next morning. He walked towards the swamp behind the school, the swamp from which the village got its name. There was a broad sweep of glittering flood water covering the area where yesterday there had been green rice shoots. They lay covered below the expanse of water. But the rice fields on the higher land were in fine condition as the water lay trapped between the bunds of each field. His vegetable plots, however, frightened him. The ridges on which he had planted his lettuces and coriander had all been washed away by the rain. The Chinese cabbages which had already sprouted lay fallen on top of each other. Some of them had broken right off and lay piled up on one side.

The young teacher took up his toothbrush and walked to the well. Here he had another shock. The well, which he had left, its mouth round, the soil nicely arranged around its rim, now looked like a shallow hole, full of water which had been caught in it. The earth had collapsed and fallen into it. The well had been about two metres deep. When he used the *khan kor* to measure its depth, the stick stirred up the mud at the bottom of the hole, now barely a metre deep. The mouth of the well, which had been about one metre and thirty centimetres in diameter, now looked like a buffalo wallow.

Everything he had expended his effort on seemed destroyed. Of the vegetables he had planted, only the chillies, the basil, the galangal and the lemon grass remained. These, the roots of which went deep, looked as if they might sprout any day now. But the coriander, the leafy vegetables, the beans, which had sprouted with gay leaves already, now all lay uprooted by the force of the rain. But, most tragic of all - for he was proud of the fact that it was the product of his co-operation with his pupils - the well lay quite destroyed, completely unusable.

'I told you so - you can't do anything with this sandy soil.' Thit Phun wearing but a *pha khaw ma* and shouldering a hoe, stood looking at the well with a taunting look on his face. 'However industrious you are, you can't compete with the elements here! I knew your efforts would be completely useless.' When he had finished speaking, he walked purposefully towards the swamp.

CHAPTER 1O

'The meeting decided that term would end on Monday and school would reopen again on the first of September,' the headmaster reported to Piya and Duangdaw that morning. 'We'll only close for twenty-five days this time for there's fear that we may not complete our one hundred and eighty days teaching this year.'

'Why must we wait till Monday? The rains have come, there's water for the rice fields. We can close tomorrow or the day after,' Piya, who did not understand the benefits of this kind of break, asked naïvely.

'This is an established custom. The school must close on a Friday, and the vacation be counted from the Monday - we then get two days extra, the Saturday and Sunday. The last day of the holiday must be on Friday, so that the new term begins on a Monday. That way we get extra days at head and tail - four days that are not counted as holidays,' the headmaster explained.

'Why must we be so meticulous in counting the days and nights of the holidays? Each year we teachers get about three months holidays over and above Saturdays and Sundays and government holidays,' Piya continued.

Duangdaw could not contain her impatience. 'My goodness, Khun Piya, everybody likes to take holidays as long as possible! I understand the headmaster. With the two days at either end we'll get twenty-nine days altogether, not just the twenty-five.

'These holidays I'd like to tour some of the more distant provinces. I don't know yet if I should ask father for extra money or not.'

'Are you going to Bangkok? Are you going anywhere or not these holidays?' the headmaster asked Piya.

'I thought I'd go home to Amnart Caroen for a few days and then go on to Bangkok. I'd like to visit Luang Lung for a few days and then I'll come back here.'

'What do you want to come back so quickly for? Or are you going to help the young girls with the transplanting?' Duangdaw laughed. 'How are the vegetables? They must be doing well with the rain.' The girl changed the subject abruptly.

'They're fine. But my well's completely ruined.'

'That's what happens when you dig a well in the rainy season. If you don't put in a support it's bound to collapse.' The headmaster gave him encouragement. 'Wait until the rains are over and we'll dig it again. We'll put in a concrete pipe this time.'

'What happened about the school? When you talked to the Section Head that day, did he say what had been decided?' Piya changed the subject to a more important matter, one which the teachers had much discussed among themselves. 'Or is there going to be a big fuss about our request for an allocation to complete the school building?'

'It's all been taken care of. I forgot to tell you that an allocation has been approved,' Headmaster Khammaw announced triumphantly. 'The Section Head said our *tambon* has only one proper building. Would you believe a hundred thousand baht? He said Sia Mangkorn has been given the contract. They should start work by October at the latest.'

Both Piya and Duangdaw were overjoyed at the news that they were going to get a new building; particularly Piya, who immediately thought that when the new building was completed he would have space to organize various other activities for the children. As for Duangdaw, though she was not preoccupied with her teaching, like any other teacher she liked to have decent surroundings in which to do her job.

'Don't forget to see they include a toilet in this place. I've heard the plans for rural schools don't have toilets - I don't know where they expect the kids to relieve themselves,' the young man advised the headmaster.

'Also ask for a new flagpole. A metal one! I'd like to plant flowers all around it - make it look nice,' Duangdaw mused.

'Oh, I thought you were going to get a job in town!' Piya teased.

'Of course I'm going to transfer,' she said, raising her voice. 'You don't think I'm going to stay here till I die, do you?'

They talked about that most important aspect of teaching and education, the official teaching instructions to teachers. The contents of these instructions were the business of educationists at the national level. They decided on the interests and aims of the education system, the kind of characteristics they wished to foster among the citizens of the nation. They decided the principles and the content of the subjects which the teachers then taught. The success of these aims did not however rest with the principles, the publications, the teaching aids, but in the teaching itself - which depended on the teachers' knowledge, their ability and their true determination.

Piya would always remember the words of one of his young foreign professors with regard to principles and methods of teaching.

'Principles are like the instruments you use to reach your aims. It is the teacher who determines the results of education. There are two vital aspects to education and teaching. First, does the teacher teach or not? If the teacher doesn't teach, it is as if he sits like a pillar, drawing his salary and waiting for retirement and pension. Education might as well be abandoned. Second, if he teaches, one must ask "What does he teach?" Does he teach merely by telling, by writing and through memory? Or does he teach through practice, by directing powers of thought? Does he make his teaching attractive - that is, does he teach people, not teach books?' he had said, punning on the Thai idiom, *sorn nangsy*. Piya remembered that he had asked for amplification and the professor had explained.

'To teach people means to teach them everything that will help them be better, have more knowledge, more ability, think better, and be more useful to themselves and to others. "To teach books" means merely to instruct them with what is in books, to have them then remember what is written in them but be unable to put this knowledge into practice.'

'I shall remember that when I become a teacher. We need to teach people, not teach books!' The words of that professor still rang in Piya's ears.

In the two months that Piya had been teaching at Barn Norng Ma Vor he had tried to improve the children in every way he could. He had instructed them and had them learn by experience, trying out what he taught them. He was an example to them to be thorough in everything they did. Under his direction they had learned about planting trees.

They had dug the holes, prepared the soil, looked for the trees and planted them. Piya had then seen that they continued to tend the young plants with care. He had taught them about cleanliness. Each day he had them line up at the well that the children themselves had helped to dig - but which now lay destroyed. At the same time, Duangdaw and the headmaster had their own way of teaching - that which was popular among the majority of teachers in the country, particularly among middle and upper school teachers. They had their pupils copy down in their exercise books whatever the teacher taught and repeat it as accurately as possible when it came to examination time.

Lunch that day had been particularly delicious. It had included *som tam*, a spicy hot dish made with shredded green papaya, spiced scrambled egg, barbecued catfish, fried crickets, and *caew borng*, a relish made with fermented fish. The three teachers ate together at the house, or perhaps more accurately, at the hut of Piya. After lunch Duangdaw was teaching ethics to the children of Primary 2. Her subject for the day was 'generosity'.

'Generosity is liberality and benevolence.' The young woman began her explanation with a definition she hoped the children would remember. The children, however, understood none of the words she used - not 'generosity', not 'liberality', not 'benevolence'.

'We should be liberal and benevolent towards each other. Whatever we have we should share with each other, we should not be selfish and just look after our own interest. He that is not generous will not have many friends.'

She then put up her original definition on the blackboard and, using the pointer, had them all read it out together as loud as they could. She had them read each word separately, twice round, then copy it all out into their soft-covered exercise books, distributed to them by courtesy of the Education Department.

'Write it out in your books. No talking! No playing around!' It was all according to the instructions of the Teachers' Manual on the subject of 'generosity'. She then read them an account from a journal about the distribution of gifts to government officials who worked on the territorial borders of Thailand. This was supposed to be an instructive example of the virtue of 'generosity'.

'Please Miss! Caw Thorng has broken my pencil,' piped up one of her charges, speaking in a broad local dialect. He brought up his pencil and showed it to Duangdaw, claiming the broad, jagged edge was the fault of his friend Caw Thorng. Duangdaw was slightly irritated but, remembering her duty as teacher, took it from him and sought out the headmaster.

'Please, Uncle, can you sharpen this pencil for me?'

'If you're looking for that silly machine, I've thrown it away, I am afraid. I don't know what they supply me with now. The pencils are just as bad. The first letter you write the point's gone. It's not just the kids, it's even the adults. Take this knife and sharpen it, let's hope it's better.' It was not quite clear whom the headmaster was blaming, for it was he who bought all the supplies for the school.

When she returned with the sharpened pencil, there was a stream of other children who wanted the same done - sorely testing her own sense of 'generosity'!

'If you've finished you can go out and play' - the magic words the pupils were always waiting to hear. In a few minutes all her Primary 2 pupils were running, screaming, playing outside the schoolhouse, in the shade. Some stood looking at Piya's well which had collapsed the previous night. Others climbed the rosewood trees and the pepper vines, giving the teachers great fears of a crop of broken legs.

'Come down at once! What do you think you're doing up there?' shouted Piya, who had taken his fourth class children to help clean the earth washed down by the rain. He ordered the children down out of the trees, at the same time thinking to himself that Duangdaw did not take much care of her pupils.

Meanwhile, Headmaster Khammaw, who always taught by the book, had the children of Primary 1. In the morning he had them do their numbers and in the afternoon practise their handwriting. After that his teaching was over. That afternoon he put up four lines on the blackboard, in large letters:

Khoo	*Mii*	*Taa*
Khoo	*Faa*	*Too*
Aa	*Mii*	*Khoo*
Aa	*Mii*	*Taa*

He used the pointer to lead the children in reading each syllable in unison at the tops of their voices - *khoo mii taa* ... Soon most of them were bawling out the meaningless syllables, paying no attention to the blackboard at all. Then, as a variation, he had some of the children, one at a time, use the pointer to lead his or her companions in the same routine.

'Master Hoam, come up and lead the class.' The headmaster called up one of the boys, speaking in dialect, in breach of Ministry of Education directions. Hoam, the leader of the class, came up and conducted the class in bawling out the syllables, using the long ruler to guide them. The rest of the class followed, each one getting up in turn from the long benches on which they all sat—three children on each.

While this was going on, the headmaster sat oblivious, smoking a cigarette of the type the villagers called *Pattimokka*. Some villagers said you could recite the *Pattimokka* in the time it took to smoke one of these cigarettes, as they were so difficult to keep alight.[1] Others said smoking one of these kept you intoxicated for as long as the monks chanted this holy text. Who knows which, if either, is the true explanation for the name; but this was what they called this cigarette they rolled themselves in banana leaf. Headmaster Khammaw was addicted to it.

Before he started on his smoke he had said, 'When you've finished reading, get out your slates and practise writing on them [the children's slates for the most part had fallen out of their wooden frames by the first week of school]. When that's done you can go out and play.'

Piya had the children of Class 4 continue with the digging of ditches they had begun on a previous occasion. He allocated four children to a ditch, each ditch to be a metre deep and a metre square. Most of the children, however, did not succeed in getting them a metre deep; though they were more successful in achieving the required

---

1 *Pattimokka:* the Canonical Buddhist code of behaviour enforced on monks, usually recited together by them on holy days.

breadth and width. While they were working Piya himself kept a close watch on the work, noting the sense of co-operation and determination the children exhibited - all of them without exception. When he saw they had finished, he called all his pupils, Classes 3 and 4, together and had them sit under the shade of a tree.

'Today we've tried out another method of working. The fourth class was divided into groups for digging ditches, and all the groups have done their work well; the ditches are all as required. The third class, who were asked to sweep up dead leaves and grass and put them in the ditches, have also done their job well. I've seen all of you, Classes 3 and 4, determined to work, co-operating together, not fighting, or each one going off on his or her own. There are two or three who didn't seem interested, who let the others do their share too. Let's hope they do better the next time. For the time being I'm not going to say who they are.'

Piya hoped that with such a lesson the children would not only learn many practical things through experience, but would also learn some ethics. This, he thought, must surely be better than giving them verbal instruction and then having them write his words down in their exercise books.

'We've dug holes to plant trees in - do you know why we don't plant them immediately? Why must the holes be so deep? And why do we fill them up again with leaves and grass?

'The reason is that the better we prepare the soil the better the trees will grow. Trees need food just as people do. The food trees need is manure. When you put in manure for the trees it must be put into the earth, as the trees take up their food through the roots. The rubbish, the dried leaves and grass we put into the holes will rot away and become manure, food, good fertilizer for the vegetation in the future. Our village soil is very sandy and doesn't have much natural nourishment for the vegetation, so we must prepare the soil well and add in the manure for the trees we are going to plant. We've now prepared many holes, and when we come back for the next term we'll be able to put in the trees.

'Many people plant trees, but they find they don't grow well because they don't prepare the soil properly. You may not believe what I tell you until you've seen for yourselves. We'll plant some trees without preparing the soil properly and then compare how they grow with the others.' He then sent them off to get themselves washed, and thought to himself that Siang hadn't been at school that day. He asked the headboy,

'Khiaw, do you know what's wrong with Siang that he didn't come to school today?'

'His mother's sick, Sir,' Caw Khiaw replied.

'Where do they live?' Piya asked.

'Not far from my house. His mother's called Mae Kham,' he replied, and rushed to join his friends at the well.

CHAPTER 11

The house was old and made of the cheapest materials. The roof was thatched with *kha* grass, the walls made of plaited strips of bamboo. The four walls of the little house which was the kitchen were all of dipterocarpus leaves. Usually, these leaves were only used for the roof or the walls of a hut, or on a temporary dwelling, or by the very poor. The area under the house was used as a chicken coop, with a row of bamboos, each about seven centimetres thick, placed one next to the other up to the stairs. At the top of the steps was attached an old black chain.

'Is this the house of Mae Kham?' Piya stopped his bicycle and addressed a woman who was feeding pigs under the granary.

'That's right,' she answered in dialect. 'Whom has the teacher come to see?' That, Piya thought, was an unnecessary question. If he had asked for Mae Kham's house he must surely have come to see Mae Kham.

However, he said, 'I've come to see Mae Kham. I heard she was ill. Is that right?'

'*Err*,' she grunted in assent. 'She's been ill a long time.' She shouted into the house, 'Phayorm, there's someone come visiting.'

Piya thanked her and walked under a gooseberry tree to the front of Mae Kham's house. He looked up and drew back in surprise, for in the house was Phayorm, the pretty girl who had drawn water for him.

'Has Khun Khru come looking for Siang?' Phayorm greeted him, smiling, her face flushed. Caw Siang, her only brother, had regaled her daily with stories of Piya's virtues, particularly his kindness of heart and industry. 'Please come up to the house.'

The young man gingerly climbed up the steps while Phayorm got herself a mat and spread it on the floor. She invited Piya to sit and turned to an old man who was seated at the other end of the house.

'Phor jai,[1] the new teacher has come visiting.' Piya turned and raised his hands in greeting to the old man. He recognized him as the *thaw cam*, the 'brahmin' priest, who had officiated at the wedding of Caw Kart, the son of Uncle 'Carn Kern; the one who had performed the *khwan*-calling ceremony.

'Phor jai is a doctor, he's come to treat my mother,' the young girl explained.

Next to the ritual expert or curer was a woman in her forties. She was thin, her face drawn and yellowish in colour. She lay on a frail, narrow bed. By her side was a large brass tray and some small containers with flowers, and small tallow candles. The young teacher guessed this was Mae Kham, the mother of Phayorm and Caw Siang.

'I heard you were ill and I've come to visit,' he said, raising his hands in greeting to the sick woman.

'Siang's gone for water. He should be back in a moment. He said he was going to set fish lines in the swamp this evening.' She referred to a popular form of fishing in the district. Lines are set up by the water's edge on short rods, each about an arm's length.

'What's wrong with you, Mother?' he asked the patient courteously.

---

[1] Lit. 'Big father'

'*Ooi*!' she cried, 'I don't know what's wrong. I've been sick like this for a long time. Sometimes I'm laid out like this, at others I can get up again,' she said softly. 'I get a stomach ache and then my whole body starts aching.'

'What do you think is wrong, Sir?' He turned to the curer.

'It's known as "the mark of the forest". If she takes this mixture for three or four days, we should know whether she's really ill or not,' the doctor replied, while grinding roots on a small stone quern and then mixing them with water in a bowl.

'Will this medicine cure this "mark of the forest"?' Piya asked, not feeling much confidence in such herbal cures. Nor was he very sure as to what this sickness the villagers called 'the mark of the forest' really was.

'This recipe comes from the city of Khon Kaen. It can cure many types of this disease - "the hooked mark of the forest", "the curled mark of the forest", of the nerves, of the ligaments, of the blood, of the wind - it can cure many kinds of disease.' The old man expounded on the virtues of his medicine.

The young teacher gazed at the healer. His nails were long. The medicinal roots he had used came out of an old cloth bag. He was not at all impressed. He thought that there could well be many types of roots and herbal medicines which were effective, but the manner in which this particular medicine had been mixed inspired in him no confidence; the long nails, the dirty black quern, the unboiled water which he had used. How could it have escaped contamination by harmful organisms? He thought of the modern doctors who establish clinics in the city; the hospitals, the health centres, the maternity centres and the rural medical officers. Barn Norng Ma Vor had none of these. His musings stumbled over the thought of Mor Sombat. Even Khru Thongsaen, the teacher of Phak I Hin, a man of education, took his wife for treatment to an unregistered doctor.

When the curer had finished his preparations he raised the bowl over his head and muttered an incantation of some kind and then blew a spell onto it - that is, he blew air out of his mouth onto the preparation. He then placed it by the sick woman's head and began the whole business again with more roots he pulled out of his bag. This mixture had some ten ingredients - roots, twigs, stalks - all completely unrecognizable by Piya. While he scraped and mixed he kept talking about his successes with other kinds of illnesses. However ill his patients, he never failed to cure them, even those who were carried out of hospital became better, though doctors couldn't do anything more for them. He treated them with his herbal concoctions and every single one was cured. Piya listened, unwilling to interrupt.

As the curer was finishing his second batch of medicine Caw Siang arrived carrying water. When he saw the teacher, the little dark-skinned boy's face broke into a smile from ear to ear.

'Siang! Come on, son, greet the teacher properly.' Mae Kham addressed her son with a diminutive, indicating he was her last born. Her words called on him to prostrate himself before the teacher in respect.

Caw Siang greeted the teacher as his mother requested and said, 'I thought I'd set the fishing lines out tonight in the swamp. May I sleep at your house so I can check the lines during the night?' The lad spoke briskly and clearly, in a fashion Piya had not heard before. Whenever he'd met him, particularly when Caw Khiaw was present, he'd had very little to say. Piya had thought him retiring.

'Goodness!' exclaimed Phayorm, aghast at her brother's words spoken to the teacher. 'Want to sleep at the teacher's house? Why don't you show some respect when you talk to the teacher?'

'Don't say that! People will think the children are my underlings. I like doing things with the kids. Fine, we can be friends now and I won't be lonely any more. But Mother's ill - won't you need Siang for anything?'

'There's nothing,' the sick woman replied. 'I've been sick so long, everybody thinks there's nothing wrong with me. I should get better when I've taken this medicine. It was just that today the pain was stronger than usual and I asked him to stay home from school to help. Go ahead, son - go and keep the schoolmaster company. Come back early tomorrow morning. Take care! Don't go out too far to set your lines, you may fall in and drown.'

Caw Siang went to prepare his lines, his creel and hoe; also his lamp - a kind used to catch frogs and fish and called a 'fish torch'.

'*Eei*! May I take some *mok pla siew* with me to eat?' Siang yelled from inside the kitchen, asking his sister if he could take some of the food she'd been cooking. *Mok pla siew* was a popular dish which could be prepared by anyone. *Pla siew* are small fresh-water fish; these are wrapped in two layers of banana leaves with salt and sweet basil or a similar herb. The packages are placed on a gentle fire and left to heat till they are cooked and give off a truly mouth-watering aroma.

'Go ahead! Just leave one for me, that's enough,' Phayorm yelled back at her young brother. 'Mother, will you eat? The barbecued fish is nice and hot and the rice has just been steamed. Go on, eat a bit,' she coaxed.

'Eh! Bring some and let's have a try. I feel like eating a bit today.' The sick woman pushed herself up into a sitting position. Her face had more colour in it now.

'If you eat properly, you'll be better in no time. When term's over I'll get some medicine for you in town to improve your appetite.' Piya tried to raise her spirits, knowing that most of all she lacked proper food.

'There are three of us, mother and children,' Mae Kham spoke softly. 'Formerly we had land and didn't need to buy rice or go looking for food. Then we had to pawn our fields to Lung 'Carn Kern. There was no money to redeem them and we lost them. Now I've got to send Phayorm to work on other people's fields and at the harvest and she gets some rice for us to eat. Before all this, when I could get about, I would collect frogs and catch fish and there was enough to feed the children. Now it's all just aches and pains and trouble - as you see. You shouldn't be impatient with the poor and the unfortunate. I'd like to ask you to take on Siang as a special pupil, instruct him and help him on a bit.'

'I, too, am poor,' said Piya, turning to the curer. 'We've got to live together and help each other, don't you agree, Phor jai?'

'*Err*!' he said, assenting. 'Where there's poverty and trouble we've got to share and help each other according to our ability.' He packed his medicines away. 'They tell me, Schoolmaster, you're a real energetic one. Take all the little kids working. Some of the parents are complaining you make their children dig ditches and clear grass. I've told them everything's fine, but some people don't understand.

They may misunderstand you. You should find some way of convincing them,' the old quack warned Piya with good intent.

Before he left the house he told the sick woman, 'Finish up these two medicines and you should be OK. You should be well in two or three days.'

Piya put Siang on the pillion of his bike, Ai Krong, and made his way back to his house. As he passed the headmaster's house he saw Duangdaw seated on the verandah reading a book. He pedalled past, not wanting to be seen by Duangdaw or the headmaster, but Duangdaw was quick-eyed enough to know that it was Piya who had hurriedly cycled past.

Back at his hut Piya lit the fire to steam rice for their meal. Siang placed his bundle of fishing rods in front of the hut and began digging near Piya's vegetable garden. As he turned over the lumps of soil, wriggling earthworms of all sizes came to view. He picked out some medium-sized creatures and put them in an old powdered milk can. When he had enough he took them out again and chopped them with his hoe into sections each about two centimetres in length. He took his bundle of fishing lines, each line attached to a bamboo pole, and baited each hook with a section of earthworm. The hooks looked like the Thai letter *vor vaen* . When he had baited all forty lines, he draped the rods on his arm and walked towards the swamp. The water had risen, almost reaching the boundary of the school grounds.

Siang chose a location which he thought suitable, where the fish would come looking for food. He released the line and firmly dug the base of the rod, which had been sharpened to a point, into the ground. He let the line sink into the water so that the piece of earthworm hung about 5 centimetres from the bottom of the swamp. He set his lines about 3 metres from each other. All forty were set up within a distance of about 150 metres. Nearby there were others similarly engaged in setting their lines and on other sides of the swamp were other groups of men with their lines.

Siang hurried back to Piya, washed his face and hands and got himself ready to eat.

'How did it go, Siang? Where did you set your lines?'

'Just behind the school. When we've eaten, let's go and have a look,' Siang invited, meaning 'let's see if we've got any fish or not'. If they had caught any, they'd collect the fish and replace the bait with a new piece of earthworm. Sometimes the bait was lost - and there was no fish. These too had to be replaced. Sometimes the fish would wiggle off the hook. Sometimes the line would break. In that case another line had to be found to replace it. The lines were usually inspected every two hours. If the fish were biting well, the fisherman might inspect them every hour. Sometimes he would have go back and forth, not getting out of the water at all. What was certain was that at daybreak the lines would have to be collected.

'Have you washed your hands yet? Come, help me bring out the tray,' Piya called to Siang, referring to the tray on which the curries and the accompaniments for the rice were arranged.

Siang picked up the basket with the steamed glutinous rice, and the dish of soup. The soup was catfish cooked with tender tamarind shoots. Piya carried out a plate with the *mok pla siew* Siang had brought with him and a little container with *nam phrik,* the spiced relishes which must accompany every meal. The two of them sat down to their meal, their appetites sharpened by the delicious smell of the *mok pla siew*. The fish lay neatly on their bed of sweet basil and chopped onions. An aroma specially designed to get the gastric juices working arose with the steam from the catfish soup. The medium-sized catfish, caught in the rice fields, were cooked with lemon grass and young tamarind shoots. When Siang had eaten his fill he quickly jumped up, washed his hands and poured himself some water. He then drew another bowl of water from the large jar and placed it beside Piya. He then gathered up his dishes and took them into the kitchen. When Piya had finished, Siang took what was left into the kitchen and washed up the dishes, for once leaving Piya without any chores to perform.

He sat a minute and said, 'Sir, let's go and check our lines.'

'What's the great hurry?' Piya knew well the excitement of boys who had set out lines in this fashion. He himself had once been one of them. As they say, 'He who sets a trap is impatient to collect his game.' Fishing lines were the same; one wanted to examine them as soon as possible.

'Oh, let's go! I'll come with you.' Piya led the way, wearing a pair of shorts and a windcheater. Caw Siang followed, wearing only a pair of shorts with an elastic waistband. The small boy hurried along, carrying the container to put the fish in. Nevertheless, he could hardly keep pace with the schoolmaster. He yelled delightedly when he reached the first line.

'It's caught, it's caught. It must be a catfish, pulling gently like that.' He rushed down and quickly pulled the rod out of the ground. He hoisted up a catfish about a span in length and put it in his container. He felt around with his hand and gently and expertly released the hook. He took out a piece of earthworm and rebaited the hook, then put the rod back in the ground in its original position.

The sun was about to disappear behind the line of trees in the distance in front of them. Black clouds moved slowly in from the south. There were flashes of lightning in the distance, but no sound of thunder reached their ears. They heard instead the sounds of the kora or water-cock *'Tum, Tum, Tum'*. The *kaput* birds hooted *'Poot, Poot, Poot'*, from the forest to the south of the school grounds. They heard the sounds of people playing in the water, carefree, the loud sounds of 'striking the water drum', that is, splashing water making a sound like the beating of a drum.

Piya followed his pupil, helping when needed, gathering in the fish and rebaiting the hooks. *'Oh, ho*! This fellow has pulled the line and wrapped it round a clump of grass. It's probably got away.' Caw Siang gazed at the rod which now stood aslant, and as he spoke he bent down and gently pulled out the grass and gingerly pulled up the rod. A *chorn* (loach) about the size of a man's forearm wriggled energetically, but the line wasn't broken. Siang gently pulled in the fish along the surface of the water. As it reached the bank he grabbed it and put it in his basket. At the end of their first round they had twelve large catfish, three *chorn* and another five *mor* (climbing fish). It was not a bad catch - twenty fish from forty lines.

'It would be nice if we got at least one *pla khaw*. I could grill it for my mother early tomorrow morning.' *Pla khaw* was a variety of carp with white scales. It was believed it was very good for the sick, probably 'the white fish from the rice fields'.

'We are sure to have one by tomorrow,' Piya affirmed his hope. 'We'll come again and have a look some time after seven.'

When they got back to Piya's house, Caw Siang poured the fish out of the creel and put them in a cane bucket with a little water. He covered it with a lid, on which he placed a heavy piece of wood. Piya changed his clothes as soon as he got home. He had slipped and fallen on the way back. He now put on a pair of jeans and a shirt open down the front. He got out another windcheater and had Siang put it on. The evening was turning cooler.

'Come on, put this on. It's baggy, but never mind. It's better than nothing.' Siang took it and pulled it over his head. He grinned broadly.

The call of a *nguang* insect - a creature like, but somewhat larger than, a cricket - trilled out of the forest south of the school. Piya didn't know what these were called in the Central language. Its call was pleasing to hear. It is difficult to represent the sound in the letters of the alphabet. It was, perhaps, like a cross between the lash of a whip and the chiming of a bell. Its call was rare outside the rainy season, and then too it was heard only at twilight, with the setting of the sun.

The light of 'Carn Khen's home came flickering through the gloom, together with the quavering sound of the *khaen* borne on the wind. Lights also appeared where villagers were fishing on the banks of the swamp and in the paddy fields. In the countryside the business of making a living went on day and night. There was no time for rest, no vacation.

Piya picked up the *phin,* the stringed instrument he had got from 'Carn Khen, and sat on the bench on the verandah of the house. He gently plucked the strings, trying out the sound. He played a catchy, lively tune. Siang sat and listened, open-mouthed, quite oblivious of himself. Siang could play the *phin* like the other boys of the village. The tune Piya played was from the touring players, the *mor lam*, to which they sang the words:

'They are open-eyed in the morning, they are open-eyed at dinner time. In the dark of night they are open-eyed.' Which was nothing more than a piece of comic nonsense.

Piya played some three tunes and asked who was the best *phin* player in the village. Siang answered, 'Carn Khen, the mad one. But teacher plays very well, too.'

That night, at about half-past seven, the two of them did another round of the fish lines. It was after eight o'clock when they got back. They had to use a light on this trip. Siang had prepared the lamp and brought it with him. It was made from an old milk can with a guard to protect the flame from the wind as well as direct the light forward, and a hand grip.

The fish were biting well and on this second trip they got thirty fish, almost all catfish.

The next morning Siang got up at five. He hurried down to check his lines by himself, dawn having already broken. He collected another twenty fish. They included five *pla khaw*, the kind he wanted to grill for his mother. Piya kept about ten fish for himself and told Siang to take the rest for his mother and sister, telling him to grill for his mother as many as she would eat. She needed to gain more strength to get better quickly. Apart from 'Carn Khen, Piya had developed the closest relationship with this family.

CHAPTER 12

The headmaster announced that school would close on Friday and reopen on the Monday, as had been expected. Duangdaw set off for Ubon as quickly as possible, going in Sia Mangkorn's landrover, together with Lung 'Carn Kern. Piya decided he would go to Bangkok, but he first had to visit his relatives in Amnart Caroen.

Piya went into the village to ask Phayorm and Siang to keep an eye on his hut while he was away, also taking the opportunity to see how Mae Kham was. She seemed better; she could sit up now for quite long periods, and her appetite had improved. He went on to the headmaster's house. He told him he was going home and then going on to Bangkok. He would not be away long, he hoped to be back in ten days. The headmaster offered to keep an eye on Piya's hut.

Early Sunday morning, Piya boarded Caw Kart's 'two-row' bus to the district town. Then he caught the bus for Ubon, changing there to continue his journey to Amnart Caroen. From the district centre it was another fifteen kilometres to his village. It was about evening when he arrived.

His family was happy to hear that he had returned to teach in his home province. Some wanted him to apply for a transfer to his home village. Others wanted to know when he was going to take a wife and start a family - in other words, 'when was he going to get married?' To which Piya answered that it would be a long while yet. Many wanted to drink with him, seeing he was now earning a salary. The villagers held that one who was earning should treat those who were not.

'Bak La,[1] you're earning many thousands now, eh?' an old lady said to him in broad dialect, rubbing his back and shoulders.

'It's not much that I get, Big Mother,' he answered evasively.

'How much is it a month?' she persisted, wanting to know.

'It's about a thousand a month,' he answered truthfully.

'Goodness, how can you spend all that?' she exclaimed in good faith. A thousand, even a hundred, was a great deal of money for the villagers of the outback. 'Give us five or ten baht for some betel and areca nut.'

Piya pulled out ten baht and the old grandmother wandered off as happy as if she had just been given ten thousand or a hundred thousand. After three days in the village he returned to Ubon and took the fast train for Bangkok, staying at the monastery where he had lived for ten years.

At the restaurant of the Pathumrat Hotel in Ubon, Sia Mangkorn, Lung 'Carn Kern and the Section Head of the Education Department sat at the table in the southeast corner. With them sat two employees of the Sia, two drivers. Their faces suggested they were professional boxers or strong-arm men.

---

1 'Little last born'

'We'll go and have a look at the site for the schoolhouse on the eighth,' the Section Head said. 'It's a pity the school's closed at the moment. There may not be any teachers to receive us. There'll probably be only the headmaster.'

'Oh, Khru Khammaw doesn't go anywhere. Day after day all he does is play *boke'*, Lung 'Carn Kern proclaimed loudly, startling the young girl who was waiting to take their order. Sia Mangkorn ordered a *baen* (a flat half-bottle of liquor), and *yam vun sen* (a spicy salad with noodles). 'Will you have liquor or beer?' He turned, addressing the Section Head - the question asked in jest, for he had decided he was going to treat them to the local whisky.

'May I have some beer?' The Section Head, who had just been promoted from the status of village schoolteacher, thought that people like Sia Mangkorn were really generous, treated one to anything one fancied.

When the drinks and food had been served, Sia Mangkorn turned to business.

'Who's on the supervisory committee?'

'I can't remember who else is on the committee. The province, the district and the school are all represented.' The Section Head added, with certainty, 'I'm on it from the *amphur*, and the headmaster will be on it from the school. There's no problem about either of us; Headmaster Khammaw is very easy to talk to. That's fine. My only worry is that teacher who was just appointed. There may be some awkwardness there. I've heard he's got new-fangled ideas.'

'So don't appoint him to the committee,' Sia Mangkorn exclaimed.

'There's not much chance of his being on the committee, he's too junior for that. What I am frightened about is that he will criticize and interfere with our work,' the Section Head said.

'Let's leave that for later.' The Sia pulled out a cigarette and one of his underlings hurriedly struck a match for him.

'I have now decided that Lung 'Carn Kern will get the subcontract. As for the timber, I'll look after that. When I've seen the lay-out, there'll be no problem - unless somebody goes to the suppression squad in Bangkok.'

'You mean you'll have the contract, but Lung 'Carn Kern will do the actual work?' The Section Head already knew the answer to that.

'That's right. I've taken the contract for this little job because I've got other business in that area.' They'd known each other a long time and Sia Mangkorn spoke openly. 'What I wanted to say today is that whatever Lung 'Carn Kern does it is just as if I do it.'

'Oh, you don't need to be worried about that. We've been associated for many years. I understand.' The Section Head, formerly a village schoolmaster, had known the Sia a long time. They had stripped the timber from many forests and the Sia had grown enormously wealthy; he was now worth more than a hundred million baht. When they had assured each other of their mutual understanding, they chatted desultorily in their boastful manner.

'Everything that goes on in the *amphur* is my business, whatever school it's at.'

Acarn Ekachai had hurried to Ubon when he heard that Duangdaw was on vacation and had returned home. His school had not closed yet as it was in a local government area and such schools followed the schedule of the schools in the provincial city. Acarn Ekachai did not know when she had gone to Ubon. He usually did, but this time Sia Mangkorn's landrover had not stopped over at the *amphur*. He had met her at their briefing at the district headquarters and had twice travelled on the bus with her into Ubon, and they had been together to the pictures once. The young man had the pretty teacher continually in his thoughts, and in his dreams.

The timbered two-storey house was in a mixture of styles. It was roofed in red tile and the walls were painted light green. It stood on Upalisarn Road, within the Municipality of Ubon. In the same compound were four 'bungalow' type houses set high off the ground and all of similar size. The fence in front of the house was composed of posts set close against each other, about head-high. The large gate was of wrought iron. On one gatepost was attached a blue plastic nameboard on which were set out in white the number of the house and the name of the owner: Koson Kaewsai.

Everyone knew this as the house of Palat Koson. The Deputy *(palat)* District Officer had been posted in many districts and had finally settled down here in the district of the provincial capital. At first he had been an ordinary deputy working his way up from among the clerks and showing proper respect for authority. When the *farang* had come and established a camp at the airfield, the *palat* had built his four 'bungalows' to rent to them. He pulled in a rent of ten thousand baht a month. He also seized the opportunity to trade in goods from the PX. This brought in another ten thousand a month. Still not satisfied, he joined up with a bunch of cronies and opened a bar to make more money from the foreigner. Profits flowed in. Palat Koson's financial standing soon far exceeded that of any other deputy - or any other government official of similar rank.

Acarn Ekachai parked his motorcycle by the gate in front of the house. He opened the iron gate and walked in with assurance, as he had already been here once before.

'Ui tai!' What are you doing here, Acarn? Please come up,' Duangdaw called loudly, putting on a pleased expression when she saw who it was walking up to the house.

'I heard from Headmaster Khammaw that you've been home since last Friday,' said the young man, who was everywhere known as Acarn. It was the custom of provincial teachers to so honour any of their number who held a degree.

'Where did you meet the headmaster, Acarn?'

'At the *amphur,* just this morning. Your headmaster turned up with Khru Piya.' The expression on the young man's face changed when he mentioned Piya's name. 'Isn't there anyone at home?'

'Mother's gone shopping and Father's gone to Barn Ha Rua instead of the District Officer. They are electing a headman,' the young girl explained. 'But how did you get here so quickly?'

'Oh, as soon as I heard you were home, I jumped on my motorbike and came immediately. These days the Highway Department has the road in good condition. It took just over two hours,' Ekachai answered proudly.

'Have you bought that bike?' Duangdaw seemed particularly interested in the motorcycle. Teachers and government servants competed with each other buying vehicles on hire purchse.

'I just got it two weeks ago. I'm still running it in, but I let it out at top speed today.' They sat and talked a while in the sitting room, sipping iced water. Ekachai got to the important point of his visit.

'It's about noon now, Khun Duangdaw. I'd like to take you out to lunch today.'

'Where to?'

'Anywhere's fine. It's up to you.'

The young woman quickly changed her shorts for a pair of flared jeans and a tight-fitting red shirt. She whitened her cheeks with powder and tied back her raven black hair in a pony tail, making her face look even more appealing. She instructed the servants and her younger brothers and sisters to look after the house and seated herself on the pillion of the new motorcycle on which the young man had just made his first payment.

'Where shall we go?' asked the teacher, in whose heart the flowers were beginning to bloom.

'I like the atmosphere of the Coconut Grove. Let's go there.'

The young woman was used to having her own way since childhood. Since she started Teachers' College she'd had many boy friends and one in particular had declared his love for her and tried to win her heart in return. She had been cool to him, however, until she came home the first time after she began teaching. She had met the young man, but he had been with a new girl. She had immediately decided that she must take up with some young man, anyone at all presentable would do, so the young man would see her with him. It was the same the previous time she had gone to the pictures with Ekachai. She'd hoped to be seen by the other young man. While Ekachai's thoughts about her were quite sincere, Duangdaw was thinking along quite different lines.

'When are you going to get yourself transferred to the city, Khun Duangdaw?' he asked, having ordered beer and fried fish.

'Father said he didn't want to bother the high-ups yet. It was good enough that I could move from the school on the border and come and stay with my uncle.' She raised her glass and sipped at her beer. 'Whatever happens, I am not going to stay for ever in Barn Norng Ma Vor.'

Piya returned from Bangkok with a guitar. He had wanted to bring back his old instrument, the one on which he had learned to play, but Caw Suk, his cousin, who had taken his place looking after Luang Lung, begged him for it and persuaded him to buy a new one. Suk had been very possessive of the old instrument and Piya had given in to his pleading, raiding his savings box for the price of a new one, a better instrument, but also more expensive.

He had not been away from the village ten days, and not a great deal had changed when he returned. It rained every day and Caw Siang set his fish lines and spent the night at Piya's hut each night. The young lad caught many fish daily, keeping Piya plentifully supplied. Phayorm and Mae Kham were also well catered for. When there were more fish than they needed, Phayorm chose some of the best catfish, still alive, and sold them in the village. Some days she sold a couple of kilos and made many baht. Mae Kham was happy and her condition improved so much she could get up and walk around.

Piya was also conscientious about visiting 'Carn Khen. He learned the older man was a great fisherman. Whereas most people fished in the evenings and at night, 'Carn Khen's method was to fish during the day. He possessed over a hundred lines and it meant that when he set his lines he expected to land at least fifty fish.

Piya was going to try to learn the art of fishing from 'Carn Khen, and went out and bought himself a packet of No. 12 hooks. Siang helped him cut bamboo poles for rods, trim them and attach the lines. They made about fifty lines and Piya tried them out, setting them up during the daylight in the manner 'Carn Khen taught him. He found he could catch at least two or three kilos a day. The teacher and his pupil got much pleasure out of their fishing.

'You've got to know the habits of the fish,' 'Carn Khen told the young teacher. 'Each species feeds differently. Usually catfish feed in deep water, serpenthead *(pla chorn)* in shallow water by the bank, but they all like to feed where there is natural food for them. It's not as if you'll find fish wherever there is water. When a fish is feeding it will swim near the bottom, so that you should place the bait either on or just above the bottom; lower the line till the bait's right down. You should also choose your bait according to the kind of fish you're looking for. If it's earthworms, choose small ones and use the whole creature - don't be stingy about it, we don't buy the bait. The wiggling will bring the fish to it quickly. When you've caught a fish, move your line to another spot, never stick the rod back in the same place.'

When he had finished explaining about fishing in shallow water, he spoke of other methods. 'But if you are fishing in deep water, fishing for catfish, you need other methods. If you want the various kinds of catfish, you must use the appropriate bait. If you fish for serpenthead during the winter, you need still other bait, and if you want *pla tuphian* (carp) during harvest time, you need a different method again. If you're interested, I'll teach you the lot in time.'

It was not only fishing with hook and line that Piya learned. During the vacation he learned from the villagers other ways of fishing, catching frogs and many methods of food gathering; for example, catching frogs, fish and birds at night with the use of a light, using traps of various kinds, *ngaep, lorp, sai, morng*.

The *li* was a large contraption for catching fish and called for the investment of much capital and labour. First a large weir is built across flowing water. When completed an aperture is made through which the water can flow. On either side of this opening, downstream, a frame of two rows of wooden stakes is constructed, to which are attached walls of closely woven bamboo strips. The walls narrow the gap between them as they move away from the weir, gradually at first, but then more sharply, till they meet, leaving open a narrow hole called the 'mouth' of the trap. To this is attached a large creel, about the size of a man, into which flow fish and other water creatures, washed down by the stream or floodwaters. There isn't a great deal to catching fish with a *li*. Once it has been well constructed all you have got to do is to go to sleep and wait for the sound of rain. Whenever it rains heavily and the water flows swiftly against the weir, it can be used. The water can only flow through the one hole in the weir, and crabs, fish and prawns are swept into the creel which lies at the end of the trap. In about two hours you can lift out the enormous creel and pour out the fish that are trapped there. Each time there should be at least a 'load' or two. A 'load' is the equivalent of a *khru*', a woven bamboo water bucket. It is one of the easiest ways of catching fish.

During the ploughing and planting, Barn Norng Ma Vor was as peaceful and silent as a deserted village. Every day most villagers set off before dawn for work in the fields, and it was dark before they returned. Some villagers moved their families to a field hut and spent the entire period there, returning only when the planting was over. Only the old and the very young of some families were left to watch the village.

Piya pedalled into the village, hoping to meet and talk to the villagers. He was disappointed, however. He met no one and most houses had their doors closed. There were few windows, and these were normally not opened. The steps which led up to the houses were mostly of the kind which leaned against the open verandah, and could be moved away from the house. A rope or chain was tied to the top step of the stairs and they were pulled away from the house, the base remaining in its original position. This is known as *ngerk khandai,* 'pushing away the steps', and is done to keep dogs and chickens from getting into the house.

He dropped in to see Mae Kham and to find out how she was getting on. He found the sick woman alone. Her pretty daughter, Phayorm, had gone off to work in the fields of Headman Lua, and Caw Siang had gone for water.

'How are you, Mother, are you getting better?' he greeted her as he sat down beside the sick woman. He handed her a paper bag with a bottle of medicine and a box of pills. 'I bought some medicine to improve your appetite, as I promised.'

Mae Kham raised her hands to her head in a *wai* and thanked him profusely before accepting the bag. Piya said, 'The mixture should be taken before meals, a spoonful at a time. Ai Siang can read the label and give you the details. The pills are to be taken after meals, one at a time.' Piya had bought a vitamin preparation and a tonic recommended to be taken during convalescence. He chatted a little while till Siang returned carrying water. Piya said his goodbyes and left.

'Are you going to set lines with me this evening?' Piya asked, while Siang was pouring the water into the jar.

'Yes, I'm going to play the *syng* with teacher,' Caw Siang smiled showing his white teeth. At daybreak, Piya walked down to the fields beside the school. The villagers, both men and women, were bent over transplanting the rice. They were all dressed in black shirts. The shirts were dyed with indigo which they themselves grew and used. The women had *pha khaw ma* wrapped around their heads and cheeks, barely showing their faces. The children were left to catch frogs in their own fashion and according to their ability. When the ploughing was over, the children took the buffaloes and tethered them on the higher land. They had finished their work in the fields and were left to graze and eat their fill. While the buffaloes were grazing, the children hunted insects in the *sark* trees.[2] Sometimes, unknown to their keepers, they'd get loose from their tethering, the rope would work itself loose or break, and

2 *Sark* - SERIANTHES GRANDIFLORA.

they would eat the new shoots of rice - sometimes devastating half a *ngarn* before anyone knew.[3]

The young man shouted a greeting to a farmer who was up to his shins in the mud, ploughing a flooded section of his field. In another part of the field women were transplanting.

'Good day, Headman, have you almost finished the transplanting?'

'Oh, it's you Schoolmaster! I wondered who it was.' Headman Lua raised the handle of the plough and took hold of the rope flanking the buffalo, to force it into a turning circle.

'It'll be many days before it's all done. It's been so hot the shoots turned yellow and died. Then it rained so hard the fields flooded and we had to wait till the water subsided.'

'Won't you come and help transplant?' the headman's wife said, standing with legs apart. She twisted her body from the bent posture of transplanting, turning towards the young girl who was working next to her. 'Phayorm, go ahead and show the schoolmaster how to transplant.'

Phayorm raised her head and grinned.

'Would you like to try, Khun Khru? Perhaps you'd better not, you'll get covered in mud.'

Piya took off his slippers, placed them on the bank and stepped into the field which was ploughed and ready for transplanting. He reached for a sheaf of seedlings from among the pile which was stacked on the curve of the bank, watched attentively by Phayorm, the headman, his wife,

---

[3] A *ngarn* is about 0.04 hectare.

and the three others who were transplanting. They all wanted to see if the teacher knew how to transplant.

'I did this when I was a kid. I think I can still manage,' he said, carrying his bundle of seedlings in his left hand and joining the team. He took two seedlings in his right hand, bent over and with the top of his thumb pushed them into the soft earth. He kept a similar distance between the seedlings and between rows, following Phayorm - about thirty centimetres between each.

'You do know how to transplant, too, Khun Khru,' Phayorm said, looking up and watching him for a moment. She bent down and continued pushing in the young seedlings. Piya finished his bundle and stopped; the bending was beginning to hurt his back and his waist. Before he could move off and visit the neighbouring farm, Headman Lua invited Piya to stay and have lunch with them.

'Don't hurry off, Schoolmaster, stay and eat the midday meal with us. Mother of Bak Khiaw,' he said, turning to his wife, 'what's for lunch today?'

'Larp thaw and *langoke* mushroom curry.' She pushed in the last seedlings, straightened up and stood on the bank. She turned towards the young teacher.

'Stay and eat with us. The *larp thaw* is delicious.' When they had finished working on that section of field it was time to break for lunch. All of them who had been 'backs to the sky, faces to the mud', were glad to stop. They washed their faces and hands and walked to the *thiang na,* the field hut, where the rice was stored, as were their implements and their food.

They had two dishes that lunch time. The first was a curry of *langoke* mushrooms. It was more of a soup than a curry, for there weren't many condiments in it. The only spices in it were chillies, onions and lemon grass pounded together. The cleaned mushrooms are put into boiling water and the spices added. *Pla ra* (pickled fish) and vegetable *(phak orbaeb)* are also added. The latter is a kind of vine with a sour flavour. What must not be neglected is the sweet basil, which is put in when the pot is taken off the fire. The *langoke* mushroom is like the straw mushroom, though bigger and of a prettier colour - white, yellow and orange. Before it opens it looks like an egg and is the size of a hen's egg. When these are cooked in the fashion described they are delicious.

The other dish was *larp thaw*. This dish is different from the various kinds of *larp* made with meat. *Thaw* is a kind of euphorbia growing near water. It consists of long strands of attractive green about the thickness of hair. It is believed to be rich in protein, but the villagers know nothing of these virtues. They have eaten it since the time of their forefathers, and they continue to do so. The preparation is very simple. The weed is washed clean. The villagers' idea of 'clean', however, is that no visible foreign matter such as mud adheres to it. There may be dangerous bacteria, but these are invisible, and to the villagers the weed is clean and may be eaten. It is then cut into pieces small enough to be picked up and eaten with a spoon. A hot, spicy fish relish known as *pon pla* is made and mixed into the greens, with chilli and onions to taste. The indispensable accompaniment is bitter gourd - the two together are much appreciated.

They sat in a circle on the split bamboo floor of the hut. Piya was so hungry he thought the food was particularly delicious, and, by the way they ate, so did all the others. Phayorm was the first to finish, which the headman's wife was quick to observe.

'Phayorm's heart is full with the one who came to help today. What do you say, Schoolmaster?'

'My heart's full too, that I could come and help with the transplanting and then come and eat with all of you,' Piya answered lightheartedly, as Phayorm looked slightly red about the face.

That evening the young teacher sat down and considered his garden of chilli and *makhya* plants, and bushes of ginger and lemon grass. They were all sprouting green shoots and leaves. When he'd had his evening meal he brought out his guitar and played a modern song to himself. He played some four or five tunes then brought out the *phin* and played a local tune. Siang did not come that day to set his lines. Piya did not know whether he had been kept with chores at home, or whether he was getting tired of the fishing.

It began to look like rain again, and soon it was falling heavily characteristic of a depression in the China Sea, there was no sign of its abating. That night he lay and listened to the sound of the rain till he fell asleep.

CHAPTER 13

Though Mae Kham's condition seemed to improve, her disease was by no means cured. So, one day, at a time when everyone was engrossed with their work in the fields or in the swiddens,[1] Caw Siang came panting to Piya's hut. It was five days before the second half of term was to begin.

'Sir, please come and look at Mother, she's in great pain.'

'What's wrong? What's wrong with her?' the young teacher asked anxiously.

'She's in pain and she told me to come and call you.' Siang looked very frightened.

Piya quickly put on a windcheater, grabbed his bike, Ai Krong, and pedalled furiously through the drizzle with Siang on the pillion. When they got to the house they found Mae Kham lying down groaning and moaning in pain. An old woman sat beside her, tending her.

'*Ooi*! It hurts. It hurts terribly! Siang, come here to Mother.' She moaned softly when she heard Siang climb up to the house. 'Has the schoolmaster come? *Ooi,* it hurts.'

Piya sat down by the sick woman. 'Where does it hurt? Try to bear up a little. I'll go and get the doctor at once.'

---

1 Rice agriculturalists distinguish between irrigated rice fields and cultivation areas which are cleared of forest and burned, and depend on rainfall for water. Cultivation of the latter type is known technically as 'swidden agriculture'.

'Bak Siang, go call Phor Thaw cam, quick!' the old woman told Caw Siang. 'Go first to his house; if he's not there he'll be in his field. Hurry there and back. Have courage, Kham, it'll be all right.'

She bent over and began kneading and massaging the upper portion of the sick woman's legs.

'Ooi! It hurts there. Gently, gently, Mae Sai.' Mae Kham closed her eyes, and her face twisted with the pain.

'How long have you had the pain like this?' Piya asked, while he looked around hurriedly. The bottle of medicine he had bought her was half empty. He turned to Siang, 'OK, go and get the old man, Siang.' He thought to himself, in a situation like this any doctor at all would be excellent.

Caw Siang rushed out of the house and into the falling rain, without umbrella or anything else to protect himself. Piya tried to diagnose the patient's condition with all the knowledge available to a holder of a teacher's diploma. He had thought at first she suffered from malnutrition - a not uncommon disability among the inhabitants of this village. He still held to this belief. But he had no idea what was causing the pain in the woman's legs. His thoughts turned to doctors, and to those available nearby. The most obvious was none other than the *mor thyan,* the 'quack' Mor Sombat, the dependable standby of the villagers of Tambon Phak I Hin.

There was hardly time for a chew of betel before the dripping form of Siang reappeared climbing up to the house. With him appeared an old man carrying a tattered paper umbrella. It was the *mor cam* the 'universal curer' of the village.

Mae Sai turned to the old man and said, 'Come on, hurry up a bit, she is in great pain.'

He folded his umbrella and put it down on the floor. He sat down by Mae Kham and placed his package of medicinal roots beside him.

'Where's it hurting now?' Mae Kham, groaning slightly, indicated the area above her knee. Piya, Caw Siang and Mae Sai sat silently, waiting to see how he would deal with the pain.

'Fill this bowl with water,' he said to Siang, handing him the brass bowl into which he'd put his medicinal roots the last time.

When the bowl came back he held it in both hands in front of him at chest level, sitting in the respectful position, legs folded under him, both feet on one side. His mouth moved silently in a *gatha* for about the space of two minutes. In the silence it seemed like two hours. He then blew on the bowl of water three times in a right handed circle. That done, he raised the bowl above his head three times. The water was now magically potent. He took some in his mouth and blew it out onto the sick woman's legs, above the knees where she had indicated the pain. This too he did three times with a clockwise motion.

'That will cure it. There won't be any pain any more.' He pulled out some betel leaf and nut, prepared it and commenced chewing.

Piya watched the performance in silence, but he was irritated. He wanted to do something, but did not know what; had he known, he would hardly have dared.

Whether it was by faith or a miracle, the woman's condition improved rapidly and the pain was soon gone.

Piya waited a while after the *thaw cam* had gone, then went home himself.

That evening Piya went down into the village and dropped in at the headmaster's house. He asked if there were any instructions from the department and then asked after Duangdaw. He wanted to know when she was expected back. The headmaster could not give him a definite answer. His trusty bike, Ai Krong, took him from there to Mae Kham's. It was just getting dark.

Phayorm and Caw Siang were having their evening meal. She called to him to come up and eat with them. 'Come in, Khun Khru, come and have some food with us.'

'How's your mother?' Piya asked, sounding genuinely concerned.

'Siang says she complained of pain again, late this afternoon,' Phayorm answered, while she checked hurriedly to see if she looked presentable. She had just bathed and changed out of her working clothes into a striped *pha thung* and a short-sleeved pink blouse.

'With what are you eating rice?' Piya asked, using the greeting universally popular in Isarn.

'We are having a bamboo shoot curry with rice.' She smiled shyly. 'Siang hasn't been to set his lines and we've got no fish.' Curried bamboo shoots were a principal dish of the villagers of Barn Norng Ma Vor, particularly when they lacked meat or fish. It was truly a dish of an ascetic for there was no flesh of any living creature in it. The shoots are sliced into thin long strips and boiled in water. When soft, the water is poured out as it becomes very bitter. Various spices are added. These are *pla ra,* pounded chilli, lemon grass and onions. The gravy of the curry is special - made with the herb *ya narng* (lady grass). This is a creeper with a dark green leaf like long feathers of a bird - about ten centimetres in length. A handful is squeezed till a green fluid is obtained, green and thick. This is strained with a piece of cloth or a strainer and the green liquid forms the gravy of the curry. Absolutely necessary to the bamboo shoot curry is *khaw bya*. This is made of glutinous rice, soaked in water till soft and then finely powdered. Some people use sliced raw corn instead. Various greens may be added, such as green shoots of bamboo, pumpkin shoots and flowers, *cha-om* which the villagers call *kha*, mushrooms, grasshoppers, or tree ants' eggs.[2] When you consider the nutrition available from bamboo shoot curry, it is probably the same as eating plain vegetables without meat - likely to cause malnutrition if it happens to be the sole diet.

Piya, who had eaten already, declined. He sat and chatted with Siang and Phayorm while they ate. It looked like rain again and he prepared to leave but just then the sick woman cried out again in pain. This time the pain seemed to strike on the cap of her right knee. Her loud cries brought the neighbours running to see what was wrong. There came Headman Lua, Thit Corm and the wife of Siangbaw, carrying a little baby. Siang and Phayorm looked very uneasy and the headman told the girl to get the old medicine man.

When Phayorm had gone, Piya decided he too should do something. He quietly climbed down the steps and left, unobserved by all but Caw Siang. The young man pedalled his bicycle towards the village Khok Klarng from which the road led to the *amphur*. He remembered that that was where

---

[2] *Cha-om* - ACACIA INSUAVIS.

Mor Sombat lived. It was nine kilometres on a dirt road and would take him about an hour. He thought he could get Mor Sombat to the village that night. The old bike, Ai Krong, didn't have a lamp, but Piya had a flashlight.

As he rode along he passed villagers returning from their fields, others going to set fish lines and some to fish with a torch and knife. There were men and women hurrying along, carrying children, leading buffaloes, carrying buckets and baskets. Between Barn Norng Ma Vor and Barn Khok Klarng were fields and forest and halfway was the village of Phak I Hin.

As it grew darker, in the silence the noise of the bicycle chain could be heard clearly as it clacked to the rhythm of the turning wheels. Frogs of different kinds gave out their distinctive cries. The green frogs with long legs that lived in the treetops croaked alternatively long and short. Piya quickened his speed as he heard the wind and rain rippling the trees. When he finally got to Barn Khok Klarng he enquired where Mor Sombat's house was and made straight for it. He had scarcely dismounted when large drops of rain began to fall.

'Is this Mor Sombat's house?' he yelled.

'Yes. What do you want?' an old man answered, and made his way down the steps.

'Is Mor Sombat at home? Can he come and look at a sick woman?' Piya still stood outside the house.

'When? Who is it? What's wrong?' Mor Sombat came out and stood, holding the balustrade.

'The sick woman's at Barn Norng Ma Vor. Please come tonight, doctor!' Piya pleaded.

'Barn Norng Ma Vor, is it?' His voice seemed cheerful. 'But it's raining! Come on up to the house first.'

'I'd better not, doctor, I want to hurry back. Go to the house of Mae Kham. It's near the headman's house. Please go tonight. I'll take care of the fee myself.'

'Aw! It's Khun Piya. I wondered who it was.' The doctor recognized the voice. He said, in a businesslike manner, 'I'll go there straight away. Will you come with me on the motorbike, or do you want to cycle back?'

'I'd like to go with you, but it'll be a nuisance coming back for my bike. You go on the motorbike and I'll pedal back.' The teacher pushed his bike under the eaves to avoid the rain. 'I'll go ahead, then. It's Mae Kham's house, near Headman Lua's. Whatever it is, please go tonight.

'Yes, I'll follow in a moment. Why don't you wait a bit and see if the rain stops?'

Exhorting the doctor yet once more, Piya pushed his bicycle into the rain and set out for home. He hoped the doctor would not fail him. He had heard people talk well of the doctor. He treated patients at a reasonable fee and was ready to visit at any time.

It was after 9:00 P.M. when Piya got back to Barn Norng Ma Vor. When he climbed up to Mae Kham's house he found that Mor Sombat had preceded him by a short while. He thought there would be a crowd at the house, but there was only Phayorm, the headman's wife and the doctor chatting quietly when he arrived. Siang and Mae Kham were asleep.

'I gave her an injection and she's just gone off to sleep.' The young doctor looked proud of himself.

'In that case, Phayorm, I'll get back home.' He was dead tired and he moved slightly, as if to stand up. 'Khun Mor, thanks very much for taking the trouble to come. Can we talk about your fee later? How are you going back? It looks as if it's going to rain again.'

'I'll have to spend the night in Barn Norng Ma Vor.' He grinned at Piya and turned to Phayorm. 'I usually stay with Lung 'Carn Kern.'

'Are you going, then, Khun Khru?' Phayorm said. 'Thank you very much for being so concerned and getting the doctor to see Mother.'

'That's OK. I consider it one of my duties - to be the guardian of my pupils.' He turned to Mor Sombat and the headman's wife. 'Doctor, Madam Headman, I'll take my leave then.'

'I'm going too. Let the doctor keep Phayorm company,' the headman's wife said with a suggestive grin.

When they had gone, Sombat and Phayorm were left to themselves with Mae Kham and Siang sleeping a little way off. Nine o'clock was late for the village. The fishermen and frog catchers were back from the fields and ready to sleep to fortify themselves for another hard day's work beginning at dawn. Rain fell heavily for a little while, then stopped. In the darkness the young girl's pretty face stood out clearly, illuminated by the light of the kerosene oil lamp.

'I haven't had a chance to see you since the wedding breakfast at Lung 'Carn Kern's', said Mor Sombat. 'I have no idea what I have been doing.'

'Thank you very much for coming. If the teacher hadn't gone to get you, I am sure you wouldn't have come.' Phayorm hung her head and stared at the floor. 'I don't know how we are going to pay for the medicine.'

'If I'd known it was your mother, I would have come myself; you needn't have sent anyone to fetch me. About the money, don't worry about that.' Sombat gazed at the young woman. 'I don't have a great deal, but let me help any way I can. If it won't bore you, perhaps I could come and visit every day. Will anybody object?'

'Who is there to say anything, except that the doctor is a great tease?'

'Won't the schoolmaster object, if I come here often?'

'What is there for any teacher to object to?' she said with sincerity.

'The one who went and fetched me.' The young doctor bit his lip, looking tense.

'Oh, Khun Piya!' Phayorm nearly laughed. 'What's he got to say. All he'll say is "Fine". He'll treat mother and she'll get better quickly.'

'What I mean is, is there anything between you, Phayorm? You're a pretty girl. Anyone's likely to be interested and help you.'

'I don't think it has crossed his mind. I respect him like an elder brother. My brother goes and eats at his house and helps him around the school.' Phayorm turned and indicated Caw Siang, who was sleeping soundly.

They chatted a while longer and Sombat bade her goodnight and made his way to Lung 'Carn Kern's house. Before he left he said, 'I'll be here tomorrow, early.'

From then on, Mor Sombat took the opportunity to come and see how Mae Kham was getting on every day. He sat chatting to Phayorm till it got quite late and people began to say he came to see the daughter rather than the mother. Phayorm was happy that her mother was getting better and enjoyed seeing the young doctor. For his part, the doctor thought his life would be complete if he could spend it with Phayorm. He'd met many young women in his time, good ones, as well as others people said were bad, but there was something about Phayorm that occupied his thoughts.

CHAPTER 14

The school reopened for the second half of term after a month's break, during which the children had helped their parents transplant and some teachers had done rice cultivation of their own, while others had gone home to visit their families. Duangdaw returned to the village with a motorcycle - a machine with a low frame, but big wheels, a type much fancied by teenagers, particularly young girls. However, she did not ride it into the village herself. Acarn Ekachai had volunteered to bring it for her. He followed her around ceaselessly, quite unaware that he had begun to get on her nerves.

The first day she rode the little motorcycle to school she was soon surrounded by the kids, who had never seen such a strange machine, nor a motorcycle ridden by a woman. They commented freely and questioned each other in the manner of inquisitive children.

'Uncle,' Duangdaw addressed the headmaster, 'when are we going to get the new schoolhouse? I hope it's built soon. I'd like to decorate my classroom to compete with Khru Piya's.'

'Why do you want to compete with me?' Piya, with raised eyebrows, turned towards the young woman.

'Well, you like decorating your classroom, and even with a dirt floor like this it looks so nice. I think Khru Piya must have studied art.' Duangdaw pointed in the direction of Classes 3 and 4 which Piya and the children had decked out with various local objects which Piya used in his instruction.

'I've learned just as much as everyone else', the young man replied. 'What we've done is not really to beautify the class; actually they are meant to be teaching aids.'

'My goodness', she exclaimed coquettishly, but with a trace of impatience, 'everything's got to be in aid of his teaching. How serious can you get?'

'The Section Head says we're going to get another teacher in place of Khru Satharn who went on transfer.'

The headmaster interrupted the chatter which seemed on the point of getting acrimonious. 'I don't know if it's to be a man or a woman.'

'It'll be nice to have a woman teacher, I'll have a companion.' Duangdaw said.

'It doesn't matter if it's a man or a woman, as long as their intentions are good.' Piya spoke, and then beat on the old hoe to call the children to class for the first session.

The new teacher was appointed at the beginning of October. His appearance and manners were *à la mode*, he could have stepped out of a pop group. Surprisingly, his hair was somewhat shorter than could be expected of a pop musician - but this was because he'd had to take a bit off before his official briefing. His shirt, trousers and shoes were so fashionable the teachers of Barn Norng Ma Vor had never seen the like.

The new teacher was called Phisit and came from another province, another area. He had become a teacher because he could not think of anything better to do. Phisit spent his first night at the headmaster's house, but the headmaster did not have a room to give him, so he took him over to the house of Headman Lua, who had. He also had a bathroom and toilet, just as the Health Inspector had recommended many years ago. The villagers expected teachers or other government officials to live in a style appropriate to their position and salary, in their quarters as well as in their diet. It was not proper to live in a little renovated hut as Piya did.

The first day he went to the school, Phisit complained bitterly about the distance from the village. 'I'll have to get myself a motorcycle to travel the distance every day. Khun Duangdaw, won't you let me sit on your pillion?'

Duangdaw felt that the young man, of about her own age, was a little too forward for a new acquaintance. After all, she had only known him a day. So, she said rather off-handedly, 'What for? I've only seen girls sitting on men's pillions. If you are too lazy to walk, go ask the headmaster for a lift.'

'Goodness, I was only joking!' Phisit, who looked like a good talker, smiled sweetly, indicating he wasn't too upset by her words, being, to put it mildly, thick-skinned. He continued in the same tone. 'Wait a month or two. When I get my salary I'll buy myself a motorcycle and you can come with me on the pillion.'

'I wouldn't sit on your bike if you paid me!' Piya saw things getting out of hand and intervened.

'Khun Duangdaw, the plants from the seeds you brought from Ubon are going to flower nicely. I saw the first flowers just this morning.'

'Where?' Duangdaw turned, eager to change the subject. 'At your house, or in front of the flagpole?'

'At my house. They just opened this morning.' Piya meant in front of his hut. 'The plants by the flagpole should bloom next week. The stalks are all nice and plump. I'm sure we'll get some nice big flowers.'

Next Monday morning as they lined up for the flag ceremony, the flowers were blooming, their colour fresh, and profusely petalled, the leaves green, with plump midribs stretching up in clumps to receive the morning sunlight. The teachers and the children gazed with pride at the results of their labour and tender care.

'Khun Duangdaw is also a great lover of nature,' Piya said, looking in the direction of the other teachers. 'Khun Phisit, let me tell you that this is all the work of Khun Duangdaw,' pointing in the direction of the flower beds surrounding the flagpole.

'Well, you see Khun Piya doing this and that, never stopping for an instant. I had to do something too,' she said, looking embarrassed.

Not long afterwards, Phisit arrived with a motorcycle and from then on he rode off to the *amphur* nearly every Saturday and Sunday. Even though he had only a teaching diploma, and a 'twilight' one at that, Phisit had a large circle of acquaintances. He went out of his way to be on familiar terms with anyone of importance and cultivated those of rank and reputation. It was not surprising that Acarn Ekachai was his constant companion wherever he went.

Phisit's motorcycle came from the same salesroom as that of Acarn Ekachai and, because of their station as teachers, they did not have to make a down-payment. But the repayments were rather high and one way and another they were paying more than ten thousand baht over the cash price; which, however, did not seem to disturb either young man one little bit.

Because he had a motorcycle, Acarn Ekachai was able to ride into Barn Norng Ma Vor every Saturday and

Sunday, seeking out Duangdaw, who now was not going home to Ubon as often as she had during the first term. What Acarn Ekachai was doing was organizing 'meals in the forest', what the *farang* called a 'picnic'. His guests were the headmaster, Piya and Phisit, and of course Duangdaw could not be left out. Often there were also teachers from Phak I Hin and sometimes teachers and officials from the *amphur*. Acarn Ekachai was always the host, providing both food and drink. He only allowed the others to help with the cooking, according to their abilities.

The weather that Saturday was beautiful. The end of October never failed with its excellent weather. Cool winds began to blow from the northeast, but the temperature was still pleasantly warm. The earth began to dry out and the rice to show ears of grain. The *kaen vaen* birds cried *'kaet, kaet'* in the trees from which they swooped on the *cipome,* their prey. The *kaen vaen* is an interesting bird. It seems to appear with the beginning of the cold winds, when its cry is heard. There are two other species of birds which appear as the ears of rice emerge. One is the *chipfyang,* a bird similar to the weaver bird but with a long tail and small beak; it cries *'ciang-ciang, ciang-ciang'* and lives on the *krachorn* beetle. The other is the *taempun* bird, dark of body with a white neck; it likes to feed on the tips of trees or among the rice plants.

That Saturday the picnic party from the *amphur* included the Education Section Head, the District Education Officer, his deputy and Acarn Ekachai, the host. As for the locals, who indirectly were forced into being hosts as well, there were the four teachers of Barn Norng Ma Vor and the teachers of Barn Phak I Hin, Headmaster Cantha, Khru Thongsaen and Khru Visarn. Although Ekachai's motive for the picnic was to impress Duangdaw with the scope of his generosity, the Section Head enjoyed picnics anyway, though he claimed he just wanted to see the site of the new school building. For the District Head it was an end in itself. It was his good fortune. He believed it was much better to be fed and entertained free of charge than to sit bored at home. It was the custom of Headmaster Cantha and his group to follow the Section Head wherever he went and try to attend to his every need. Headmaster Khammaw, however, considered it his duty to entertain superior officers, and even though Ekachai proclaimed himself host, Khammaw, as a local, could not agree to this. He had therefore provided a tender young calf for their enjoyment.

Phisit was content to enjoy himself, eat his fill and join in all the fun. Duangdaw, however, was not only bored with Ekachai, she could not stand sight nor sound of the Section Head. She had spent a long time preparing the food for the occasion and, being tired, had asked three young women from the village to come and help at the picnic itself. They were Sommai, Khamkong and Phayorm.

The one who had to force himself to join the gaiety of that day's picnic was Piya. He knew well that a calf cost about 1000 baht, and divided between the four of them would cost 250 each. There were other expenses besides. Each of the four teachers of Barn Norng Ma Vor would at least be up for 300 baht each. The headmaster had paid for everything, but would collect his money from the others at the end of the month. It could be said they had got off lightly, for Acarn Ekachai, who had set it all up in the first place, was paying for the drinks including the liquor and the soda.

The group had settled down in the shade of a large tree, not far from Piya's hut and the home of 'Carn Khen. A large cane mat had been spread on soft grass. Round about were the yellow flowers of the 'ringworm' grass and the whites of the 'grey-haired' grass covering some of the fields like a carpet.[1] These fields were not black with mud, lying too high to be flooded. Around the swamp the ears of rice were beginning to show - though they were still bright green and the stalks still stood quite straight. In the middle of the water, red and white water lilies stood, their petals still folded, the colour barely distinguishable. A gentle breeze brought the smell of earth and wildflowers. The two education officials, the Section Head and the District Education Officer, had just arrived. They sat, cross-legged, turning towards the waters of the swamp. Phisit, officious as usual, picked up the whisky and served the Section Head the first glass.

'Actually, Khun Duangdaw should be serving you.' Phisit spoke for the sake of speaking, his tongue knowing no restraint. 'But the whisky should taste all right, Section Head, even though it's only me serving.'

'Watch what you say, Khun Phisit,' Duangdaw said, annoyed.

Phisit was not interested. He was getting ready to put a tape in the portable radio/cassette player. He turned on a Thai song in contemporary style, a current hit.

1 'Ringworm grass' - XYRIS INDICA; 'grey-haired grass' - probably a species of CYPERUS.

'It's mine,' he said proudly, in answer to the Section Head's enquiry. 'I just bought it from Chai Sawad's, the same time I bought my motorcycle. It'll be a long time before I'm through paying for it all.'

'That's fine,' the Section Head responded. 'Those who buy things, even spending ten, twenty thousand, they show everybody they've got good credit; they know how to find happiness. '

'What's to eat today, Headmaster?' the District Head asked of Khammaw. 'A little ox,' he replied, lapsing into dialect.

One blow of the hard wooden stake, about the size of a man's leg, pierced the breast of the unfortunate calf and it fell dead. Thit Phun, who was the executioner, picked up a knife and slit the skin of its belly right up to its dewlap. Here was a piece of flesh, or, more correctly, a lump of lard, fat or tallow called 'the tiger weeps'. He cut this out and then sliced it into small pieces. They shared these and chewed and ate the meat, or fat, just as it came. They ate it as tigers would. It was said that any tiger, on killing its prey, first ate this part. If for some reason it did not get it, it was so disappointed it would roar its head off. After that, the leader of the *boke* school, just as expert at slaughtering and butchering cattle as at playing *boke* or cards, using a big knife, opened up the creature's ribs and exposed the internal organs. He cut out the liver, which still appeared to be palpitating, and brought it out on the palm of his hand. He sliced it and distributed it among the gathering. They shoved it in their mouths and chewed it, swallowing with relish. This was slaughtering and eating a calf in the fashion of Barn Norng Ma Vor - in the true and original fashion.

Caw Siang, Caw Khiaw the son of Headman Lua, and a little crowd of children stood round watching the slaughter and the feasting on raw flesh by the adults, with open-eyed interest. Piya saw them and called: 'Khiaw! Siang! Come here and help me gather some firewood.'

As they went towards Piya, Caw Siang looked at Khiaw and said, 'The headmaster told us we shouldn't eat raw meat, but there he is eating raw liver!'

Not much happened at that forest meal, that 'picnic', that day. They ate their fill, then some of them sat down to play cards. The men who were not playing stretched themselves out to sleep. The women and the children gathered up the dishes and set to washing them. Duangdaw and the other three girls picked up the dishes, the pots, the rice, other food left over and walked back to the village. Phisit offered to take Phayorm back, but she refused. Undaunted, he followed her.

'We really live close by, we're neighbours, Phayorm. I was very lucky to be sent to this village.' Phisit attempted to chat her up.

'What's close is our houses. Our hearts are miles apart,' Sommai, the one with the eloquent tongue answered for her friend, whose cheeks showed a faint red. 'I'm afraid it's like the ancients said - "You may live near the forest, but your house may still be dilapidated. You can live by a great river, and lack fermented fish. You can live by the lac beetle, but your dyes may still not turn red"'.

Sommai's harsh words abashed the young man and he turned back to his proper place.

Acarn Ekachai tried to follow Duangdaw, but she was tired of his possessiveness and took no notice of him. She had no intention of having any kind of relationship with him. She had only gone out with him with the idea of disconcerting her old admirer. Now he hardly gave her any peace at all and she was eager to be rid of him. People like Duangdaw were not likely to be patient with those they disliked.

'I don't think you are getting much time for your work, coming to see me so often,' she said to him that evening.

'*Oi*! I've a lot of free time. The headmaster's only given me one subject to teach - English language. Apart from that, I help with some research at the *amphur*. I am at the *amphur* as often as I am at school. When I get bored I go and have a beer at the market. I do as I please.' He went on, 'If anybody interferes with me, I'll resign. I can easily get a job in a General Education Department school.'

Her considerable dislike for the man was rapidly turning into a positive hatred. As the teacher was speaking, the young woman's thoughts turned to another young teacher who had not pursued her or even shown any special interest in her. She thought how different he was from other people. Just at that moment the young man himself appeared astride his bicycle, Ai Krong.

'Acarn Ekachai,' he said to the other man, stopping in front of the headmaster's house. 'The Section Head said he would go on ahead. He's probably at Barn Khok Klarng by now.' Piya remounted his bicycle.

'Just a moment, Khun Piya!' Duangdaw called to him. 'Where have they decided to put the new school? Did they agree to my suggestion?'

'The Section Head chose the site you suggested - facing the road into the village. They'll begin work in two or three days.' He got on his bicycle and rode off.

CHAPTER 15

Mor Sombat came to see Mae Kham nearly every day, though it was clear it was the daughter rather than concern for the mother's health which brought him. He had thought Phayorm was attached to some other young man, but he soon realized that she had yet to fall in love with anyone. She was beautiful and had most attractive ways, modest and unassuming. Her mother related to him the tale of her husband who had run away and taken another wife, leaving the three of them to a life of hardship. Without relatives or friends, Phayorm had grown to be unnecessarily hostile to all men. There was but one man she respected, even worshipped, but as an elder brother - Piya who, she believed, had brightened her mother's life, brought her out of her illness. In fact, her mother's improvement was probably the result of Mor Sombat's attentions - or even perhaps those of the village healer, the *thaw cam*. But to her, Piya was like a god, though she did not dare think too much about it, other than to realize that he showed interest in her mother and young brother and made them all very happy.

Mor Sombat was a decent man. He had great sympathy for the poor; whatever wealth he himself may have had, he still toiled endlessly, caring for the villagers without much rest, taking whatever payment or reward was offered, sometimes barely getting the cost of the medicines he gave them. His father wanted him to save his money, get married and start a family, but he had not found anyone he wanted to marry. He dreamed about building his fortune by qualifying in the arts of traditional Thai medicine, but this still remained only a hope.

Mae Kham's condition improved. One day the parasite in her bored its way out the top of her knee. That day Piya too had been at the house. Mae Kham complained of an irritation, an itching and as they sat around, the head of the worm suddenly appeared. Phayorm had grabbed a needle and poked at the skin around the creature. She had been quite terrified, her heart pounding. She grabbed the creature's head and, gently, pulled it completely out of her mother's leg. Piya quickly drew out a piece of paper from his pocket and wrapped the worm up to show to his pupils.

After that, Mae Kham had no more aches and pains. As for her thinness and lack of strength, this too slowly improved. Piya and Mor Sombat had her eat as much frog and fish as she could get, not stinting at all. As her condition improved, so did the relationship between Phayorm and Mor Sombat.

'I've brought you a disease-causing parasite to look at, today,' Piya said to his pupils when they met the next morning before school, as they now did regularly. He held up a little transparent bottle in which he had put the worm in water.

'This parasite came from a patient who was really sick - from the mother of master Siang. We call these *tua cit*. This is a visible disease-carrying creature. Like other disease-bearing creatures it enters our bodies through the mouth, in the food we eat. This type is mostly found in water creatures such as fish and prawns. When we eat raw fish or prawns we let them get into our stomachs and intestines. It then bores its way through the wall of the intestine and gets into the body and can go anywhere - it just depends on where its head points. If it gets to the brain, the patient dies. Elsewhere it causes great pain and discomfort. Sometimes it just stays still and the patient may not feel a thing. Occasionally it comes out through the skin. When that happens, like this one, the patient may count herself very lucky.'

He passed the bottle for each of them to have a look, but they all crowded together making sounds of surprise and revulsion, so he continued talking. 'If you don't want *tua cit* to get into you, it's very simple. Just don't eat raw food, particularly raw fish and raw prawns. Who among you eats these things?'

Silence. No one answered.

Finally Caw Khiaw, the class leader, piped up. 'I've seen many people eat them, but they're too frightened to answer. I've eaten raw prawns.'

'Well from now on I advise you not to eat raw fish, prawns or shell fish. Apart from *tua cit,* there's the 'leaf parasite'[1] which enters the liver. Here in Isarn many people die each year of 'leaf parasites' in the liver. When I go to the *amphur* next I'll borrow the preserved liver from the health clinic. You can see the parasites in it - just like this *tua cit*.

'It's frightening,' said Caw Siang. 'This thing was the cause of my mother's pain. I'm sure she'll get better now.'

When one had the title *khru,* teacher, it did not matter much how good or bad the person was. The villagers of Barn Norng Ma Vor counted it much more honourable than the business of cultivation and ploughing fields. Older folk liked to have a son-in-law or daughter-in-law who was a teacher. The girls wanted to marry male teachers and the

---

1 Liver fluke.

boys female teachers. The truth of this applied to Duangdaw, Piya and Phisit. All three of them were seen as very desirable partners by the young folk of opposite sex. As for Duangdaw, compared to the villagers she stood out like a bright star in the heavens. It was difficult to see any young man considering himself her equal and wooing her. They would at least fear that hanging around might annoy her. The only ones who may have thought themselves worthy were Acarn Ekachai and Phisit. But Phisit knew he could not compete with Acarn Ekachai before he ever got into the ring. Since the day of the picnic he had directed his thoughts elsewhere.

He thought he would do better with the village girls. Many could be compared to the flowers of the forest - pretty and with a natural freshness. Moreover, each one of them was interested in the teacher. At first he directed his attention towards Phayorm, whose attractions were pleasing to all sorts and ages. Living close by he observed her character and her circumstances and decided that to win a girl like Phayorm one had to play it cool. It would need time and effort. There was no use getting excited and trying to take her by storm; but as it was a pity to give up altogether, he would make of her a long term project.

Phisit's time attending night school at Teachers' Training College had given him an education in different types of women, women of various temperaments. He was not averse to telling anyone who would listen that it would be difficult to find anyone who knew women better. Whatever the truth of the matter, this was his view of himself. His attentions, deflected from Duangdaw and Phayorm, turned towards another of the young women who had helped out at the picnic. This happened to be

Khamkong, a round-faced girl with short hair and a clear skin. Using his persuasive tongue and pleasing words he so charmed her that in a few days the girl could do nothing but dream of him day and night.

One Saturday he persuaded her to go to the *amphur* where he would meet her on his motorcycle, out of sight of relatives and friends. From there they went together to Ubon. Khamkong had been deceived by Phisit's declaration of love and believed him when he told her he'd love her all his living days.

'Aai Khru,' she addressed him, respectfully yet with intimacy, calling him both 'elder brother', a form of address commonly used by women to lovers and husbands, and 'teacher'. 'You really will take me to your home?' She didn't sound entirely certain, though the young man had told her he would take her to visit his parents.

'Are you scared? Are you scared of my father and mother?'

'I don't dare! I am afraid they'll see the truth - I'm just a village girl.' She seemed to lose her courage entirely. 'Aai Khru, please take me back home.'

Aai Khru smiled to himself. He had got her here, why on earth should he take her back?

'If you don't want to meet my parents, I won't take you. Let's wait for a better opportunity. Let them know about you first and give them a chance to get used to the idea. Let's go to the cinema first. Then we'll go back.'

It was five o'clock in the afternoon when they came out of the cinema. Phisit informed the young girl they'd had bad luck.

'We can't make it back tonight. We'll have to go early tomorrow morning.'

'My father will kill me if he knows I came with Aai Khru,' Khamkong said.

'Don't worry. I'll talk to Phor Buntham myself,' the teacher said, referring to her father. He tried to pacify the girl by promising, 'As soon as we get back I'll get my parents to ask for you in marriage.'

'Where are you going to take me now, then?' she asked, concerned.

'If you are frightened to come home with me ...' he said, pretending to consider, though in fact he had no home in Ubon, at all,' ... I can't think where we can go. Don't you have any relatives in town?'

'Goodness, I don't know anybody here. If it had been the *amphur,* I know some people there.'

So by this superior strategy, Phisit got the young girl to the Nine-Storey Hotel in the centre of Ubon. She was then a virgin of eighteen rains and had never before had anything to do with a man.

On the return journey Phisit took her as far as the *amphur* and then made her take the minibus of Caw Kart back to the village of Norng Ma Vor. She took with her the consequences of his sincere assurances.

Phisit stealthily observed her from a distance, and saw she had safely boarded the bus. The young teacher, well-versed in the tricks of the male, mounted his motorcycle and made for the boardinghouse behind the *amphur* school at which Acarn Ekachai lived.

'Phi', he greeted Ekachai. 'One's done already.' Ekachai, who was not much older than Phisit, had no difficulty understanding him. 'I only wooed her a few days and off we went to town. I don't know how I'm going to get out of it. You'll help me think of something.'

'Hey! We've got to celebrate this.' The Acarn was of similar temperament and he expressed his pleasure. 'But you're not going back to Barn Norng Ma Vor today, are you?'

'Tomorrow morning will do. I'll go in a bit later after the headmaster has run off to play *boke* as he does every day. What have I got to be frightened about?' Phisit spoke confidently. 'There's only that madman Piya there. He's at the school at the crack of dawn. I don't know what heavenly bliss he hopes to get with all his diligence.'

One of the many endearing qualities of rural folk is their straightforwardness. Khamkong had no hesitation in telling her father and mother all that had happened. Thit Buntham danced in rage, as if he were possessed. He rushed to Headmaster Khammaw and demanded an immediate settlement of the affair.

'Headmaster, you've got to see this is settled satisfactorily - otherwise it's death!' Thit Buntham delivered his ultimatum. The headmaster was stupefied. He did not know what was going on.

'What is all this, Brother Thit? Who's going to die, then?'

The whole story of Phisit and Khamkong was then relayed in a whisper from the mouth of one to the ears of the other, accompanied by the pleas of the narrator.

'Not a word to anyone, *na*! You must try to keep this from the bosses, Headmaster!'

Phisit was not an honourable man. He was not going to admit Khamkong's story. He solemnly denied every word of it. Khamkong could only weep. Her father stormed and raged. It finally went to the headman, who considered the matter was rightly his to decide on, being the government's representative. Headmaster Khammaw could not decide who was telling the truth and who was lying. Duangdaw and Piya, however, had not the slightest doubt about Khamkong's story.

Phisit's credibility collapsed at once, however, when Caw Kart gave his evidence. Kart, the son of Lung 'Carn Kern, told the meeting gathered to hear the complaint:

'I don't know who's right or wrong, but I saw I 'Kong go off with Khru Phisit, and the day she returned he brought I 'Kong along, but let her get on the bus by herself. Khru Phisit parked his bike and waited by the shop of Tia Cai Di. Where they'd been, of course, I don't know.'

Caw Kart gave his evidence and went to Buntham and sat beside him. He whispered to the older man: 'This business with the teacher is as good as your numbers coming up in the lottery. Take it to the *Nai Amphur* - he'll be sacked for sure. You get as much money as you can from him.'

Thit Buntham stood up and walked to the middle of the room and said for all to hear: 'Never mind what anybody says. If Khru Phisit doesn't consent to marrying I 'Kong and making a settlement according to custom, I will take this matter to the *amphur* and I'll make him see black, see red.'

The headmaster called Phisit to him and whispered a few words in his ear. He turned and announced loudly: 'OK! Headman Lua, Thit Buntham, brothers, sisters, uncles, aunts - for wherever I look, I see we are all relatives! I've talked to Khru Phisit. He wants to beg forgiveness for his wrong doing. Whether it be in money, bracelets for the arms, rings for the fingers, that depends on us; we'll decide what's suitable.'

There was a murmuring among the crowd and Caw Kart and Thit Buntham began whispering together again. 'OK! Let's do it like this.' Thit Buntham spoke not taking his eyes off Caw Kart. 'What's done, is done and can't be washed away or made to disappear. As the father of the injured party, I demand, as appropriate compensation, five thousand baht.'

The murmurings became louder and everyone looked at Phisit who had gone quite pale.

After much talk and many bottles of whisky, which Phisit would have to pay for, it was finally decided that the damages would be reduced to two thousand baht. The headmaster knew it would not be possible to lower this figure and he advised Phisit to agree at once.

It turned out that Phisit did not have this amount of money and the headmaster suggested he borrow from Lung 'Carn Kern. The young spark drew the line at this further loss of face and went off to the *amphur* in search of Thawkay Mui Kuang - the king of money lenders, well known to teachers in the district.

However, even though Phisit had gone through this disastrous experience, he was incapable of learning a lesson from it. It all arose out of the proximity of his place of residence to Phayorm's house. The young teacher could not resist ogling and chatting up pretty girls. The girl herself was quite scared of him, but she did not know how he could be avoided. After all, the house of Headman Lua, in which Phisit lived, was adjacent to her own.

Mor Sombat, in the meantime, was assiduously wooing Phayorm, ever solicitous and frequently there chatting with her. Phayorm too was beginning to know him better and had decided he could be trusted, like Piya. She took her disquiet to Mor Sombat, who, already being suspicious of everyone where Phayorm was concerned, became quite angry and resentful towards Phisit. He felt he could easily slash Phisit across the face with a knife but, not knowing what else he could do, he bore his resentment in silence.

Piya decided that Phisit was one of those who pursued his pleasures paying no attention to his surroundings, circumstances or the opinions of others. Phisit continued his mode of behaviour unchanged, despite his loss of reputation and money. He flirted with and wooed the village girls without discrimination. It became clear soon enough that not one of them was interested in the teacher any more. Even the young woman, Sommai, she of the sharp tongue and sharp wit, was too afraid to bandy words with him. But Phisit had yet to reach self-awareness. Whatever other people thought of him, he maintained his cheerful happy-go-lucky manner.

At the beginning of the harvest, life in the village is always peaceful and satisfying. Nature is bountiful at this time, rice in the fields and fish in the waters. After the transplanting the villagers cut rushes of a kind known as *phy* or *kok,* triangular in cross-section.[2] These are dried in the sun and then cut into strips for the weaving of mats. Some households keep silkworms, feeding them on mulberry leaves which they pick in the forest. The young girls spin the silk thread. Some weave cloth on looms set up under the houses. All these are women's tasks. The men look after

2 *Phy* or *kok* - species of CYPERUS.

their hill farms, their paddy fields, their cows and buffaloes. They watch the level of the water in the fields, letting it in and lowering it as necessary. They keep weeds away from the rice, weeds such as the *phak i hin* and the so-called 'ringworm grass'.[3] Others catch fish, using lines, traps or nets, catch pigeons and other birds such as kingfishers and species of rollers. Everyone had some occupation - in the countryside working for a living was one of the joys of life.

Phayorm helped Mae Bun, the headman's wife, with weaving mats. She was both helper and partner. She went out and gathered the rushes from the swamp, put them out to dry, then stripped them. When the mats were woven they divided them between the two.

The loom for weaving the mats used a reed about a *wa* (approximately two metres) in length, equal to the breadth of the mat. Phayorm sat behind the loom under the house of the headman. The loom for weaving mats is very low, barely off the ground. The thread used is made of hemp, about the width of a match stick. A shuttle is not used in weaving the strips of sedge through the string; instead, a piece of bamboo the size of a schoolmaster's pointing rod. It is pushed through the loom followed by the strip of sedge. Two people are needed - one to push the stick, the weaver to pull the strip through.

Phayorm was the weaver, the headman's wife the other. The two of them worked skilfully and fast, maintaining a perfect rhythm. The partly woven mat had an attractive design of yellow, gold and red. Mae Kham came down the steps of her house, sat down and watched her daughter at work. The old woman's eyes had the expression

---

3 *Phak i hin* - MONOCHORIA CYANEA.

of a sick person, but her complexion had improved considerably.

'Eh! You can get up and walk about a bit now! Getting stronger!' Mae Bun shouted to her in greeting. 'You lot should eat more - more rice, more fish. When you're better we'll go and collect bamboo shoots one day - make a fine curry.'

'Since that parasite came out I haven't had any pain at all. I don't know whose medicine it was that did the trick - *Phor Thaw cam,* Mor Sombat's or Khru Piya's,' Mae Kham explained.

'Talking of Mor Sombat and Khru Piya! One of them's going to be your son-in-law?' She turned to Phayorm. 'Or, what do you say, Phayorm?'

The young girl of the smooth complexion, so different from the dark complexion of her young brother, Caw Siang, made no reply. The sound of an old motorcycle ground its way up to the house. Mor Sombat dismounted and came towards them smiling, carrying some brown paper bags.

'Weaving mats, Mae Bun?' he said to cover his embarrassment.

'He sees it and still asks,' Mae Bun retorted. 'Have you come to heal the sick or to weave mats?'

'Whatever you want me to do, Mae Bun, that I'll do,' Sombat volunteered. He sat down and gave Mae Kham one of the bags.

'Mother's better now. I was so glad, I thought I'd buy you a small present. Here's a blouse to wear to the *kathin* festival. One for Phayorm too. I hope you'll like them.' He passed the other bag to Phayorm. She looked as if she was undecided about accepting it. When Mae Bun told her to take it, she did so nervously, then raised her hands in a *wai*.

'Thank you very much. I don't know how to thank you enough. All I can say is I'm very grateful.'

'May you attain much merit, son.' Mae Kham raised her hands over her head. 'I can't even pay you for treating me, and you bring rice and gifts for us. May you always be prosperous and have an illustrious future.' She ended with the conventional sacerdotal blessing - *thern*.

'You don't need to talk about all that.' Mor Sombat sat down next to Phayorm. 'Khru Piya offered to pay my entire fee. But I can't take it from him or from anyone else.'

'You didn't bring anything for me, Mor Sombat?' Mae Bun asked, joking. 'If you don't have a young daughter nobody pays you any attention.'

'Don't you have a son, a schoolteacher, then?' Sombat said, smiling. 'Oh, you mean Schoolmaster Two Thousand.' Mae Bun knew he was referring to Khru Phisit, whom many people now referred to as 'Mr Two Thousand', since his payment of the compensation. She laughed and said, 'My son's only skill is in spending money.'

When school was over, Phisit went back to his lodgings at the headman's house to change his clothes. He stopped to greet Phayorm, who was working below the house, as usual. He bathed and put on fresh clothes. He chose a fashionable, coloured shirt. He came down the steps and sat by Phayorm, chatting to her, completely ignoring the headman's wife, who was weaving with Phayorm. He was there but a moment when he decided this was not much fun and decided to pay Duangdaw a visit. He got on his motorcycle, even though the headmaster's house was quite close by and he could easily have walked. Duangdaw had not returned from school and the young man kicked his motorcycle into life again and headed for the school.

Phisit found the two of them, Piya and Duangdaw, training the children at sport, quite unaware of the time. Piya was supervising the boys at football and Duangdaw was playing 'chairball' with the girls.

'What's going on? Haven't you gone home yet, Khun Duangdaw?' Phisit yelled, sitting astride his motorbike.

'Oh! Khun Phisit, come here. Come on and help us a bit. I'm not very good with sport.' Duangdaw beckoned him with a nod of her head.

'Goodness, what's the matter Khun Duangdaw? Are you now going to follow Khun Piya's foolishness?' He walked towards her and said, 'I've never seen teachers anywhere stay at school till four o'clock. It's only the mad ones like Khun Piya who are so conscientious. Are you now going to join him?'

'I'm not trying to be a model teacher at all, and I'm not following anyone's madness!' The young woman tossed the ball, spinning, into the air. 'Playing with the kids cures the boredom and it's better than sitting doing nothing in the house.'

'In that case let's go for a ride on the motorbike.' Phisit spoke as if he had the answer.

'You go ahead, then, by yourself,' she said, as if indifferent.

When they had finished with the sports, Piya suggested a drink of water at his hut. They walked, close together, across the field, across the top of the hillock on which the school stood. The evening sun threw long shadows behind them. A wind blew from the swamp drying the sweat off their bodies, making them pleasantly cool and comfortable.

'Isn't the weather nice?' Duangdaw said. 'You shouldn't overwork yourself, Khun Piya, always so lively and active.'

'But you've been lively and active too. You should see yourself, cheerful and carefree.' Piya spoke, not looking at his companion.

'Oh! Khun Piya, you know how to look after a house,' she said, taking a glass of water from him. 'Thank you. And you're a musician, too!'

Piya did not answer, but picked up the *phin* and the guitar.

'Which one can you play? Can you manage the guitar, Khun Duangdaw?' he said, holding the guitar out to her.

'You go ahead. I'd like to hear a song. Sing whatever you like, Khun Piya.'

'What songs do you like, Khun Duangdaw?' He strummed the guitar.

'Anything at all. I like all kinds.' Duangdaw picked up the *phin*.

'OK.' Piya sang a song he was teaching the children at school. It was a merry tune and a lighthearted song, and the young woman listened attentively till it was over.

'Oh, that's excellent. You could make a living at it. I would like to learn the guitar. Sing another one, then let's listen to this chap here,' she said, gently striking the strings of the *phin*. He played another song on the guitar, then a few on the *phin*. It had become quite dark now and Piya suggested Duangdaw should return to the village.

'Don't think I'm chasing you away, Khun Duangdaw, but it's quite dark and you should go back. They'll be expecting you. I'm having *mok pla* tonight, I don't think you'll like it very much. I won't ask you to stay for dinner.'

'Look at that. He won't even invite me, so that I can refuse him to his face,' she teased.

He escorted her to her little motorcycle, which was parked not far away. Before she left, he picked a red flower from one of the beds planted by the pupils, and gave it to her.

'You like flowers, don't you? Let me give you one. Now don't take it and throw it away!'

Duangdaw took it, not showing her feelings. She thanked him and rode off. She did not turn back to look at him, though she dearly wanted to.

CHAPTER 16

The earth began to dry out as the rains ceased towards the middle of October. The timber lorries and the ten-wheeled transport lorries were seen in the village nearly every day as they passed by the school on their way into the depths of the forest. Sometimes there were long-wheel-based landrovers with darkened windscreens, passing swiftly the same way, or open pick-ups with two or three men seated in the back. Sometimes on the return journey the landrover or pick-up would stop at Lung 'Carn Kern's house and there would be much drinking and smoking.

The building of the schoolhouse also began. Piya and Duangdaw directed the builders to the site and gave them other directions. The Section Head had at first wanted to raze three large trees, but Piya had seen this would not be necessary if the site were moved ten metres to the east.

'Please have them spare those three trees, Headmaster,' Piya had pleaded. 'The children use them for shade when they play, and during their rest periods. If we have to plant new ones it'll be tens of years before they're this size again. They are so rare too. Particularly this large 'fish-yam' tree[1] - it's the only one of its kind in the whole area. The flowers smell so sweet!'

'But the Section Head ordered them cut and the building to go there. I don't like questioning the boss's orders.' Headmaster Khammaw did not look happy.

'I don't see there's going to be a big difference if the school is moved ten metres. We've got about a hundred *rai*,

---

[1] 'Fish-yam' tree - FAGRAEA FRAGRANS.

we don't have to build just where the trees are. The Section Head doesn't seem to like trees. It doesn't worry him to have them cut, he sits there in the *amphur*. But our kids and the teachers are here all the time. Why should we have to destroy something that is of such use to us?' Piya voiced his displeasure, his voice growing louder and louder.

Duangdaw, who had been part of the discussion from the first, tried to introduce some reason into the argument when she felt things getting unpleasant, and suggested that the climate might be affected.

'I feel we ought to spare the trees; after all, they can't be moved, but the school can be built anywhere.'

'What do you say, Khru Phisit?' The headmaster turned to the young man, who appeared uninterested in the discussion.

'Who? Me? Anything's OK with me. But what do we want to cross swords with the Section Head for? I think we are getting excited over nothing.' He got on his motorcycle and started it.

'But I beg of you, Khru jai, don't let them cut these trees.' There was a note of urgent pleading in Piya's voice. 'If they build where I say, these two trees will be by the corner of the school and that one will be about fifteen metres away, behind. I'll talk to the Section Head myself. He can tell the workmen to resite the plan. Khun Duangdaw *na!*' He turned to the young woman, calling on her support.

'Let's do as Khun Piya says, Uncle.' The headmaster looked uncertain.

'What do you say, Lung 'Carn?' The headmaster addressed Lung 'Carn Kern, the man who would actually build the schoolhouse. Lung 'Carn had subcontracted the building from Sia Mangkorn and was mainly concerned with his own convenience.

'Let's do as Khru Piya says. We won't have to waste time cutting the trees. That "duck foot" will take at least half a day.[2] Let's do as Khru Piya suggests and leave it at that.'

The plans were resited, the foundations dug and the building proceeded apace, there being no need to drive in piles as in Bangkok. The soil of Barn Norng Ma Vor, especially on top, was sandy. Below it was laterite, in some places quite deep, at others very shallow. Even though the plans for the school specified the use of piles, the contractors and the officials at *amphur* level knew there was no necessity for their use. The money allocated for this purpose was profit for the contractor. The timber for pillars, floorboards and roof timbers, such as the joists, cross beams, tie beams, the purlins and rafters, was transported in large ten-wheeled lorries and dumped higgledy-piggledy by the old school building. There was no fear of its being stolen, for everyone knew the timber was the property of Lung 'Carn Kern.

The workmen built themselves a lean-to as a temporary dwelling near Piya's hut, giving him some companionship during the evenings and at night. Some evenings he invited them over for a meal, others he wandered over to them, taking his food with him. One of the workmen was an expert on the *khaen* and Piya was always at him to play.

In addition to Piya and the other teachers, it was 'Carn Khen who took on the job of unofficial supervisor and giving advice. After all, he lived quite near the building site. He came along every evening to walk around and examine

---

2 'Duck foot' - VITEX LIMONIFOLIA.

the work. Piya observed that the timber being used was of excellent quality and had come from a sawmill, quite unlike the handsawn timber one usually saw in the district. He silently congratulated the contractor for providing such good quality timber, but as to whether the quantity provided was in accordance with the plan or not, he had no way of knowing.

'They should use double beams if they're using crossbeams of this size, not single ones like this,' 'Carn Khen said to Piya. 'Do you know how many and what size the plan specifies?'

'There should be a copy at the headmaster's, but I think he said the Section Head has taken full responsibility for the construction. I think he's coming to have a look on Saturday.'

'But I think we should take an interest and tell the builders. The school belongs to the villagers, to everyone. We can't just let them build it any old way, not worrying as long as it's done.' 'Carn Khen walked back to his house, preoccupied with his own thoughts.

The Section Head arrived with Sia Mangkorn and one of the teachers who worked in the *amphur*, in charge of finance and construction. He was thirty-eight years old, the nephew of the Section Head - Sawad by name. He was known to all as hatchet man for the Section Head. He followed him everywhere - to the Provincial Office, on visits to other *amphur*, on school inspections. He had the authority to order meals for the Section Head and to pay out money. He ordered teachers to put on food, on behalf of his boss, and before leaving he saw they did not forget to have parcels of beef, grilled fish, duck's eggs, fresh fish, fruits and vegetables placed in the pick-up for him. Most of all,

Khru Sawad liked to go on school inspections with his revolver strapped to his side.

Lung 'Carn Kern, the sub-contractor, had a young pig slaughtered to welcome the Section Head. They sat down to eat on the lawn by the school, not far from the workmen's lean-to. The food and drink, the liquor and the soda were brought in Caw Kart's 'two-rower' bus. Headmaster Khammaw and the other three teachers were at hand to wait on the Section Head and see to his every need. Even though school hours were over, Duangdaw and Phisit were expected to take care of various odds and ends. This Phisit was certainly pleased to do. He liked the idea of hanging around the Section Head as much as having a free feed. As for Duangdaw, she would have liked to have gone home, but the headmaster asked her to stay back and help, keeping the Section Head's glass filled up with liquor.

'Why do you want me to fill his glass for him? Hasn't he got hands of his own?' She sounded sullen.

'Goodness, have a little consideration for your uncle. You know that's our custom. Show some patience,' he pleaded. He finally persuaded her, much against her will, to go out and join the circle of drinkers on the lawn.

'Hasn't Acarn Ekachai come?' Phisit asked Khru Sawad. 'If he was coming, he should have arrived by now. Last time he caught me with a full hand three times.' He referred to a game of rummy.

'Acarn Ekachai! I understood he'd get here before evening. We're going to have fun tonight. I heard the Section Head say he's going to stay here tonight.' Khru Sawad grinned and his gaze strayed towards Duangdaw.

As he wandered round the foundations of the new building, Piya decided he would ask the Section Head for details about the building materials.

'Section Head, Sir. I feel these crossbeams are smaller than they should be. Small ones like this are usually used in pairs.'

'They've estimated all that! This size is more than sufficient.' The Section Head was not very interested. 'A hundred children are not likely to bring the building down.'

'People like Sia Mangkorn are careful to follow the details of a contract. Isn't that so, Sia?' Khru Sawad walked about elbow's length behind the Section Head with the construction magnate. 'You don't need to worry about it, Khru Piya. Teachers should only be concerned with their duties, their teaching. Don't get too involved in the villagers' affairs.'

'Certainly teachers like me must be interested in the affairs of the village! Teaching is not our only business. I am supported by the taxes of these villagers.'

'Piya, whom is Duangdaw calling? I think the food must be ready.' The headmaster intervened before the argument could get any more heated.

The Section Head's party sat down to their liquor and barbecued pork in the grounds of the school. As it grew dark the headmaster volunteered to get a pressure lamp so they could continue their party, but the Section Head preferred to move to the headmaster's house. Lung 'Carn Kern, who was paying for the festivities, intervened. He said, as he was the host, perhaps it would be better if they all went to his house. Sia Mangkorn too preferred the latter arrangement. The whole party moved *en masse* to Lung 'Carn Kern's, except Piya and Duangdaw; they decided there was no further call on their services and asked permission to go home.

Tonight was the full moon of the eleventh month, the day celebrating the end of Buddhist Lent. Young and old, lads and lasses, men and women, were off to the monastery for merit-making ceremonies. The main event of that night's ceremonies was the *tai pratheep; tai* meaning 'to light, to make bright', and *pratheep,* 'a flame'. The festival signified the beginning of the winter season, the season of the harvest. Ceremonial halls or pavilions were erected in the compounds of monasteries, in which were placed Buddha images and the accoutrements of worship. The altar was specially made of banana trunks on which the votive candles and incense were placed. They were stuck into the banana trunk and lit, each person making his or her offering. The combined effect of all these had a brilliance and beauty all of its own. There were also offerings of flowers. Besides ordinary flowers, there were the 'rice flowers', that is, ears of rice still unopened, called *marn khaw.* Each farmer chose an ear from his field to offer on this occasion. This offering was believed to ensure an abundant harvest. The lads and lasses put on their best clothes to go to the *wat.* Some of them went in groups, each one carrying a lighted candle. Some played the *khaen* or strummed the *phin.* They played Jew's harps and kept time, beating sticks and clapping hands. From time to time the more highspirited let off firecrackers, frightening the young girls. The cool, fresh night, the light of the full moon, was a perfect setting for the camaraderie among fellow villagers.

Mor Sombat, Phayorm and the young girls who were her friends were headed towards the *wat;* all except Khamkong, who had done little but look miserable since her experience with Khru Phisit. There were Sommai, Khamkhian and three other young girls.

'Isn't Phayorm's blouse nice?' Sommai exclaimed as they set out. 'I haven't seen this one before. I'd really like to know if it's the doctor's blouse or the teacher's blouse.'

'I think it's the doctor's. Right, Phayorm?' Khamkhian, her next door neighbour, giggled softly.

'A pretty blouse like this, I suppose, must be the teacher's,' Mor Sombat joked, hiding the anguish he was feeling. He thought the teacher the young girls were talking about must be Piya. The blouse was in fact the one he himself had bought her. Despite the moonlit night and the atmosphere of religious devotion and goodwill, in Sombat's heart there was only a sullen resentment. His gaiety was only on the outside.

In the main monks' residence was a pressure lamp which lit up the area in front of the building. The old people and women had made their offerings of incense, candles and flowers and were seated around in large numbers. In the middle of the large yard in front of the monks' residence was firmly planted a bamboo post about the thickness of a man's leg and two metres high. On it hung a large basket in which there were various kinds of food, packets of boiled rice, wrapped rice cakes and a large bunch of bananas.

When the monks had finished chanting and the religious rituals were completed, the time for merrymaking had arrived. The highspirited young men got ready to show off their skill in front of the girls and compete on the bamboo post. The prize was the basket of food. It was not worth a great deal of money, but the lads were more concerned with the honour of winning in front of that audience.

The head monk asked them if they would like to compete one by one, or in a catch-as-catch-can free-for-all. The youths were unanimous that they would like to display their individual skill competing one at a time. Piya, who had been one of the first to arrive for the rituals, was the popular choice to be on the committee, and was happy to agree.

A number of young boys and teenagers tried their luck climbing the bamboo pole, but none of them could. The pole had been well greased with coconut oil. The idea was to climb to the top and reach for the things in the basket. None of them was successful, though some asked for and got two or three tries.

But Barn Norng Ma Vor was not without its strategist. It was finally Caw Khiaw who conquered the pole, getting a bit of added assistance by deciding to keep his shorts on to counteract its slipperiness. Using his climbing skills and his strength, the eleven-year old son of Headman Lua and the leader of the school walked away with the prize.

Piya saw Phayorm and Mor Sombat in their own little group and guessed at the state of affairs. He decided against going up and chatting to them. He shouted a greeting to them and went and sat with a group of old folk.

He left the *wat* about nine o'clock and on his way home passed the house of Lung 'Carn Kern. The pressure lamp was still burning brightly and from inside came the sound of loud voices. He recognized Phisit's voice and guessed he was very drunk. Ai Krong, his bicycle, passed the headmaster's house. There was no light showing in Duangdaw's room. She had gone to bed, he supposed. He regretted he had not asked her to accompany him to the *wat*. He blamed himself for his lack of courage.

He passed the house of 'Carn Khen. The house glittered with little lights. The occupant was also celebrating the festival of lights. The sound of the *khaen* playing 'The Lullaby of the Deserted Mother' drifted on the cool wind. The pathos of the melody struck a chord in Piya's heart and he went sadly off to bed.

The construction work went on apace. In ten days the sheets of corrugated iron were on the roof. The floor of the upper storey was soon laid - work went on day and night almost as if the work had to be completed before the end of the budget year. Piya was amazed, and wondered what the hurry was about. But he dared not ask. He was still curious, however, and felt there must be a reason.

Winter is the season for growing vegetables in Isarn. Piya set to work planting all kinds of vegetables in the patch of ground by the side of the hut in which he lived. He re-dug the old well which had collapsed in the rains. He had not dug very deep when he struck water which he could draw and use. This time he used timber which he had begged from the construction workers to line the well to prevent the sides collapsing. He had at first thought of getting a concrete pipe and using that to line the well, but he did not have the money for that, so used the timber instead. This appeared successful. Around the top of the well he built up the area of soil and kept it in place with laterite. He poured concrete over this, making a platform around the well which could be kept clean. The school now had a well of its own, giving water for drinking as well as washing. However, the children and the villagers referred to it as Khru Piya's well.

Piya planted vegetables for the kitchen - onions, lettuces, coriander, beans and pumpkin. In addition, he prepared about a hundred ditches for watermelons. He had used many full Saturdays and Sundays preparing the soil. For the watermelons he dug broad ditches, about an arm's length in depth. He mixed in animal manure which he got from the headman and the headmaster, and filled up the holes with soil. In each ditch he put three seeds, the seeds he had acquired from the Agricultural Station. Some days Siang and Phayorm came to help; so did Caw Khiaw and the other kids when they could get away from their parents.

'You don't really need to come and help,' Piya said to the young woman. 'If Siang comes and helps, that's enough. I don't like some of the things I've heard people say.'

'Mother told me to come and help, to make some return for all your help. I, too, think of it all the time,' Phayorm said earnestly. 'You've been very good to my family. Are you bored then with my company?'

'It's not like that at all, Phayorm.' The young teacher decided to speak out. 'I'd like you to come and help every day. Draw water, cook, all kinds of things. But people say there are those who don't like you helping me. You can come and help, but let's do this!'

'Do what?' The young woman put down the hoe she was using.

'If anyone asks you, say I've hired you to do the digging for me. In fact, I think of us as partners. Any money we get we'll divide equally.'

'I am not concerned with that. I am not even certain we are going to get any crop. I've never seen anyone plant watermelons at this time of year. I just see you cultivating so diligently I want to help. If you want me to tell people you are employing me as a labourer, I'll do what you want.'

'Don't misunderstand, Phayorm. I just don't want there to be any unpleasantness because of other people's gossip.' Piya straightened up and looked with satisfaction at his watermelon garden.

Duangdaw was bathed and dressed and did not know what to do with herself. She got on her little motorbike and rode out of the village. Seeing the weather was fine, she made for the school. She got to the top of the hill and stopped, then immediately turned round to return to the village. That was when Piya saw her.

'Khru Duangdaw! Come here a moment! Where are you hurrying off to?' Piya beckoned and called to her. But she revved her motorbike and sped away towards the village.

'I know now why you don't want me to come and help,' Phayorm said, smiling.

About six o'clock that evening Mor Sombat arrived at Phayorm's house and Mae Kham told him she was out. Sombat looked disconcerted. He wanted very much to meet the young woman.

'Do you know where she went, mother?'

'She went to get water, as usual. But I hear she's also helping Khru Piya with his vegetable garden,' she said, repeating what her daughter had told her. 'Little Ai Siang always goes with her too.'

Mor Sombat was about to start his battered old motorbike when Phayorm arrived carrying water. He dismounted again, looking sullen.

'I hear you've been going to school every day, Phayorm.'

'I went to help Khru Piya plant watermelons. Why?' she answered innocently, carrying the water up to the house. 'Come on up to the house. Where are you hurrying off to?'

Mor Sombat did not answer, but climbed up to the house and sat down, leaning against a pillar.

'What's wrong, Mor? You don't look well. Have you eaten yet?' She spoke, unaware of the other's thoughts.

'Not yet,' he replied curtly. 'I'll go eat at Lung 'Carn Kern's in a moment.'

'Aw! Why? Yesterday you said you would eat here. I was going to make *orm kop* with *kayaeng*[3] leaves, the way you like it. Why don't you eat with us?' She spoke as she put away her buckets and carrying stick.

'Where's Siang gone?' he said, to make conversation, but his voice was still sullen.

'Khru Piya wanted him to sleep there tonight. At dusk he is going to Grandmother Pui's funeral house.'

'Is Grandmother Pui dead, then?' The young doctor looked distressed at the news of the death of a woman he had treated. It was an opportunity to change the subject of conversation which had brought unpleasantness from the moment they met that day. The tension lessened considerably.

---

3 *Kayaeng* - LIMNOPHILA GEOFFRAGI. *Orm kop* - a frog curry with thick gravy.

Mor Sombat realized full well that Phayorm loved him. He was very much in love with her. Great love could bring great jealousy. He had promised the girl that he would find money to marry her as quickly as possible. He now pursued every way he knew to make money - including gambling. He now played cards frequently, whenever anybody invited him to. He also began to pour large sums of money into the lottery, buying many tickets each time, sometimes also buying numbers on the illegal lottery; all in the hope of winning a lump sum of money, but never with any success. It was a period during which the young doctor was overwhelmed by love and misery; misery over how his love could be fulfilled and how he could get enough money to get married.

One of his pupils had brought news to Piya that the boy's grandmother, Mae jai Pui, had died that afternoon. Piya had to attend the funeral. The old lady had always been very kind to him with her household utensils and food when he had first moved to the school.

He had his evening meal and left Siang to watch the house, telling him to go straight to bed, as he was likely to be late returning. He mounted his bike, Ai Krong, and made for the village.

There was a large noisy crowd at the funeral house. The deceased had been a woman of some importance and had many relatives. The corpse lay in a coffin covered with a white cloth. A number of people were cutting coloured paper into wavy strips to attach to the outside of the coffin. This work required considerable skill and it appeared that 'Carn Khen was in charge of the group. Everyone knew of his skill in making paper patterns and carving the sections of banana trunk into elaborate decorations for the coffin.

But he had to be invited in a way which satisfied him. If not, he would not come. It was not that his services were expensive. If he was satisfied he would not charge a *satang*. While he worked he talked to no one. He drank a little whisky. Others had the task of sitting by him, watching and passing him his instruments as he needed them.

The wake, at which neighbours and friends gathered at the house of the deceased while the corpse was still there and the relatives in a state of grief, was known as *ngan hyan di*. *Ngan* means 'celebration' or 'the expression of sympathy'; *hyan di,* 'the good house', referred to the house at which there had been a death. The name denied the evil (of death) and instead asserted the coming of good fortune to the household. It was an ancient custom. When the villagers heard of a death they flocked to give their help, performing whatever task had to be done. Those who could not perform strenuous tasks performed lighter ones. They brought food, rice, fish, fruit, to feed the guests that would arrive. They all stayed around to prevent the bereaved being lonely and to ease their grief.

The host had provided an ox and whisky was brought from the distillery in large quantities. When the monks had chanted from the *Abidhamma*[4] it was time for the guests to enjoy themselves. They played various games, 'tiger eats pig', *mark harp,* 'tiger eats ox' - all board games like chess. The young lads and lasses had fun with riddle competitions between teams, girls versus boys. The winner, as his or her reward, could slap the hand of the opposing team member. The young men reckoned this a bonus, as they could hold a young girl's hand whether they won or lost. The older folk

---

4 One of the three main collections of Buddhist scriptures.

sat around and read old stories from palm leaf manuscripts, intoning the words with a pleasing melody. The others sat listening silently. There were many of these stories.

The wake for Grandmother Pui was in keeping with the times. In addition to the games and activities mentioned, there were also two card schools in the house and two schools of High-Low in the yard. The host could not chase these entrepreneurs away; instead they too had to be supplied with food, liquor and soft drinks. Piya sat watching 'Carn Khen carving and decorating the banana trunks. In the other corner was a card school. There was Thit Phun, Mor Sombat, Caw Kart and Khun Phisit. Headmaster Khammaw was holding the pack. Near them was a group of women wrapping little packets of betel leaf with nut and other condiments for chewing, rolling the locally-grown tobacco into cigarettes and stringing garlands of flowers which would be used as offerings and to decorate the coffin. Phisit was clearly drunk. He talked loudly, played carelessly and sat as if he were going to fall over the women who sat near him. It happened that the one seated nearest him was Phayorm. It was no surprise that Mor Sombat was watching everything with keen eyes.

'Move back a little please, Khun Khru.' Phayorm moved her body to avoid Phisit's pressing against her.

'Just a little, *na*! Pretty one. I don't see the tiniest bit anywhere!' Phisit deliberately slurred his speech. He pretended he was uninterested in what she had just said. He pulled out a twenty baht note from his pocket and said, 'I'll bet the twenty. Thish hand'll win. The girl's gi'n me luck.' His speech was slurred. Mor Sombat ground his teeth till his molars stuck out of his cheeks. The headmaster dealt the cards, two of each, and nodded to the first, who was Thit Phun.

'I'll stay,' he said, placing his money on top of his cards.

Phisit came next. He slowly raised the corners of his cards to see what they were, taking so long about it that everyone else became quite furious. Finally, he nodded his head. 'Another card, closed.'

The headmaster dealt him a card and Phisit went through the same act, as slowly as before. He nodded. 'Another card.'

The headmaster turned up the last card, which was a two spot. Phisit slammed down the four cards in his hand, face upwards, bending backwards and shouting, 'Twenty-one! do you see? The girl brought me luck. Go on, nudge me again, pretty one!'

Mor Sombat seemed about to jump up and kick Phisit's backside, but he managed to control himself. The card game proceeded, with many of the players becoming more and more annoyed.

'Teacher! If you're drunk, go home and sleep it off. You can even sleep here, nobody will say anything.'

'I'm not drunk. Who says I'm drunk? Thish one drinksh, never drunk.' His voice was thick.

Piya, seeing that things looked bad, asked Phisit to go home with him. But Phisit was obstinate. Piya said goodbye to his hosts and left. It was about nine o'clock. He stopped at the headmaster's house when he saw Duangdaw seated on the verandah.

'Not yet asleep, Khun Duangdaw?' he said, leaving his bicycle against a coconut tree by the steps and climbing up to the house.

'I've got to watch the house tonight. Uncle and Aunt have gone to the funeral house. I Si has gone with them.' She moved, to give him room to sit.

'I haven't been to Ubon for two weeks, I've got no cakes for you. There's some nice *khaw maw*. Would you like some?' She got up and walked into the house, using a torch to light her way. She returned in a moment carrying a brass tray. On it was the green rice, looking soft and smelling delicious. The *khaw maw* of the northeast was made from rice which was not yet ready for harvest. The rice was roasted in its husk and then pounded and winnowed to get rid of the chaff. This left the *khaw maw*, green and ready to be eaten. The best *khaw maw* was soft and green; it smelled beautiful, without any chaff in it and not lumpy.

'Did Mae Phan make this?' he asked - Mae Phan being the headmaster's wife.

'Khamkong brought it this evening,' she said, passing the bowl to Piya. 'It's such a pity about her. Before all this happened she was so lively. Now she looks as if she is about to cry all the time. Khru Phisit should not be allowed!'

'I don't like to condemn a fellow teacher, but I think he's done us all great harm. I feel ashamed to face the villagers when I think of it.' Piya picked up some of the parched rice and put it in his mouth. 'Khun Duang,' the young man spoke and then fell silent, avoiding Duangdaw's gaze.

'Yes,' she said, then she too was silent. 'You can call me Aew.'

'OK. Khun Aew. But I think I prefer Duangdaw.' Piya slowly turned his face towards his companion. 'However I say it, it doesn't sound right. Well, Khun Aew, do you still think you'll get a transfer from here?'

'It doesn't matter now, whether I get transferred or not. It's very pleasant here. I don't mind staying. Why do you ask?'

'I thought at first Khun Duangdaw, *eh-i!* Khun Aew, wouldn't stay here even a month.' Piya was still uncertain about using her more intimate name.

'But I see now you love and trust the kids and the villagers. Am I right? Khun Aew?'

'You may be right, you may be wrong. Wait and see.' She smiled shyly. 'Goodness, if I knew I was being observed I would have put on an act for you. What a pity I learned too late.'

On the night air there came the sound of a *khaen* and the smell of night flowers. From the funeral house came the sound of loud voices. Both of them were silent for a while, and suddenly from the funeral house there was renewed shouting and hullabaloo as if a fight were taking place. Someone rushed past the house and yelled. They could scarcely understand, but it seemed he said, 'Someone's broken Khru Phisit's head!'

They shouted a warning to each other in concern and Piya leaped from the house and rushed towards the noise. Duangdaw followed, shouting 'Don't! Don't go!'

Piya paid no heed to her and vanished into the darkness. He was soon at the funeral house. A crowd stood outside the house shouting at each other so Piya could not understand a word. Phisit was being helped up the steps of the house, his face covered in blood. He looked both drunk and hurt. Piya rushed and grabbed him on one side, helping the others take him up the steps.

'What happened, Khun Phisit?'

'He went for a piss in the banana grove,' someone explained, 'and somebody hit him over the head, or slashed him with a knife - I don't know. He's covered in blood.'

Under the light of the pressure lamp Piya and the headmaster took charge of him. With some fear they examined their colleague for a wound. Headmaster Khammaw yelled for someone to get medicine for the wound. Piya examined the unfortunate man, but found no wound on his head or face. He examined his neck, his shoulder, his arms and his body. He then smelled the blood and began to laugh.

'Never mind the medicine - he's got red medicine all over him already.'

'What's this?' said the headmaster, looking closely at Phisit's neck.

'This is some red medicine - not blood.' Piya couldn't stop laughing. 'You can open your eyes and get up, Phisit. Someone's really played the fool, I don't know who. He's had a good joke and frightened the lot of us.'

Some joker had taught Phisit a lesson. He'd been hit over the head with the stem of a papaya filled with some red liquid and attached to a split bamboo. When it struck his head it had made a frightening noise and he had yelled at the top of his voice. The pain of the blow and the red liquid made him think his head had been split open. He had been too scared to open his eyes or examine himself to see what had really happened. Everybody had a good laugh at Phisit's expense and went back to their merrymaking.

CHAPTER 17

The new school building progressed splendidly, according to plan. Its growth was like that of the vegetables in the school garden, or like Piya's watermelons. They all seemed to flourish together. Both teachers and children were pleased. Everybody was pleased that they could soon use the new schoolhouse, but Piya and some of the children were also happy that the vegetables they had planted were beginning to bear fruit in their own gardens as well as in those of their parents. Piya had the children cultivate vegetable gardens near the school and these too were showing signs of abundant crops. There were luscious red tomatoes, the greens of the onions and garlic stood tall, collecting the dew in the early morning. Smooth-skinned cucumbers hid under green leaves. Piya pruned the watermelons, cutting and throwing away one fruit from each vine. The children complained bitterly.

'You've got to cut away one fruit from each vine; that's how you get big fruit. If you leave them all on they've all got less food and none will reach their proper size,' he explained.

The teachers and pupils collected their produce. They took it home to their families to eat at home and took some for their midday meals at school. The children loved to come early to school and admire the vegetables. The watermelons had been planted later than the rest, but the fruit slowly grew larger. Every day they watched their crops grow - they hardly left them for a moment, except at night.

'If we can sell our watermelons and our vegetables,' Piya said to the children, 'we'll keep chickens. I'll show you how to rear chickens. We can't do it yet because there's no fence round the vegetables. But as soon as the vegetables are all harvested, next term, we'll all have at least one chicken each.'

Piya had got seed from the Agricultural Station for his watermelons. The 'Charleston Grey' and 'Sugar Baby' varieties he had planted were ripening beautifully, repaying the care lavished on their cultivation, the preparation of the soil, the pruning of the flowers and the spraying of insecticides.

Phayorm particularly was overjoyed at the success of the project. She had maintained her close relationship and respect for Piya, even though Sombat now made it known to everybody that he was going to marry her. When the first watermelon was picked, Piya cut it in two and gave half to Siang to take home to his mother and sister, making both of them very happy.

It is usual that where there is affection, there will also be dislike. Some villagers and the children saw Piya as a lovable teacher. These people felt quite the opposite about Phisit. But there were others who disliked Piya. They did not show their feelings, but the consequences soon showed.

One morning, after New Year's day, which by chance happened to be the festival of *khunlarn* - the day on which the villagers celebrated the completion of the harvest - Piya had a nasty shock. The previous night a folk drama troupe, *mor lam,* had played in the village and Piya had returned home about ten o'clock. When he woke he found that many of the watermelons he had been waiting to pick for sale and for the kids to eat had been stolen. Piya thought it would be impossible to find out who had done it, just as it had been impossible to find out who had clouted Phisit over the head. He kept cool and broke the news to his pupils, looking quite his normal self.

The kids were very disappointed and wanted something done about it. Piya took the opportunity to give them a homily on stealing, on wickedness and virtue. They listened in silence, as old people listen to a sermon. 'Carn Khen came by and was upset when he heard the news. He spoke privately to Piya.

'Don't be discouraged, keep on battling. There's at least one person here who appreciates what you're doing.'

'What are you digging, Siang?' Duangdaw asked the young lad who was Piya's usual companion.

'I'm digging *cipome,* Khun Khru,' he said, squatting on the ground, digging with a small spade with a handle about a metre in length. 'They are good in the winter and great to eat when roasted.'

He dug down a span's length and found a creature, much like a grasshopper but brown in colour and somewhat bigger. He grabbed it and put it in a little creel, then began looking for a new hole. Duangdaw picked up the creel and had a look. *Cipome* were a crawling mass inside the creel.

'Oh, oh! You've got a lot. How long have you been digging?'

'Since school was over.'

'Are you digging them for Khun Piya, or are you going to eat them yourself?'

The yellow pick-up belonging to the Section Head came tearing from the direction of the new building, now nearly complete. As it came up to them, Khru Sawad, the Section Head's hatchet man, who usually acted as his driver, saw them and turned the wheel towards them.

'What are you doing, Khun Khru?' Khun Sawad greeted her in an ingratiating manner.

'I'm watching the boy dig up *cipome,'* she replied brusquely. 'Is the Section Head going, then?'

'Yes, we are going back now. Let's have a look, have you got many?' the Section Head called to Caw Siang.

The boy, looking frightened, handed him the creel and stood by silently.

'Are you selling them, Bak Siang?' Bak Siang happened to be a common way of addressing young boys. The Section Head did not know Siang by name.

'No, Sir, I'm just digging them to take home to my mother.'

'You! You can dig some more.' He turned to his chauffeur.

'Wad! Is there anything we can put these in?' Khru Sawad searched the vehicle and came up with an empty plastic bag. He took the creel from the Section Head and poured out the wriggling insects and handed back the creel with two baht to Siang.

'OK. Take the two baht, Bak Noi! That's more than enough.

'He drove off, uninterested in the looks of the boy and the young woman who stood staring after them, quivering with anger.

'Hey, what a smart uniform we have on today!' Caw Kart's bus screeched to a halt by Piya. 'Are you going to collect your pay?'

'The headmaster wants me to collect the salaries for him,' Piya replied, climbing into the empty back section.

Thit Phun, seated in front, said, 'What class are you, then? Stripes like this must mean many thousand a month,' he teased.

'It's not even many hundreds. Just enough to eat from day to day.' Piya had taken a dislike to this man from his first meeting and tried to avoid any conversation with him.

The 'two-rower' reached the *amphur* at 9:00 A.M. sharp, just in time for Piya to attend the regular end-of-month meeting. At the *amphur* office a crowd of government officials was milling around, all dressed in khaki uniforms. The shirts and trousers of some were quite distinctive in their unusual shades of khaki. The office of the Education Officer was strangely quiet. There were only the District Head, his assistant and a clerk. The office of the Section Head, however, was alive with people coming and going, drawing textbooks, writing materials, chalk. Others were working out the deductions from their salaries for the month just gone. Khun Sawad looked busy. He was responsible for the finances of the entire district. In any month he handled many hundreds of thousands of baht - the salaries, the pensions, orphans' funds, payments for medical expenses, scholarships and the funds of the Savings Co-operative.

On the board outside the Section Office was a notice detailing the scale of deductions. It said:

Scale of Payments and Deductions for the Month.

TBS	32.50 Bt.
Association	3.00 Bt.
New Year	20.00 Bt.
Teachers' Day	40.00 Bt.
Children's Day	15.00 Bt.
Nai Amphur's Farewell	40.00 Bt.

Piya read the notices pasted on the board, but could not understand many of them, particularly the list of salary deductions. He asked Headmaster Cantha, who was busily parcelling a set of books and a box of chalk, 'Oh, Headmaster, can you explain these deductions to me? Khru Sawad is insistent that each school have its accounts correct and ready for him. I'm afraid I'll waste his time.'

'Oh! It's Khru Piya. I didn't recognize you. Where's Headmaster 'Maw gone then, that he's not here?' Headmaster Cantha looked up from his boxes of chalk. Headmaster 'Maw was Headmaster Khammaw.

'My headmaster said he was too tired to come. He asked me to come instead.'

'That list doesn't mean that everyone has to have all those deductions,' Khun Cantha explained. 'That TBS, for instance, is the Teachers' Benevolent Society. Only the members need pay that. I think only Headmaster 'Maw is a member from your school. The Association is supposed to help improve our wages and conditions. Everyone has to be a member whether he likes it or not. There have been many who tried to get out of it, with no success. That twenty baht for New Year is for the celebrations put on last New Year. We had a stall at the Provincial Office which lost money. The *Amphur* asked us all to meet this by paying twenty baht each. The last headmasters' meeting agreed to this. It was the same with Teachers' Day and Children's Day - two districts joined together and the Section Head still complains that we're short many hundreds. The *Nai Amphur's* farewell - only those who attended have to pay that. I don't think anyone attended the dinner from your school. You don't have to worry about all this, Khun Sawad has all the accounts.'

'Thanks very much.' Piya was still not quite clear about it all.

'What about people like me? What do I have to pay? I'm not yet a member of anything.'

'Oh! What you will have to pay for certain is the Association fee, the charge for New Year, Teachers' Day and Children's Day,' Headmaster Cantha said, putting the last knot in the string around his parcel.

'Every time I come to the *amphur* I've got to carry back one thing or another - it's always many kilos. The exercise books and texts are bad enough; sometimes there's chalk on top of it. Then there's all the material sent out by various departments and ministries. They seem to compete with each other in sending us this stuff, they must think we have nothing better to do than read it all. Sometimes I feel like bundling it all together and selling it off by the kilo as wrapping paper.'

'What's the chalk like this time?' Piya asked of the issue he'd just taken. 'The stuff we're using is as hard as rock. It can't write, but it's first-class for breaking. I don't know whether it's a rip-off by the buyer or the factory.'

'It's always like that. What can you expect of things handed out free?' Headmaster Cantha complained.

Walking slowly up the steps to the verandah of the District Office came a fat man with a crew cut and gold teeth. He was carrying a bundle of small notebooks. He greeted Khru Cantha.

'Hasn't Khru jai Khammaw come today?'

'This is Khru Piya who's come in his place,' he replied, pointing.

'Is that right? Did he say anything?'

Piya looked closely at the man's face. 'He asked me to do all kinds of things. Is there something you wanted?' he asked abruptly.

'It's about Khru Phisit's money.' The man's face took on an innocent expression. 'I'd asked the Section Head to deduct it from his salary, but now the Governor's office has forbidden deductions from teachers' salaries. I want you to pay me from Khru Phisit's salary. We agreed on this earlier.'

'But Khru Phisit hasn't said anything to me. I think you should arrange this with him.' Piya was not having anything to do with it. 'How much is it?'

'It's quite a bit. The payments on the motorcycle, the radio, plus the interest, it's about a thousand.'

'I can't pay that without authority from Khru Phisit,' Piya said, and turned towards the entrance of the meeting hall.

The monthly meeting of teachers was attended by headmasters or their representatives, so that the number of those attending was equal to the number of schools in the district. The fat figure of the Section Head walked into the hall and sat down with Khun Sawad, known to all present as his hatchet man. The buzz of conversation faded away. The meeting began with the announcement of new regulations and a statement of policy as it affected the country as a whole, the province and the district.

The Section Head read the statement and then went on to the details of monthly deductions from the teachers' salaries. He listed them and explained their necessity. Although the Governor's office had forbidden deductions, the Section had the right to make them. This Khun Sawad announced boldly with a voice conveying absolute conviction.

Piya looked as if he was going to raise his hand to ask a question, but Headmaster Cantha poked him in the ribs and whispered to him to keep quiet. Piya restrained himself.

When the Section Officers were done, the Education Head spoke to the gathering on 'Adult Education' - a subject in which the teachers present showed very little interest. The District Health Officer had his turn next and spoke on the dangers of the liver fluke and how it could be avoided. The Agricultural Officer at the Development Office spoke briefly on the formation of farmers' groups. The District Officer closed the meeting with an exhortation to those present to dedicate their efforts to the well-being of the nation; although they had a short wait before this took place while he returned from a visit to a nearby village. While they were waiting, an insurance agent took the opportunity to distribute leaflets to the gathering advertising various kinds of insurance which his company thought the teachers might need.

The *Nai Amphur* began speaking at 11:30 and went on till 12:15, when they broke up for lunch. The Section Head announced that they would meet again that afternoon at 2:00 as the Provincial Director of Education wanted an assessment made of the standard of Primary Education. Salaries would be paid after this and all the rural schoolteachers would be able to pay their debts as was expected of them.

In fact, Khru Sawad and an assistant began paying salaries during the lunch break as they were concerned they might otherwise run out of time. Piya decided to do without lunch and joined the queue to be paid. It appeared that their salaries this month were to be 'docked' as Khun Phisit had spent more than he earned. At the provincial level they had deducted some hundreds of baht from his salary of about a thousand as repayment of an emergency loan he had taken from the Teachers' Co-operative. This deduction had been a condition of the loan. There was, in addition, his club bill in Ubon and his credit purchases from the co-operative. He had all the *amphur* deductions on top of that. These added up to more than his pay. It was his colleagues who would have to take the consequences. Salaries were paid out according to the school and the total deductions were made from the total amount paid to the teachers of any one school. If one of them had overspent they were all 'docked' to make up for it - and there was little they could do about it.

Piya knew nothing of all this. When he drew the money and worked out how much each should get, he realized that Phisit had eaten into everybody else's, but he did not know what could be done about it except to go back to the village and extract payment from the culprit at some later date.

He took the money and hurried to get himself a bowl of noodles in the restaurant opposite the District Office. The noodle shop also served other kinds of food and was full of teachers come to collect their salaries. The owner of the shop was a Vietnamese who had begun by only serving noodles, but when he had seen that people enjoyed eating *larp* and other local dishes he had set himself up to make *larp, koi* and meat soup, greatly increasing his trade. His food was much appreciated. It is Thai custom that any shop selling food must also sell liquor, and so it was here.

The headmasters who had just been paid ordered bottles of liquor with their food, even though it was midday and very warm. With their craving satisfied, also went their sense of responsibility and sense of time. Many of them did not make the afternoon meeting.

'Aren't you coming to the afternoon's meeting, Headmaster Cantha?' asked Piya, when he saw that it was almost time.

'No, I don't think I'll go.' He sat, fat in his uniform with two stripes, his face red. 'There won't be anything much. That Supervisory Unit bunch is always the same. A bit of airy-fairy nonsense, nothing of any use. Are you going?'

'Yes, I thought I'd go and listen. They are talking about school standards, aren't they?' He got up and left.

'Khun Khru! Just a moment.' It was Khru Phisit's creditor. 'What about Khru Phisit's money?'

'Khru Phisit is already overdrawn, there's no money for anything Thaw kay. You'd better go talk to him yourself.' He walked to the meeting hall for the afternoon's session.

After the meeting the senior headmasters and others who liked to keep the company of their superiors gathered in the Thai Lert Rot restaurant, the best in the *amphur*. Compared with other border districts of the same level, this restaurant was considered very good, certainly good enough for the Governor to have lunch there when he visited. It had a reputation for Chinese-style Thai food, Chinese food made in Thai fashion, which could be had in restaurants throughout the country. In the provinces this type of food is considered superior; local food such as *larp, koi,* barbecued chicken or *som tam* is considered fit only for villagers. The regular customers of Thai Lert Rot were mostly government officials and teachers. Occasionally there would be a travelling salesman, a forestry inspection unit, or a mining team joining them. The real regulars were the local district government officials and the police. The teachers and education officials would appear on special occasions, such as payday at the end of the month, or some celebration.

Today there was a lot to celebrate. Three teachers had been awarded special middle school teachers' diplomas. Up to about 1958 whoever achieved this diploma was appointed directly to the Third Class of the government teaching service. It had great prestige. It still had enough prestige to be the occasion for a celebration. Another three had been appointed to headmasterships. All this called for special celebration. The unfortunate six were hosts. Those invited were the Section Head, the District Education Head, the *Nai Amphur,* Khun Sawad, and six other teachers from the administration branch, and the presiding heads of groups of schools. As for others who wished to join in the merrymaking, the organizers, having sympathy for the six hosts, charged them forty baht cash to cover the cost of the meal. The six unfortunates would be responsible for covering the rest of the bill. Many of the headmasters, not specifically invited, and their representatives, stayed over to join in the fun - including Headmaster Cantha from Barn Phak I Hin. He persuaded Piya to stay for the party too. Piya, who had to wait for the headmaster to get a lift back home, was forced into joining him in sponsoring one of the celebrating teachers.

Acarn Wichai, the Education Department Supervising Officer from the provincial headquarters, finished his talk on standards for primary schools and not a single question followed. The monthly meeting came to an end and the headmasters trooped out to the Thai Lert Rot where some of their number were 'keeping the engine warm'. In the lingo of the provincial teachers 'keeping the engine warm' meant many *baen.*

Piya and Khru jai Cantha got to the restaurant at about four o'clock. The Section Head, the District Education Head, the *Nai Amphur* and his underlings arrived about fifteen minutes later. In these border districts it was not possible to predict when work would cease in the government offices. Some days they would work till dusk. Usually, they stopped in the early afternoon, as soon as there were no more members of the public with jobs to be done. On Fridays they stopped work at noon, for some officials lived in other districts and they had to get home. In this district they called Friday 'little Saturday' for it was unofficially a half day.

Everyone, dressed in uniform, was seated round a long table which stretched almost out of the restaurant. Thaw kay Yun, who had learned how to cook when he was just a lad in China, smiled broadly, showing his gold teeth. He would take at least two thousand baht today.

The *Nai Amphur* was, by custom, seated at the head of the table, flanked by the Section Head. Next to him sat

Khun Sawad. Opposite the *Nai Amphur* sat Acarn Wichai, the Supervisory Officer of the Province, an unexpected guest. One who never missed an occasion of this kind was Acarn Ekachai, the only graduate teacher in the district. There were three women in the party, from the Education Section. One of them, still unmarried and pretty, sat opposite the *Nai Amphur,* pouring his whisky and mixing it with soda.

The eating went on apace. The food ordered was all Chinese, and it vanished in the twinkling of an eye as the headmasters gobbled it up - whether from hunger or because it was particularly delicious was impossible to tell. When all the dishes were done, there was food left only in front of the *Nai Amphur*. Piya sat next to Headmaster Cantha and had taken a few mouthfuls of food. He felt he should not compete in the scramble with the headmasters - after all, he'd had experience as a temple boy. He sat and observed them all and thought to himself, 'Is this what they mean by "eating like rural teachers"? It's shameful that they should put on an act like this for those from other departments to see and despise us.'

Khun Sawad, who had taken over the arrangements and ordered the food, now became Master of Ceremonies. He stood up and explained to everybody the reasons for the celebration. He called on each of the unfortunate hosts to stand up and be applauded. Then he turned to the *Nai Amphur* and respectfully and eloquently called on him to address the gathering. Part of his eloquent invitation went, 'We teachers must be united, must make sacrifices, must patiently bear our hardships, and be a shining example to our pupils and our fellow citizens.'

When the *Nai Amphur* had spoken, the Master of Ceremonies invited each of the distinguished guests to speak, each in order of importance - the Section Head, the District Education Officer, the Supervisor, the senior teacher of the Non Du commune, of Dong Sawan, of Phak I Hin, then rapidly through the eight groups of schools. Twelve of them spoke, and then it was the turn of the six who were being honoured with the dinner - altogether eighteen of the forty-two who were at the dinner spoke; a good example of a teachers' dinner.

As it grew dark, the headmasters who lived in other areas began leaving for home; some on motorbikes, some by 'two-rowers'. Those who lived far away would spend the night here at the *amphur*. There was too much chance of being robbed of their salaries travelling at night.

As the crowd dispersed, Piya took the opportunity to talk to the Section Head about the school building. He spoke very respectfully, 'Section Head, Sir! I asked the contractor for our school building about a toilet for the school. He says it depends on you.'

'It all depends on the agreement. I can't do anything to contravene it.' He placed his right hand eloquently over the front of his shirt.

'But in the plan there doesn't seem to be any toilet at all. If he builds it now, before the building's over, I am sure he won't lose any money. Please speak to him, Sir,' he pleaded.

'You like to make complications, don't you?' The Section Head raised his voice. 'Your school has been there many years, many 'lives', without a toilet. Now you've got a new building. If you want a toilet, build it yourself.'

Piya's face froze. He regretted waiting till the *Nai Amphur* had left. If he had been there, perhaps they would have heard the *Nai Amphur's* opinion. When he saw there was nothing to be gained talking to the Section Head, he sought out Khru jai Cantha and asked when he was going home.

Khru jai Cantha looked tense and his breath stank. He had changed his mind and decided to stay the night.

'It'll be better if we go back tomorrow morning. If anything happens on the way back, it'll be trouble. Last month there was a hold-up and they robbed the headmaster of Khemarat of his salary. And the month before, there at Sri Muang Mai, the headmaster was robbed and brutally murdered. Let's play it safe.'

'It's up to you, Headmaster.'

Piya was baffled. Though he wanted to return home, there was no way he could. There was no regular bus nor even a 'two-rower'. There was only one trip a day into his village - Caw Kart's 'two-rower' which left the *amphur* at three o'clock each afternoon.

'But where are we going to stay?'

'Oi! There are lots of places. You can sleep at someone's house,' he said generously, 'or there's the hotel'.

The only hotel at the district centre was a large wooden two-storey building with numerous rooms. On the ground floor was the restaurant and shop run by the owner. The guests' rooms were upstairs, each with its own bathroom. Opposite the hotel was the bus stop for buses going to Ubon - this the populace called *khiw rot,* 'the bus queue'. Piya and the headmaster shared a room.

Piya bathed and put on his old clothes - he had not come prepared to spend the night. He came downstairs and walked out of the hotel, strolling in front of it, finding nothing better to do. He saw Acarn Wichai talking to two other young teachers in Thai Lert Rot and greeted him.

'Where are you staying, Acarn?'

'The hotel,' he said, pointing to where Piya had come from. 'I put my things away this afternoon. Sit down.'

Piya sat down and one of the other young teachers ordered another glass for him. Chatting to Acarn Wichai he learned that 'supervision' was an educational activity, the duty of the Supervisory Unit under the jurisdiction of the Ministry of Education, just as 'administration' was the business of the Administrative Unit of the province, with the Section Head and the Provincial Administrative Head in charge.

'It's just too much,' Acarn Wichai complained, about the supervisory work in general. 'There are over a thousand schools and we have only ten officers. There's no way we can visit all the schools - and our annual budget is tiny.'

Piya, however, did not understand why they needed an annual budget, why they had to visit schools and what they did when they did visit. He had some vague ideas about it, nevertheless. He had heard the headmaster talk about the Supervisory Unit and when he was a student at the Training College, they had lectures on the Unit. But he had never really understood what they did. He learned now from Acarn Wichai that they were supposed to help teachers with their teaching, help them in educational matters, but Wichai did not explain what this help might be. Ever keen to learn, Piya invited the other to visit the school at Barn Norng Ma Vor. The other promptly agreed. He could visit what school he pleased, when he pleased, as long as it was convenient.

Piya went back to the hotel at 7:00 P.M. sharp, and went to his room. The door was closed and bolted from the inside. He knocked and a voice answered, 'Is that Piya? Go down and get yourself an iced coffee or something. I've got some important business.'

Piya recognized Headmaster Cantha's voice and had a good guess as to what his business was. He went down and ordered himself a drink as he had been told. Half an hour or so later the headmaster came down the stairs grinning broadly. With him was a young girl whose appearance branded her unmistakably as of only provincial standard. They joined Piya at his table.

'Well, are you interested?' The headmaster was very pleased with himself and nodded his head at Piya in encouragement. The girl just sat smiling knowingly. 'If you'd like to chat with little sister here, I'll go take a stroll.'

'No, I don't think I will,' he refused, smiling in embarrassment. 'I'd better get to sleep, I'm terribly tired.'

He did not sleep well that night. There were creaks and rattles from the adjoining rooms nearly all night. He had the money, his salary and that of the other teachers, in the pillow case and his thoughts kept returning to the school, his hut, which he had left without anyone to watch it. And he could not keep his thoughts away from Duangdaw, despite the fact that he had vowed to himself he would take no interest in any woman until he was twenty-five years old. He saw in his mind the faces of the two girls - Phayorm, pretty and demure, but living in poverty and hardship, and Duangdaw, with a different kind of beauty, a different charm and a much higher social position. He also saw the face of Caw Siang, the little lad with trustworthy eyes, and then 'Carn Khen, a man completely dependable. As he thought of these, his friends, or more, their images slowly faded from his mind and he fell into a sleep about one o'clock in the morning.

CHAPTER 18

Piya left the next morning with Headmaster Cantha and Acarn Wichai, who had come on his motorcycle from Ubon. The headmaster had invited Wichai to visit his school in Barn Phak I Hin and he asked Piya to stay for lunch.

'I'd better get back as soon as possible. The headmaster must be worried. This is the first time he's asked me to collect the salaries. He must be standing staring down the road by now.' He made his excuses and set out on foot from Barn Phak I Hin, leaving Acarn Wichai to follow.

When he got to the school it was about noon and Duangdaw was by herself in charge of the children of all four classes. They were merrily playing as they pleased. The young woman had not known what to do with the lot of them and had let them out to keep themselves amused.

'The headmaster and Khru Phisit went off to Phor jai Phan's field at ten o'clock,' she said. 'What happened last night? Where did you sleep?' 'At the *amphur*, with Khru Cantha.' Piya had a worried expression on his face.

'What did they go to Phor jai Phan's field for?'

'The kids said he's emptying his fish pond - there must be a party as usual. Khru Phisit said he'd come and pick me up at the lunch break to go and eat there.' She looked at her wrist watch. 'It's about noon now. You'll come along won't you?'

'What's going on - we all go to eat and drink and leave the school to look after itself?' He sounded quite disgusted.

'Goodness, Khun Piya!' she remonstrated. 'We're only going during the interval - not the whole day. Phor jai Phan told me yesterday to ask you along. It's not far, we can walk.'

Just then Phisit arrived and sounded the horn of his motorcycle. He sat astride his bike as if quite uninterested in Piya's return. Piya, furious, stalked off towards his hut, saying curtly, 'Go on, Khun Duangdaw, you don't need to wait for me.'

She stared after him, not understanding what that was all about. Then decided to sit on Phisit's pillion - but she was quite upset.

At Phor jai Phan's fish pond about twenty people were busy around a fire, barbecuing and cooking fish. Some were sorting out fish, others catching fish in the pond, which was almost a *ngarn* in extent. The fish were mostly catfish and serpent head; also *pla mor* (a climbing fish), but these were small in size as they were only a year old.

The headmaster sat on a mat spread under a combretum tree near the field hut, with Phor jai Phan and Phu jai Lua. In front of them was a large pot of liquor and a number of aluminium bowls.

'Has Piya come back from the *amphur?*' was the headmaster's greeting to Duangdaw.

'He's back. He says all our school salaries have been docked. I don't know what I had to pay for.' She sounded as if she did not know what it meant.

'Eh? Who's gone and got our salaries docked? There are just four of us.' He looked towards Phisit who had parked his motorbike under another combretum tree and was walking towards them. 'I expect Phisit has fouled things up again.'

They had a picnic lunch there, in Phor jai Phan's field, and Duangdaw hurried back to the school. The headmaster asked Phor jai Phan's nephew to take her on his old motorbike and she got back at 1:00 P.M. sharp.

'You go ahead,' he had said. 'Phisit and Uncle will follow shortly.' Duangdaw knew well that neither of them would see the school again that day. She had seen many of the gambling school sitting down to eat and thought to herself there would be no stopping them till night fell. 'Is something wrong with your bike, Khun Khru? You didn't bring it to school today,' Phor jai Phan's nephew asked Duangdaw. The young man had left school after MS4 - the eleventh year of school - and had not found a job yet.

'Nothing's wrong, I just left it at home this morning and came in with the headmaster.' She continued, 'What are you doing these days, Somsak?'

'Nothing at all. I want to sit for the Teachers' Training College again next year. This year they let the *tambon* council make the choice and they played their favourites as usual.' The young man, disappointed in his desire to study for the Teachers' Diploma, sounded bitter.

'If you've got time to spare, come along and help with the preparations for the school opening.'

'I'll be glad to. If there's anything I can do, please let me know, Khun Khru.' Somsak sounded pleased at the idea.

Acarn Wichai, who worked in the field of Adult Education, was the first supervisor to visit the school at Barn Norng Ma Vor. Headmaster Cantha brought him there at two o'clock that afternoon.

'Are there just the two of you?' the young visitor asked Piya and Duangdaw.

'Four. One for each class. But the headmaster and another schoolmaster have gone out on official business.'

They settled down to a chat roaming over many topics concerned with education - what was happening at provincial level, who was being transferred and when. They talked about the new projects of the Ministry of Education, their implementation in their own province, and were pessimistic about the future of rural education. Finally, they got on to the attempt to encourage the reading of newspapers in the villages. This was a project of the Adult Education Section which was concerned about the failure of many adults in the villages to maintain their literacy.

'This project must be a co-operative one between the public and the government. If the public wants newspapers to read then they must get together and build a hall or some suitable place to be used as a reading room. They can then apply for a vote to supply two newspapers a day, which the villagers must look after and make the best use of they can,' Acarn Wichai explained to Piya and Duangdaw.

'You mean they've got to build the reading room before anything else?' Piya asked, interested.

'That's right. They've got to build a hall first.' Wichai continued, 'But it doesn't have to be a new hall. They can either repair or extend a hall they already have - nearly every village has a public hall. It's got to conform to the standards laid down by the Adult Education Section: it must be large enough, it must have provision to store the newspapers and to put them out for reading, it must be in a central position, and it must have a committee responsible for its upkeep.'

'Isn't that interesting?' said Duangdaw, looking at Piya. She turned to the visitor, 'And how will they send us the papers, and who chooses which newspapers we'll get?'

'Oh, that depends on you. You get the villagers to choose what they want. You can choose any newspapers you like. You arrange with the agent at the *amphur* to send them. At the end of the month he takes the receipt to the District Education Office and gets his money.' Acarn Wichai mentally considered the road into the village.

'You've got a bus coming in every day, haven't you?'

'Yes, it makes the trip every day. It's a local man. He goes to the *amphur* in the morning and comes back in the afternoon.

'Fine. That makes it very convenient.' Wichai cultivated their enthusiasm. 'If you think it's possible, explain to the villagers. If you like I can come and talk to them too. When you've got the place ready let me know. I'll support it for this financial year. It will be a boon to your fellow villagers.'

When Wichai had left, Piya felt he had acquired responsibility for yet another project. He was already committed to the raising of chickens at the school when his vegetables were all harvested. His tree planting endeavours were beginning to show a result. The mango and the tamarind trees which the children and he had so laboriously planted, digging ditches and patiently preparing the soil, were growing larger day by day and had already begun to branch. Each tree had a group of children in charge of it. They competed with each other in watering the trees and putting on fertiliser. They were so keen, Piya sometimes had to stop them overdoing the fertiliser. It was a source of great satisfaction to them, for they could clearly see the fruit of their labours.

Meanwhile, Piya and Duangdaw, who seemed to do things together much more often these days, had persuaded Lung 'Carn Kern, Sia Mangkorn's sub-contractor, to build a latrine for the school. This was more convenient sanitation than the pit latrine the school already had. The old one lay some way from the school and not many people used it. Most of the children were a bit frightened of walking out into the bush. This structure was the product of Piya's endeavours. He had built it not long after he moved to Barn Norng Ma Vor. It would not be wrong to say he had built it largely for his own use.

The chicken-rearing project began with the construction of a small coop near the school and his hut. He told the headmaster this would be part of the regular activities of his class, Primary 4. When the coop was ready he asked his pupils to each get a chicken from around the village, from family, neighbours, or friends. He added to these by buying hens and chickens, using the money made through the sale of their vegetables and watermelons. He had enough money to buy two hens and twenty medium-sized chickens, each about the size of a pigeon. The chickens fed around the school compound and were also hand fed morning and evening. He gave them bran and chaff and vegetable peelings. Leaving chickens free to feed was common village practice in the period after the harvest. The farmers led their chickens out on their rice fields to feed on fallen grains of rice and caterpillars and other insects which abounded there. Piya was much taken with this practice and decided to give it a try.

It was not too many weeks before the children became caught up in this new activity, and the chickens thrived on their enthusiasm, getting bigger daily. The males began putting on bushy tail feathers and their red combs grew bigger. Some began crowing. The faces of the hens too seemed to grow red and their feathers glossy in the bracing climate and with the abundance of food. They thrived. The children and the teacher never ceased to delight in gazing at all this, the visible outcome of their efforts in planting watermelons in the months gone by.

Duangdaw had begun teaching her class, Primary 1, more and more in the manner of Piya, getting the children to learn by engaging themselves in various tasks. She paid more attention to her pupils as individuals. She became stricter with those who were weak in their work and fostered the brighter children. She now went home to Ubon not more than once a month and since the New Year - it was now mid-February - she had not been home once.

On Saturdays and Sundays Piya and Duangdaw usually went to the school to watch the progress of the building, which was now nearly complete. They encouraged the workmen, who were mostly villagers from Barn Norng Ma Vor, to pay attention to detail, now to this, now to that aspect of the building; the tables, the chairs, the bookshelves and the shelves for equipment. In their spare time they also prepared teaching aids, prepared maps and charts, made models and puppets. They were limited only by the limits of Piya's skill. They sometimes consulted 'Carn Khen and sometimes enlisted his aid. Duangdaw, who had at first not shown much interest in teaching or working around the school, began to derive more satisfaction from all this and began to enjoy it very much.

Acarn Ekachai visited the village occasionally and then was not seen for days. He realized that Duangdaw had no interest in developing their friendship beyond its present level. As for Phisit, since becoming ensnared in debt he had cut down on his high living, but satisfied his craving for the good life at the expense of village society. Wherever there was an alms-giving or any festivity which involved food and strong drink he was always there, ever ready to help the hosts with their celebrations. His constant companion in this activity was Headmaster Khammaw, who was addicted to bootleg liquor, cards and the local game of *boke*.

The villagers soon observed that though the school was supposed to have four teachers, only two of them, Piya and Duangdaw, took their job seriously. The two others were often away from the school, but no one said anything. Such behaviour was very common among village schoolteachers in the rural areas distant from the district centres. Whenever they saw a conscientious and hard-working teacher, everyone would comment, 'Goodness, how diligent you are, Khun Khru!'

Many thought Piya and Duangdaw were 'fans',[1] but one thing confused some. This was the close relationship between Piya and Phayorm's family. Piya acted as if he had joined this family of mother and two children. He brought them rice and presents, sometimes for the mother, sometimes for the children. They in turn did him favours of the kind villagers often did for each other, sending him mushrooms, bamboo shoots, frogs, fish, tubers and other foods of forest villagers, which Caw Siang took to him. Sometimes Phayorm herself took him the gifts, but

---

1 Lovers, or betrothed; a term current throughout the country.

whenever she did go she made sure to have a friend go along with her.

It was still cold, early in February, and one day after school Piya and Duangdaw were watching the children flying kites in the school playground. Not only was it colder than usual this year, but the wind was blowing later. Usually the cold wind died down towards the end of December; occasionally it was in late or mid-January. But this year it was February and the wind was still strong enough for flying kites.

The villagers of Barn Norng Ma Vor fly kites in the winter. Their kites are special in that they carry music-making instruments on their heads. These are known as *sanu* and shaped like a bow, *thanu,* whence their name probably came. The 'string' of the bow is made of the centre rib of the sugarpalm leaf or of the coconut, or sometimes of a thick strip of rattan. The bow is tied to the top of the kite. When the kite gets up in the air the wind vibrates the string of the *sanu* creating a rising and falling note, pleasing to listen to.

Caw Siang, Caw Khiaw and company were competing with each other flying their kites in the playground. The competition consisted in comparing the height attained by each kite - each one starting off with the same length of string. Caw Khiaw's kite had not only flown higher than everyone else's, it had also caught a favourable wind and the *sanu* was giving off a plaintive lullaby.

'Isn't it a lovely sound?' Duangdaw had her head back, staring into the sky. 'They fly this kind of kite in Ubon too, and the *farang* who rent our houses say the noise is deafening. I can't understand how they could think that.'

'Our experiences are not the same. What's pleasing to the ear, what's tasty, what's good, what's beautiful, all these must be different for different nationalities. I am afraid that they've now brought their planes, their jets, to disturb the people of Ubon. In five or six years we'll think those noises are more pleasing than the sounds of the sanu.' Piya's gaze was directed far into the sky.

'Khun Piya,' she said, changing the subject, 'there's something I want to do, but I don't know how to go about it. I'd like to consult someone with experience.'

'And who's that?' said Piya, still gazing into the sky.

'Khun Piya, of course!' She laughed softly. 'Don't think I'm being flattering. I'm sure you can help me decide.'

'Is it something to do with you?'

'You could say it's something to do with me, but it's really to do with all of us.' Duangdaw went on without pausing. 'I'd like to set up a reading room in the village, you know, like the Supervisory Officer said that day. What do you think of it?'

'I think we should talk to the headman and some of the other elders. I think you could talk to the villagers, Khun Aew, better than I could.' He used the name 'Aew' as he had agreed he would, but it was not often he did so. It was only on occasions when he felt it was right, special in some way.

'I'll try, but you must help me, Khun Piya.'

Within ten days the job of building a reading room had begun, after Duangdaw had obtained the agreement of the headman and the villagers, at a public meeting, to use the hall in the middle of the village.

It was usual for a village to have a central hall, a public place, the common property of the village, serving a variety of purposes. It was an overnight resting place for travellers and the site for public meetings. This hall was about six metres square in area and raised about a metre off the ground. It had no walls and Duangdaw persuaded the villagers to put up walls on three sides. On the fourth side they used a row of evenly-spaced poles to construct a balustrade. They also made benches lined with bamboo slats to sit on, a cupboard to store the newspapers, shelves for books, and stands for placing newspapers on. Phor jai Phan and Somsak, the young unemployed youth, took charge of all the work.

When the work was done, Piya and Duangdaw wrote to Acarn Wichai asking him to come and have a look, to see if the facilities would reach the standards necessary for an Education Department grant. The Supervisor came to examine the work as soon as he got their letter.

'I think everything is up to standard, but now we've got to follow government procedure. We've first got to send in a request to the *amphur*. The *amphur* collects these from many villagers and forwards them to the *changwat*. The *changwat* considers which requests should be approved and then sends them up to the Adult Education Section. It will be some time before our budget is approved. I'll try to make this one special. I'll see if I can get our office to advance the money so that we can pay it back later when the vote comes through. I heard they are coming soon from the *changwat* to open the new school building; we should seize the opportunity and suggest the Governor unveil the board for the newspaper reading room at the same time.'

From then on the villagers of Barn Norng Ma Vor had two newspapers a day. At the meeting of villagers Duangdaw announced that Somsak would be in charge of the reading room, would take care of the newspapers, keep the accounts, receive donations of books and magazines, keep a tally of the daily use of the room - in fact, take care of anything that needed looking after. The newspapers ordered from the agent were chosen by Duangdaw and Piya.

Duangdaw chose *Thai Rath* and Piya, *Siam Rath*.[2] In addition to these, Duangdaw brought in journals and magazines she had bought in Ubon and which she had finished reading. Piya wrote to his colleagues and teachers in Bangkok asking for old books and magazines, and many of them obliged. The reading room began to look more and more like a library within just a few weeks.

As Duangdaw and Piya worked at their various tasks, acting in a way that rural teachers were ideally expected to, they seemed to have an effect on the headmaster and Phisit as well. Their behaviour began to change and they began taking more interest in the school. Phisit's philanderings did not cease, but became less frequent, as did his drinking. His attendance at school was much better, he was now usually there from the time school started till closing time.

The day of the official opening of the school drew closer. The District Section Head and his side-kick, his hatchet man Khun Sawad, came to inspect the school and ordered the headmaster to attend to a number of things in time for the big day.

---

[2] The former, the leading popular daily, the latter, the serious, national newspaper associated with the statesman and scholar, Kukrit Pramoj.

'We're going to invite the Governor to perform the ceremony. If he comes for the opening it'll certainly be a big event. Everybody who's anybody will want to come along too. There must be no problem about the arrangements or about the cleanliness of the building. As for the food, I think I'll get a woman from the *amphur* to come and do the cooking. I'd like the pupils and the villagers to put on some good entertainment, as many items as possible. The headmaster and the teachers will be in charge of that.'

The 22nd March was fixed as the day for the celebration. The pupils would all have finished their exams by then. Headmaster Khammaw and the other teachers worked hard. They cleaned up the school grounds, swept up the dead leaves and branches, dug out the stumps of dead trees, planted flowering plants, built a temporary shed for the ceremony, rehearsed their pupils, and wrote up a number of boards, including a list of the names of all who had made contributions and one extolling the generosity of Sia Mangkorn, the contractor, who had donated a 400-gallon tank for drinking water for the pupils, tables and chairs for the teachers and a cupboard for storing books and papers. All these were the results of Duangdaw's pleadings with Lung 'Carn Kern and Sia Mangkorn himself. After all, the Sia was a frequent visitor to the village, often spending the night at Lung 'Carn Kern's.

Piya worked at having the building and grounds in order and Duangdaw at the performance to be given by the school children. Phisit, in quite unaccustomed fashion, helped both of them, and the preparations went along nicely, according to plan.

One day, about three weeks before the opening, Headman Lua summoned a meeting of villagers to hear the Section Head and one of the Assistant District Officers, who had arrived in the village without warning.

'I hear from Phu jai Lua that the village is to celebrate *Maha Chart* on the twelfth night of the waxing moon - very near the date of the school function,' the Assistant District Officer said to the meeting. 'I would like to have these two celebrations on the same day and make one big occasion of it. We'll then be able to show all the important guests from the *changwat* our sense of togetherness and also give them a glimpse of the traditional customs of this area. Do you think this will be possible?'

Lung 'Carn Kern spoke out before anyone else could express an opinion.

'I agree with the *Palat Amphur*. Let us all do our best to help him in this.'

When Lung 'Carn Kern expressed an opinion, it was for the villagers to follow. 'Agreed! We'll put back the *Maha Chart* four days to the first night of the waning moon. Let everyone know,' Headman Lua announced to the assembled villagers. 'I ask a favour of you all, my brothers and sisters. Let this celebration be as impressive as we can make it.'

The Section Head added, 'Whoever among you in Barn Norng Ma Vor or in Tambon Phak I Hin is skilled in making fireworks and in playing the *seng* drum, I ask him to do his best for the occasion. I'd particularly like to have the *seng* drum exhibited - I know we can do it. The *Nai Amphur* specially mentioned it, as His Excellency the Governor is very interested in local customs.'

'But I thought the playing of the *seng* drum was held in the sixth month during the rocket-firing festival.' Piya had jumped up and spoken without any warning. 'I thought the *Maha Chart* has only the procession of the Lord Vessantara and the procession with the chapters of the *Maha Chart*. That's all.'

'That doesn't matter.' The *Palat Amphur* supported the Section Head. 'I've never seen the *seng* drum since I was transferred here. I'm sure Phu jai Lua will arrange it.'

'Perhaps we can do it, but the *seng* drum hasn't been played in these parts for a long time. The experts no longer stay home, they go off to Bangkok or I don't know where. All the old customs are disappearing.' He turned to the meeting. 'That's it! The Vessantara celebration, the *Maha Chart* this year will be held on the first night of the waning moon to coincide with the opening of the new school. And we'll have the *seng* drum. I ask all of you to help, for the honour of the village.'

Piya stopped off at the headmaster's house on his way home. Duangdaw had not gone to bed and he stayed a while talking to her on the verandah.

'What was the meeting about?' she asked.

'The celebration for the new school.' He went on to relate to her what had happened. He concluded, 'This has now become the business of the whole village. It's going to cost quite a bit, but we Thai are like that - whatever the occasion we like a lot of ritual, as big a celebration as possible. We can't bear to cut anything out.'

'What's this *seng* drum?' Duangdaw asked. 'I've heard them talk about it, but I've never seen it.'

'I haven't seen it either,' the young man admitted. 'I only know it's an old custom of Isarn. *Seng klong* is to compete at beating the drum - *seng* means 'to compete'. But how they compete we'll have to wait and see.'

'It must be fun to watch. But this kind of thing is for the children. None of us are really interested.'

The Section Head's pick-up drew up in front of the house and Piya, knowing who it was, hurriedly said goodbye to Duangdaw.

'Aw! Are you going already?' Khun Sawad, the Section Head's strong-arm man said, mockingly. 'Stay a while, Khru.'

'I don't think so. I've got to get up early tomorrow morning. Please excuse me, Sir,' he said to the Section Head, raising his hands in greeting. The Section Head came up the steps with Headmasters Khammaw and Cantha and Khun Sawad. In the rear followed Phisit.

When he got home, Piya walked over to have a look at the chicken coop - counting his chickens, making sure they were all there. He was constantly expecting some loafer or other to raid the coop for a snack to accompany a drinking party. And so it had happened. As he flashed the torch into the coop he realized at once he had been robbed. He counted his birds and found three had disappeared. He had no doubt they had been stolen, but he did not know what he could do about it except go to bed and sleep.

Early next morning he told his pupils in Primary 4 that their chickens had been stolen.

'Perhaps they weren't stolen, perhaps a snake, a dog or a jackal got them.' He tried to give them a better view of the world.

'It's a shame,' said one lad with a sorrowful look on his face, 'my "Ai Mon" was just beginning to grow a comb.'

'Don't be sad, Bunmi. I'll buy a chicken to replace your Ai Mon - also Sompong's and Mali's,' Piya consoled the kids. 'If someone has really stolen the chickens, they will surely suffer for it.'

Later that same morning, in the forest behind the school, the gambling school was settling down to a game of *boke*. Thit Phun was the banker as usual - today Mor Sombat had joined the group.

'Bad luck today. I'm having fives against me all morning.' Thit Phun laughed raucously.

'Enough!' The noise from the circle got louder. 'You took the teacher's chickens, you didn't even select the bigger ones.'

'They're not the teacher's!' Thit Phun opened up the *boke*. 'They're mine! All cooked and ready to eat!'

CHAPTER 19

Though Headmaster Khammaw was not usually very enthusiastic about his work, about his teaching or the progress of his students, he was seized with great anxiety when he heard that his superiors, particularly the Governor and the Provincial Director of Education, were to visit the school. This resulted in his ordering his teachers and the pupils to have everything arranged in a manner he thought would please the important visitors. His understanding of what was necessary was to have everything in place, everything clean, everything according to the rules. The teachers were to have their uniforms in spotless condition, every detail according to the regulations. He worried about Phisit and Duangdaw - for these two did not like wearing uniforms at all. They too, however, conformed with the headmaster's wishes.

Phisit had a uniform tailored at a shop at the *amphur*, paying for it on hire purchase. The trouser legs were cut a little wide, as was the fashion. Duangdaw went in to Ubon and ordered a uniform at her usual tailors, to be made in a hurry.

In addition to ordering the teachers to wear the uniforms, the headmaster also had both teachers and pupils practise greeting their visitors so that etiquette would be strictly observed. The teachers had to rehearse their individual parts in the celebrations, the headmaster even writing his instructions down and having the three subordinate teachers commit them to memory.

'Repeat your programme over and over till you've got it perfect. Don't let what happened to Khru Kaen and Syksa

Man happen to you,' he said to the three young teachers. 'Khru Kaen learned his speech, but got confused. When he had to greet his supervisor he mixed up the names and said, "I, your humble servant Nai Man". Instead of saying his own name, he used the name of the *Syksa*. Don't you start daydreaming, Phisit.'

'No. But don't you daydream either,' Phisit said jokingly, knowing the headmaster was in a good mood. 'Don't write your lines the wrong way round.'

The villagers were in a ferment over the preparation for the celebration of *Maha Chart,* the festival honouring Lord Vessantara. Any kind of celebration was spoken of as a 'merit-making' or acquisition of merit (*aw bun*). They considered them all occasions in which their participation would bring them merit and therefore a better destiny either in this life or in a future one. In Barn Norng Ma Vor there were certain kinds of food which could not be omitted on these merit-making occasions. One of these is a noodle dish popular throughout the country, *khanom cin* (lit. 'Chinese cakes'), but known locally as *khaw pun*. Another is *khaw tom mat,* glutinous rice cakes wrapped in banana leaf. There were no special rules about other foods and sweets - all the villagers demanded was that they be good to eat and plentiful.

The making of *khanom cin* is a job for the women. The rice is soaked and then pounded in a stone mortar until it is like flour. This is left to stand in water, then kneaded. When thoroughly kneaded, the rice dough is put into a press called a *fiang* which turns the dough into the familiar firm threads of noodles. When the *khanom cin* is ready, it is served out on large flat bamboo trays.

There is not much to the making of *khaw tom mat*. Milled glutinous rice is packed in banana leaves with ripe bananas inside. Black beans may be added if desired. The entire packet is boiled in water and may be kept for many days.

All these are usually prepared on the day before the festivities are to take place. As the appointed day for the joint celebration - the merit-making and the opening of the school - approached, the villagers seemed to work more and more frenziedly. Caw Kart's bus went to the *amphur* two or three times a day. People were increasingly going in to shop for foods, for tools and materials, and some to bring back goods for sale in the village. Young girls bought new skirts and blouses, Mae Kham bought cakes and sweets to retail, and Headmaster Khammaw ordered liquor and soda by the crate. No doubt this liquor was 'joint property', for the cost was divided equally among the teachers.

Phayorm helped Mae Bun, the wife of Headman Lua, to make *khanom cin,* and Mor Sombat was always in the village, not on medical duties but merely to watch over his loved one. Whenever he could he joined Thit Phun and the gamblers, playing *boke* or playing cards, drinking, having a great time.

Headman Lua, Lung 'Carn Kern and the headmaster discussed at length the arrangements for receiving the Governor in the headman's house. Everything was in order, but what exercised them was the *seng klong* - the drum-beating competition. Many villagers would be invited to compete. When the event actually took place however, it was expected that the hosts would maintain their prestige and be the team to win. For this purpose the expert was summoned back to the village from Amphur Kansalak in Sri Saket province, where he had gone to cultivate swiddens.

'Brother Khune, the officials are coming to see the *seng klong* in our village,' the headman explained. 'As you are the acknowledged expert, having defeated everybody else in the *tambon,* we depend on your skill to meet the challenge to our village. I have assured Sia Mangkorn of your ability and he intends wagering many hundreds of thousands on you. When you win you can be sure of a few thousand yourself. I hope you are in good strength and in good form.'

'Since I went to Kansalak I've done nothing but fell trees and dig ditches. I haven't touched a drum. Can I beat the rest of them Phor Phu jai? Don't make me go into that competition.'

'Don't worry! You've never been beaten yet in this district.' Lung 'Carn Kern slapped the unassuming young man on his sturdy shoulders. 'If you win, Sia Mangkorn will reward you well.'

The festival of *Maha Chart,* the honouring of Lord Vessantara, was an annual event falling in the third or fourth month (March-April) when the flowers begin to bloom. The weather turns warm, the dry season sets in, and the forest is full of beautiful flowering trees of various kinds. The red flower of the red cotton tree blooms in competition with the flame of the forest on the edge of the fields.[1] The yellow laburnum flowers on the hillocks wave like garlands in the warm breeze.[2] As for the *lamduan,* the *khatkhaw,* and the *khainaw,* though their hues were not bright, their fragrance each evening was wafted on the breeze.[3] They were particularly strong that evening when the villagers took Prince Vessantara in procession back to his city. The youths and lasses made the most of the occasion.

The important event of the festival was the recitation of the sermon of *Maha Chart* - the tale of the last incarnation on earth of the Lord Buddha before his birth as the Prince Gotama who would reach enlightenment. The thirteen chapters of this sermon must be recited in one day. While the recitation proceeds from the elaborate preaching chair, the villagers take their offerings in procession to the monastery. This is called the *kanlorn.* The preaching is done with monks and novices taking turns. When the procession enters the monastery, the offerings are given to whichever monk is reciting at the moment. The chief almsgiver takes the offering to him and makes the presentation in appropriate fashion. *Kanlorn,* which may be translated as 'a ghostly sermon', refers here to the element of surprise in the almsgiving - the monks are not told in advance - hence the name given it by the villagers of Barn Norng Ma Vor.

The preparation of the offerings for this 'ghostly sermon' was a major task. Some made their offerings in the

---

1 Red cotton tree - BOMBAX MALABARICUM; flame of the forest - BUTEA FRONDOSA.

2 Yellow laburnum - CASSIA FISTULA.

3 *Lamduan* - SPHAEROCORYNE CLAVIPES; *Khatkhaw* - RANDIA SIAMENSIS; *Khainaw* - VITEX GLABRATA.

shape of an elaborate casket, some in the form of a chariot, some hung their offerings on a tinsel tree and some made them in the form of an animal. But of most importance are the various things which are offered. Together with foodstuffs and useful articles, the one thing which cannot be omitted is money. There is much competition as to whose offering is the most attractive, which the largest.

Public entertainments are also *de rigueur* - films, shadow puppet theatre and traditional forms of theatre such as *mor lam* and *liké*. These the villagers saw infrequently. The mainstay was always the *mor lam* - whether presented by a group or by a pair, whether the play was about adulterous love or competition for a husband, local *mor lam* or *mor lam* of whatever kind, the troupes of players accompanied by the *khaen* must always be there, however much the story and the style of presentation might differ.

The committee, on this occasion, decided on a *mor lam* group, rather than a couple - a group with an established reputation from Amphur Khamkhuankaew in Yasothorn province. The task the villagers were finding most onerous was the arrangement of the drumming competition which, according to tradition, should have been held with the fireworks festival in the sixth month. Nevertheless, they had agreed to put on the competition and they were determined it be done well. Villagers in the commune Phak I Hin, as well as others in the district, expressed their wish to enter the competition. The festival of Lord Vessantara and the opening of the school would be a grand occasion and everyone was looking forward to it.

The celebration would take place at two locations - at the school and at the *wat*. For the most part the villagers took care of the preparations at the *wat,* particularly in erecting the pavilion for the religious rites, decorating the monastery hall with garlands of flowers and illustrating the story of Lord Vessantara on cloth banners encircling the hall - like the pictures painted on the outside walls of many temples in Bangkok. At the school, the teachers from villages in the commune spent many days preparing the venue for the grand opening.

Headmaster Cantha and Khru Visarn slept at Headmaster Khammaw's house the whole week before the big day. During the day they helped construct the temporary pavilion in which the ceremony would take place; they decked the compound with strings of flags and ornamental trees uprooted entire and brought specially for the occasion. The Section Head and Khru Sawad came every other day without fail to inspect the progress of the preparations.

'We must prepare a *bai si* and perform a *su khwan* ceremony for the Governor. Prepare the tray for the ceremony to look as nice as possible.' The *su khwan* is a traditional Thai ceremony in which the *khwan* or life force of the individual is 'recalled' or strengthened. The *bai si* is a tree made of tinsel and highly ornamented which must accompany this ritual.[4] The Section Head went on, 'Get all the old people in the village to tie goodluck threads round the wrists of the Governor and the other important officials. Get every old person in the village, no exceptions. Have them dressed up properly. The Governor is very keen on old ceremonies and local customs.'

The result was that the headmaster, Piya and Duangdaw had to run around cajoling the old folk in the

---

4 *Bai* is apparently a Khmer word meaning 'rice', *si* or *sri* is a Sanskrit-derived word meaning 'auspicious'.

village to set up a *su khwan* ceremony for His Excellency the Governor.

'You'll come along, won't you, Mae jai Kham?' Piya said to one old lady. 'The first night of the waning moon; I'll remind you again before the day.'

Duangdaw was kept busy preparing the children for their performance on stage. Another group of teachers from nearby schools worked hard at building the stage, painting notices and arranging the display of gifts presented by Sia Mangkorn.

It was fortunate that the pupils' examinations were past and done with. The teachers did not have to worry about their teaching. It was a long-established tradition that once the examinations were over, so was the business of education. The aim of education was the passing of exams. When the exams were held, half the job was done, and when the results arrived it was complete. The responsibility of learning was over for the pupils, and for the teachers, that of teaching.

At last the big day arrived. The school festivities began on the first day of the feast of Vessantara. Early that morning the loud sound of drums and cymbals proclaimed the start of the merit-making. This first day was known to the villagers as *wan home*, the day of coming together. Everyone prepared food to receive guests from other villages. In the evening the Lord Vessantara was taken in procession 'from the forest to the city', the procession formed of monks and laymen, girls and boys, young and old. The 'forest' was the edge of the fields, where the laymen sat in a circle round the monks, in the shade of the trees. The sound of the monks chanting was compelling, like the sounds of lamentation. When the sun finally disappeared behind the distant line of trees, the procession of Lord Vessantara made its way into the village. The villagers carried with them flowers of the forest, which would be offered in worship.

That same day the school would celebrate the unveiling of its new name board. One thing of great importance, which foiled the hopes of the Section Head but brought satisfaction to the headmaster and the teachers, was the inability of the Governor to attend.

'His Excellency cannot come today. The Minister has arrived for an inspection and both the Governor and the *Nai Amphur* have been summoned to a meeting,' the Education Officer told those gathered to welcome the Governor at the *amphur*.

'Should we go on Section Head?'

'What a pity!' the Section Head grumbled. 'Never mind! Your being here is as good as the Governor,' he said to the Provincial Education Officer. 'It's all arranged and ready at the school.' He put on a welcoming face, determined not to offend the gathering of notables.

The Education Officer's party set off for Barn Norng Ma Vor, the Section Head's pick-up in front followed by the Education Officer's jeep. The laterite road was known as 'Kukrit's road', being one of the results of Kukrit Pramoj's rural development programme during his term as Prime Minister. The villagers had helped construct it, in line with government policy. It was criticized as being unsuitable for vehicular traffic, but for the rural folk it was of great importance as it linked many villages of Phak I Hin with the *amphur*. As they went away from the *amphur* the potholes, too, rapidly increased.

'I haven't been on this road before,' the Education Officer said to the Section Head, who was seated opposite. 'Oh, you've got a sawmill too! You wouldn't want to talk about a road like this, full of potholes.'

'Yes, Sir, it's Sia Mangkorn's mill,' the Section Head explained.

'How long has that been there?' He stared at the piles of timber and the smoke which drifted out of the chimney. 'It's forest all the way from here to the frontier—is it not?'

'Yes, it's deep forest beyond Barn Norng Ma Vor - there's nothing there. When you're free I'll take you to shoot some langurs, there are some left still. But I myself have never been beyond Barn Norng Ma Vor,' the Section Head fawned, contradicting himself.

The two vehicles swiftly passed fields and scrub on either side of the road. At the school a large crowd waited, hungry, but unable to have their midday meal before the guests arrived.

The pupils lined the road from the foot of the little hill all the way to the school. Piya had argued that this was now an obsolete practice; the policy-makers and education authorities had forbidden the use of school children for mounting such guards of honour. But Headmaster Khammaw had insisted. He claimed that since the school was established, in fact since the founding of the village, there had never before been a Governor or other high official visit the village.

They had waited a long time; both teachers and pupils were feeling the strain. The children had played around and their clothes, all freshly washed on the teachers' instructions, were dirty again, covered in sweat and dust.

The loud booming of a drum from the *wat* brought the tired children back to some semblance of life.

The welcoming party seated in the pavilion where the ceremony was to be held was also getting somewhat impatient at the long delay. The Governor was due at noon, and there was still no news, no sign of his arrival. They had all been waiting, expecting him to arrive at any moment. There were the government officials such as the District Education Officer, and the other departmental heads at district level, the teachers - all of them in uniform. They checked, each one, to see everything was in order - the pips and stripes on their epaulettes, the black ties around their necks. They felt the tails of the shirts, to see they were neatly tucked into trousers or skirt. They awaited the arrival of the chief guest.

The person assigned to look after the public address system took off the tape which had been relaying music through the loudspeaker, and tried out the microphone, making certain it would be working when the important guests arrived. The female schoolteachers who had arranged the flowers on the main table, hurried to rearrange the roses, trying to have them look their best.

At about 12:15, a long-wheel-base landrover with five doors slowly crawled up the hill accompanied by shouts of 'They've come! They've come!'

All eyes followed the vehicle and everyone checked themselves once more, hastily pulling at ties and uniforms. The landrover passed up between the rows of school children and came to a halt in front of the pavilion.

The first to dismount was a fat man, fair complexioned and wearing a short-sleeved shirt, white with light blue stripes. Its style and the quality of the cloth proclaimed it expensive. His grey trousers were beautifully cut and appeared completely suitable for a man his age - which was about forty. It was Sia Mangkorn.

'Sawatdi khrap,' he said in greeting, moving his hands, palms together, to acknowledge everyone in the pavilion. 'I thought His Excellency would be here already. I tried to get here in time.'

'He hasn't arrived yet. The Section Head went to meet him at the *amphur,* but they're not here yet and there's been no news.' The District Education Officer stood up and beckoned. 'This way, Sia.'

Sia Mangkorn looked around the gathering with the air of a man of power and importance. His bodyguards separated and sat around him like ornaments setting off his magnificence.

Shortly afterwards the Section Head's pick-up and the Provincial Education Officer's jeep arrived. First out was the Education Officer, dressed in a brown safari jacket. He was closely followed by the Section Head. They were accompanied by six others from the provincial administration and the *amphur*. Khru Sawad drove the Section Head's car and parked it under the shade of a 'fish oil' tree. He sauntered back to the pavilion, trying to look important.

'His Excellency had to attend a meeting at the *changwat*; the Minister's here on inspection. His Excellency asked me to take his place.' The Education Officer took the cold towel Duangdaw held out to him respectfully, on a tray, and sat down.

The ceremony began immediately. The Section Head conducted the proceedings. He told of how the village of Norng Ma Vor got its school. The Provincial Education

Officer answered and then pulled the cord which released the cloth covering the name board of the school fixed to the wall of the building. He then cut the ribbon across the steps and led the official party into the building to look around. The school was as spotless and beautifully arranged as the village schoolteachers could manage.

'It's all the best timber, both the floor and the walls,' the Section Head announced to the company.

'Sia Mangkorn had the contract - you don't have to worry about a thing.' The Section Head turned to the Sia, who was walking next to him. 'Isn't that true, Sia?'

Sia Mangkorn grinned. 'I suppose you'll have to look to Lung 'Carn Kern, the major sub-contractor.'

When the distinguished guests had examined all four classrooms they formally made presentations to the school. Sia Mangkorn, as usual, was most conspicuous with his presentations. The names of the donors had been carefully inscribed beforehand. Their gifts included a large iron tank for the storage of rainwater, four sets of tables and chairs for the teachers, and a cheaper set of chairs for visitors. The furniture had been placed in front of the pavilion, but the tank had already been installed in position under the eaves of the school, mounted on four legs.

When the gifts had been offered by their donors and received on behalf of the school, the names of those who had donated money for buying school equipment, and for bursaries for children who needed help, were read out. The list included those who had already made donations and those who had indicated an intention to do so.

The Provincial Education Officer had subscribed 150 baht. Everyone applauded noisily. Sia Mangkorn had doled out just a 100 baht note - not wanting to outface the chief guest. The Section Head, the District Education Officer and the other officials, the teachers and villagers who attended the ceremony, all made contributions, showing their goodwill, each according to rank giving between 10 and 50 baht.

One of the last names read out surpassed the other contributions by far. An old pupil gave 500 baht. The young lady, now known as Raphiphan, known in the old days as Phan, had had the fortune of making a good marriage. She had married a *farang* and was at the moment visiting her village, back home from America.

They all ate lunch and then the distinguished guests made their way to the *wat* to watch the drumming competition, specially arranged for the Governor. Though the Governor had not come, the competition could not be cancelled, for drummers and their contingents of supporters had gathered from many villages.

The Education Officer's party arrived at the *wat* about 3:00 P.M. while the competitors were trying out their drums. The many drums filled the compound of the monastery with their beat, high notes and low, the overall effect most pleasing. The drums used in the competition are known as *king* drums. In the dialect of some villagers the consonant *k* became *ch* and the drum is known as *klong ching* - but not, however, in Barn Norng Ma Vor. The *klong king* was much like the drum seen up front in a modern band - often played when the singer pauses during a song. It is a single-faced drum, broad on the playing surface and narrowing towards the bottom, but not as long as the drums used by drummers in a band. It is, however, played in the same manner, being set on the leg with face upwards and played with a stick which is known as a 'drumhammer'.

Competing with this drum calls for both athletic ability and art. The skill of the competitor begins with choosing the tree, its characteristics set out in the old texts. The tree must then be cut in the specified manner and all the rituals carefully observed until the drum is complete. A similar meticulous procedure must be followed in the choice and fitting of the skin. From start to finish everything must be done strictly according to the texts. At the end of each season of competition the drum is placed in the *wat* for safe keeping and each year, when the competitions come round again, the drums are dusted off and the playing skins restretched.

The skins are stretched by pouring water over the wood of the drum, which makes it expand, and then placing the drum out in the sun, which shrinks the skin. The tighter the skin the better the music.

'King, king, king' is the sound the drum makes in competition. If a drum sounds *'tun, tun, tun'* or *'tyng, tyng, tyng'* it means it cannot be used.

The competition is decided by the loudness of the drum and its ability to hit the sharpest, highest note which the listeners find pleasant - particularly the ears of the judging committee. The loudest and the sharpest - that is the winner, and he would require much strength in the beating of the drum. If his body were not strong and had insufficient endurance he would face defeat, however good his drum. As for the manner in which the competitors showed off their skills, this was a matter for the spectators, who would have their own views as to how the competition should take place. The competitors could play one at a time or all together. Everyone, competitors and spectators, committee included, would have to stuff their ears with cottonwool lest their eardrums be damaged.

When the drummers were ready a young man came running, out of breath, to Phu jai Lua and Lung 'Carn Kern, who sat in the Education Officer's circle.

'Something terrible's happened, Phor Phu jai, Phor Lung 'Carn! Aai Khune, our drummer's gone away!'

'What's that?' Lung 'Carn Kern exclaimed, startled. 'Where's Aai Khune gone?'

'He went back to Kansalak - sometime before noon.' The lad came out with it, anxiously. 'Someone came and told him his wife had a baby.'

'Didn't he say anything?'

'I was busy with the arrangements at the school. How do you think I could keep track of everybody?' The headman scratched his head. 'What shall we do, Lung 'Carn? Can we get someone else in his place?'

'Death! This time for sure!' Lung 'Carn swore, looking towards Sia Mangkorn. 'The Sia put on a thousand with Barn Phak I Hin - then increased it by five thousand. What do you say, Khru 'Maw? Whom can we get instead of Aai Khune? Come on, think!'

'I don't know. Of the younger bunch there's no one who can play the drum. Of the older crowd there's only 'Carn Khen, the mad one. His skill with the stick is equal to any, but I don't know if he's strong enough these days.' The headmaster gave his views of the matter.

'True. So get him at once,' the headman agreed. 'But this fellow - if he gets offended he won't come, even if you send an elephant to drag him. I think I should go myself this time.'

Phu jai Lua set off for 'Carn Khen's house, but as it happened he did not have to go far. 'Carn Khen had himself come to see the competition. It was not easy. The headman was joined by Piya and Phisit in cajoling him, and finally he agreed. He would play the drum in place of Caw Khune on behalf of the village of Norng Ma Vor.

The sound of the six drums grew dangerously loud and the committee of experts from the various villages gave the signal for each drum to be played by itself. Each one was given about two minutes to display his highest skill and his greatest strength. They then played all together again with the committee standing in their midst. They conferred and finally made their decision.

The enjoyment of the spectators came not only from the excitement which the rhythm of the drums instilled in them; many of them could appreciate the skill of the individual players too. The villagers of Barn Norng Ma Vor, to a man, put their support behind 'Carn Khen. Young and old crowded behind him, cheering on their champion, the man they all called 'mad'.

With a flourish of his arms, 'Carn Khen wielded the drum sticks rhythmically and untiringly. The sound of the drum of Barn Norng Ma Vor was louder and sharper than all others. Its sound was heard as clearly as possible, despite the ears all protected with plugs of cotton wool. His supporters began to smile as his striking of the drum increased in speed and intensity, just when some began to tire and their drumming faltered. Others were still as energetic as he, but their drums were inferior and their beat was soon drowned in the sound of his.

The drum of Barn Norng Ma Vor, the more it was played the louder it grew; and the drummer, the longer he played the more energy he seemed to have. His efforts were answered by a *'Hoo Hiu'* from his supporters, watching him from the side lines.

It was finally 'Carn Khen who was announced the victor - and with him every villager of Barn Norng Ma Vor. And the one who raked in the money, with no effort on his part, was Sia Mangkorn who won five thousand baht. When the result was announced, flushed with victory, Sia Mangkorn pulled out a one hundred baht note which he gave 'Carn Khen as reward. The victor took it, indifferently, and shortly afterwards bought cakes and sweets for the full amount, handing them out to a crowd of children who swarmed around him happily, till the money was all gone.

One who was quietly happy about the victory was Piya. It was the first time he had seen such an event and he went up to 'Carn Khen and congratulated him with all sincerity.

While 'Carn Khen was busy buying sweets for the kids, the microphone crackled with the announcement of the results. The first prize went to Barn Norng Ma Vor, the second to Barn Khok Klarng and the third to Barn Phak I Hin. The announcer invited the drummers to come up and receive their prizes. There were prizes for the village and the individual drummer. Cups were awarded to the villages placed first, second and third, donated, respectively, by the ex-member of Parliament for the district, a member of the Provincial Council and Sia Mangkorn. The prize for the individual drummer was a parcel wrapped in gift paper. It was thought the parcel contained towels. 'Carn Khen went up and received his prize with no change of his usual expression. When the Education Officer had handed out the prizes, the announcer went on, 'Now Mor Sombat will donate a prize for the runner up from Barn Khok Klarng.'

Mor Sombat who was seated with the official party looked flabbergasted. Those around him, thinking he had arranged it all beforehand, applauded loudly and pushed him from behind, helping him to stand up. The drummer from Barn Khok Klarng, the runner up, came out and stood in the centre of the crowd, grinning broadly.

Mor Sombat whispered hurriedly to Sia Mangkorn, 'Sia, lend me a hundred baht, please. I don't know who the announcer is, he's really pulled a fast one on me.'

Sia Mangkorn reached into his pocket and pulled out a red note. Mor Sombat walked out and handed the money to the runnerup amid the loud applause from the villagers of Barn Khok Klarng, who thought he was making the presentation of his own free will.

Piya walked back to the school with Phisit to prepare the evening meal.

'Khun Phisit, why did you announce that Mor Sombat was going to donate a prize? Did he tell you to? It looked more like a trick you played on him.'

'Yes, I really got him, didn't I?' Phisit said with satisfaction. 'I've been waiting for a chance to get my own back on him for a long time. Someone told me it was that quack who hit me over the head that time.'

'Is that how a teacher gets his own back, then?' Piya stared at his colleague, as if not comprehending.

At the village hall, which had been converted into a reading room for daily newspapers, Duangdaw, Phisit, Somsak and Piya had prepared for a visit by the Education Officer on his way back from the *wat*. They were keen he should see what the villagers had done for themselves. The great man, however, stopped but a moment, as if grudging the time. He was of the opinion that the provision of daily newspapers to the village came under the Adult Education Section and had nothing at all to do with him.

Duangdaw briefly related to him the manner in which they had acquired the reading room. She spoke with pride as she felt she had been the spearhead and the chief organizer of the project. She did not give a thought to whether the matter came under the jurisdiction of the Ministry of Education or some other ministry. If asked, she would have said the benefit was to the citizens of the village and they were part of the Thai nation like every other citizen.

'They are all very keen. When the newspapers arrive they sometimes come close to quarrelling over who gets the paper first. Isn't that right, Somsak?' She turned to the young lad who had volunteered to help with the reading room. He, however, had nothing to say. 'They are very keen on discussing the news, too.'

'Watch out! You let these village folk read newspapers, soon they'll think they have the answers to everything,' the Section Head said to no one in particular.

The distinguished guests walked from the reading room to the school, where a table had been prepared for their dinner. A portable power generator was roaring a little way away and the school grounds were illuminated with electric light for the occasion. The pupils' tables, still unused for any school work, had been brought out and arranged into one long table, now covered with a white table cloth. The Education Officer sat at the head of the table, the Section Head at his left, with Khru Sawad, his bodyguard, next to him. On the Education Officer's left was an empty seat. Next to this sat the District Education Officer, who had felt all day as if he were in the middle of a forest with strangers. He did not deal with teachers in his job.

'Wad, go and call Duangdaw! Tell her to sit here,' the Section Head said to his henchman, pointing to the empty chair. The trusty hatchet man quickly walked with self-importance to the school house, which was temporarily being used as the kitchen. He was soon back with Duangdaw, who had a rather dirty face. She had been cooking under the directions of Headmaster Khammaw's wife, the head cook for the occasion. '

'Khun Khru, sit here next to the Education Officer and make sure his glass is kept filled up with beer,' the Section Head instructed her.

She sat down and raised her hands in greeting to the Education Officer. It was the second time that day she had greeted him thus.

'A pretty girl next to him to pour his beer should do his appetite no end of good. What say you, Section Head?' Sia Mangkorn spoke loudly across the table.

The young woman frowned when she heard him, but suppressed her anger, sitting quietly.

'Do you visit your father in Ubon often?' the Education Officer asked, speaking to her as a child, using the expression *nu*, 'mouse'.

'These days I don't go very often.'

'You don't want a transfer yet? If you are satisfied to stay here, please ask to stay on. I am sick of everyone wanting a transfer to the city. There aren't enough places for them.' He said what he always said to teachers wanting transfer, suspecting that Duangdaw would use the opportunity to wheedle a transfer out of him.

'I wanted a transfer at first, but now I think I like it here,' she replied. 'Syksa, Sir, why don't you change places with me?' Khru Sawad spoke to the District Education Officer, at the same time standing up and walking round the head of the table. The District Education Officer made way for him. Duangdaw was now between the chief guest and the Section Head's drunken hatchet man. She was sickened by the smell of drink on his breath and by his leering countenance, but at the same time tried to parry his impertinent suggestions. He deliberately tried to annoy her and when he finally brought the light close to her to read the palm of her hand, she said, 'I think I should go and see what's happening in the kitchen.'

She excused herself and walked away with a scowl on her face, not waiting for a reply.

Phisit and Piya had been watching from down the table and they got up together and followed Duangdaw into the school house.

The food came dish by dish till the long narrow table was full. There was *larp, koi* (another salad-like dish, made with seasoned, raw meat), liver *koi,* barbecued meat and barbecued tripe, meat soup and tripe soup - everything made with beef. The liquor was placed in bottles on the tables - 'round' bottles. For the head of the table there was beer, which had been standing on ice since before noon.

When everybody had begun eating, to the accompaniment of a folk melody over the public address system, Khru Sawad got up and walked to the lavatory behind the school house, accompanied by two of his colleagues from the *amphur*. They knew from past experience that when the Section Head's buddy was drunk there usually was trouble.

In the gloom behind the school, not far from where the cooking was taking place, Duangdaw, returning from the toilet, barged into Khru Sawad, just the man she was trying to avoid. She was startled and cried out, not knowing who it was. It was nothing more than the involuntary cry of someone taken by surprise. Sawad, who was very drunk, groped in front of him with his hands - with no clear idea of what he was doing. At this, Duangdaw really screamed. Phisit and Piya rushed out to see what was happening and arrived on the spot at the same time as Sawad's two companions. Phisit grabbed at the drunk's arm, meaning to lead him away. But he was slow in holding on and he missed, staggered, and fell. Piya, not taking care, caught a blow from his other fist. All this sounded like a fight in progress, sounds of blows, cries and moans - and above it all rang out the sound of a shot.

Duangdaw continued to scream. When others rushed to the scene they found Khru Sawad with his head bleeding, blood streaming down his cheek, and his revolver in his hand. But there was no sign of who had split open his scalp. The Education Officer, the Section Head and the others came to have a look. They all seemed terribly excited, jabbering at each other, but nobody understood a word.

'Headmaster Khammaw, you find out who's responsible and let me know within a week,' the Section Head stormed, in a fury.

They walked back to their food, leaving a few others to find medicines and dressing for the wound. Khru Sawad was almost sober.

The atmosphere of the celebration had lost its sparkle. The stage show put on by the pupils was excellent. They had practised hard and many of them were naturally talented. But the guests could not find any interest in it at all.

Those who had earlier decided to stay the night in the village, changed their minds and made their way to the *amphur,* leaving the teachers and the villagers to clean up after them and enjoy the village festivities by themselves.

The one who had no thought for any entertainment was Headmaster Khammaw, who did not know where to begin looking for the culprit who had split Khru Sawad's scalp. Who would confess his guilt?

CHAPTER 20

'It was I,' Phisit said, 'I broke Khru Sawad's head.' The headmaster, Duangdaw and Piya looked bewildered, particularly Piya.

'Thank you very much, Phisit.' Piya looked on his colleague with more friendly feeling than he had ever felt before. 'I can't let you take the blame, because it was I who struck the blow.'

The headmaster and Duangdaw looked even more bewildered.

'You give me a headache.' The headmaster scratched his head viciously. 'Why must you compete to be the villain of the piece?'

'It was I who struck him. You'd better believe me, Headmaster!' Piya spoke with conviction. 'I've hated the very sight of him for a long time.'

'I don't care who hit him, but I am not going to allow Khru Piya to take the blame,' Phisit said firmly. 'I have too much respect for Khru Piya to let him be branded with this. I've got many bad marks, another one won't matter.'

'Let it be, whoever's guilty, whoever's innocent. Khru Sawad got a broken head.' Khru jai Khammaw sounded somewhat uncomfortable. 'He deserves more broken than that. Let's see what he'll do about it.'

Because Khru Sawad and the Section Head realized that a long drawn out attempt to get the truth out of the young woman might reflect on them, they let the matter drop. But they were determined to get their revenge on the teachers of Barn Norng Ma Vor one way or another. Khru Sawad was certain it was either Phisit or Piya who was responsible. The fact that he had no evidence only strengthened his determination.

There was only a week left before the school closed for the summer. An emergency order came from the *amphur* that the pupils were to be examined in 'behaviour', and were to have physical training every day in accordance with the policy of instilling patriotism and good citizenship, which the new minister in charge of education had formulated. He had set out with enthusiasm to build up the nation by distributing pamphlets and training and examining the young.

The headmaster discussed the order with his teachers without a great deal of enthusiasm.

'Every time there's a change of government, a new policy is announced. We unimportant people have got to follow, whether we agree or not. I ask Piya and Phisit to discuss this among themselves and train the children as much as they think necessary. As for the examination in etiquette, we can only proceed as always.'

'Hasn't the *amphur* sent a manual?' Piya asked, concerned. 'The regular schools have had a manual setting out the standards for physical education distributed to them last month. It seems only right we should get it too.'

Phisit spoke up. 'Our school is far from civilization. Who's so interested that they'll come and inspect us? Whether we train the kids or not, who's to know? But for the sake of the kids, we should at least train them according to what we ourselves learned. Don't worry, Headmaster, I'll take responsibility for this.'

Though they had finished their exams, the kids came gladly to school. They enjoyed their lessons in the new building. The headmaster took the new bell out of the cupboard. This was a gift to the school from one of its old pupils who was now labouring in Bangkok. The old hoe which had served as a bell was duly thrown away. They lined up and sang the national anthem and performed their religious observances. Phisit, wearing his new uniform, walked out and stood in front of the lines of children. He announced in a loud voice,

'Khru (here meaning himself) has some good news for you. From today I am going to take you in physical training every morning before we go into class. This is to help make you all fit and strong. We'll begin today. I'll first show you how to do the exercise. You'll then follow me slowly. When you know the exercise, I'll blow my whistle to give you the rhythm. OK! Let's begin.'

Phisit showed them the exercises he remembered from when he himself was a student. There was the raising and lowering of arms, jumping, bending the body, legs apart, legs together - all of which most of the children found quite easy. Even those who made mistakes enjoyed it all, for it was something new.

The sun was already hot at 9:00 in the morning when Siang came running and joined the ranks of schoolchildren. He was not happy at being late and he was hot and sweaty, having run a long way. He jumped and swung with the rest of them until the final exercise. Phisit increased the speed of the exercise, quickening the blasts on his whistle. Siang collapsed in a faint, unseen by the teacher. As soon as the exercise ended the children broke into a confusion of shouts and questions.

'Teacher! Siang has fainted!' Khiaw, the children's leader, yelled above the confusion. The others crowded round to have a look. Phisit pushed his way into the crowd and Piya, who had been watching from the verandah of the school, came rushing down the steps. Phisit carried Siang under the shade of the 'fish oil' tree. Duangdaw and the headmaster came together, yelling to the kids to stand back and make way.

Siang responded to their attentions and sat up, looking around before meeting Piya's eye. Piya rubbed the young boy's head and said softly, 'What's the matter Siang? Are you better now?'

'Yes.'

'Aren't you well? Have you eaten this morning?' he asked anxiously. Siang hung his head and did not reply. Piya knew what the answer would be.

The objects Piya had brought to class that day were shadow puppets made of cardboard. 'Carn Khen had drawn the pictures and cut them out. The class sat silent, all eyes on the giant bird which Piya held up before the class.

'This bird is the chief of birds. It has great power, but it uses that power to bully other birds. They are all frightened of it and it thinks it can do as it pleases. Well, who is going to be this bird?'

The boy Bunmi raised his hand and quickly came up and took the puppet. Piya took out another piece of cardboard cut in the shape of a little bird.

'This is a little bird who has been bullied so much by the big one that he can't stand it any longer. He has asked all the other little birds to join him in fighting off the bully.'

Piya brought out three more figures of little birds. 'In the end the big bird is defeated. Who's going to take the part of the little birds?'

A number of children quickly put up their hands, some of them jumping up in their excitement. Piya called up two girls and two boys. The big bird and the little ones carried on an argument in the local dialect, much to the amusement of all the children, before they began their battle. The kids enjoyed themselves, changing over the control of the puppets, everybody getting a turn.

The teacher then asked them to summarize the lesson they had learned. Each one had his own version and Piya wrote them up on the blackboard. Finally he said, 'He who has little strength, if he combines with others and uses his intelligence, he can overcome the powerful bully.'

On the last day of the school year, the four teachers of Barn Norng Ma Vor School were thoroughly perplexed by an emergency order from the *amphur* for Phisit to go on transfer to Barn Dong Khaen. This school was a small school on the international frontier, about fifteen kilometres away from the village of Norng Ma Vor. There was no road between the two villages, except a cart track and footpath. It was the most depressed of schools and the farthest away from the *amphur*.

'I don't think anyone goes there for anything,' Phisit said bitterly.

'Why should you bear my misfortune. It's better if they ordered me to move there,' Piya said, taking the order and looking through it again.

'What kind of justice is this? It's just to harass! If they want to transfer someone, they do it as they wish. They act without any principles, without any consideration of the law,' Duangdaw said passionately.

'That's it! It's their law,' Piya exploded.

The headmaster said nothing. He was quite confused. Phisit summed it up.

'When you become a rural teacher there is no authority you can go to for justice. Whatever they order, you've got to follow. Whenever you are ordered to go, you must go. There is no part of Thailand to which they can't send a rural teacher like me.'

Piya took Phisit's hand and held it firmly. 'Khun Phisit, I don't want you to go. We've just begun to work well together. Whatever happens, we are still teachers together in the same *amphur*. We must work together. We'll have to fight the system again and again! I hope you won't give up. As for me, even if there's no one to help, I will continue the course I have decided upon.'

CHAPTER 21

One of the timber lorries that regularly passed Barn Norng Ma Vor on their way into the forest was stuck in the sand in front of the school. The huge logs of timber had been too heavy and the truck could not pull itself out. Piya looked at the logs reflectively, but Duangdaw was merely excited by their monstrous size.

'Oh, ho! Who would have thought there were trees that size? They are frightening.'

'I think there are plenty of trees that size in the forest near the frontier. I keep wondering whether that timber was legally felled.' Piya spoke softly and went up and closely inspected the protruding ends of the timber. He did not see any indication that the timber had been examined and stamped. The young teacher shelved his suspicions for the time being.

'Are you going home to Ubon when the term ends, Khun Aew?' asked Piya, changing the subject.

'I'll go in four or five days' time. Are you going anywhere or not, Khun Piya? If you don't have anything special, you can come to Ubon with me.'

"Carn Khen invited me to go and see the dammar tapping in the forest. I'd said I'd go. I think he's going tomorrow morning. I should be able to go to Ubon with Khun Aew.'

The young woman hid her pleasure with the trace of a smile. 'If you can stay a few days in the city, I'll take you to Hart Wat Tai, or we can do a trip down the river Mun or go to Kaeng Saphy ... it depends on whatever Khun Piya likes. I'm sure we'll have fun.'

'I'll go anywhere Khun Aew recommends, as long as your father doesn't object. I must go on to Bangkok and then go home to Amnart for about a week. After that I'll come back here.'

Before they parted at 'Carn Khen's house, the young woman turned to Piya, looking serious and anxious.

'I don't like your going into the forest at all. I don't know whether the stories the villagers tell are true or not - but you shouldn't be reckless.'

'You shouldn't worry, Khun Aew. There's probably nothing to it. I too would like to know how much truth there is in what they say. It can't be true that the forest spirits seized those dammar tappers who vanished. We've got to stop believing in ghosts and spirits with painted faces. I am sure there's some other explanation.'

'I don't want to believe in them either, but the villagers believe in them absolutely.'

'The forest's mysteries, as well as its riches, are being destroyed daily. Perhaps tomorrow I too will know the truth.'

'Carn Khen appeared and called to them both to come up to the house. Duangdaw excused herself and indicated to Piya not to keep the other man waiting.

The uninhabited part of Tambon Phak I Hin was luxuriant forest, a dark forest that stretched to the international boundary. At the edge of this forest, villagers took over pieces of land, burning and clearing it for the cultivation of a variety of crops. Most of them were migrants from other districts where drought prevailed and the soil had become impoverished. Amphur Hua Taphan and Sarmsit were two of these districts. Despite these clearings, the forest still looked like a forest. As one went deeper, it stretched dank and dark to the frontier. There were no villages, no farmers, no squatters. The only men who dared enter the depths of the forest were hunters, the collectors of forest produce, and the tappers of dammar. Many of them had amazing and mysterious tales which they recounted to friends and neighbours. There were tales of huge trees inhabited by ghosts, fierce animals and the abundance of forest fruits, nuts, roots and other products. But no one else was interested enough to go see for themselves. For the most part they collected mushrooms and bamboo shoots and tapped dammar at the forest's edge.

The tapping of dammar was a pursuit of some importance for the villagers of Barn Norng Ma Vor. The method employed is to cut a groove deep enough for the resin to exude. Usually the grooves are cut about a metre off the ground. The area around the cut is burned and then left for two or three days. The resin oozes out and hardens in the groove. Each one knows his own groove and there is usually no infringement of others' claims. The resin is collected in a container made of a section of bamboo called the *bang khi yarng* ... 'a section for the exudation of the *yarng* tree'.[1] The resin may be sold or used by the collector himself, for instance mixed with the crumbling wood of decayed logs to be used as fuel for a torch, or mixed with pitch for sealing the tiny gaps in the wicker water scoops, or for varnishing boots.

Lung 'Carn Kern bought the dammar from the villagers, collected it in large barrels and sent it on for sale

---

1 *Yarng* tree - DIPTEROCARPUS ALATUS.

to the provincial town. In fact the collecting of dammar required permission from government as the dipterocarpus was a protected tree, and tapping or felling was strictly forbidden without the permission of the Minister of Agriculture.

The villagers, however, continued their tapping without any application for permission. They believed it was a right they had inherited from their ancestors. There was much tapping of the dipterocarpus and felling of various species of trees for house building - some of it legal and some of it not. After Sia Mangkorn had established a sawmill near the *amphur*, the villagers were much harassed by officials of the Forestry Department who prosecuted them often for illegal felling. Many decided it was better to give up the illegal felling and buy their timber from the sawmill. It was now generally known that in this area it was only Sia Mangkorn who would be given rights to fell timber. Sia Mangkorn also had mills in Amphur Amnart Caroen and Khemarat, as well as in Yasothorn province. He was one of Isarn's most powerful timber merchants.

In March there had been many stories circulated causing great excitement about villagers collecting resin and other forest products being taken by spirits in the forest. The inhabitants of villages such as Norng Ma Vor were very frightened and no one dared go deep into the forest by himself, even though it was only rumour and no one knew for certain who it was that was actually lost in the forest or taken by spirits until, four or five days previously, a villager, Thit Liang, had gone by himself to collect dammar, as was his practice, and had not returned. Some said a tiger had got him and others that he had been captured by terrorists. Most, however, believed the forest spirits were responsible.

Piya had been interested from the first and had made extensive enquiries to get at the truth. He had even gone to Thit Liang's house and talked to his wife and children. He now felt he had a good opportunity to pursue the matter further. He jumped at the chance of going into the forest with 'Carn Khen.

The two of them left early the next morning, taking a cart track into the forest. The track was criss-crossed with traces of other cart tracks hauling timber to and fro. The forest had begun to shed its leaves. They saw various species of dipterocarpus and leguminous trees, *daeng, tengrang, takhian,* and *makha,* huge trees which had escaped the attention of fellers and tappers;[2] rosewood and blackwood trees, so valuable that it was said the timber was sold by the kilogram.[3] There were also gigantic trees whose names were unknown to them. Their branches and leaves intertwined, creating a cool shade under their canopy. The purple flowers of the *tabaek* and *inthanil* alternated with the red of the cotton tree - a sight quite beautiful to see.[4] Green pigeons and woodpeckers, one species of which was fast disappearing from the forests of Isarn, flew past, screaming in competition with the jungle fowl whose cries came fluttering through from hidden corners of the forest.

From the first moment that Piya entered the deep forest

---

2 *Daeng* - XYLIA XYLOCARPA; *tengrang* - SHOREA OBTUSA; *takhian* - HOPEA ODORATA; and *makha* - INTSIA BIJUGA. The last identification is uncertain.

3 Rosewood - DALBERGIA COCHINCHINENSIS; blackwood - DALBERGIA OLIVERI.

4 *Tabaek* and *inthanil* - two species of LAGERSTROEMIA.

he was enraptured by the trees, the flowers, the fruits he had never seen before and whose names, to him, were quite unknown. The cool shade of the trees and the gentle calling of the birds filled him with such contentment that he quite forgot the world outside until they finally reached the site of 'Carn Khen's tapping activities. They stopped, and Piya helped the older man collect the resin and put it in his bamboo containers, the *bang khi yarng*, of which he had brought four. They were all finally filled.

'How long ago did you come and tap these, Uncle?' said Piya, referring to the deep incisions at the base of the huge *yarng* trees.

'I made them last year. Only four or five of them are mine.' Piya looked at the other trees with the crevices burned black in them all around.

'What about those there, whose are those?'

'Oh, they belong to various others. We all know our own trees, and when the time for collecting comes no one will steal from someone else's,' 'Carn Khen answered.

Piya mused, 'That's good. So far from anyone's sight and yet no one steals from the others. We village folk are to be admired. Not like townsmen - always fighting and grabbing for their own advantage.'

'But nowadays we too seem to be getting like that. The more civilized we get, the more we seem to think only about ourselves.' 'Carn Khen replaced his four bamboo containers leaning against the floor of a *yarng* tree. He spread out his *pha khaw ma* on the ground and from it took a packet of rice. 'OK, let's eat. We'll pick some ginger flowers and some sweet vegetables later and make our way back in the afternoon.'

While they were enjoying their midday meal they heard the sound of a large vehicle travelling in low gear coming towards them, then going on deeper into the forest. Piya stared in the direction of the sound, but could see nothing, and they were left with no idea of what it was or where it came from.

'Do lorries come in as far as this?'

'Oh, it's the loggers. I suppose it's Sia Mangkorn's lorry.'

'Carn Khen rolled a ball of glutinous rice in the palms of his hands and dipped it in the relish. With it he picked up a fried grasshopper and put it all in his mouth.

'Does Sia Mangkorn have a franchise for this forest? I thought it was a reserve.' Piya seemed puzzled.

'I don't know. You've seen it too, Khru, haven't you? The lorries carrying trees out of the forest every day? Since last year. All big ones, too.' 'Carn Khen chewed a piece of pickled vegetable as if it had lost its savour.

Piya raised the bamboo container and poured water into his mouth; then poured some over his hands and washed them.

'I'll walk round here a bit. You go along, Uncle, and gather your vegetables. Let whoever gets back here first, wait for the other.' Piya stood up as he spoke.

'Don't go too far, you'll get lost,' 'Carn Khen warned as Piya scrambled past a huge creeper.

As he picked his way through the undergrowth, Piya's thoughts were on the lorry which they had just heard, but which was heard no longer. He soon stumbled on a track on which he thought he could make out the recent marks of a large vehicle. He followed it for not more than five minutes when he heard the sound of heavy machinery and the felling of trees. He stealthily made for the sounds, making his way through the scrub, no longer following the tracks of the lorry. He paid no attention to the twigs and thorny branches that seemed to grab at his arms, legs and face.

He finally got to a spot from which he could see a large opening. He saw large trees lying felled on the ground, smaller ones lying on top of them, all scattered around in disorder. He looked towards where three timber lorries were parked, sheltered under a cloth canopy. Workmen were using motor-driven saws, topping off branches and cutting the trees into logs. The noise was considerable, reverberating through the forest.

As Piya was taking all this in with great excitement, a landrover crawled into the clearing and parked beside the lorries. Curious, and wanting to see better, Piya crept closer, in quiet terror. Soon the motors stopped.

'Where is he? Where is the bloody spy, the bloody intruder? Bring him here at once,' Sia Mangkorn yelled at the top of his voice, turning in Piya's direction. Two workmen with guns pushed a middle-aged man into the clearing. He looked thin and dried out and his hands were bound behind his back. Piya crouched down low, careful he made no sound, fearful the workmen would see him. Twenty metres away he could see the unfortunate man was Thit Liang, the villager who had disappeared while collecting dammar five days ago. Imagining what might happen to him if caught, Piya froze in fright, he couldn't blink and he dared not breathe.

'You couldn't leave things alone. You had to come and spy, come and see what's none of your business. You wanted to die like the others.' Sia Mangkorn poked his finger towards Thit Liang's face.

The unfortunate man fell on his knees and pleaded for his life. 'Oh Lord! Please don't do anything to me. I didn't mean to spy on you, Sir. Please let me go. I won't tell anybody.'

Sia Mangkorn yelled back at him. 'Impossible! If I let you go all it needs is for you to open your mouth once. There's no other way but to kill you - put an end to this business.'

The colour fled from Thit Liang's face and his body broke into a sweat. He shuffled forwards and fell at the feet of the timber king of Isarn. He gasped out between sobs, 'Please don't kill me, Sir! If you're frightened I'll talk, let me stay here and work for you. I'll stay here in the forest. I'll do anything you want. I don't want any pay. Just let me live.'

Sia Mangkorn was silent. He looked thoughtful. Ai Uam, the foreman, a villager from Barn Phak I Hin, looked at the Sia and said, 'That's a good idea. This fellow is not dangerous. I know him well. If you kill him, it will be like killing a dog. It's better to make use of him. I'll see he's OK.'

'Are you certain, Ai Uam?' The Sia hesitated, staring at Thit Liang. He thought of all the other villagers he had ordered killed. 'If you're sure, take care of it. But don't let him leave the forest.'

'Oh, Sir! I won't let him out of my sight during the day. At night I'll chain him up.'

CHAPTER 22

Piya and Duangdaw came out of the restaurant of the Ciaw Ki Hotel, walked down the lane by the side of the nine-storeyed Ubon Hotel and came out on Brahmarat Road. They stopped at a draper's and entered the shop, which stood at the corner of a short street connecting Brahmarat with Brahmadera Road. While Duangdaw was choosing a dress material, Piya excused himself and sought out a nearby photographer's. He bought an Instamatic camera, a film and flash equipment, then hurried back to Duangdaw, who had not yet finished her business.

While they were in Ubon, Duangdaw had invited some of her friends to accompany Piya and her on a trip to Hart Wat Tai, hiring a boat to take them down the Mun river. The following day they had gone, the two of them, to Kaeng Saphy in Amphur Phibun Mangsaharn, with Duangdaw's younger brother driving them. After three days in Ubon, Piya left for Bangkok and spent five days there. On two of these he sought out a friend who worked on a newspaper and regaled him with stories of Barn Norng Ma Vor, saying he would send him more details when he got back.

As soon as he got back to the village he went to 'Carn Khen, taking him a palmleaf manuscript he had got for him.

'I've bought you a copy of the Legend of Siaw Sawart, Uncle.[1] I thought you'd like it. I've heard you talk about it

---

[1] Siaw Sawart: an Aesop-like character who in folk tradition is the teller of fables and morality tales. He is said to have been the younger son of a family in Benares (in India). He travels to the court of Champa as a young lad, and through his wisdom becomes its Chief Minister. The stories show some relation to Buddhist and Indian sources such as the epics, the

so often. This copy has been translated from Dharma characters.' Dharma characters were the ancient script in which the scriptures, sermons and Jataka tales of the life of the Buddha were written by the people of Isarn.

'Thank you very much. I've wanted this for a long time. It's an old story from Isarn and it has so many things in it young folk should know. It's very difficult to get nowadays; the new generation doesn't seem to know it at all.' 'Carn Khen looked very happy.

That evening Piya took his old bicycle, Ai Krong, and went off to the headmaster's, and to Phayorm's. He had presents for the headmaster, and for Mae Kham and for Phayorm. He chatted a while with Mae Kham and Phayorm, then went off home. He felt lonely and wished the new term would begin quickly, missing Duangdaw. There were ten more days to go.

Piya had barely left Phayorm's house when Mor Sombat arrived.

'I came to get some money from Uncle Campa, he's owed me for many months now. He wants me to wait till his daughter gets back from Bangkok. The village is really deserted. It looks as if everybody's gone off to work in Bangkok.' Mor Sombat sounded discouraged. He stared at the new brown paper bag which stood next to Phayorm.

'What's that bag?'

'Khru Piya brought us presents.' She picked up the bag and passed it to her lover. The unlicensed doctor did not

---

stories of the lives of the Buddha and other collections. The reference here appears to be to a Lao text. One such text is available in a French translation by Anatole-Roger Peltier: *Le Syvsvāt* (Paris: École Française d'Êxtrême-Orient, 1971).

look very pleased. He looked into the bag and passed it back.

'Put it away. It should keep you pleased a long time.'

'There's nothing! He brought a present. I had to take it. We respect each other. I don't see anything wrong. Don't get the wrong idea.' Phayorm was familiar with her lover's jealousy.

He turned to Mae Kham. 'I thought I'd get my parents to come ask for Phayorm's hand in marriage before the month's over. I think I'll be able to find enough money by then. I don't want to wait any longer.'

Mae Kham nodded. 'That depends on Mor, what Mor thinks is suitable. I too would like to see my daughter settled. It'll ease the worry.'

At dawn Piya set off into the forest on the route he had taken before and in a few hours he reached the logging camp. He found himself a suitable vantage point, unseen by the labourers, and photographed the men at work, the forest round about the workmen's shelters, the equipment and the lorries. He used up his film. When he was satisfied he returned the way he'd come.

Piya was now convinced that Sia Mangkorn was using his position and connections to fell timber illegally and transport it to his sawmills for processing, after which it could no longer be identified, leaving the legal timber, duly stamped, to lie outside the mill to suffer the effect of rain and sun. The timber that the mill worked day and night was all illegally felled. Piya did not know whether the officials concerned knew about all this, whether they were accessories, whether they were ignorant, or if they just ignored it. He did see, however, that the Sia's workmen were not interfered with at all; none of them was ever arrested nor, it seemed, were his sawmills even inspected.

Piya decided he had to make this business public. The destruction of forests was much in the news in every part of the country and he felt he had to do what he could to combat it. He had heard tell often enough that the conspiracy between powerful business interests and government officials to illegally clear forests was at great cost to such things as the building of roads, dams and reservoirs and the establishment of settlement projects. He had now come across an example himself. Aware of his responsibility, as a teacher, as a Thai citizen, he was determined he would see this through to the end. He would fight them to the best of his ability.

He had his film processed at the *amphur* and from among the prints he chose those which had come out most clearly and sent them off with a letter to his friend, the newspaperman in Bangkok. The letter elaborated on the conversations the two of them had had while Piya was in Bangkok. The letter ended with an injunction not to disclose the name of the informant, merely to say the events took place in a southern *amphur* of Ubon Rajathani Province.

Two or three days before school re-opened Piya was seated in the village newspaper reading room chatting with some villagers about the items of news in the day's various papers. In fact, he wanted to see if the newspaper carried his story and, if so, how it had been presented.

'It's the third hour already,' one of the villagers said as he entered, meaning it was 9:00 A.M. 'Hasn't the bus come yet? Uncle's going to wait for the paper, here. I want to see whom they've shot next.' He turned to Piya, 'How's it going, teacher? What's happening to the country? It's nothing but robberies, murders and rapes every day. How's it possible?'

Piya smiled at him. 'It's always like that, Uncle Chan. We read the newspapers now, so we know all about it. When we had no newspapers to read, we never heard of these things. Only what happened in our neighbourhood.'

'Since we got these newspapers, it's opened our eyes and ears to a lot of things. Makes us feel we live in a huge world, much bigger than before,' another villager chimed in, looking with interest at a picture on page four.

'Eh! Do all the women in Bangkok wear these little trousers, then, Khru?'

Piya laughed out loud as he glanced at the picture of swimsuited girls on the page of the newspaper. 'It's not like that at all, Phor So. It's only some people who dress like that - when they go swimming in the sea. People dress in Bangkok the same way they dress in our province.'

Caw Kart screeched to a halt in front of the reading room, poked his head out of the vehicle and tossed out two newspapers.

'There was no *Thai Rath* at the shop. I brought the *Daily News* instead.'

Somsak, the young lad who looked after the newspapers, ran out and picked them up.

'Why wasn't there a *Thai Rath,* Phi Kart? Have they been closed down or something?'

'They said at the shop that someone - I don't know who - bought up the lot in town. There's no *Thai Rath* to be had anywhere in the province. Nobody knows who or why.'

The new house stood in a spacious garden on the banks of the river Mun. The view of the river from the verandah was superb, but the owner, who sat there, Sia Mangkorn, did not seem at all entranced by the view. He was yelling angrily at his underlings.

'Don't you see? They'll drag me by the neck to jail! This will destroy the lot of us! Go and find out who the bastard is who took these photographs.' He flung the newspaper at his three employees, who sat stony faced in front of him.

'Read it you clots! It doesn't say where, but anybody reading it - those officials will know it's me. I've tried to buy up all the copies since early this morning, but I don't know if we got them all or not. They'll soon be here in procession, those bastards from the Corruption Suppression Unit.'

'I think it must be the local correspondent, Sir. I'll go and check it out,' one of his employees volunteered.

'I checked out all the correspondents already - I think they're OK, but I can't be sure. You go and investigate, Ai Song. When you find who's responsible there'll be a big reward.'

He sent them off with their orders and retired to his bedroom with a headache.

The day school re-opened Duangdaw handed Piya an old newspaper.

'Have you read this paper, Khun Piya? It's two or three days old; I think this refers to somewhere near here. I thought you might like to read it.'

'What news?' Piya took the newspaper, excited. When he saw the headline and the page one picture, he quickly tried to hide his feelings, put a normal expression on his face.

'Massive Destruction of Forests Discovered in Ubon. Influential Magnate Directs Operations.' He read out the headlines and put the newspaper on the desk, looking carefully at the picture, which showed felled timber lying all over the place, the workmen's lean-to and the timber lorry, its number plate clearly visible.

'I suspect the 'influential magnate' is Sia Mangkorn,' Duangdaw said. Headmaster Khammaw joined them. He looked at the newspaper and said: 'Oh! This must be why Sia Mangkorn sent him over to come and ask questions in the village. It can't be anyone from here who sent the news to the paper. I am inclined to worry about Phisit. If he's done something stupid here, it won't be a laughing matter.'

Piya avoided the headmaster's eyes. 'This doesn't say anything about where it is. There's no mention of Sia Mangkorn's name - or anybody else's name; there's no allegation of criminal behaviour against any particular person.'

The Governor looked up from the large file on his desk and looked at the man who entered with an expression of displeasure.

'Please sit down, Mr Mangkorn.' The magnate sat down, but first raising his hands in the overelaborate greeting characteristic of many successful merchants. The Governor got up from his desk and walked over to the sofa and sat opposite his guest.

'I am very concerned about this newspaper story. There's an investigation team due from Bangkok on Friday. This government's taking the matter of the destruction of forests very seriously. This is going to cause me a lot of trouble.'

'Sir, you can't believe these newspaper stories. They could have taken those photographs anywhere and then claimed they came from this province.'

'But the number plate in the picture shows clearly the vehicle's from Ubon. Or are you suggesting the photographer fitted it with false number plates?' The Governor was not convinced. 'You can see it, can't you, Sia?'

'You're very observant, Sir, just as a top administrator should be.' The merchant smiled sheepishly. 'I think I know the people coming from Bangkok. I'll try to settle this without making difficulty for you, Sir.'

'That's fine, but the fact that the newspapers printed the story is enough cause for me to worry. Whatever its truth, the Ministry's going to take me to task,' the Governor complained. 'I'm leaving for Bangkok this evening. You find some way to settle this, Sia. Oh! And I beg of you, please send that BMW to Bangkok for four or five days.'

Piya rolled the newspaper tight. The photograph he had taken was on the front page of the newspaper with the largest circulation in Thailand, with the story of illegal felling of timber. This was a commonplace for readers throughout the country. Such events were frequent, reported from every corner of the land. But for Piya it was a major affair. No one knew he was the photographer, that it was he who had given the story to the newspaper. He took the paper to 'Carn Khen.

'Look at this, Uncle.'

'Let me read it.' 'Carn Khen took the newspaper and read the story carefully. He smiled, and then said, 'Who else is going to be sorry about this besides Sia Mangkorn? You're responsible, aren't you, Khru?'

'Think what you like, Uncle. If I was really responsible, do you think it was the right thing to do or not?'

'If you really did it, that's good. But please take care. These people have a lot of power.' 'Carn Khen's tone became very serious. 'If you have any trouble, I'll always be ready to help.'

CHAPTER 23

'How's it going, Ai Song?' Sia Mangkorn stubbed his cigarette out in the ashtray. 'Where did you go? And what have you found out?'

'Nothing yet, Sir. I talked to nearly all the newspaper reporters in the province, but I couldn't find out a thing.' Ai Song, who had formerly worked for *farang* at the air base, sat on a chair in the corner of the room.

'The reporters all get a white envelope from me regularly every month. I don't suppose it's any of them.' The Sia's mood seemed to improve.

'Get them to try and help you. If you don't get any results, you'll have to start on the villages. You get some results quick, or I'll have to sack you.' He spoke half-seriously - then gave a loud laugh.

That same day Ai Song and two stony-faced gunmen arrived in Barn Norng Ma Vor. They met with the Sia's hirelings and hangers-on in Lung 'Carn Kern's house. Among them were Thit Phun and Mor Sombat.

'If we cut away the undergrowth, there's only one path we can follow. We've got to admit that the one who went into the forest and took those photographs is either a resident of this village or passed through here on his way, or flew in in a helicopter over this village,' Ai Song said, summarizing his deductions to the gathering. 'For my part, I'm no good at investigations; my business is killing. I'd like us all to co-operate with this investigation. When we've got the culprit beyond doubt, leave the matter of reward to me. The Sia has instructed me not to stint. I am the Sia's agent. Let everyone know that the one who finds out who other in an effort to protect what they had and to earn a livelihood.

He thought about his own part in the doings of the year, what he had put into his work for the school and its pupils and the various benefits that had ensued. Even though it had not all been his own work, he could not but be proud of his part in it. Much of it had been done on his initiative. The children loved him; most villagers saw him as a teacher devoted to his work, trustworthy, worthy of respect. And now he was engaged in a new campaign, by accident almost, and without intending such involvement. But he had known from the first that this affair would not end with the newspaper story. The people engaged in the business of destroying forests, at the level of the *amphur* and at the level of the province, were scurrying around concerned lest the details of their activities would become public knowledge.

Piya knew that Sia Mangkorn was furious, that he had sent his men to find out who had been the instigator of the story. He was therefore not as careful as he should have been. Worse than that, overjoyed and proud of the consequences of his actions, he planned to circulate the story more widely and bring it to the attention of an even higher level of politician and official.

As Piya sat listening to the sounds of the crickets, Caw Siang came walking across the field, whistling and carrying a basket.

'Hello Siang. What have you got in the basket?'

'Mother sent you some food, Khun Khru.' He put the basket down on the bench which stood on the edge of the verandah.

took those photographs and who sent them to the newspaper will get a reward of two thousand baht.'

Mor Sombat dropped in to see Phayorm after he left the meeting at Lung 'Carn Kern's. Then got on his motorcycle and left for the *amphur*. His destination was the photographer's. He chatted awhile with the owner-operator of the shop, but got no information from him. He was quite unwilling to say anything at all or cast any light on the subject of Mor Sombat's enquiries. The latter was on the point of giving up, but the thought of the reward renewed his determination. He thought he might make enquiries in the city, but remembered that there were scores of photographers - small shops that provided a thirty-minute service for identity card photographs, and big ones that took and processed colour pictures. He went back home turning over many names in his mind, but he could not decide which of them was likely to be the guilty one.

It was almost dusk and the crickets could be heard in all the big trees around the school. Piya sat on the verandah of his little hut thinking about the year that was fast coming to an end - it was almost a year since he had first come here as a teacher. In that year he had encountered many people, in varying situations, most of whom seemed bound to an endless wheel of poverty and hardship. He had seen the suffering caused by sickness, pain and ill health; the stupidity, ignorance and small-mindedness of the villagers; a school which had been little more than a temporary shack, a headmaster that cared for nothing but gambling; a tractable bunch of pupils; devout villagers and business magnates who destroyed the environment and exploited their fellow citizens; and everybody engaged in a struggle against each

'What is it?' Piya stood up and came to have a look. 'Oh! It's fried *cinun*. I like that very much. What's in the package? It looks like pork with bamboo shoots.'

'It's *mok* with red ants' eggs,' Siang replied, smiling.

The young man's mouth watered when he smelled the aroma of the red ants' egg preparation which came from the packages. He had not had this for a long time.

'You shouldn't have taken all this trouble. Who got the red ants' eggs?'

'Phi Phayorm collected the red ants' eggs. Mother and I went digging for the *cinun*. We got a whole bucket full,' Siang said proudly.

'Have dinner with me, Siang,' Piya invited.

'Thank you, I've already eaten. I'll go get some *kadon*[1] vegetables for you to eat with the fried *cinun*.' He rushed off to the *kadon* plant behind the old schoolhouse, which had just put out tender new leaves. He soon brought back a handful of leaves which he washed at the water jar and then brought to Piya, arranged on a plate.

'I am going home now.'

'Just a minute. Take these dried bananas to your mother.' Piya picked up two plastic bags of dried bananas, put them in a paper bag and handed them to the boy. He usually kept a stock of dried bananas in his house, it being impossible to get any other fruit in the village, particularly during the dry season. The dried bananas from Khemarat were his usual dessert. Every time he went to the *amphur* he laid in a stock.

Siang took the paper bag and ran off towards the village. The sun slowly disappeared behind the distant trees

---

1 *Kadon* - leaves of CAREYA HERBACEAE.

and the sound of the crickets died away. The bells and clappers hung round the necks of the cows and the buffaloes sounded *'kring, kring, kok, kok,'* along the road to the village. Mor Sombat had taken his motorcycle along the sandy shortcut to the village and arrived at the house just as Siang did.

'Where've you been, Siang?' the unlicensed doctor asked as he parked his motorcycle.

'Khun Piya's.'

'What's that bag?' He stared at the paper bag in Siang's hand.

'Dried bananas. Khun Piya gave them.'

'Let's see.' Sombat pulled the bag in a friendly manner and looked inside, but it was what was on the outside that excited him. In large letters, the bag proclaimed:

Phorn Silp - Indoors and Outdoors Photographers.
Developing and Printing. Black and White and Colour.
Agents for all kinds of Photographic Equipment.

'Is this Piya's bag then?' Mor Sombat asked, keeping the excitement out of his face.

'Yes,' Siang answered briefly and took the bag up to his mother. Mor Sombat followed him up the steps.

'Well, well! Gifts come often to this household,' he said to no one in particular.

Phayorm was lighting the kerosene oil lamp. 'What gifts?'

'That there! Siang's brought something else from Khun Piya.' Sombat pointed to Siang.

'Oh! Mother sent Khun Piya some *cinun*. He must have given Siang some sweets.' Phayorm sounded annoyed.

'Oh, I see. You have this regular exchange of food, do you?'

'Goodness! Once in a while. Mother went digging for *cinun* today and she sent some up to Piya. I don't see anything wrong in that.' Phayorm looked angry.

'Fine, fine! I didn't say anything,' Mor Sombat protested in a loud voice. 'Have you eaten yet, Mother? I've brought some beef from Phak I Hin. Will you make some *larp* for us to eat?' He turned towards Mae Kham, speaking in a softer voice. He took the parcel of beef and walked into the kitchen as if he was a member of the family.

After Siang had gone, Piya had his evening meal and then walked over to look at the chicken run. He checked that they were all there, then strolled across the school grounds. The full moon had risen over the trees and bathed the high ground in a cool light. The two school buildings, the old and the new, stood like two representatives of different generations from some distant age. From 'Carn Khen's home the notes of the *khaen* could be heard over the silence. Piya stopped and turned towards the house from which the music came. It was but a short way there, but his feelings prompted him to make for the village. He locked his hut and set off for the house of Headmaster Khammaw.

He passed children at play in the yards of their homes, calling to each other in their high-pitched voices. Piya hoped they would not see who it was. They recognized him, however, stopped playing, whispered to each other and greeted him respectfully as he passed. Piya acknowledged their greetings and walked on.

'Have you gone to bed yet, Khun Aew? Come out and look at the moon. It's very beautiful,' he called out as he climbed the steps of the house.

'Oh, you are in time.' Duangdaw opened the door of her room and came out. She was wearing a wide-necked red blouse and a cloth striped black and yellow. A faint fragrance of perfume hung about her. 'Some people are lucky wherever they go. I've got some cakes for you today.'

'Did you make them yourself, or did you buy these?' Piya teased, as he knew Duangdaw was not much of a cook.

'You watch out, or I won't give you any.' She picked up the mat and took it out on to the uncovered part of the verandah. 'Come, sit out here, it's better. The moon's beautiful. You should have brought your guitar, Khun Piya.'

'I am very happy these days. I like this life, close to nature. I think Khun Aew likes it too.' He looked around. 'Where's the headmaster gone?'

'Oh! I don't know, he went out to dinner. I think he may have gone to the headman's.' Duangdaw gazed up into the sky, the clouds shining like cobwebs, now, with the light of the moon.

'If you lived in a big city I don't think you'd get to see the moon like this. The more I think about it, I don't think I want a transfer from here.'

'You really feel that, Khun Aew?' Piya said quickly, but hid his joy. 'Rural teachers have got to find their pleasures in the work they do and in the natural beauty of their surroundings. The gifts of nature and all the other good things we find around us, can bring us happiness.

There's no need to struggle for a transfer to the city - or to the *amphur*.'

'Sometimes I think you love your work more than anything else around you. If I'm wrong, please excuse me.' The young woman pursued the opportunity. 'Sometimes it seems you have no heart.'

'I have one, but sometimes I don't know whom to tell what's in it,' the young man said earnestly.

Duangdaw served out two plates of a sweet made from bananas, then went in and poured out two glasses of water from a jug.

'Aunt Caem sent in two bunches of bananas. I made this when I got back from school. I wanted to send you some, but I thought you may have a favourite student with you and I changed my mind.'

'You can't be sure of anyone.' The young man laughed. 'Come on, give it to me. You might change your mind and I won't have any at all.'

'Wait a moment. Speak nicely or you won't get any.' The two of them chatted on till it was nine o'clock. Piya walked home and was both annoyed and angry to find his hut had been broken into for the second time. His possessions had been searched and scattered about. However, nothing was missing. The intruder, or intruders, had clearly been looking for valuables. They had taken nothing when all they found was books, old clothes and musical instruments.

The young man thought he might go tell 'Carn Khen, his nearest neighbour. But he changed his mind as there did not seem any necessity for it. He went to bed, and despite his anger, he fell asleep about midnight.

CHAPTER 24

'The Governor and the Chief of Police are still blaming me - as if I were some stranger,' Sia Mangkorn complained to his associates. 'These high officials are so bloody sensitive, they've got so excited about this story in the newspaper that they aren't paying any attention to much more important things. And no one knows who the rascal of a reporter was either.'

'Hell, Sir, this government has taken the whole business of forest preservation very seriously. There are stories from every province and the big boys are being watched to see if they are hand in glove with the timber merchants. Wait till they cool down a bit. It's natural they get excited,' one of his partners advised the Sia.

'This is only a newspaper report - and it doesn't identify anyone. There's nothing for us to worry about.' Another of his colleagues tried to pacify him.

'I am not worried. I am abused day and night. I sometimes think I'll have to present them with a Mercedes Benz before I get any peace.' The Sia sipped his tea.

'The newspapermen are just the same. If you start feeding them, they want to be satiated. Otherwise they start barking. But I am sure this is not their work,' the first partner observed.

'No. Look at the pictures. They were taken way up near the border. I don't know, could it be one of our men?' the Sia's younger brother said.

'Whoever it is, he must be caught. I am so furious I'll chop him into little pieces. Damn him!' The timber king of Isarn seemed to tremble as he spoke.

An underling came in looking excited. 'Mor Sombat from Barn Norng Ma Vor wants to see you, Sia.'

'What about?' He looked angry.

'I don't know, Sir.'

'Go and ask him, then,' the Sia's younger brother snapped. The servant left, expressionless, and soon came back.

'Regarding the newspaper story, Sir.'

'Bring him in at once,' the 'Sia ordered in a low voice. Mor Sombat sat down in an overstuffed chair and looked round the airconditioned room. He looked excited. Before he could speak, Sia Mangkorn asked, 'Well, have you got some new information?'

'Yes, Sir!' he reported. 'At first I was only suspicious, but last night I searched his house and I've got certain evidence now.

'Who?'

Mor Sombat looked round at the others in the room and then looked at the Sia, who nodded.

'Go ahead, they are all with us.'

'Khun Piya, the one who lives near the school at Barn Norng Ma Vor.' Mor Sombat controlled his nervousness and related the story of his investigations.

'From the first I suspected it was a teacher from that area. Ordinary villagers don't have cameras. When I happened to see a paper bag from a photographer's I searched his house when he'd gone off to chat up one of the girls in the village. I found the camera and the box in which the film came, but I didn't find any pictures or the film itself. It's enough. I am sure he's the guilty one. Another thing, this fellow has many strange things about him - it's very suspicious. Sometimes I think he's some kind of spy or a student come to stir up trouble.'

'But don't do anything yet. Just keep him under close observation. If we are wrong, things could get worse, there could be more trouble. When we are certain we'll get him.' The boss gave his opinion.

Piya did not make a complaint to the village headman. Nor did he say anything about his house being broken into and his possessions searched, to anyone, not even to the headmaster or Duangdaw. He did not discover that Mor Sombat was the culprit, nor that the *mor* was now his continuous shadow.

Since he had sent the pictures to the newspaper and thrown everyone into confusion after the story was published, the young teacher had expanded on the story in the form of letters to the editors of several newspapers. He related the illegal, destructive and criminal doings of the timber magnates, including their abduction and murder of peaceful villagers. Because he had actually seen them working, Piya could specify the names of those who were missing, but he still did not mention the name of the one ultimately responsible. But he did mention the *tambon* and the *amphur* in which the happenings had occurred. He then waited to see what would happen, making sure to read the newspapers in the village each day.

Mor Sombat now visited the village much more often than he had in the past. After about two weeks the newspaper published Piya's letter. The villagers were even more excited, for there in print was the name Barn Norng Ma Vor. This became a matter of general excitement.

'I thought at first some fierce forest spirits had abducted poor Thit Liang,' Phor jai Phan muttered. 'But now it seems it was those pestilential evil spirits that destroy the forest.'

'Phor jai, you shouldn't be in too much of a hurry to believe it all. You've got to be careful with what you read in newspapers,' Somsak cautioned. 'It may just be an attempt to make trouble.'

'What? How can you not believe? If it's in the newspaper it must be true. If it wasn't true they wouldn't print it!' Phor jai countered.

Mor Sombat hurried to Ubon to report to Sia Mangkorn.

'That bloody animal's done me again.' The Sia was beside himself with rage. 'Have you read today's paper? He knows everything - as if he lives and eats with me. He'll soon announce my name too! Well, Mor Sombat, what other news do you have?'

'I watch him every day. There's nothing really unusual, except that he reads the newspapers every day. And one day he sneaked off to the *amphur* by himself.'

'What did he go to the *amphur* for?'

'I followed him, but I got there too late. I just saw him eating *larp* with a bunch of young teachers in Tia Chai Di's shop. He even invited me to eat with them,' Sombat reported.

'Eh! What if it's not him?' the Sia's younger brother asked.

'I say it's him! I got him talking about forestry - he has lots of opinions about that.'

'What did he say?'

'He said forests cause the rain.'

'Bloody mad! I think we'll get more than this,' he insisted. 'Go try the reporter at the *amphur*. I think he said there's a teacher at the *amphur* who's also a newspaper reporter. That lot, they like writing and barking a lot!'

The rains fell during the sixth month. The hot parched earth became cool and moist again, green with the new shoots of grass which had been waiting for the rain. The young green leaves of the tamarind appeared - delicious, boiled with little golden frogs. Piya arose to the freshness of the new day. He walked, admiring the flowers and the vegetables which had responded to the rain, as if eager to hasten the recovery of all convalescing patients. A timber truck had appeared and stopped in front of the school. He walked around it, but could not make out if anything was wrong, if it had bogged down in mud or sand. He asked the driver and all he said was

'It stopped'.

The young teacher could not help staring long at the gigantic lengths of timber on the truck. He wanted to go back to his hut and get his camera, but feared he would be seen taking photographs. If the lorry was still there that evening he would take some photographs and send them on to the newspaper. He was so proud of the results of his activities, so overcome with officiousness, he did not realize he was being constantly watched.

The morning wore on; it was noon, then afternoon, and the lorry still stood there. No one came to repair it, no one even watched it. It was evening and Piya went home and ate. Rain fell gently and lightning split the sky. Frogs croaked loudly, glad of the rain. Piya got ready his camera and the flash which came with the Instamatic. He waited for the heavy rain to ease, to go out and take his photograph.

It was after eight o'clock and the rain still fell. Lightning crashed into the fields. Piya crept close to the lorry, chose himself a suitable position and waited till his excitement lessened. He chose the moment of a flash of lightning to snap the camera. Immediately he found he had to scamper away for there was the sound of yelling and the beat of running feet coming towards him.

'Catch him, don't let him get away.'

The young teacher ran as fast as he could. He set off as if for his house, but then changed his mind and, using the darkness to conceal his destination, he made for 'Carn Khen's house. His pursuers rushed towards the school, as if hoping he would run in that direction.

'They are going to catch me, Uncle!' Shaking, Piya asked, 'Let me stay here tonight.'

'Carn Khen, still thoroughly bewildered, looked at the young man, now soaked from head to foot, and asked

'What's wrong? What are you running like that for, as if chased by tigers or elephants?'

'I went to photograph that timber truck opposite the school and the whole lot suddenly came chasing me.' The young man handed the camera to the other. He looked thoroughly frightened.

'Don't be frightened. Calm down. You'll stay here tonight. If anybody tries to make trouble, I'll take care of them.'

Thit Phun, Caw Kart and Mor Sombat, when they lost Piya, made straight for his hut. They found it empty and were more than ever convinced he was the one they were looking for. The hut was unlocked and they seized the opportunity to examine it at leisure.

'You see, he's gone and his camera's gone; there's only the film container here,' Mor Sombat pointed out with satisfaction. 'I am going to Ubon tomorrow; Ai Phun, Ai

Kart you'll come along? The Sia should at least give us a thousand or two.' He wrapped the film container in a piece of paper and the three of them left, satisfied.

CHAPTER 25

'You need have no doubts now, Sia. Khun Piya is certainly the one you want.' Mor Sombat unwrapped his paper and took out the film container. 'The three of us hid and watched all the time - from when Ai Kuai pretended the lorry broke down, from early morning till evening. It was night when he came out to take his photographs. He ran off. We chased him to his house, but couldn't catch him. It's clear, he's the one responsible for it all.'

'I too have suspected him for a long time,' Caw Kart was not to be outdone. 'Whenever he went to the *amphur* he had to go to the photographers.'

Thit Phun must also have his say, 'Truly, if I hadn't been stoned on ganja last night, we'd have had him for sure.'

'We'll deal with him! Can we get him out of Barn Norng Ma Vor?' It was half question, half order.

'I think you should go and see his superiors. Get him transferred,' Caw Kart gave as his opinion. 'If you want us to deal with him we may have to use force, threaten him with a gun.

'Do what you like. As long as he doesn't remain there. But I can't go and see any officials at this time.' Sia Mangkorn counted out some five-hundred-baht notes and handed them to Mor Sombat. 'Here's two thousand. Divide it among yourselves. When you chase him out of there, there'll be more.'

Since the road was improved and vehicular traffic could come and go without much difficulty, commercial vehicles selling all manner of goods became increasingly frequent in the village. Some sold goods on credit or on hire purchase - such things as large water jars from Ratburi, cane mats from Phimai. Sometimes they brought films for screening in the village and sometimes entrepreneurs would show films, making a small charge for entrance. They used the school grounds as an open air theatre and charged two or three baht per person. They never made much out of this, at best four or five hundred baht a night.

That night Benchaporn Cinemas, the largest of travelling cinema companies, was screening a film called 'The Bloody Land', a film full of violence, slashing and thumping. As the hero was surrounded by a mob of villains who attacked him without compunction, the sound of shooting on the screen seemed to grow louder and louder - 'Bang, bang, bang'.

The spectators watched, excited, but unsurprised, thinking it was the hero's offsider shooting on screen. But finally, they all grew quiet and frightened. The film stopped. Caw Uam, Sia Mangkorn's foreman, took hold of the microphone and announced: 'Brothers and sisters of Barn Norng Ma Vor' - he sounded like a politician soliciting votes - 'I must apologize, brothers and sisters, for having interrupted your enjoyment tonight. I have something I want to say to you all. You don't need to fear anything from us. In the past we have all lived together without any trouble, each one minding his own business. Then they sent two teachers to the school here, Khun Piya and Khun Phisit. We all thought they were teachers for the pupils only, but that was not the case. The two of them began interfering in all kinds of things, causing great trouble to the people. Things were so bad they had to transfer Khun Phisit to a distant village. As for Khun Piya, he had the people do all kinds of things, all of course for his own benefit. We had all to spend our hard-earned money. He lived off the products of the handiwork of all of you, brothers and sisters. Khun Piya pretended he did these things for everyone's benefit, but it was really for his own. Headmaster Khammaw knew Khun Piya's plans, but he didn't know how to stop them. Khun Piya is a deep one. He wanted to live by himself so he could carry out his secret plans.

'We've found out he's a Communist. The Communists have sent him here to incite disaffection among the villagers. All the tactics he's used are those of the Communists. If you think carefully you will see his strange ways. He doesn't like to drink with his fellow villagers. He likes to pretend to be doing all kinds of things, so that people will praise his diligence. But really he only wants to brainwash our fellow villagers. Just think: what is it Khun Piya has done for this village of Norng Ma Vor? He has only exploited the labour of our children and our grandchildren. Growing vegetables, growing watermelons, keeping chickens - he used his pupils for all of this. The new school house! Khun Piya pretends he's the one who got the money for the new building. In truth he did nothing. All he did was take timber from there to build his own house and make chairs and tables for himself. Let's chase this man away from here.'

When Piya and Duangdaw first saw what was happening, they got away from the film crowd as quickly as possible. They went straight to 'Carn Khen's house. Ai

Uam's voice could still be heard detailing the crimes and failings of Piya. But he did not mention Duangdaw's name at all. Meanwhile a group of youths, thoroughly annoyed at the interference with their entertainment, tried to yell down the speaker, exhorting him to 'get lost'. But they too fell silent, seeing Ai Uam's supporters were too many for them. Those who valued a quiet life, silently left the crowd and went home. The employees of the travelling cinema did not know what to do except to allow the intruders to use the microphone. Some villagers went along with the speaker and began to mutter among themselves, criticizing Piya; but those who were on Piya's side, and many who would rather remain neutral, fled the school compound as quickly as possible.

Duangdaw's body shook in fright. She clung tightly to his arm all the way to 'Carn Khen's house.

'Khun Piya, what did you do to them? Why didn't you say anything to me?'

'Quiet! Don't be frightened.' 'Carn Khen spoke fiercely. They could hear the sounds from the school grounds in the distance.

Get rid of Khun Piya! Where is he? If you are innocent, come show yourself! If you don't, that's proof you're a Communist.'

The efforts of Ai Uam and his men were having success. At least some of the villagers were being incited to side with Ai Uam and agree to chasing Piya away. When they saw they were having success, they quickly piled into their pick-up and made for the village. The cinema men quickly folded up their screen, collected their equipment, and left.

'Carn Khen dressed hurriedly.

'The two of you stay here. Don't leave under any circumstances. I'll go find the headman. Put the lights out.' He hurried away. They heard the yells from the men in the pick-up as they circled round the village, calling on the people to drive away Piya.

Duangdaw snuggled up to Piya until they were pressed tightly against each other.

'Khun Piya, I don't know why they are doing this. I've never seen anything like this. What'll happen if they come here?'

'Cheer up! Don't worry. Let whatever happens, happen. I'll try to do the best I can.' He moved closer to her and tried to calm her. She was shivering as if cold, and he rubbed her to warm her.

'If anything happens, I want you to know, Khun Aew, that I only wished the best for the village. If I die, I'll die happy, just being with you like this.' They were silent and all they could hear was the sound of their heated breath and the pounding of their hearts.

'Phu jai Lua! Beat your gong, quickly!' 'Carn Khen ordered the headman, as if he would take no denial.

'What's the matter, 'Carn Khen? What's happened?' The headman jumped up from where he had been lying, face downwards on the outer verandah.

'Didn't you hear the gunshots, the yelling over the loudspeakers? I don't know who they are, they are trying to drive away Khun Piya! Beat that gong and get the villagers to come and protect him. If it's possible, send someone to get the police. If we allow such things to happen, our society, our security, will become like a house without beams, without joists.' 'Carn Khen did not delay. He grabbed the hammer and beat the *korlor* with quick, repeated beats, signifying trouble.

In no time at all the villagers who had returned from the aborted cinema show gathered at the headman's house. Headmaster Khammaw looked around anxiously, looking for Piya and Duangdaw. When he did not see them, he rushed off to the school, thinking they may have hidden themselves there or in Piya's hut.

Headman Lua asked the villagers to make their views known. 'Carn Khen stood on the verandah of the house, the centre of attention. About a hundred people, adults and children, were gathered there, most of them just come from the interrupted film show.

'I am a citizen of Barn Norng Ma Vor. I was born here, I grew up here, and here I will die. I live peacefully, and it's a long time since I caused any trouble to anybody. Today I ask your permission to speak.'

The villagers were silent. There seemed to be unspoken agreement that this was a man of importance and they were going to listen to what he had to say. 'Carn Khen, the man they called 'mad of the spirits', looked out over the crowd.

'I'd like to say now what I haven't said for many years. Everyone here knows full well what happened here in Barn Norng Ma Vor today. Those of you who went to the cinema know that a bunch of people tried to incite us villagers to chase out Khru Piya. They tried to do this with force and intimidation. I don't know who they were. But I know that what they did was wrong. I ask you to resist them without fear of any person that may stand behind them. Brothers and sisters, those of you with human hearts, those of you who uphold the *Dhamma,* know that Piya is a good man. Khru Piya has done much good for the school.

He is beloved of the children, because he truly has the qualities of a teacher. He is an example of decency, of trustworthiness, of perseverance, of diligence. Our village and our society needs people like this. But his wishes conflict with the interests of those with power and influence - don't make me mention names. He is now in danger because evil men have been annoyed. Will we now allow this man from another village, who has sacrificed so much for our development, to succumb to this danger? Do you, the villagers of Barn Norng Ma Vor, want to fall into the power of brigands?'

'Where's Khru Piya, then?' a voice shouted from the darkness.

'Let those who love Khru Piya follow me!' 'Carn Khen descended the stairs and made off for his house, followed by men, women and children in procession. Some of them stayed behind, wondering which side to take. He mounted the stairs of his house like a commander leading the troops.

'Khru Piya, Khru Duangdaw, we're here! You don't need to be afraid!'

They emerged from inside the house together. 'Carn Khen lit lamps, the large group of villagers stood crowded together below. Piya regained his composure, but Duangdaw was still disturbed and frightened by what had happened in the crowd, but also by what had happened between the two of them. But she too found enough inner resources to hide her feelings.

Piya walked to the edge of the verandah, wanting to thank the villagers gathered below, realizing they had come to show their support. They were those who loved and respected him. His enemies in the village were keeping quiet, seeing they were outnumbered.

'Thank you, brothers and sisters. Thank you all my pupils.' Piya spoke with feeling. 'Carn Khen jumped up when, a few seconds later, a gunshot sounded, 'Bang'.

Everyone screamed, those outside as well as those inside. 'Carn Khen fell face downwards. Piya bent over and took hold of him. Those below thought Piya had been shot and set up a howl. Duangdaw screamed and embraced Piya - she too thinking the young man had been shot. The confusion did not last long. Everyone soon knew that 'Carn Khen had been shot on the tip of his shoulder, the bullet grazing it and causing profuse bleeding, but he made little fuss about it. No one knew whether the gunman had tried to kill Piya or 'Carn Khen.

'You keep saving my life, Uncle!' Piya prostrated himself in thanks to the older man.

Headmaster Khammaw rushed up the stairs of the house, now deeply disturbed about the safety of his niece and of the young man who had become so important in the running of his school.

'Aew! Piya! 'Carn Khen! What's happened? Is anyone hurt?' He forced his words out, gasping 'Ai Sang, Ai Lat, Ai 'Sak! Hurry! Go, get some water! Get some medicine! Ai Nuai! Ai Thaen! Go and get Phu jai Lua! Quick!'

CHAPTER 26

'You should go and stay somewhere else for a little while, Khun Piya,' Duangdaw announced firmly. 'I think it's much too dangerous to stay here.'

'I want to stay here and fight them to the very end,' the young man said with determination.

'You can't do that. Your life's still valuable to many. Listen to me! Go and stay in my house in Ubon for a little while. I'll write out your application for leave.'

'You go, Piya. You don't need to worry about the leave application. Just wait till they quieten down and then you can come back.' The headmaster sounded very concerned. Piya looked at 'Carn Khen.

'You don't need to worry about me, Khru. I'll be fine. I think it's good if you go away for a little while. You can then come back and take them on again,' 'Carn Khen advised.

Before dawn, Piya left on his old bicycle for the *amphur,* accompanied by Somsak, the boy who looked after the newspaper reading room, on another bicycle as companion. Duangdaw and 'Carn Khen waved him goodbye. They planned his early departure so that the villagers would not know where he was. At the *amphur* he left his bicycle with an acquaintance and took the bus to Ubon. He made for Wat Sawarng Arom, where he usually stayed when he was in Ubon. He agreed with Duangdaw that he would leave a message at her home if there were any news and she would call in and pick it up herself.

Mor Sombat sat in Sia Mangkorn's house in the provincial capital, looking depressed. He had hurried there after the happenings at Barn Norng Ma Vor - happenings which he had planned and for which he was entirely responsible.

'I've had enough, Sia. It's too much for me. I didn't realize it would get to the stage of murder. I'm not doing any more.'

'Khun Sombat, you want money, don't you? You are already fully involved. Even if you withdraw now you are still guilty. But if you continue to help us there's money in it for you. You think about it carefully before you decide. You have two choices. One, you will have enough money to marry the woman you love and get your own back on the man you mistrust. The other, you get no more money and you're guilty of attempted murder. I can prove you're the man who tried to kill 'Carn Khen. Will you take ten thousand baht and get yourself a wife or will you go to jail?'

'You want me to kill him then, Sia?' the unregistered medico asked, though he already knew the answer. Instead of answering, Sia Mangkorn pulled out a bundle of purple notes and dropped it on the table in front of the young man.

'I can get Ai Song to do it too. But Ai Song doesn't recognize him too well. If he makes a mistake there'll be more chaos. Here, take this ten thousand. When it's done, there will be more.' He turned and went into his bedroom, leaving his new gunman to decide for himself.

Phayorm lamented for Piya, every day, in Mor Sombat's presence, unaware that the one she loved was about to murder the one she worshipped.

'I am so sorry for Khun Piya. In spite of all the good he's done, there are still people who hate him. They have no gratitude, no justice.'

'You miss him do you? If you miss him, why don't you go to him? Or don't you know where he has hidden himself? I've never seen a coward like him,' Sombat said offensively.

Mor Sombat tried every way he could to find Piya. He had decided he would have to do away with the schoolteacher. If he did not, Sia Mangkorn would see he would get into trouble for the crimes he had already committed. He was not certain whether this was in the Sia's power or not, but he feared the magnate more than he feared the consequences of killing Piya. What tipped the balance however was the thought of the money and the desire to get rid of the man he thought was a rival for the love of his woman. He could not get out of his mind the belief that Piya was trying to take Phayorm away from him.

Nevertheless, Sombat was an ordinary man who had never before considered murder. Sometimes he wondered to himself why he should have to kill Piya. He had never before even killed any large beast such as an ox or a buffalo. But then he thought of all the reasons for the murder. His mind tumbled from one view to another. In secret he sought out Ai Song, Sia Mangkorn's usual gunman.

'You must help me out of this. Otherwise I'll be dead for sure. All the money I get from the Sia I'll hand over to you. The only thing I ask is don't tell the Sia you did it.'

'Why shouldn't I tell tell him I did it?' This fellow was suspicious too.

'I suppose he thinks dogs like that are not worthy of a gunman of your station.' Sombat tried to soft-soap him.

'Where is he now?'

'Who knows? He may have run away to Bangkok. Or some other province. But I'm sure he'll return. He loves that school of his. Can you ask the Sia for permission to go and stay there for a short while?'

'That's fine. I haven't killed anyone for many months now. It's been boring. My hand needs the practice.' The gunman stroked his hand with anticipation as he spoke.

Things turned out as Mor Sombat had anticipated. Piya had been in Ubon five days when he got a letter from Duangdaw.

> Dear Khun Piya,
> I miss you very much. Everything seems normal now. The children complain so much about your not being here, they seem to do no studying at all. I don't think you should return yet, but everybody misses you.
>
> Missing you terribly,
> Aew

Piya got the letter when he went to Duangdaw's house in Ubon. As soon as he had read it he went back to Wat Sawarng Arom, bade respectful farewell to the head monk and took a bus back to his school - all on the same day. He got to the *amphur* when it was almost dark. He wanted to continue on to the village, but changed his mind. He decided to set out the next morning, going straight to school in time for the morning session. He stayed overnight with his friend.

He woke next moring at 4:00 A.M., took his bicycle, Ai Krong, and set out for Barn Norng Ma Vor. His thoughts went out to his pupils and the young woman who was waiting for him. At Barn Khok Klarng he happened to cross paths with Mor Sombat. They stopped and spoke for a moment, then parted. A few minutes later, Mor Sombat turned his bike and returned the way he had come. He pretended he had forgotten something and speeded his bike up towards Barn Norng Ma Vor. Piya had no thought of danger, suspected nothing. His thoughts were only on the school, on his pupils, and on Duangdaw. He rode through the village and had started the ascent to the school when there was the crack of an old World War ll rifle. Just one shot. The bullet ploughed into the young teacher's chest and through his body. His body was thrown back and off his bicycle, Ai Krong, and he lay still on the ground, blood gushing.

Duangdaw shrieked as she jumped at the sound of the rifle, as if she knew what had happened. The children streamed out, running one after the other, children and teacher dreading what they would find, heedless of danger to themselves.

'Khun Piya! You've gone from me!' Duangdaw hugged the corpse to her, not caring who saw. The others stood, completely silent as if hypnotized. At last Caw Siang spoke:

'Khru Piya is dead. Who is going to teach us now?'

'I am here. I'll be here with you always.'

The young woman cradled the body, now bereft of consciousness, as a little girl would cradle a beloved doll. She sat there surrounded by children who could not understand why someone like Khru Piya should be shot and killed.

GLOSSARY

aa *ʔaa* :
Uncle. There is some dialectal variation in the use of this term. Author appears to use it to mean 'father's younger brother'.

aai:
See **ai**.

ab nam ab tha *ʔaab naam ʔaab thaa* :
An 'elaborate colloquial' form of 'to bathe': **ab** - 'to bathe', **nam** - 'water'.

acarn *ʔaacaan* :
A learned person. In the novel a schoolteacher with a university degree. Any university teacher below the rank of full professor. *Also see* **'carn.**

ai *ʔai or ʔaai* :
Term of address used for males, usually as a prefix. May be derogatory, or indicate equality and intimacy. In dialect, 'elder brother'. Where this meaning is obviously intended, written **aai**. *Also see* Introduction.

ai krong ʔaai krooŋ :
Name author uses for Piya's bicycle. **krong** - 'to rattle'.

amphur *ʔamphəə* :
I.Thai administrative unit below provincial level, district. 2. The administrative office of such a unit. 3. The town or general locality in which this office is situated.

aw bun *ʔaw bun* :
To get merit, in the Buddhist sense.

baen *bɛɛn* :
Flat. Term applied to the flat bottle in which Thai whisky is sold. A half-bottle. A full bottle is a **klom** 'round' and a quarter is **kak.**

bai si *baai sii* :
Lit. 'auspicious rice'. Ritual offerings made during **su khwan** (q.v.) ceremony.

bak *bak* :
Dialect. Prefix used with name in address to young boys. Similar to some uses of **ai** (q.v.).

bak la *bak laa* :
(See above) **la** - 'last born'. A term of familiar address, used to young boys. **bak noi** - 'little boy'.

bang boke *baŋ book* :
Section of bamboo used as a container in **boke** (q.v.).

bang khi yarng *baŋ khii jaaŋ* :
Section of bamboo used for collecting dammar (the resin of the **yarng** tree).

barn *baan*:
House, home, village.

barn norng ma vor *baan nooŋ maa voo* :
Name of principal village in story—'village of the swamp of the mad dog'.

boke *book*:
A gambling game in which players wager on the fall of four counters.

bot *boot*:
The consecrated building in a monastery in which monks are ordained.

caew *cɛɛw*:
A type of relish. Also **caew pla daek.**

caew borng *cɛɛw bɔɔŋ* :
A relish made with **pla ra** (q.v.).

cam *cam*:
Dialect. **mor cam** (q.v.) or **thaw cam** (q.v.). Traditional curer, using both herbs and magical techniques.

'carn *caan* :
Abbreviated form **acarn.** In local usage a man who has been a monk and has been specially honoured by **villagers.** *See* Introduction .

caw *caaw*:
Here used as a term of reference prefixed to the names of males, usually children or young men.

cedi *cedii* :
Spired dome, usually housing relics, in Buddhist architecture.

changwat *caŋwat* :
Province, provincial administration office.

chorn *chɔɔn* :
Type of fish, loach.

cinun *cinuun* :
Type of edible insect.

cipome *cipoom* :
Type of edible insect.

cudci *cutcii* :
Type of edible insect.

di *dii* :
1. Good. *See* **ngan hyan di.** 2. Gall bladder.

'dorng *dɔɔŋ* :
Abbreviated from **kradorng** (q.v.). **kin dorng** - 'wedding'.

err *ʔəə*
Word (or sound) indicating assent.

fan *fɛɛn* :
From English. Girlfriend, boyfriend, lover, betrothed, currently also used for husband, wife.

farang *faraŋ* :
Westerner, European.

fiang *fiaŋ* :
Press for making noodles.

gatha *kathaa* :
Magical text, spell.

hak *hak* :
Dialect. Equipment for winding spun thread onto bobbin.

han *han* :
To turn, revolve. Here used to mean 'turn meat on spit'.

harn *haan* :
To divide, to share.

I *ʔii* :
Prefix used with various names of plants and animals. Used with human names it is the female equivalent of **ai** (q .v.).

I thaw *ʔii thaw* :
The name given the headmaster's motorcycle. **thaw** - 'old person'.

kaen vaen *kεεn vεεn* :
Species of bird.

kanlorn *kanlɔɔn* :
Lit. 'the ghostly sermon'. Type of almsgiving held in connection with **Maha Chart** (q.v.).

kaput *kaput* :
A species of bird.

kathin *kathin* :
The ceremony of presenting robes to monks at the end of the so-called Buddhist Lent (the annual three month retreat during the rains).

kha *khaa* :
Type of grass, IMPERATA CYLINDRICA, used for thatching roofs.

khaen *khεεn* :
A musical instrument of northeast Thailand. Pan pipes.

khan khor *khan khɔɔ* :
Pole with hook on one end used to attach pail for drawing water from well.

khan mark *khan maak* :
Container for betel leaf, nut, instruments and accompaniments for chewing.

khanom cin *khanom ciin* :
Thai-style noodle dish.

khaw bya *khaaw* (sometimes *khaw*) *bya* :
Powdered glutinous rice.

khaw maw *khaaw maw* :
Green rice, roasted and pounded. In dialect, **khaw pun** (*khaaw puun*).

khaw tom mat *khaaw tom mat* :
Glutinous rice cakes wrapped in banana leaf.

khi *khii* :
An excretion; odd (as opposed to 'even'). In the latter sense, dialect **khik**.

khi fa *khii faa* :
fa - 'sky'. Lit. 'excretion of the sky'. Dialect for 'clouds'

khiw rot *khiw rot* :
Bus station. **khiw**, from English 'queue'; **rot**, vehicle.

khorn *khɔɔn* :
Hammer.

khorn ti korlor *khɔɔn tii kɔɔlɔɔ* :
Hammer to beat the **korlor** (q.v.).

khru *khruu* :
Teacher. **khru jai** - headmaster.

khru' *khruʔ* :
Closely-woven basket used for carrying water.

khu *khuu* :
Pair, even.

khun *khun* :
Title used before name; polite form of second person address.

khwan *khwan* :
Thai concept of soul, life-force.

kin *kin* :
To eat. **kin dorng** *see* **'dorng.**

king (or **ching**) *kiŋ* :
A type of drum.

klong *klɔŋ* :
Drum.

koi *kɔi* :
Dish made of minced meat.

kong *koŋ* :
Dialect. Equipment for spinning thread.

kop *kop* :
Frog .

kor *kɔɔ* :
The name of the first letter of the Thai alphabet.

korlor *kɔɔlɔɔ* :

A hollow piece of wood used as a gong for summoning villagers to meeting.

korng *kɔŋ* :
A container.

kor torng *kɔɔ tɔɔŋ* :
Dried banana leaves.

krachorn *kracɔɔn* :
A species of beetle.

kradorng *kradɔɔŋ* :
Carapace. *See* **'dorng**.

krong:
See **ai krong.**

kuti *kuti?* :
Monks' residence in a monastery.

lai khup *laai khup* :
Woven bamboo screens.

langkha *laŋkhaa* :
Roof.

langoke *laŋook* :
Type of mushroom.

larp *laap*:
Dish made of usually raw, minced meat.

larp thaw *laap thaw* :
Dish made of the long strands of a species of EUPHORBIA.

law *law* :
Granary (dialect).

li *lii* :
Weir built for catching fish.

like *likee* :
A type of Thai folk drama.

lorp *lɔɔp* :
Type of fish trap.

luang lung *luaŋ luŋ* :
'Venerable Uncle'. Respectful term for a senior monk.

lung *lung* :
Uncle. Elder brother of mother or father.

mae *mɛɛ* :
Mother.

mae jai *mɛɛ jai* :
'Big mother'. Respectful term of address for older woman.

Maha Chart *mahaa chaat* :
'The great life'. The celebration of Prince Vessantara, the last incarnation as a human of the Buddha (Gotama) before the one in which he reached enlightenment.

makhya *makhya* :
Fruit of the SOLANACEAE family.

makok *makɔɔk* :
Fruit, SPONDIAS PINNATA.

marg i *maak ʔii* :
A game.

mark harp *maak haap* :
Type of board game.

marn khaw *maan khaaw* :
Unopened ears of rice.

mok pla siew *mok plaa siw* :
Fish steamed with herbs in banana leaves.

mor *mɔɔ*:
1. Doctor, title used for a variety of healers. **mor cam** *See* cam. *See also* **thaw cam**.
2. A species of climbing fish.

mor lam *mɔɔ lam* :
Type of folk drama typical of northeast Thailand.

morng *mooŋ* :
A type of fish trap.

mor thyan *moo thyan* :
An unregistered medical practitioner; a 'quack'.

M.S. (mor sor) *moo soo* :
Initials standing for **matayom syksa** - 'middle school'.

muang *myaŋ* :
A Thai political unit. A city. **Amphur muang** the district of the capital city of the province.

na naʔ :
Final particle often used to soften a statement or question.

nai amphur *naai amphəə* :
Administrative head of the **amphur.** District Officer.

nam phrik *naam phrik* :
Various kinds of hot chilli sauces, any hot relish.

nang khi hart *naŋ khii haat* :
Skin from back of pig's neck.

ngaep ŋɛɛp :
Type of fish trap.

ngaep sai kop *ŋɛɛp sai kop* :
Device for catching frogs.

ngan hyan di *ŋan hyan dii* :
Dialect. A wake. **ngan** *see* **ngarn; hyan** (**ryan**) house.

ngarn *ŋaan* :
1. Work, activity, ceremonial. 2. A measure of area about 0.04 hectare.

ngerk khandai *ŋəək khandai* :
Dialect. 'Pushing away the steps'. To move steps away from the house to prevent dogs, poultry etc. from entering when occupants are away.

nguang *ŋuaŋ* :
A cricket-like insect.

orm *ʔɔɔm* :
A type of curry.

palat *palat* :
Deputy, assistant.

pha khaw ma *phaa khaaw maa* :
A waistcloth.

pha thung *phaa thuŋ* :
A woman's waistcloth.

phak i hin *phak ʔii hin* :
1. Name of a village in the story, name of the tambon in which Barn Norng Ma Vor lies. 2. A plant sometimes used as a vegetable.

pharn *phaan*:
A tray on a pedestal.

phi *phii*:
Elder brother or sister. A respectful term of address.

phin *phin*:
A stringed musical instrument. Also **syng** or **sung.**

phor *phɔɔ*:
Father.

phor jai *phɔɔ jai*:
'Big father'. Respectful term of address to an older man.

phra khru *phraʔ khruu*:
A title conferred on monks.

phu jai (barn) *phuu jai baan*:
Village headman.

phy *phyy*:
Rush used for basket weaving.

pla daek (caew pla daek) *cɛɛw plaa dɛɛk*:
See **caew.**

pla ra *plaa raa*:
Fermented fish, used as a condiment.

ponglang *pooŋlaaŋ*:
A wooden gong.

pon pla *pon plaa* :
A relish made of fish.

pungki *puŋki?* :
A basket for hauling earth.

saeng *sɛɛŋ* :
Timber used for protective wall in well.

sai *sai* :
Type of fish trap.

samlor khryang *saamloo khryaŋ* :
A motorized trishaw.

sanu *sanu* :
Type of kite shaped like a bow **(thanu)**.

sarng *saaŋ* :
Dialect. A well.

sarng saeng *saaŋ sɛɛŋ* :
Well with protective timbers.

satang *sataŋ* :
One hundredth of a baht.

sawatdi khrap *sawatdii khrap* :
A polite form of greeting.

seng *seŋ* :
Dialect. To compete.

sia *sia* :
A Chinese derived term for a business magnate.

sokalek *sokalek* :
A type of **larp** using thin slices of meat.

som tam *som tam* :
A hot spicy dish made with shredded green papaya.

sorn nangsy *sɔɔn naŋsyy* :
To teach.

sorng thaew *sɔɔŋ thɛɛw* :
'Two rows'. A 'utility' converted for passenger transport.

su khwan *suu khwan* :
Ritual strengthening an individual's life force. Fixing the **khwan** q.v.

syksa *syksaa* :
1. Education, short for **syksathikarn.** 2. 'Education' as in Ministry of Education. 3. Education officer.

taempun *tɛɛmpun* :
A species of bird.

tai pratheep *tai prathiip* :
A festival of lights.

takror *takrɔɔ* :
A Thai game played with a ball of woven cane.

talung *taluŋ* :
A species of langur.

tambon *tambon* :
Administrative unit often translated as 'commune'. Administrative division below the level of district, a collection of villages.

tarng barn *taaŋ baan* :
Net for trapping birds.

than *than* :
Sir, a deferential form of address and reference.

thar narm *thaa naam* :
Waiting one's turn for water at the well. **thar** - 'to wait'.

thaw *thaw* :
Old person. Title of respect.

thaw cam *thaw cam* :
Village officiant at ritual, known as 'brahmin' in urban Thailand. *Also* **mor cam.**

thaw kay *thaw kɛɛ* :
A businessman (from Chinese).

thern *thəən* :
A word spoken at the end of a blessing or invocation.

thiang na *thiaŋ naa* :
Hut in fields for storing farm implements, etc.

thit *thit*:
Title for a lay man who has spent time in the monkhood. cf. **'carn.**

thor *thɔɔ*:
Dialect. A hollow cylinder used to line a well. Thai: a punting pole.

tia *thiaʔ*:
Father (Chinese). Here used as a title for a Chinese shopkeeper .

tua cit *tua cit*:
An intestinal parasite.

twilight:
From English. To attend nightschool - **rian twilight**.

ui tai *ʔui tai*:
Exclamation!

vor vaen *vɔɔ vɛɛn* :
The name of the letter of the Thai alphabet with a sound between the English v and w.

wa *waa*:
A measure of length, about two metres.

wai *wai*:
The gesture of greeting.

wan home *wan hoom* :
'The day of coming together'. The first day of **Maha Chart** (q.v.).

wat *wat* :
A Buddhist monastery.

yam vun sen *jam vun sen* :
A spicy noodle dish.

yarng *jaaŋ* :
A large resinous tree. DIPTEROCARPUS ALATUS.